IMPERIAL GLORY

GUN AND BAYONET lost, Dennett fell down the earth slope behind the fire-step and the ork rolled with him, both of them punching, scratching and kicking at the other with all the strength they could muster. Its barks and grunts filled his ears, its pungent fungoid smell invaded his nose.

They hit the ground tangled together, the ork pressing down upon him. It heaved and Dennett felt his throat tighten, and then a sudden release as his chinstrap broke and the ork ripped the helmet from his head. The xenos monster towered over him in the night and gripped the helmet with both hands, ready to smash it down on Dennett's head and break his skull apart. Dennett scrabbled in the dirt behind his back for anything to defend himself with, but he was too slow and the ork hammered down with a cry of victory.

A WARHAMMER 40,000 NOVEL

IMPERIAL GLORY

Richard Williams

BLACK LIBRARY

With thanks to Jules, McCabe and Fiona.

A BLACK LIBRARY PUBLICATION

First published in Great Britain in 2011 by
The Black Library,
Games Workshop Ltd.,
Willow Road, Nottingham,
NG7 2WS, UK.

10 9 8 7 6 5 4 3 2 1

Cover illustration by Clint Langley.

A CIP record for this book is available from the British Library.

ISBN13: 978 1 84416 889 7

Distributed in the US by Simon & Schuster
1230 Avenue of the Americas, New York, NY 10020, US.

See the Black Library on the internet at
www.blacklibrary.com

Find out more about Games Workshop
and the world of Warhammer 40,000 at
www.games-workshop.com

Printed and bound in the US.

IT IS THE 41st millennium. For more than a hundred centuries the Emperor has sat immobile on the Golden Throne of Earth. He is the master of mankind by the will of the gods, and master of a million worlds by the might of his inexhaustible armies. He is a rotting carcass writhing invisibly with power from the Dark Age of Technology. He is the Carrion Lord of the Imperium for whom a thousand souls are sacrificed every day, so that he may never truly die.

YET EVEN IN his deathless state, the Emperor continues his eternal vigilance. Mighty battlefleets cross the daemon-infested miasma of the warp, the only route between distant stars, their way lit by the Astronomican, the psychic manifestation of the Emperor's will. Vast armies give battle in His name on uncounted worlds. Greatest amongst his soldiers are the Adeptus Astartes, the Space Marines, bio-engineered super-warriors. Their comrades in arms are legion: the Imperial Guard and countless Planetary Defence Forces, the ever-vigilant Inquisition and the tech-priests of the Adeptus Mechanicus to name only a few. But for all their multitudes, they are barely enough to hold off the ever-present threat from aliens, heretics, mutants - and worse.

TO BE A man in such times is to be one amongst untold billions. It is to live in the cruellest and most bloody regime imaginable. These are the tales of those times. Forget the power of technology and science, for so much has been forgotten, never to be re-learned. Forget the promise of progress and understanding, for in the grim dark future there is only war. There is no peace amongst the stars, only an eternity of carnage and slaughter, and the laughter of thirsting gods.

11TH BRIMLOCK
(CONSOLIDATED)
- 660.M41 -
REGIMENTAL FORCE ORGANISATION

| HQ | CO: *Colonel Arbulaster*
2nd: *Major Brooce*

Senior Commissar Reeve |

Line Infantry
Major Brooce

Dragoon (Chimera) Company
Major Brooce

Line Company
Captain Fergus

Dragoon (Chimera) Company
Captain Deverril

Line Company
Captain Tyrwhitt

Line Company
Captain Wymondham

Line Company
Captain Gomery

Line Company
Captain Ingoldsby

Line Company
Captain Colquhoun

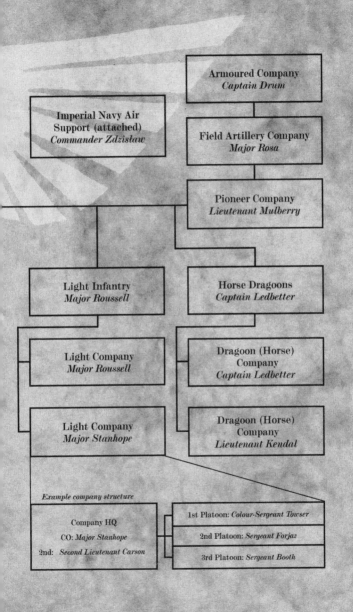

Armoured Company
Captain Drum

Imperial Navy Air Support (attached)
Commander Zdzisław

Field Artillery Company
Major Rosa

Pioneer Company
Lieutenant Mulberry

Light Infantry
Major Roussell

Horse Dragoons
Captain Ledbetter

Light Company
Major Roussell

Dragoon (Horse) Company
Captain Ledbetter

Light Company
Major Stanhope

Dragoon (Horse) Company
Lieutenant Kendal

Example company structure

Company HQ

CO: *Major Stanhope*

2nd: *Second Lieutenant Carson*

1st Platoon: *Colour-Sergeant Towser*

2nd Platoon: *Sergeant Forjaz*

3rd Platoon: *Sergeant Booth*

BATTLE HONOURS

11th Brimlock Consolidated Regiment*
Ellinor Crusade – 660.M41

643.M41	Mazari
644.M41	Kaswan Bay
645.M41	Yaarvagnari
647.M41	Carrion Stars
649.M41	Mespots (merged with 191st, 282nd and 317th Dragoons)
653.M41	Kotal
654-6.M41	Azzabar (merged with 920th Armoured)
656.M41	Ordan (merged with 92nd Line)
657.M41	Charasia (merged with 412nd Line)
657.M41	Takht (merged with 83rd Line and 1331st Ogryn Auxilia)
657.M41	Kam Daka (merged with 47th, 110th Line and 821st Artillery)
659.M41	Kandhar (merged with 13th Dragoons, 56th Horse Dragoons, 74th Line and 713th Heavy Pioneers)

Note that due to vehicular losses, the 'Dragoon' designation was removed in 656.M41

'We ain't much on paper. A single regiment, a dozen companies, a few detachments of support. Bits and bobs. Not much on paper.

'But you take a million men and you throw them into the fight. And you keep 'em fighting 'til for every ten you started with you got only one man left. 'Til just the toughest, just the smartest, just the bleedin' luckiest are still breathing.

'And then you send them out again.

'And of the ten men who thought they were tough, nine find they weren't tough enough; of the ten who thought they were smart, nine find they weren't smart enough; the ten who thought they were lucky find their luck runs out.

'Imagine who you've got left after that. And then you send them out again 'til you've only got one in ten of those still kicking.

'That's us. That's the Brimlock Eleventh.

'We ain't much on paper, that's true. But that's the only place we ain't.'

Trooper Rit 'Mouse' Chaffey
Brimlock 11th Imperial Guard regiment, Ellinor Crusade

PROLOGUE

THERE IS A tradition amongst the crusading regiments of the Brimlock Dragoons. When each new recruit leaves Brimlock for the first, and almost certainly last, time they are told to look at the planet behind them. Then they are told that that planet is no longer their home. From that moment, their home is whatever ground they stand on, the ground they fight on, and the ground that they die on.

Major Stanhope watched on helplessly as, below him, his men found their final homes. The fight was hopeless, they had known it from the start, but they were standing fast and fighting hard. By the God-Emperor, they were showing the enemy how hard a Guardsman could fight. But one by one they fell and, as each one succumbed, Stanhope felt another part of his soul cut from him. He knew that when the last was extinguished there would be nothing left inside him.

He ached, he burned to be down there with them. To

fight beside them, to share these last moments and then march alongside them into the Emperor's light. But they had forbidden him, they had entrusted him with a task to give their expenditure purpose. He could not resist them. He held the colours, the immortal pride of the regiment, in his hands and, above, the shining lights of a salvation beckoned to him. But Stanhope knew he could not be saved. And yet. And yet.

God damn me, Stanhope thought, and he took hold of the first rung and began to climb.

Charasia – 657.M41 – Year 18 of the Ellinor
Crusade

'YOU HAVE YOUR orders, lieutenant!'

'They're being slaughtered!'

'I can see just as well as you can.'

'*You* might be willing to stand here like a gawping fool, captain, but *I*–'

'You take another step, lieutenant, and I will shoot you where you stand!'

Captain Blundell-Hollinshed-Blundell of the Brimlock 11th raged at his insubordinate second-in-command. He had not drawn his pistol, but his threat was very real. He glared fiercely at the other officer: a second lieutenant named Carson. Carson was one of those, Blundell knew, who would never amount to anything, who in eighteen years had never been decorated or promoted, and who would most probably be put up against a wall after this campaign if he was not forced to gun him down in the next few seconds.

There was a look in Carson's eye, Blundell could see. That stare. Cold, yet calculating. Blundell tried not to glance down at how close Carson's hand was to his own gun. Everyone knew how fast Carson was supposed to be, how he had survived so long. It didn't matter, Blundell told himself, this would not be settled by speed. It was a matter of authority and unless Carson wished to place himself in the hands of the crusade's commissars, he would back down.

'Return to your position,' Blundell ordered, keeping his voice calm. 'And we will stay in the line until we are *ordered* to do otherwise.'

Carson did not move and Blundell refused to repeat himself. Instead, the lieutenant slowly turned and looked across the valley to where the 11th's Boy Company was being gutted.

The Boy Company, or the probationary unit to give it its formal name, was an inevitable part of the decision, poorly made in Blundell's opinion, to allow a portion of the Guardsmen's wives to accompany them on crusade. Their offspring earned their keep as soon as they were old enough to carry, until, as adolescents, they were permitted into the Boy Company to prove their worth and become proper guardsmen, or alternatively to stay fetching and serving all their lives.

That burning desire to prove themselves sometimes made them fearless, but it was no substitute for experience.

They should have been kept to the rear, that is if anyone could tell where the rear was, or where the front was for that matter, in this damn irritating war. The Brimlock assault had soon booted the Karthadasim soldiers and their mercenaries off Charasia, but they'd left their guns for these pesky indigenous tribesmen who took great delight in snapping at their liberators even as the Brimlock Guardsmen tried to pacify each region.

And now, Blundell considered, the tribesmen had bit on a juicy target. They'd sprung from some hidey-hole after the main bulk of the 11th had passed and struck the rear of the column. The sergeant major in command of the Boy Company had been sniped in the first volley, a mere second after one of the boys had saluted him, unknowingly giving the sniper his target. Without the SM, the company had collapsed. The officer-cadet had tried to organise return fire, but he too had been struck as soon as he had started shouting orders. At that, the rest of them had dived for whatever meagre cover they could find. The ones who raised their guns and tried to shoot were the first targets. Quickly they were down too and the Charasian tribesmen could start leisurely picking off the boys who were cowering, second by agonising second.

They were in a dreadful pinch, Blundell knew, but he also knew that it was almost certainly a diversion. There was most likely a far larger enemy force, just waiting for him to move his company out of position, to have him expose them, before launching their attack. How did he know that? He didn't. But he trusted in his chain of command. He had sent his report to Colonel Arbulaster and the colonel would decide. Until then, his last orders were to maintain his position in the column and he would do so, until he was ordered otherwise. That was the duty of a Guardsman.

Orders and discipline. That was what made the Brimlock regiments great. That was what held the line at Defiance, that was what had carried them over the trenches at Torrans, and that was what Blundell had tried so hard to impress upon his unruly second lieutenant and the rest of his company.

Carson was still standing there, still obviously nursing a spark of obstinacy. Or posing, Blundell considered, one hand resting on the butt of one of his holstered pistols and the other clasping the back of his untrimmed blond hair. No doubt trying to draw the men's attention to their confrontation. Well, it was not a confrontation Blundell intended to lose.

'Return to your post, lieutenant,' Blundell instructed. 'You shall not issue any orders to any man until I say otherwise. Understand me? Dismissed.'

'Captain,' Carson muttered, and walked back to his men. No, Blundell corrected in his own head, slunk back to his men. He was definitely beginning to master the man.

His men; yes, that was the problem. When Blundell's own regiment, the 92nd, had been dissolved after the bloody crossing over the Katee on Ordan and had been subsumed into the 11th, he had suspected that he would be given a command at the bottom of the barrel. He had not been mistaken. His fellow 92nder Gomery had warned him. Gomery had told him that the rest of the regiment called it Carson's company, despite the fact that a second lieutenant, and certainly one with such a stain on his reputation, would never be allowed a command.

Gomery had told him that Carson's men were devoted to him. But Blundell could tell that that wasn't true. His men had just grown used to him; that was all. Carson curried their favour incorrigibly, allowing them far too great a liberty and irreverence. Blundell himself had already heard a nickname some of the men had put about for him, 'Blunder', and he intended to come down with the severest sanctions the next time he had so much of a whiff of it. And trash encouraged trash; Blundell had been lumbered with several survivors of the regiments from the debacle on Cawnpore. One of them, a corporal named Gardner from the 412th, had emerged particularly maladjusted and without use.

A few of the company showed promise, however. His steward, who'd acquired the name 'Mouse', seemed a salt-of-the-earth, hard-working fellow, whilst

Colour-Sergeant Towser, or 'Old Red' as the men called him, was an inexhaustible pillar of strength and fortitude. Blundell did not doubt that it was he who had kept the company effective in spite of Carson's indulgence. It was these kind, of men who were the rocks on which Blundell would build the new spirit of the company. He had disciplined them mercilessly on the journey from Ordan to Charasia and drilled out their bad habits and eccentricities, and here on campaign it was paying off. They were obeying his orders in spite of the tribesmen's provocation and, for all his posturing, their lieutenant could not fight it. Carson had become an irrelevance.

Blundell watched Carson until he had returned to his assigned position, ensuring his obedience. Blundell then returned to his vox-operator to wait for the colonel's orders. The distant cries of the wounded and dying boys gave him no pleasure, but at least the pitiful situation had allowed him to crush the last traces of Carson's influence. By the end of this campaign, no one would be talking about Carson's company any more; it would be known by its proper name as Blundell's company, and it would be he who would take them on to glory.

A few minutes passed and still there was nothing from the colonel. Still the boys were suffering. A doubt emerged, unbidden and unwanted, into Blundell's mind. He had won the point with his lieutenant; he had no further use for delay. If only the colonel would reply he could be calm. Whether it was to hold and defend their position against some attack, or to strike out and drive the tribesmen away themselves. Blundell did not care which way. He just needed to be told.

He caught a particular look in the eye of his vox-operator. He stared at him in reply and the operator quickly focused back on his machine. Blundell wanted to question him, wanted to tell him to make sure it was working properly, ensure he was using it correctly, but he knew such questions would be redundant and might be taken for the first signs of panic. He knew he had no choice in the matter. He had told them all to wait for orders; he could not now countermand himself. He could not tell them to wait for orders and then decide that orders were not necessary. If they weren't, then he should have moved at once, and as he hadn't, that meant they were.

He stood and faced away from the decimation of the boys, staring at the rest of the regiment. The other companies were manoeuvring, dust-coloured Chimeras transporting some platoons, others marching on foot, a few of the horse dragoons galloping on their mounts, but none of them were coming back towards him. From where he was, he could not discern the pattern in their movements, but he continued to stare into the distance beyond as though he could see some enemy force to which they were responding.

He peered from the corner of his eye in the direction of the regimental colours where he knew the colonel must be. He strained as though he might pick out Arbulaster somewhere within the group, then see him stoop down so as to pick up the vox and give him his orders.

Blundell looked down expectantly at the operator. Still nothing. Now, Blundell suspected, he was beginning to look like a fool. The whole company must have realised that there was no immediate threat to their front, and that the closest enemy was behind and filleting the regiment's sons. Blundell knew that some of his men had sons in the Boy Company. Sergeant Forjaz was one. What could he possibly say to him if the worst happened? How could he explain why he held him back, why he held the whole company back, when they could have intervened? He knew he could not possibly countermand what he had previously said, but how could he explain that to a father who had lost his child?

Still no orders! Blundell clenched his jaw tight. He should not have been placed in this situation. Arbulaster should not have done this to him. He should have replied. There should be orders!

He turned around, ready to snatch the vox from the operator's hand and demand answers from command, when he caught sight of what was happening. Help had finally arrived. A platoon of Guardsmen had ghosted along the side of the valley. They were moving fast, but carefully. Blundell could believe that the Charasians, from their positions, would not even catch a glimpse of them, and yet within a couple more minutes the Guardsmen would be right on their flank.

Suddenly, it all became clear. Evidently, the Charasians could see his company further along the valley. They would see his company move as soon as he gave the order and disappear once more. So, instead, the colonel had left his company in position, letting the tribesmen believe they were secure, whilst he brought another force in to catch them before they could run and annihilate them.

Blundell knew he should never have doubted the colonel. He only wished that on this occasion it could be another company acting as distraction, whilst *his* men went in for the kill.

He paused a moment as he caught sight of the distinctive pair of pistols that one of the attackers had holstered on their hips. He looked sharply down at his company in their positions. Carson, Forjaz, Red, nearly a platoon, they were all missing. Furious, he turned back to the attack just about to begin. Damnation, they *were* his men!

* * *

CARSON SCRAMBLED OVER the rocks at the head of his men. He hadn't given any orders; he hadn't needed to. His men knew what was happening, and they knew what to do. Every single one of them was a veteran. Every single one had been fighting since the first campaign of the Ellinor Crusade to here. They'd been soldiers for more years than everything else they'd ever been. He had left his position on the line; Red had gone with him, and the men silently laid down their packs and followed after. Words were simply no longer needed.

He had led them hard south, taking them around onto the reverse of the ridge that led back down the valley. They ran in amongst the stacks and rock chimneys which made the craggy terrain look almost as though it were a field of giant wheat made of stone. They went fast, swarming up the slope and over the broken, treacherous ground. Their step was sure, their movement confident and quiet. Anything they had been originally issued which rattled or clinked or flapped had been secured or disposed of long before.

The men grouped automatically in their sections, each man knowing his place in formation behind his corporal. The corporals focused ahead, each one forging his own path so as to avoid congestion or bottlenecks that would slow their advance or draw the enemy's eye. The sections rushed through concealed gullies, the men tightening into a column to thread their way through narrow gaps between chimneys and then dispersing back into formation once on the other side. They kept low over rises to reduce their profile and, no matter how steep their path became, they always kept their lasrifles in their grasps.

They went fast. Faster than they should. Faster than doctrine allowed. Carson knew it was a risk, but neither he nor any of his men could abide any further delay.

Their attack was a strike to the throat that would take grip and then throttle the life from their foe.

It was a risk that paid off. Whilst the Charasians had some fine shots amongst their kind, Carson knew they were not soldiers. The tribe-males had allowed their attention to focus entirely on their victims in the Boy Company; they all wanted to score a kill against their liberators. They thought they had hidden themselves well, but the faint discharges from the Kartha weapons their former overlords had left them were all Carson needed. Their very firing stances, low and crouched over, helped conceal the Brimlock platoon as it closed in on them from their left and behind. There were only a dozen or so metres left between Carson and the rearmost of the Charasian positions and still no warning had been shouted. Just like their targets a few minutes earlier, the Charasians did not stand a chance.

Carson did not need to order the attack. He merely had to think it. His men acted as he knew they would. They sprinted the last few metres and launched themselves at the enemy. The heavy butts of lasrifles smashed against the backs of unprotected Charasian heads, smashing their skulls or knocking them cold so there would be no shouts of pain when the lasrifles were reversed and bayonets impaled their flesh. One realised the danger a moment too soon and Carson heard a xenos shriek that carried over the sound of the continual gunfire.

Grenades, Carson thought, and he saw them fly down into the midst of the Charasian hiding places. Their firing stopped and for a split second there was no sound but a single voice gabbling xenos words. Then there was the *crump-crump-crump* of the detonations and blood-mist sprayed into the air. The screaming began for real: screams of pain from those struck and of panic from those who had been so confident a moment before, but were now realising the peril they were in. They were turning, desperate to target the threat that had appeared right behind them.

Volley, Carson thought, and las-shots from Brimlock rifles flashed around him. Through the spurs and jagged outcrops, few struck true, but the crack of the shots as they splintered off rock and the hiss of the air as the beams passed nearby convinced the remaining Charasians that they had been outflanked by far greater numbers than a mere platoon. There was no return fire. The Charasians were surprised, a few of them were dead, but the rest were safe in their dug-in positions. If the Brimlock Guardsmen hesitated, gave them even a minute to recover and collect themselves, the Charasians could have stayed put and unleashed a withering fire on the Guardsmen now so visible coming over the ridge above them.

His men had to charge, Carson thought, and that was exactly what they did. As his men leapt down upon their targets, Carson launched himself into a knot of the tribe-males. They were still standing, turning, fumbling to bring their weapons around against the new threat. Carson's pistols were already in his hands. He clenched the triggers, once, twice and a third time, and the bodies of three of the xenos fighters smacked down onto stone, their faces and chests incinerated by the heat of the las-beams.

There was a sharp, shocked inhalation of breath behind him. He whirled about. Another Charasian had been hidden in the shadow of an outcrop. It was younger, this one, and for a split second Carson paused. His gaze locked with the wide, black-eyed xenos. Its youth was not relevant; it was carrying a gun, it would not get any older. Carson fired. He did not look to see that it hit, he knew it had.

He flattened himself against a rock, taking cover in

exactly the same position that his enemy had been in a few seconds before. He listened and the only sounds he could hear were the shots of Brimlock lasrifles and the crunching of stone underfoot as men charged in behind him.

He looked up. All across the slope the Charasians were on their feet and running east, staying on the side of the valley, fleeing from Carson's men above them and the Boy Company below. It was only now that he could see how many of the enemy there had been. Over a hundred of them were running from the thirty Guardsmen who had attacked them. The Brimlock Guardsmen, winded and unable to keep up, kept firing at the backs of those in flight. Every Charasian tribe-male they killed at this moment was one who would never return to strike at them in the future. Carson saw Forjaz, his bayonet and rifle barrel drenched in the blood of the xenos who had been shooting at his child.

'Sergeant!' Carson called over to him, his first word since he had worked away from Blunder. 'Take a section, check on the boys.'

Forjaz stared for a moment, still wrapped in his paternal blood-rage, then blinked and nodded gratefully. Better that he knew as soon as he could whether his son was living or dead.

The sound of Brimlock las-fire lessened as the surviving Charasians went to ground, disappearing amongst the same kind of rock chimneys and gullies that had hidden Carson's own attack. They would not go far, they did not need to. They knew the country far too well to be rooted out by off-worlders. A few of them at least would turn back so as to stall any pursuit of the main party and perhaps even to creep back and take their attackers off-guard.

It was a merciless war, on both sides, and Carson

suspected he would soon see how little mercy his own side had, for Blunder had finally ordered the other two companies to move and they were coming back for him.

CAPTAIN BLUNDELL REGARDED the awkward reunion of Sergeant Forjaz with his bruised, bloodied, but still living son: man and boy, both shaken, yet both firmly restraining the emotions going through them. Blundell looked away from the embarrassing scene and instead shot a scorching gaze up towards the rocks where Carson, Red and the rest of their platoon were still holding. Blundell would be damned if he was going up there to haul the second lieutenant down again. Carson had to come down to him, and he would wait until he did so and then throw the book at him.

Blundell was furious. The captain did not care who Carson had saved; he was finished in this company. With the help of a senior officer or two – Major Roussell was another who detested Carson – the second lieutenant would be finished in this existence as well. He would be handed over to the commissars and they would put him up against a wall and be done with him.

This waiting game he was playing was not going to save him. Lord General Ellinor himself could appear and could not save him from the facts. Carson had defied Blundell's orders and that was it. His life was forfeit, and a thorn in Blundell's side would finally be removed.

'Captain,' someone alerted him. Blundell looked about. A trooper was walking towards him from second platoon. It was that piece of Cawnpore detritus, Corporal Gardner.

'Captain Blundell,' Gardner said, raising his hand and saluting him.

Blundell automatically snapped off a quick salute in reply. 'Yes, what?'

And the carefully aimed shot from a Kartha rifle burned through the back of Blundell's head and blew his face out from behind.

CHAPTER ONE

The Fortress of Kandhar – 659.M41 – Year 20
of the Ellinor Crusade

THE CONQUEST OF Kandhar by the Ellinor Crusade ended not with a bang, but with a crackle. It was the crackle of the flames from the funeral pyres that burned twenty metres high around the ruins of the enemy's last stronghold, cremating the bodies of friend and foe alike. They lit up the dark sky and their light reflected off the low-hanging clouds bathing the cold valley with their warm glow.

The trooper watched them burn through the wide hole in the side of the manor house. He sat in comfort, sunk down in a red, velvet chair. Someone had lit a fire in the fireplace to keep the place warm against the cool night air. The men, the rank and file, were huddled around the pyres, the bodies of their dead comrades keeping them alive. But no officer could be expected to debase himself in such a manner, and so the manor house had been appropriately refurbished.

The trooper gazed at the small but happy fire in the

fireplace, and then looked outside at the great vengeful flames soaring up in giant columns towards the heavens. There was a beverage on a side-table near his right hand: a good, fine-cut glass with a measure of heavy liquid the colour of oak. It sat there untouched as he drank in the view instead. This was one of the moments, one of the moments of wonder that needed to be savoured.

'You got the drinks? Where's a good spot?'

'Over there by the fire?'

The two officers stepped lightly towards the fireplace, looking to take their ease in the chairs around it. The trooper was sitting so low in his seat that the first of them did not see him until he had nearly sat down in his lap.

'Oh! Apologies, I didn't–' It was then that the officer took a good look at the trooper, as much as he took a good look at anything, and he saw his dirty face, his battered uniform and, most importantly to him, the insignia of a private.

'What are you doing in here?'

The trooper did not respond.

'Do you hear me, man? Officers only in here. Get back to your section.'

The trooper's heavy eyes stayed staring at the fire.

'He looks pretty far gone,' the officer's friend said. He had noticed the stains on the trooper's grey fatigues: sweat, smoke and most definitely blood. 'Maybe we should leave him to it.'

'Damn him!' the officer replied. 'He's just playing dumb. I'll have your name and regiment, man, and your commanding officer will have a mite more, I'll warrant, after I've had a word with him.'

The trooper still didn't reply; in fact, he had not moved an inch, even to blink, during the entire confrontation. The officer's friend shook his head and went to get a steward.

'Name and regiment, soldier!' The officer tried to sound commanding, but the order came out as petulant.

'Very well, I'll find it for myself.' The officer reached for the tags around the trooper's neck. He leaned in and suddenly yelped in pain. The trooper's hand was clamped around his wrist, twisting it into a lock. The trooper's head whirled around, he blinked and stared wide-eyed at the officer.

'What's wrong with you?' the trooper asked, his tone one of genuine concern. 'Why are you shouting?'

'Unhand me, you dog, or I'll have you on the wheel!'

'Is there a problem here, sirs?' One of the heavy-set, politely threatening stewards closed in, the officer's friend behind him.

The trooper saw what his hand was doing and released his grip. The officer shrank back, cradling his injury and spitting nails.

'I want this private's name and regiment,' he ordered the stewards, 'and then I want him slung out of here!'

The trooper stood and presented himself. 'Major Stanhope, commanding the 1201st.'

'That's a lie!' the officer blurted out. 'There's no such regiment. Not on Kandhar at least!'

'Sir,' the steward began. 'Sir?'

It took a moment for the officer to realise that the steward was focusing not on the fraudulent major but on him.

'What?'

'Major Stanhope is currently seconded to the 371st, whom, I believe you'll find, *are* on Kandhar. Now,' the steward raised his hand for two of his colleagues to approach, 'it will be no trouble for us to arrange chairs for yourself and your friend with a very pleasant outlook upstairs.'

'No,' the officer retorted.

'Sir?' the steward replied with seemingly infinite patience.

'You'll not fob us off. He assaulted me.'

The steward allowed a moment to pass to indicate his silent disappointment.

'In that case, I shall have to ask you to vacate these premises before continuing any further.'

'Very well.' The officer turned to the trooper only to discover he had slumped back down in the chair once more. He contained his irritation and rested his uninjured hand significantly upon the hilt of his sword. 'Major Stanhope, if that is who you are, you will accompany me outside. Do you have a second you wish to contact?'

Stanhope did not reply. He was gone again, once more gazing at the fire.

The officer walked round pointedly to stand right in front of him. Stanhope blinked back and the officer gritted his teeth and repeated his challenge.

'Of course. Of course,' Stanhope replied and stood up.

'Do you have a weapon,' the officer said disdainfully, 'or do you need one to be provided?'

'You're right. You're right. Got to have a sword or might get you into trouble. Had a sword somewhere... Where's it gone?' Stanhope turned his back and bent down near double, searching under his chair, and incidentally displaying his trouser-covered rump to his opponent.

'Ah, there it is!' Stanhope saw the unusual thick sword with its distinctive inward curve entangled under the chair and reached in, grabbed the hilt and gave it a tug. It slipped out halfway and then stuck fast. He grunted in annoyance and took a second grip with his other hand.

'That's a fell-cutter,' the friend exclaimed. 'He's a bloody fell-cutter!'

'Blessed Marguerite!' the officer gasped.

There was the smash of glass and the bang of furniture being knocked hastily to one side.

'Aha! Got it!' Stanhope declared as he pulled the sword free with a great ripping of fabric. He waved it triumphantly in a small circle above his head and then turned his attention back to his challenger. Or, at least, where his challenger had been.

Stanhope looked about in sluggish confusion. The steward righted the table and chairs that the officers had toppled in their flight.

'Can I get you another, major?'

Stanhope looked down at the empty side-table.

'Did I have one already?'

'Yes, sir. The glass broke.'

'Oh, sorry about that,' Stanhope said. 'I suppose I'd better have another then.' He reached into his pocket.

'No need, sir,' said the steward, bowing: the coin that the major had given him for the first drink had been enough to cover a round for an entire platoon.

'Take it anyway.' Stanhope pressed another coin into his hand. This one was enough for a whole company.

'As you say, sir.' The steward vanished and Stanhope settled back into his chair, jamming his sword underneath again. The fresh drink appeared on the side-table.

'Shall I stoke the fire for you?' the steward offered, reaching for one of the lance heads propped up beside it.

'No, no, leave it be,' Stanhope replied, as he returned to his moment. 'It's happy.'

Medicae Station, Kandhar

THE MAN WHO would become known as Blanks opened his right eye a fraction. They'd finally turned the luminators down. He scanned the room; all the medicae were gone and the wounded were in their beds. He held his breath, listening intently to the sounds of their breathing. None of them snored. Any troopers who snored had been killed many years before. Hopefully, the medicae had drugged them to keep them quiet just as they had been doing to him. He raised his hands a few inches from his bed and felt the tug of his restraints. There had been some kind of panic today. More wounded arriving. Many more. The medicae had not paid him much attention and had forgotten to shorten his wrist straps after his meal. It was his opportunity.

The medicae were lying to him. They had told him that he had lost his memory because of his injuries and yet he had no injuries. How could he have lost his entire memory and not have a scratch on him? He had been injured before, he had scars, but they were all long healed. He had tested every part of his body and everything functioned as it should. He was not wounded, he was not sick, and that meant they were doing something else to him.

When he had first awoken, he had tried to break free, but he had been too confused and there had been too many medicae standing ready, and so he had been restrained. One of the medicae had tried to comfort him, telling him that the paranoia would fade in a few days and then he could be released back to his regiment, but then another one had said that his regiment were all dead. He asked them why he was being kept here; they said they were only keeping him until he was fit, but he was fit already. More lies. He asked to see his service docket, but they refused. When he continued to ask, they stopped listening to him and started drugging him until he stopped. Tonight was the night that he was going to find out the truth.

He slowly arched his body up. His bedclothes rustled slightly as they slid down him. He pushed his hands behind his back, the fingers from one hand stretching to reach the restraint on the other. It took nearly half an hour to undo one; his muscles should have been screaming, but his body was strong.

Once one restraint was off, the others quickly followed and then, at last, he was out of bed. His legs wavered a moment as they readjusted, but then they responded. He had obviously not been off them long. Another lie. He took a blanket from the bed and padded softly along the ward and out through the door.

There was no alarm. There was no guard. There were wounded, however. There were wounded everywhere: lying on pallets, slumped against walls, standing and trudging slowly down the corridor. The ones nearest him looked up plaintively for a moment, but then saw he was not one of the medicae and so ignored him. He threw his blanket over his head and shoulders and held it close. He started trudging as the other walkers did, looking for his path.

He had tried to get information from the others in his ward, but they had all been officers and uninterested in conversing with a private soldier. However, they had been free enough in talking with one another and he had gleaned the information he needed from that. There was a blue line painted on the floor ending at his ward. He shuffled along it, passing soldier after soldier, bandaged, missing limbs, burned, and with every other injury he could conceive of. None of them were screaming, none of them were crying out, but there was a general groan of suffering that permeated the air. There were no medicae, no one tending to any of them.

He reached a junction and there the blue line intersected with a half-dozen more. A thick red line terminated in another ward the size of a cavern: double, triple-stacked with pallets and more men upon them.

There were more than a thousand of them in that one room alone. It was not his destination. He found the thin grey line and started following that. There were no wounded along this path and so he picked up his pace. He jogged lightly down the empty corridors until he found his destination: the records room. In there, he had heard, was a service docket for every patient within these walls. The door was locked, but he was not going to be halted now, so close. He forced his way in and flicked on the emergency luminators. There they were.

There were thousands of them. Maybe tens of thousands of them. But they were all ordered and filed. He ran through the aisles until he found the right rack. He searched through them, looking for his service number. There it was. There he was.

He pulled the docket clear and poured the contents out onto the floor. The top sheet was a medical report. It was obviously new; it had nothing on it since a week before, nothing he did not already know. Behind it, though, was his service record, with his number at the top. He picked it up and began to read. Name: Stones, John. Rank: Private, Grade Primus.

And that was it. Every other section, every other page, was entirely blank.

Cloud Hills, Kandhar

CARSON AND RED met the officers from the 29th early in the morning in a wooded grove in the lee of one of the hills. There was no other place to go where they could not be seen.

As the two parties came closer, Red muttered to Carson. 'I reccied the woods already, sah. Nothing. You'll be alone.'

The officer in the lead, Captain Ross, saw them

approach. 'A colour-sergeant?' he said, talking of Red, but goading Carson. 'Could you really not persuade a real officer to stand by you?'

Carson would not normally have wasted a second on such a jibe, but today he wanted to relish this. He could feel the fluttering in his body. The anticipation. This might be his last time for a while.

'A staff lieutenant and a quartermaster?' Carson retorted, noting the insignia on Ross's companions. 'Could you really not persuade a real soldier to stand by you?'

Ross gave a chuckle that had no trace of humour and started to shuck off the heavy winter coat he was wearing.

'Your chaps got off pretty lightly so I hear. What was the bill in the end?' he asked Carson.

'Fifteen in the company,' Carson replied, 'about a hundred for the Eleventh overall.'

'Sounds like you were a bit careless with your platoons, eh?' Ross said, but Carson knew that he was in no position to stand upon his high horse this time.

'Heard you got a bit of a bloody nose yourself,' Carson replied, keeping his tone light and well-mannered.

'Took us by surprise with that sally at Thal, is all. Caught us out of position. Eighty per cent across the Twenty-Ninth.'

'Bad luck.' Carson said, but Ross waved it off.

'It was the ones that broke who got it.' Ross said with a smile of vindication. 'My chaps held together. Wasn't so bad for us.'

'There's a bit of gold piping to it though,' he continued. 'There's not much of the Twenty-Ninth left; it means that Command is going to sit us down and send back our colours.'

Carson scoffed openly at that. 'They'll just merge you with another regiment and send you on to the next one.

Just as they've done with all of us a dozen times already.'

Ross curled his face in a grin. 'That's not what I hear coming out of Command. Word is that the Twenty-Ninth is being set for garrison duty.'

'Garrison duty…' Carson could not believe it was being considered.

'That's right. The colours go home. I stay here. Twenty-five years, twenty years on this crusade and five before that, and after all that the Guard and I are finally saying good-bye. Might be the Eleventh as well. But your lot still have some fight in them, don't they? Should have been smart like me, Carson, and been a bit less careful with your men.'

Carson had no response to that.

'Let's get to it,' he said, unbuttoning his jacket and throwing it down onto the ground.

The quartermaster cleared his throat. 'I believe, sirs, that I'm required at this time to ask you to confirm that you are acting of your volition and both intend to proceed.'

'I do,' Carson said quickly. The fluttering was in his blood now. The familiar excitement pulsed around his body.

'Oh yes,' Ross confirmed.

'Very well,' the quartermaster sighed. 'On your honour, sirs.' He set off out of the woods; the other officer followed. Red hooked Carson's jacket up off the grass and went after them. Carson and Ross were finally alone.

'So this, dear friend,' Ross said, 'will be our last time. No holding back, eh?'

Carson could not have agreed more. 'No holding back.'

A FEW MINUTES later, Carson emerged from the woods. Red handed him his jacket and Carson gave him a curt nod of thanks. The other two officers, pale-faced, went to collect their friend's body.

News of the death of Captain Ross came as little surprise to his fellows in the 29th. Carson's reputation as a duellist was well known, infamous even. It was his duelling, or at least one particular duel in the first year of the crusade, that had finished his career and consigned him to live out the rest of his career at his present, lowly rank.

Ross had already walked out with him three times, each time coming back wounded and defeated, but still nursing his grudge against the deadly lieutenant of the 11th. At least, his fellows said, this last time Ross had done the decent thing and waited until the end of the campaign.

In past times, twenty, fifteen, even ten years before, the officers of the 29th would have felt slighted at such a defeat. A deadly feud might have erupted, more duels might have been fought, more officers incapacitated or killed. But now, here at the end, none of them was willing to pick up Ross's cause. Strangely, the idea of confronting a man who had survived two decades of war across the most lethal battlefields and shooting him dead for the sake of honour was less appealing at their age than it had been in their youth. They were tired and they had had enough.

The 29th was struck off the order of battle, their colours were returned home to form the core of a new regiment in a future founding. They were settled on Kandhar, there to keep in check the native human tribes liberated from the Karthadasim. The officers of the 29th and the other garrisoned regiments soon established themselves as the new noble elite of the world and began indulging in the rewards peace offered, that so few of them had survived to enjoy.

And the same fate should have been awaiting the long-serving officers and men of the 11th as well, if there had been any justice in the galaxy.

CHAPTER TWO

Imperial cruiser Relentless, *Kandhar low orbit*

THERE WAS NO justice in the galaxy, Colonel Arbulaster decided. If there had been then he would not have been rousted from the midst of the victory celebrations, then forced to endure an hour's shuttle journey into orbit, and all on the general's whim.

He stepped onto the hangar deck and was greeted by a young Navy officer. Arbulaster hid the scowl of annoyance he had been wearing ever since he'd received the general's summons behind his bushy moustache and wearily returned the youth's salute. He introduced himself as acting sub-something or other, but Arbulaster never had much patience for the titles and ranks of the Imperial Navy. As far as he was concerned, as the colonel of a Brimlock regiment, the only ranks he needed to know were those of ship's captain and higher.

The youth led him off the hangar deck, making polite small talk as they went. Arbulaster limited his responses to small affirmative grunts as he fought down the nausea caused by the flight and his preceding celebratory excesses. He resisted the urge to plug his ears against both the youth's chatter and the deep-pitched, omnipresent pulsing of the engines which churned his stomach.

They arrived on the command deck and the background pulse became a cacophony created by the constant chatter of the hundred or so crew crammed into the area, all punctuated by a diverse succession of trilling alarms, all obviously routine given the lack of interest the crew appeared to show. Arbulaster did not know how the Navymen could stand it. Every inch of space on the deck had a purpose; it was packed with consoles and arrays, some sunk into the floor, others climbing into small towers. The walls themselves were covered by bank after bank of logistician and cogitator rows, all appearing to be frantically busy even though the ship, as far as Arbulaster could tell, wasn't doing anything. The bridge itself arched over the width of the deck and above it hung the Imperial aquila, its sculpted wings just as wide as the bridge itself, keeping watch over them all.

The youth asked him to wait and then excused himself. Arbulaster paused a moment and then took a few steps over to one of the more reflective consoles. Whilst trying to maintain an air of interest in the crewman's operation, he surreptitiously checked his appearance. Hang the inconvenience of the early reveille, if he had been brought here for the reason he expected then it would all be worth it. The rumours had been rife amongst the regimental commanders: the general was standing the Brimlock regiments down; assigning their old, tired Guardsmen as permanent garrisons to the worlds they had won. His days in this seemingly endless crusade, the magnum opus of Lord-General Ellinor, were done. He had survived. He had survived.

His men would live out their days here on these

fringe-worlds and help bring them into the Imperium. Arbulaster, however, was going home.

'Arb!' a familiar voice called to him. It was Colonel Thabotka, descending from the bridge, a hand out-stretched in salutation.

'Good morning, colonel.' Arbulaster forced a smile and returned the greeting.

'Is it morning?' Thabotka replied breezily. 'I can't tell a thing aboard these crates.'

Arbulaster was glad that the ship's captain was still up on his dais and out of earshot of that last remark. Thabotka was not a Brimlock officer. He was, in Arbulaster's opin-ion, with his manners and his casual familiarity, not a Brimlock officer in almost every respect. Instead, he was from Hellboken, one of the dozen other planets which had contributed Guardsmen to the crusade. Despite this, and even though they were of equal rank, Arbulaster knew well enough to treat him with a great deal of courtesy, for Thabotka was on the general's staff. It was they who were making the decisions on which regiments were staying and which were fighting on.

'Listen, Arb,' Thabotka continued blithely, 'the gener-al's real wrapped up right now; these negotiations have been nothing but delay after delay. I'm here with his regrets, but so you don't have a wasted journey, he'd like me to have this chat with you instead.'

'Of course,' Arbulaster replied. He felt his chest tighten. Thabotka was the kind of man who would begin by say-ing how much he liked you, and finish by sticking you a task as rotten as a gangrenous leg. He was more than a staff colonel, he was the general's personal enforcer. When there were rewards and medals to be given, the general appeared. If an unpleasant conversation was to be had, he sent Thabotka.

They left the command deck behind and adjourned to

one of the chambers set aside for the general's use. One corner of the cabin had a pict viewer playing the latest transmission of the Voice of Liberation with its regular thundering denunciation of the crusade's foes. The rest of the wall-space was festooned with trophies of animals and xenos. In different circumstances Arbulaster, a game hunter himself, would have been most interested in examining them more closely. As it was, he kept his attention fixed upon Thabotka.

The staff colonel muted the pict viewer, picked up a small case of lohgars from the desk and offered one to Arbulaster. Arbulaster picked it up and caught a strange scent from it.

'Exotic, isn't it,' Thabotka remarked. 'You know where it's from?'

'No,' Arbulaster said as he accepted Thabotka's light.

'It's from right here. From right on Kandhar,' Thabotka said. 'Turns out the humans have been growing it here ever since the Great Crusade. Before that even. Even the Karthas liked it.'

Arbulaster grunted. 'Hard to imagine us all sitting down with the xenos and sharing a puff.'

Thabotka gave a chuckle, both friendly and insincere. 'I like you, Arb. It's always a pleasure when our paths cross.'

Arbulaster stayed quiet as Thabotka lit his own and carried on, chewing the words out with the lohgar still in his mouth. 'The general needs you to do him a favour, Arb. He needs you to do the whole crusade a favour.'

Arbulaster didn't dare draw breath.

'You ever heard of Voor?'

'No,' Arbulaster replied.

'No reason you should.' Thabotka continued. 'Never heard of it myself until a few days ago. Pioneer world. Colony set up about a century ago, sent out from Frisia. Mostly uninhabited. Turns out, though, that we may have left a bit of a mess there.'

'Have we ever even set foot on it?'

'Didn't need to. An orkoid ship, or rok or whatever they call it, crashed there about a year ago. The general reckons it's probably a leftover from that ork armada which crossed our path back in '56.'

'I thought Ingertoll and the Navy got 'em all?'

'So did I, Arb. So did the general. But with Ingertoll and his staff biting it in the fight, who did we have who knew for sure? Captain Marcher says that the Navy knew. He says the Navy reported to Command. Maybe they did. Back then all I know was that every single eye at Command was focused on Cawnpore, Carmichael and the 67th.'

'I wasn't there,' Arbulaster said quickly. 'The Eleventh was fighting on Ordan for most of '56.'

Thabotka chuckled again. 'You know, Arb, of all the Brimlock officers I've met, I've never met one who was on Cawnpore. I find that a truly amazing coincidence considering how many Brimlock regiments we sent there.'

Arbulaster bristled at that. Rank had its privileges, but he could not remain silent at Thabotka's insinuation.

'I am certain that you have access to my service record if you doubt my word, colonel.'

Thabotka held up his hand in mock defeat. 'Of course, of course, Arb. Never doubted you. Never doubted you at all. And that's why the general trusts you with this Voor business. There's probably nothing to it. Command reckons that none of the orks even survived the crash. You'll just need to head over, fly the colours, let these Voorjers feel protected.'

But his reassurances fell on deaf ears. Arbulaster knew that Crusade Command was notorious for filling their briefing dockets from the closest source of information to hand. Arbulaster had seen dockets chock-full with detailed information about tithing, imports and exports and the names of long-dead governors, whilst only vaguely alluding to certain facts, such as the planet's highly toxic atmosphere, freezing temperatures, constant darkness, perennial monsoons or tunnelling hyper-predators.

'If none of them survived, why isn't Command leaving this to the local PDF?'

'They don't have them. No PDF. No Administratum. No arbitrators. Not even an Ecclesiarchy mission.'

'Nothing?' A suspicion slid into the back of Arbulaster's mind. For a world, even a colony, to have no trace of the Imperial institutions had a most definite implication.

'That's right, Arb. Appears our Voorjers are very keen on their *independence*.' Thabotka's stress on that last, near treasonous word was unmistakeable. 'But the general is a generous man, so he's going to give them exactly what they're asking for. And that brings me on to the other favour you can do him.'

ARBULASTER CLIMBED ON board the shuttle taking him back to the planet's surface and back to his regiment. He held his orders, both sets of them, and also a listing of the officers and men who were being reassigned from other regiments to replace his losses. He had not glanced at it yet, and even if he had, the names of Major Stanhope and of Private 'Blanks' Stones would have not yet meant anything to him.

Troop ship Brydon, *transporting Brimlock 11th en route to Voor*

BLANKS HAD COME to miss his paranoia. The unnerving fiction that everyone had been out to get him was starting to feel strangely preferable to the truth that everyone, absolutely everyone, was entirely uninterested in him. The men of the second platoon of Carson's company were not malicious, they were simply unrelenting in their apathy towards him. He hadn't needed to have picked up his nickname from the blank pages of his service record; it could easily be used to describe the expression in the face of every man in the platoon to whom he started speaking.

The mystery of his service record had at least been resolved. Apparently, his had never made it to the medicae station, but the officials had filled one in for him as a placeholder while waiting for a reply from Crusade Command. As soon as that had come in, they brought it to his bedside. Blanks had read it carefully. It was the typical banal record of a soldier who had fought for nineteen years and yet never been promoted. There was a list of campaigns, a smattering of minor disciplinary matters, a single limp commendation and that was all. What a great disappointment it had been to have the great question of one's life answered and to be revealed as such a mediocrity.

He had stopped causing trouble then, and when he was finally discharged with orders to report to the 11th, he went without a fight.

He no longer even felt bitter towards his platoonmates. He had started to understand what they had gone through during the crusade, what he must have gone through as well, but with the blessing that every trauma, every stain on his memory had been wiped clean. When he had first joined the platoon, he had put his kit down on an empty bunk, only to have the man on the bunk above scream at him to get out of his mate's place.

Blanks had got up and the man had instantly fallen back to sleep. He would have no recollection of the incident in the morning. Blanks had eventually found space at the far end of the room near the ogryn, who appeared to have attached himself to the platoon. No one slept there except Gardner because of the smell. And, he learned later, no one ever slept in the empty bunk below the man who screamed at him, because his mate had been hit by an eldar needle-shot on Azzabar that had burned him alive from the inside.

The subsequent days in the *Brydon's* hold had been little different. The company had a regular routine of drill, exercise, meals and rest. Blanks followed along as best he could. A trooper named Mouse introduced him to the gambling games they played, to fill up the empty time in the evenings. The other troopers took an interest in him long enough to win his back-pay, and then they closed their company to him again.

Blanks did not care about the pay. It was in regimental scrip that couldn't be used anywhere that had anything worth buying. He did not even miss the conversations that he'd had whilst he'd gambled it away. They had been awkward. The men of his platoon spoke in their own language of short, truncated sentences, whose fuller meaning had been established over the years that they had been in one another's company. Their words were riddled with obscure references to battles long-fought and men long-dead. During one game, another trooper had walked past, looked at the position on the board and made a noise like a straining animal. The other players creased up in laughter and Blanks could only stare on while he waited for the game to continue. But that one occasion where Mouse had asked about him had been even worse.

'You don't know anything?'

Blanks fished out his tags. 'Just what's on here. Trooper John Stones. Thirteenth Dragoons.'

'The Thirteenth?' Mouse said. 'I heard they all bit it in the drop on Jug Dulluk last year.'

'That's what I've heard as well.'

Mouse paused at that, frowned and unconsciously tucked his lower lip behind his teeth in thought.

'You don't remember anything?'

'No.'

'What's the first thing you remember?'

'Waking up in a medicae station on Kandhar.'

'And what happened then?'

'I was tired. I fell asleep.'

Mouse asked again and Blanks told him what he could. While the 11th and the 29th and every other Brimlock regiment that had survived the crusade completed the lengthy process of reducing the fortress-world of Kandhar, he had been tucked up safe in a bed, trying to bring the man he had been back from the darkness. None of the medicae knew how he had come to be there; their only interest was keeping him quiet and then turfing him out. The 13th Dragoons had been wiped out, so there was no one there to ask. But even that small piece of knowledge caused him trouble.

The grey-haired sergeant of the second platoon, Forjaz, had called him aside:

'This thing, about you being one of the Thirteenth.'

'Yes, sergeant?'

'Don't spread it around any more.'

'I haven't,' Blanks said. 'I haven't spread anything, sergeant. I don't know anything, just that that was my last regiment.'

'That's what I'm talking about. Don't spread it around any more.' Blanks still did not understand. 'I'm only looking out for you. They can be a superstitious lot, Guardsmen. They hear you're the only survivor of a regiment that got hit, it starts them thinking.'

'Thinking what?' Blanks asked.

'That maybe you think you're special?' Forjaz replied, irritated at the question. 'Maybe you think you've been touched by the Emperor?'

'I don't, sergeant.'

'Or that maybe you're lucky? The kind of luck that means you'll walk away even when the rest of your platoon bites it.'

'I don't think that at all.'

'Good,' Forjaz said bluntly. 'But maybe some of the others do. If they think they've got a man of destiny amongst them, it starts them thinking. It starts them thinking that they don't want to be the trooper that takes the shot that was meant for you. That they don't want to be the trooper who follows you on some mad charge that means their death and your glory. They don't like men with a destiny; they tend to get everyone else around them killed.'

'I don't,' Blanks stated. 'I don't think I have a destiny. I just want to serve.'

Forjaz paused a moment. 'Who?' he quizzed. 'Who do you think you serve?'

It was a question Blanks hadn't expected. Guardsmen served. There was a never a question of who; you served Him. 'The Emperor,' Blanks said.

'Wrong,' Forjaz corrected. 'Out here, there is no Emperor. You serve me. You serve the lieutenant. You serve the platoon. You serve the man beside you. That's how we make it through. All together. You understand me? If you wanted to be a hero, you shouldn't have joined the Guard.'

PERHAPS, BLANKS CONSIDERED, Forjaz had had good intentions. But it was plain even to Blanks that if Forjaz knew something, it would have gone around the company a dozen times already.

Forjaz was the only man left in the company whose wife and children had won the ballot to travel with the regiment. His family, along with the others, were required to keep their own company. His wife worked for the gastromo, his daughters helped the medicae and his son was himself a cadet-sergeant in the Boy Company, soon to join the ranks as a full Guardsman. They were kept separate on board ship from the unmarried men and those rest periods when the men talked, Forjaz spent in the married men's quarters.

It was this that made him an odd man out. He ran the platoon with precision and efficiency, and could bawl a private out with the best of them. But unlike Lieutenant Carson, whom the men adored, and Colour-Sergeant Red, who struck terror into them, Forjaz was only ever simply obeyed. The men of second platoon respected his rank, but he was not one of them.

Forjaz might have been an odd man out, but he certainly was not the oddest man out in the platoon. That honour belonged elsewhere.

'Yes, I'd agree. It's too late for you now,' Ducky, the company medic, told Blanks as he waited with the rest of the platoon for their routine examinations.

'What?'

Ducky hissed through his teeth as he studied the chart in his hand. 'We're going to have to take that foot.'

'What? What's the matter with my foot?'

'It's quite abnormal, I'm afraid. Almost mutated. The toes are hugely splayed and elongated. Your big toe is nearly entirely dislocated. I'm surprised you can even wear those boots.'

'The boots feel fine. My foot feels fine. Which one are you even talking about?'

Ducky stared down, then stared at the chart, then turned it upside down.

'Ah, my mistake, trooper. That's a very healthy-looking hand you have there.'

There was a chortle from the other men, not so much at the laboured wisecrack, but at Blanks's confusion.

'Are you really the medic?' he asked.

'That's what it says on my badge.' Ducky replied. The lanky Guardsman with the permanent half-grin proudly displayed a piece of white plastic he had pinned to his uniform. It had 'MEDIC' handwritten on it in black ink and a crude copy of the medicae helix drawn below.

'That's not official,' Blanks said.

'Are you trying to be funny?' Ducky replied sternly.

'No.'

'That's a shame. I need all the help I can get.'

And so it went with Ducky. If you got him alone he could be serious and sensible enough, but put him in front of a group and he couldn't help performing. The constant barrage of puns and jokes were almost involuntary, a nervous tick developed either as a symptom of his madness or as the only way he had kept himself sane all these years.

When working, however, Ducky could be very serious.

'Are you having trouble remembering anything that's happened since?' Ducky examined Blanks's torso. His chest was as big as a barrel and had old scars and burns enough to make his skin look diseased. Whatever the problems with his mind, Blanks's body was in great condition, especially amongst the ageing Brimlock troopers. Doubtless that was the reason that the old hands of the platoon had given him no trouble when he joined.

'No. That's been fine.' Blanks sat up on the slab in the tiny med-chamber the regiment was allowed. 'The medicae before, they told me it was probably shock. That it might just be a matter of time.'

Ducky ignored him. 'And you don't remember anything before. Nothing of your old regiment? Nothing of Brimlock? Not even a sight or a smell? Nothing in your dreams?'

'No, it's all blank.'

'Hence the name.'

'Yeah,' Blanks said, ruefully. 'Why do they call you Ducky?'

'There, my friend, you have a choice between the mundane and the slanderous,' Ducky said, studying the auspex readings on the panel beside him. 'The mundane is that my name is Drake and that your average trooper is unable to resist such an obvious soubriquet. The slanderous is that I am a coward who tosses away his lasgun and ducks for cover at the merest hint of an enemy.'

'And that's not true?'

'Oh, no, it's true. But the reason I do it isn't because I'm a coward.'

Blanks thought on it a moment. 'Why is it then?'

'It's because I don't want to kill people.'

Blanks laughed out loud, but Ducky was serious.

'That's another joke, right? It's a good one.'

'I've seen a lot of men die. Some of them even had my hands in their chests as they went. But none of them died because of me. And that's the way it's going to stay.'

'You've never killed at all?' Blanks said in disbelief. 'How long have you been in the Guard?'

Ducky looked up from the auspex readings. 'I'm only a Guardsman because they put the pen in my hand and the gun to my head and I didn't want to put them to the trouble of cleaning my brain off the wall. Humanity owes the Emperor its existence, and He can have my life if He so chooses. But I can't give Him another's. It's not my right.'

Blanks was stunned. He had never heard such sentiments expressed before. Had he been a commissar he would have been obliged to execute Ducky on the spot. Killing, especially killing enemies of the Imperium, was not an ethical dilemma, it was a religious imperative.

'I'm surprised you've lasted this long, if that's what you believe,' Blanks said.

Ducky was not fazed by Blanks's attitude. 'I think,

private, as you come to know this platoon and this company, you will find that there is one and perhaps only one characteristic that all of us share.'

'And what's that?'

'That we do what it takes to do what we do and live with ourselves afterwards.' The smile had vanished from Ducky's face.

'Can we just get this over with?' Blanks stood up, eager to be away from the medicae bay and its strange occupant. 'When's my memory coming back?'

'Are you sure it isn't already? You certainly salute well.' Ducky's voice had a touch of a sneer.

'I guess you'd just call that habit,' he spat back.

'Well, I'd call it an automated learned response personally, but that's why I'm the doctor and you're the patient.'

Blanks felt his hands clench into fists. 'When, Ducky?'

Ducky examined the auspex readings one last time. 'Your memory's not coming back.'

'Not ever?' If this was another of Ducky's jokes, Blanks was going to deck him.

'Would you like a second opinion?'

'Yes!'

'That uniform does absolutely nothing for your complexion.'

A few moments later, Blanks had stormed away, venting his irritation on the examination slab rather than Ducky's face. Left alone, Ducky sighed and shook his head. He felt sorry for the trooper, but there was no doubt. The signs of Commissariat mind-cleansing were there if you knew what you were looking for, and no Imperial medicae was going to try to reverse it, so that was that. He could only wonder what the poor wretch had ever done to deserve it.

CHAPTER THREE

IT WAS AT times such as these that Arbulaster rued the great distance between himself and Crusade Command that prevented him from reaching out and throttling the boneheaded incompetents who worked there with his bare hands. Discreet inquiries! That was what he had wanted. Discreet inquiries! A scratch of someone's back, a word in the right ear. He most certainly had not wanted this!

He paced, furious, back and forth in front of his second-in-command, Major Brooce, who was holding the two offending communiqués. The first was from the office of the High Admiral stating that all battleships capable of planetary bombardment were fully engaged and that none could be spared to make a round-trip to Voor, even just to bomb a small part of it. The second one was from the office of the Imperial Governor of Voor, who had been copied in on the first communiqué which included a lengthy study demonstrating that any such bombardment on the scale necessary would cause such ecological damage to the planet as to force the colony to be abandoned. It included a short personal note from the governor herself, somewhat wryly observing that they had only begun colonising the world a century ago and that she had wondered how long it would take the Imperium to want to start blowing pieces of it up. That note had been copied into the office of Lord-General Ellinor.

Discreet inquiries. That was what he had asked for. But how could he wield his influence effectively from inside this rust-bucket of a ship, speeding into the abyss? Thabotka had certainly known what he was doing, packing them off so quickly; with a few weeks on Kandhar near the general, he might have manoeuvred himself out of it altogether. Even if not his men, at least himself.

'Shall I take care of it, sir?' Brooce offered.

'And how would you do that?' Arbulaster replied, still seething.

'Clarificatory communiqué to all parties concerned citing that the original request was truncated, mistranslation by the astropath concerned; strongly refuting any suggestion that you will not be carrying through your duty to the greatest capacity possible. The usual.'

Arbulaster thought on it. 'Yes, yes, Brooce, take care of it exactly like that. Good. Very good.'

Brooce had learned a lot from him, Arbulaster decided.

'Yes, sir,' Brooce said. 'And, sir? The officers have arrived.'

'What officers?'

'The new officers, sir. Your personal interviews. We have delayed them as long as we could.'

'Oh, Blessed Marguerite, if I must I must.' Arbulaster found such rituals excessively tedious and entirely pointless. He could make a far better judgement of a man after observing him in action for ten minutes than he could after days of courteous conversation. Then he remembered exactly who he had been given, and the details he had read in the service records. Perhaps it would not be entirely pointless in that particular case.

'Get them together, Brooce,' Arbulaster said, retreating behind his desk. 'And tell Parker to save you-know-who for last.'

MAJOR STANHOPE SAT in the colonel's antechamber with the five other transferring officers. He had been waiting a long time and the benches around the sides of the small room were not comfortable, but he did not mind. A steward had come round and offered them tanna, and the other officers chatted amongst themselves as their drinks were poured. Stanhope heard their conversation, the careful verbal reconnaissance that each man was performing, testing the ground, determining their rung upon this new ladder. They noted the rank markings, they noted the medals, they noted the insignia of their former regiments. They asked innocuous questions in order to determine who had been promoted to captain first, who was assigned command of a company first, who had been the first to see combat. Such things mattered to them, even here at the end.

Except, of course, it was not the end. Not for them, perhaps. They all knew it was to be the last campaign of the old Brimlock 11th. But after it was done and the men were granted their release, the regiment's colours would be sent home, laden with its battle honours, and would be used to raise a new Brimlock 11th. And the colonel and a few chosen others would accompany them as the colour-guard. Of the ten million men who had left Brimlock at the beginning of this crusade, only the colour-guard would ever set foot on their home world again. There they would be fêted, rewarded, promoted, and then they would form the elite of the new regiments, reborn under colours soaked in history, and they would go and wage the Emperor's wars in another part of the galaxy.

None of the other officers spoke to Stanhope, but that was fair as he did not speak to any of them. They noted his rank, they noted his medals, but then they noted his old insignia and the thick curved blade hanging from his belt frog, and they knew that he was no competition. Stanhope did not notice their glances; instead, his eyes were fixed upon his drink. He had put a blob of honey on the inside of his cup and watched the thick, golden liquid slowly ooze down towards the brown tanna. They touched and, for a few moments, the honey retained its shape like oil in water, one liquid separate within another; then they intermingled and the honey disappeared.

The door to the colonel's office opened and the adjutant poked his head out. He called for a Captain Ledbetter and the officer dressed in the uniform of a cavalry captain put his cup to one side and, with a trace of self-satisfaction, followed the adjutant in. The jaws of the other officers tightened a fraction and they occupied themselves so as to appear nonchalant. As Ledbetter went in, they all heard the colonel's voice raised in hearty salutation.

One by one, the other officers had their names called and they walked through the oak-panelled door. Stanhope blinked and realised that he was alone. He looked down at the undrunk tanna in his hand. It was cold. He put it down and decided to stand. He stamped his feet a little to quicken the blood, and stretched and adjusted the fell-cutter in its scabbard, so it hung flat against his thigh.

* * *

'I'M VERY PLEASED to be here,' the officer enthused. 'The Eleventh has quite a reputation.'

Arbulaster tried to recall the name of the officer he was interviewing. He stole a glance at the docket on his desk. Ah yes, Lieutenant Mulberry of the sappers, being consolidated from the 713th Heavy Pioneers. He should have guessed it from the beard; it seemed to be part of the uniform for sappers, though in Mulberry's case it appeared to have grown through an omission to shave, rather than through any deliberate intent.

'Glad to hear it, lieutenant,' Arbulaster replied, hoping that Mulberry wasn't going to try and reach across the desk and shake his hand. 'The 713th had quite a reputation as well, hope you're going to keep our standards high.'

'I've certainly got a lot of new ideas to try out, sir,' Mulberry beamed.

New ideas, Arbulaster thought? That sounds like the last thing the regiment needs.

'New ideas?' Arbulaster said. 'That sounds like just the thing the regiment needs.'

'I'm so pleased to hear it,' Mulberry replied and Arbulaster saw his hand come out from behind his back and begin to reach across.

'Dismissed!' Arbulaster snapped and Mulberry jumped to attention, saluted and strode out. The adjutant closed the door behind him. 'Shall I send in the last one, colonel?'

Arbulaster looked down at the sole docket left upon his desk.

'Hold on a moment.'

'Of course, sir.'

Arbulaster picked the docket up and flipped it open to the service record. Stanhope, R. B. de R. H. 639.M41, a second lieutenant with the newly raised Brimlock

33rd assigned to the Ellinor Crusade: 642, promoted to first lieutenant after the assault on Ketta and awarded the Bronze Halo; 643, awarded the Abject Hope in the storming of the fortress-city of Hanzi; 645, promoted to brevet captain during the action on Dahar; 646, awarded the Ellinor Star for the counter-boarding of an enemy cruiser in the Bukhat system; 649, promoted to major and given command of a whole regiment of margo auxilia, the 1201st. Then the Brimlock Crown, the Victory Laurel, the Bellum Opus, induction into the Order of St. Marguerite.

But, after the 1201st was dissolved after Ghilzai, nothing. Nothing for the last four years except for a litany of transfers. Stanhope had been bounced from one regiment to another, each colonel moving him on as soon as they could.

There were no citations, no reprimands, no rationale, nothing on the docket at least, but Arbulaster had heard the stories. Dereliction. Desertion. Insubordination. Intoxication. Assault. He had wondered why an officer with such a reputation had not been despatched by a commissar or a provost. That was one favour which his contacts at Command had been able to grant. A brief reply had come back: someone watched over him.

Stanhope, whether he knew it or not, had a guardian angel. And Arbulaster had not survived as long as he had by defying the angels. He didn't have to like it though.

Arbulaster composed himself. 'Very well, Parker.'

The adjutant nodded, showed Major Stanhope in and then exited discreetly. Stanhope stood at attention in front of the desk.

'Stand easy,' Arbulaster ordered automatically.

So this was the wretched Major Stanhope. Arbulaster was not surprised and not impressed. He had made the effort to shave on this occasion, but his cheeks were hollow and his reddened eyes sunk deep in their sockets. His uniform had obviously been fitted in more fortunate times and now it sagged slightly where a once-powerful frame had wasted away.

Arbulaster let the silence linger. He had found no quicker, more effective means of gaining the measure of a transferring officer: whether they shifted a fraction with discomfort; whether they, Emperor save 'em, actually started talking unbidden. Stanhope did neither, he merely stood easy, hands clasped loosely behind his back, his eyes focused on a point slightly above the colonel's head. No, Arbulaster realised, they were not focused, they were glazed.

'Damn it, man, are you on it now?'

'On what, colonel?'

Arbulaster could not bear to spend any more time with this man. He cut to the chase.

'I don't care who you were, major. I don't care what you've done. You are an officer under my command and that means you have two gods: the Emperor and myself. But unlike Him, I am a benevolent god. There are a hundred reasons why I might shoot you, but there's only one for which I'll damn you and that is if you do anything that results in the disruption of my regiment. You understand me?'

'Yes, colonel.'

'We have a vacant company command for you,' Arbulaster said with reluctance. 'Lieutenant Carson has been managing the shop there for the last few years. Done a damn fine job of it too. They're good men. They don't need much officering. Should suit you well as you ain't much of an officer.'

Stanhope did not respond despite the slur and so Arbulaster finished him off.

'One last thing, Stanhope. If you would be so kind as

to arrange matters to ensure that, after today, I never see you, never hear from you, never read your name, and am troubled by as few reminders of your existence as possible, I would consider it a personal favour.'

'I'll try my best, colonel.'

'See that you do.'

Arbulaster found that Major Stanhope was as good as his word. He absented himself from the colonel's world and the colonel returned the favour by pointedly omitting to endorse the transfer orders that would allow him to take command. Arbulaster had enough to fill his time as he swung the 11th's last campaign into gear.

The governor of Voor, despite their earlier 'miscommunications', proved helpful enough and, as the *Brydon* emerged from the warp, transmitted all the terrain information they had. The rok had landed on one of Voor's secondary continents, covered with forest or jungle. Arbulaster set his men to work to assess the most likely drop-sites. He had no intention of landing on the coast and spending weeks, more likely months, trekking inland. He would drop in, as close as was safe, and have the whole matter concluded in days.

Alongside the officers, there were new men to integrate into the regiment: two full companies of infantry under Captains Tyrwhitt and Wymondham, a few more of Mulberry's beards and, to Arbulaster's particular satisfaction, Captain Ledbetter's horse dragoons.

Arbulaster had been a horseman himself in the Brimlock planetary militia before the crusade was called and he was commissioned as a major in the armoured fist companies of the 282nd. He was not, despite appearances, one of those befuddled backward commanders that Brimlock occasionally produced who were convinced of the ultimate battlefield supremacy of the man on horseback. Ledbetter's horsemen would be useless in the jungles around the rok's crash-site, but afterwards, once the rok was taken, they would be indispensable.

Arbulaster sat at the heart of the whirlwind of planning and preparation, making quick yet confident decisions, with the assurance of great experience. He found that old feeling of the excitement and anticipation of a new campaign buzzing within his bones, and then he realised that it was for the last time. And then, despite his frenzy of activity, there was one, even older feeling that he had thought he had long overcome and yet now could not shake: fear.

One could not be afraid of one's death in the service of the Guard. Your chances of survival were too far beyond your control. One only had to step into the wrong drop-pod, the wrong transport, the wrong piece of ground. One could not do that for twenty years and fear for one's life each time, not and keep your mind together. But now this was the last. Now he could see how close he was. Now he realised the value his life could have if he could survive it all just one more time. He was marching into battle: some men would die, one of them would be the last. He could not let it be him.

Finally, five days after the *Brydon* had entered the edge of the system, it reached orbit and the 11th began their deployment. Despite all their preparation, the orks and their rok would have to wait a few days more. The 11th were not descending on them. They were descending on the governor.

CHAPTER FOUR

THE BRIMLOCK 11TH paraded in a precise column through the dusty main street of the capital, Voorheid. Arbulaster had ordered the column with a great deal of care so as to make the most impact on the rag-tag inhabitants of the capital. At the fore came the regiment's company of horse dragoons, the self-ordained elite of the Brimlock regiments, resplendent in their ceremonial armour. Behind them came the infantry, nearly eight hundred men marching in step with lasguns shouldered and fierce expressions on their faces. And then, the finale, the regiment's vehicles: the Chimeras which bore the infantry to battle, the Griffons with the gaping maws of their heavy mortars, and then the mighty Leman Russ battle tanks of the armoured company, which could grind the entire city beneath their tracks.

At the very head of the column were the regiment's colours: a single banner portraying the image of Brimlock's patron saint, Saint Marguerite, crested by the double-headed Imperial eagle and, on each side of her, stylised images of the ornate rifles for which Brimlock was renowned. In battle the colours were kept carefully sheathed until the critical moment when they might be unfurled to inspire the men to victory; on occasions such as this they were displayed by one of the horse dragoons, guarded on either side by the four colour-sergeants of the regiment, and at the head of those was Arbulaster himself.

Not all was quite how he might have wished, of course. The horse dragoons who had originally been mounted upon magnificent greys, through replacements and generations of breeding, were now a patchwork of different colours. At least, however, the horses still ran, which was more than could be said for many of the regiment's vehicles. The armoured company were the remains of the 920th Armoured, which had been folded into the 11th after Azzabar. They were a hodge-podge of different models and classes, all requiring constant maintenance from their crews and the regiment's tech-priest.

The transport Chimeras were in an even worse state, having been cannibalised to keep the tanks of the armoured company functioning. At the beginning of the crusade, the regiment had been equipped with enough Chimeras to carry every man as a dragoon regiment should. The men, however, lasted longer than the machines and so now there were barely enough to carry two of the ten infantry companies.

As for the men themselves, while they all appeared to wear the classic uniform of the Brimlock regiments, twenty years of repair and replacement had left every man with slight variations, whether in pattern or material or colour. The differences even extended to their insignia, as the stubborn veterans of the other regiments that had merged into the 11th kept something of their original regimental markings, merely shifting them to make room for the new. Simply by examining the uniforms alone one could trace back the hundred or more regiments which had now merged into one. Arbulaster understood the men's recalcitrance; he himself had been loath to give up the insignia of the 282nd even after its losses on Mespots had led to its dissolution.

The trained eye, then, would have identified the many signs of wear upon the 11th, but the trained eye would also have recognised what else those signs indicated: that these men were survivors and killers in equal measure.

The people for whom Arbulaster had arranged the procession, however, were far from trained. The ragged occupants of what laughably passed for Voor's capital city watched from the side of the street and the windows of the squat buildings. Their clothes and their skin were marked with dirt. Even though the Guard had come at their invitation to rid them of a foe that threatened their lives, their mood was quiet, their eyes hidden by the shadows cast beneath their wide-brimmed hats.

None of them cheered. None of them doffed their hats. None of them even called out in praise of the Emperor. Arbulaster had taken the effort to make the procession appear more as a parade than an invasion and had had Captain Drum play a triumphal hymn over the vox-casters on his tank, but it made little difference to the sombre expressions of the crowd. They simply stared.

Arbulaster knew what these people were and he knew what they were thinking. They were not pioneers, they were escapees: men and women who had thought to flee the strictures and the duties of citizens of the Imperium by running to this virgin world, leaving all the institutions they loathed behind.

For a hundred years or so they had been allowed their liberty. Now, they thought, here the Imperium was finally coming after them. First the Guard, then the Administratum with its tithes, and then the Ecclesiarchy with its witch-hunts. And then what would follow after? No matter what Arbulaster did, the colonists of Voor would always resent him and his troops, and so he had organised this display of strength. Let them resent him if they must, but they would fear him too.

Arbulaster glanced over to where the governor was watching them. She would know that this was not simply a procession; she would know that Arbulaster had called her colonists here so that they might meet their new masters.

Voorheid, Brimlock landing area, Voor pacification
Stage 1 Day 2

'I HEAR YOUR colonel near got his arse bit off by the governor's pets yesterday.'

Carson turned from watching the Valkyries landing and taking off around him to the Voorjer scout beside him.

'I didn't hear that,' Carson lied. He had heard it; everyone in the regiment had heard of the altercation between Arbulaster and the governor in their private discussions. Apparently, Arbulaster at one point had cause to raise his voice and had inadvertently awoken the governor's pair of leathertooths which had been asleep beneath her desk.

Carson did not know if the colonel had actually been injured, but he understood that his exit from the interview had been extremely swift.

'I hear Sarel and Hendril still got bits of his breeches between their teeth,' the scout carried on, highly amused. Her pronunciation of Low Gothic was harshened by her clipped and guttural Frisian accent

Carson left the scout's jibing alone. Her name was Van Am and she was one of the Voorjers who had been living on the Tswaing continent before the rok's crash, now assigned to help guide the 11th through the terrain and lead them to the orks. She was young, not particularly pretty, but with an attractive youthful vigour about her, and at present she was extremely nervous.

She tried to hide it behind an aggressive, no-nonsense demeanour, but in doing so she made her anxiety all the more obvious. Obvious to Carson at least. He doubted that the rest of the 11th's pathfinder detachment had even acknowledged her existence.

The pathfinder detachment consisted of Mulberry, his bearded sappers and, as far as Carson could discern, enough plans and print-outs to paper the hull of a battleship. They were still poring over terrain maps and arguing over the best place to site the regiment's operational base, even though in a few hours' time they would be there to see them in person.

Carson was there to protect them in case they needed to descend to the jungle floor. Major Brooce had told him he had been assigned because the colonel had particular faith in him. Carson suspected it was more likely that no senior officer had been willing to be cooped up with the 'beards' for most of the day.

With the pathfinders wrapped up in their own disputes, and with their Valkyrie pilot delayed, it left conversation between him and Van Am regretfully inevitable. Regretful because, as Carson was perhaps the first representative of the galaxy-spanning regime known as the Imperium of Man she had ever personally encountered, she appeared determined to convince him of the many betrayals of her people by that same Imperium.

'Don't take it personally, lieutenant,' she concluded. 'I didn't trust you before I met you. I thought it was a mistake inviting you in the first place. We should have dealt with it all ourselves.'

'Do you really think you would have been able to?'

Van Am gave a short snort of irritation. 'That's just what I expected from your kind. You can't conceive that anyone could take care of themselves without being in the grip of the Imperium, without the high and mighty Guard to rush and protect them, without your witch hunters and your judges burning out the innocent along with the guilty, without your priests preaching blind devotion to your dead Emperor. You think we're soft? Have you any idea what we've been through here? What we've had to struggle through and survive? How many we've lost just to make this our home? Of course you don't.'

Mercifully at that moment Carson saw their pilot, Zdzisław, approach and Van Am went quiet.

'Commander!' Carson called to him. 'How are you today?'

'It's a beautiful morning, lieutenant.' The mechanical Zdzisław stood at attention and snapped off a crisp salute. His chin was freshly shaved, his ashen hair was neatly combed and his right eye still twinkled blue, and that was perhaps all that was left of the original man. Everything else had been constructed afterwards. The rest of his face, his arms, his legs were metal; Navy bionics in the critical places, hand-welded plates and gears in the rest. They were his legacy of twenty years secondment to the Brimlock 11th.

Carson caught the look of restrained horror on Van Am's face out of the corner of his eye. 'Are you all set?' he inquired.

'We've the party plan already; shouldn't take more than a few hours once we get the old bird in the air.' Zdzisław's natural voice had been lost during the raid on

Kaswan Bay and instead his words emanated in a toneless electronic dirge from a vox-box fitted in his throat. What made it all the more eerie was that Zdzisław, to appear more human, had managed to wire his metal jaw to move, but could not synchronise it with the words. It flapped randomly as he spoke, as though he were a puppet laughing madly at its own joke.

'You know about the aerial disturbance around the crash-site?' The rok itself was still generating an interference field which stretched out for miles around it, preventing any flyers from coming close.

'The governor's office has given me what they have. They don't have much, but our path should be safe.'

'Excellent,' Carson replied and finally turned to the Voorjer woman who was still gaping horribly at this man who had been so violently disassembled and so painstakingly put back together. 'Holder Van Amersfoort, this is our pilot, Squadron Commander Zdzisław.'

Zdzisław politely held out the metal bones of his hand. **'Good morning, ma'am.'**

Van Am had enough sense about her to take hold of the cold grip and shake it. Her movements were as mechanical as the pilot's.

'It's holder actually. The correct title.'

'Apologies, holder.'

'Van Am,' Carson continued the introductions, 'is the governor's granddaughter.'

Zdzisław let his head fall a fraction and then jerked it back in the approximation of a nod. **'Pleasure to meet you.'**

Van Am stared at Carson. 'I never said that.'

Carson held her stare lightly. 'Do you really think that I'd allow myself or my men to go into danger alongside someone without knowing exactly who they are and what they might do?'

Van Am blinked. 'No. I suppose not.'

'Perhaps a rule to live by, then,' he told her curtly and then followed Zdzisław towards his Valkyrie. Van Am went after them and received a second shock when she saw Zdzisław's flyer. Many pilots, over time, grew attached to a particular craft. They would name it, record its victories, even start to believe that its quirks and defects were part of its own personality. Zdzisław had gone further. Much further. He was not fond of his Valkyrie, he was in love with it, worshipped it, was obsessed with it. Over the years he had painted every inch with lavish, elaborate, sometimes explicit, talismanic images. Each one he considered a labour of love, a symbol of his passion and gratitude for every occasion that the Valkyrie had taken him into battle and brought him home again.

The other pilots kept their eccentricities far better hidden, yet still Zdzisław had been promoted to squadron commander, in part because his devotion made his Valkyrie the most reliable, the most exceptional vehicle in the flight.

Van Am, however, had no clue as to this. She could only watch as Zdzisław went through his regular rituals of stroking and caressing the flyer's nose, whispering into one of its vents, whilst his co-pilot performed the more mundane pre-flight checks.

Those completed, they took off, leaving the huddled settlement of Voorheid behind, and were soon jetting over the blue ocean. Van Am had taken a seat opposite Carson, but stayed silent throughout the trip. Carson was content not to have to shout over the Valkyrie's engines and instead turned his thoughts to a more serious matter than how to handle a young woman frightened for her world. That matter was his prospective commanding officer, Major Stanhope.

The colonel had warned him about Major Stanhope,

or rather he hadn't. A Brimlock officer, when speaking to his junior, would never malign another, especially when that officer was the junior's commanding officer. It simply wasn't done. But the fact that the colonel, when he told Carson of the new appointment, did not recommend Stanhope as 'good' or 'solid' was far more damning than a whole litany of indictments from an officer of another world.

Stanhope was not one of us, Arbulaster had told him. Carson had heard that charge levelled at several officers during his career, applied to weak-kneed saps who fainted at the first sight of the enemy, to shell-shocked officers who spoke to flowers and expected a reply, to psychotic butchers who smeared themselves in blood and declared themselves the Emperor's True Prophet. It was an accusation that meant nothing in specific and everything in general.

Carson's relations with the former company commander, Captain Blundell-Hollinshed-Blundell, who was as ill-fated as he was ill-named, had started badly and continued in the same vein. The captain had been appointed towards the end of the Ordan campaign; Carson had returned with his company foetid and coated with mud from a long patrol slogging through the Katee river delta. Rather than present the company to their new commander in their bedraggled state, Carson had given them a few hours to rest and clean themselves up. Blunder nearly charged Carson with mutiny as a result for retaining command for that time.

Blunder's drilling had not been petty vindictiveness, though; it had been ambition. It was an ingrained, insatiable ambition amongst the officer corps. Each one wanted promotion. Each one wanted to be part of the colour-guard. All of them craved the immortality that glory would bring with such a fierce desire as to push them to insanity. And none of them hesitated to spend their men's lives in their quest, especially now in the crusade's last gasps where colour-guards were going home after each campaign.

Such immortality, however, almost invariably came at the cost of the lives of the men who served under them.

Carson had expected the same from Stanhope, but when they finally met that morning, he had been surprised.

'Lieutenant Carson? Major Stanhope,' Stanhope had introduced himself at breakfast in the officers' mess.

Carson rose to stand to attention, but Stanhope stopped him. 'No need for that,' he said. 'I don't want to disturb.'

Instead, Stanhope sat down with him. Carson regarded him as he adjusted his sword as he sat. He looked tired, even for early in the morning, and his uniform was rumpled as though he had slept in it.

'It's good to meet you finally,' Stanhope said.

'Yes, major,' Carson replied. 'You were on the *Brydon* with us?' Carson had been waiting for the major to appear for weeks on board the ship, but he had never emerged.

'The colonel tells me that there is some kind of administrative delay in signing the transfer papers. It appears I'm still not officially part of the regiment and so obviously can't take command of the company. I thought it best for the men that I not be hanging around while my status was still… uncertain.'

His sentiments made perfect sense, yet Carson still instinctively disbelieved him.

'I hope my absence did not cause you any problems,' Stanhope concluded.

'Not at all.' Carson found the honorific 'sir' on his lips, but could not bring himself to use it for this man. 'And have the administrative delays now been overcome?'

Stanhope didn't reply, he was staring at Carson's breakfast. 'Would you like me to call a steward over?' Carson offered.

Stanhope looked up, puzzled. 'If you'd like something to eat?' Carson continued.

'No, no. I've eaten already,' Stanhope replied. His eyes rolled lazily in their sockets as though searching for something in his own head. 'The administrative delays, no, I'm afraid not. Tomorrow, the colonel says.'

Arbulaster really was playing Stanhope along as long as he possibly could, Carson considered. He waited for Stanhope to continue, but the silence stretched between them. Stanhope appeared to have no other conversation besides his initial objective and Carson did not want to continue eating while being watched. Instead, he stood and Stanhope instinctively did the same.

'If you'd like to inspect the men first, major, I would be happy to arrange it.'

'What?' Stanhope said, surprised. 'No, that's fine, lieutenant. I'm happy to wait until everything's official.'

'Very well,' Carson said; again the 'sir' stuck behind his tongue. Instead, he saluted. Prompted, Stanhope saluted in response and then walked away. Carson stayed standing until the major left the mess and then sat back down, shaking his head, to finish his breakfast.

'We're getting close,' Van Am shouted, bringing Carson back to the present. 'Look out the window.'

Carson did. For a split-second it looked like they were flying over a grey continent of dark tangled rock. They were clouds so thick as to appear almost as though the flyer could land upon them. They stretched across the entirety of Carson's view, from one end of the horizon to the other.

The Valkyrie descended beneath the clouds and Carson

caught sight of the black water of the ocean beneath. Then, in an eye-blink, they crossed the coast and were over the jungle.

He realised Van Am had leaned forwards and was staring out of the same porthole.

'We'd barely touched Tswaing when the rok hit,' she said. 'We had just a few settlements on the coast. We thought we might be finished when we saw it coming towards us. First reports said it might be a planet-killer, thought we might have to abandon the place, everything we've done here. But the impact wasn't as big as we'd feared. It had slowed itself down as it entered our atmosphere. I tell you, we thanked the Emperor then, thought it was a miracle.

'These clouds, they formed after it hit. After the fire. The jungle didn't burn easily, but then the temperature dropped, and that and the lack of sun are slowly finishing the jungle off.'

Carson glanced at her. She took it for concern.

'Don't mistake me. That was lekker by us. We would have had to clear the jungle anyway. The cold killed the disease bugs, forced the critters to move north to where it's warmer. We even thought we could move up our timetable to expand.

'Once the fire stopped, we sent out a flyer to inspect the crash-site. That's when we discovered the interference. The first flyer didn't come back, we didn't know what had happened to it. Its vox cut off and we never heard from it again. The second we sent was a lot more cautious. As soon as the pilot felt the controls go, she dived and headed clear.

'We sent in a group on foot. They made it all the way to the impact crater, didn't see a single ork. The rok had buried itself under the ground.

'They should have left it buried, but they didn't know

then that it was the orks. They were just trying to find the source of the flying hazard. They found the rok quickly enough, the interference was coming from inside. They went in and there they found them: thousands of orks all dead, all dead from the impact. Piles of them in every pocket in the rok. Caverns full of war machines smashed beyond repair. They searched for whatever was generating the interference, but you can't tell ork tech from junk and so they decided to blow the whole thing.'

'Why didn't you?' Carson asked.

'We're farmers, lieutenant. We didn't have anything that would make a dent in it. We told your crusade. It crashed here because of you, we figured the least you could do is get us the explosives to finish it off.'

'And did we?'

'What do you think? Our request's probably still on the desk of some doos at your Command. We were still waiting when our men on the crater got hit. The resupply team found them all dead. Clubbed to death most of them, others nearly torn apart. All their rifles, all their weapons gone. That's when we first saw them, the orks. We didn't know what they were, but we knew they weren't native. The resupply team didn't hang around to ask questions. We reported that to your crusade as well and that's when they started talking back. Not help, just more questions. More delays.

'Fok to that, we said. You weren't going to lift a finger. We'd sort it ourselves. It took a couple of months, but Grandmother got a hundred men off the farms and sent them over. By that time, though, the orks had the crater. Our boys couldn't even get close. Their boss was a muggie, didn't have the nerve for a real fight. He lost a few men and turned them round and ran. That's when they came and took us from the villages on the coast. Said they couldn't be sure that the orks wouldn't cross half the continent to butcher us in our beds.'

Van Am was interrupted by Zdzisław's voice crackling around the cabin.

'We're over the first prospect point. I'll open the hatch to allow you a better view.'

The occupants of the Valkyrie attached themselves to safety lines and the rear hatch opened. The green canopy appeared almost grey in the dim light. It covered the landscape like a sea, pooling into the deep crevices and breaking around the peaks showing the bare soil, baked hard by the now absent sun.

Mulberry and his beards were quickly standing near the edge, alternately checking their auspexes and peering out of the craft to try and see the jungle floor. It was soon apparent that they were not happy and Mulberry returned up the craft to Carson.

'This is all dashed useless I'm afraid, Carson. Can't see a dashing thing down there in this light. And there's certainly nowhere to land. We're going to have to go out on the dangle, I'm afraid.'

Carson nodded and passed the message through to Zdzisław to be ready to have the team abseil out. He worked his way to the rear and started clipping himself on. Van Am followed him and did likewise. He leaned over and took her hand to stop her.

'Ma'am, no disrespect, but you're not going down there.'

He expected her to snap back at him, but she just snorted in derision. 'As I said, lieutenant, it's holder. From landholder. No disrespect, but this is my land and no offworlder is going to tell me where I cannot go. But I'll let you drop first, so if there are any fearsome critters you can shout us a warning as they take a bite out of you.'

Carson relented. He let her go and returned to his own harness. 'So long as there aren't any leathertooths,' he said. 'I hear they find the arses of Brimlock officers extremely tasty.'

That took the Voorjer girl off-guard. Van Am did not know if the Brimlock officer was joking with her or mocking her, and his dead-calm expression gave her no clues.

'Your man, the muggie,' Carson said, switching the subject. 'He wasn't wrong. I've fought orks. I've seen what they do. They care little for their own lives. Even less for those who aren't of their kind. Some fights you can only win by not starting them in the first place.'

'Maybe,' Van Am said. 'But if you stay dependent on others to fight your battles, to protect what you call your own, can you ever consider yourself truly free?'

Carson could not help shaking his head at that. In all his years, he had never heard such naïveté. On Brimlock, in the Imperium at large, freedom was not even a luxury, it was a myth. But he could see the conviction in the girl's face and knew better than to try to dissuade her.

Survival, that was all that mattered. Your own and those for whom you cared. That was why he was still fighting. He'd had it confirmed with the medicae before he left Kandhar; one way or another this was to be his last campaign. The only thing left that mattered to him was that his men survived, and he would allow no idealistic Voorjers, no glory-seeking officers and certainly no dried-up, defunct commanding officers like Stanhope to threaten that.

With that in his mind, he checked that his pistols were fastened securely by his side, tugged on his harness, took a hold of the rope and jumped down through the trees of Tswaing.

CHAPTER FIVE

IT HAD TAKEN two further days of pathfinder flights before an acceptable landing site had been agreed. Arbulaster signalled the *Brydon* to ready the DOV and finally signed the transfer orders allowing Major Stanhope to take command of Carson's company.

Carson was already awake when the notification arrived. Now he had given up on the medicae's ineffectual drugs, he found he only needed a few hours a night. Along with the notification was the standard form request from Stanhope for a handover inspection. Carson glanced at them and took them straight to Red.

The handover inspection from one officer to another was a serious event; new commanders took it as an opportunity to pick as many holes in the unit's readiness as possible, for after this they were liable for any flaw or defect the unit possessed. The unit's sergeants took it as a personal crusade to ensure that as few flaws were found as possible. Red rousted Forjaz and Booth at once and the three sergeants then woke the whole company and had them cleaning their body armour, polishing their lasguns and buffing their helmets within a few minutes.

They were glad they had done so, for when the time came and the company stood to attention outside the makeshift barracks, they discovered that Major Stanhope was not the only new member of the regiment present: a dozen yards back Commissar Reeve was also watching the proceedings, his visor down against the sun.

The commissar had also joined them after Kandhar and he had already made an impression on the men. He was an easily recognisable figure. He dressed in the ubiquitous uniform of a commissar: black cap, black coat, black boots. His one touch of personalisation, however, was that his coat was studded with skulls: hundreds and hundreds of miniature skulls.

The skulls were not for decoration, they were kill markings. Except for a commissar they would not have been kills. They would have been executions.

'First platoon, ready for inspection, sah,' Red told Carson and Stanhope. Stanhope nodded and led Carson down the line without stopping until he reached the end. He looked back and Carson waited for some comment, but there was none. Instead, Stanhope simply passed to the second line.

Forjaz then stepped forwards. 'Second platoon, ready for inspection, sir,' he said. Stanhope acknowledged him and started again, Carson a step behind. There came a point, Carson knew, when dirt became so ingrained in a fabric, or gunk so fouled a machine, that it could never be fully cleaned or made to operate again. The same was true of certain members of the company who, after twenty years of combat, had developed such dysfunctions that they could never fit back into the clean-cut press mould of the model Imperial Guard infantryman.

Marble could never be stopped from jury-rigging any weapon he was given in order to improve it, Zezé from sweating through any uniform he wore in minutes and Repton from hissing when he spoke through the wounds on the side of his face. Nothing could be done to make the lumbering ogryn Frn'k at all presentable, nor to tear him from the side of his adopted brother, Gardner. Blunder had nit-picked a list of issues as a long as a lasrifle, but Stanhope merely walked past them with no expression, his face waxen.

For a moment, Carson believed that the entire inspection would pass without incident, but then Stanhope stopped in front of Ducky.

Ducky stood perfectly at attention, his equipment all present and correct, with one glaring exception.

'Where's your weapon?' Stanhope asked.

'Sir, it's missing, sir,' Ducky snapped back.

Carson could see Reeve over Stanhope's shoulder focusing on the major. Technically, a soldier could be shot for losing his weapon, yet Ducky had declared it as easily as he might have commented on the weather.

'The campaign hasn't even begun, private. When did it go missing?'

'Sir, on a pathfinder flight yesterday, sir.' In fact, he had hurled it out into the undergrowth as soon as his feet had touched down in the jungle. Ducky, thankfully, did not share that detail.

'And you have requested a replacement?' Stanhope readied to move on.

'Sir, no, sir.'

The reply brought Stanhope up short. 'You've not?'

'Sir, no, sir.'

'And why is that?'

'Sir, I don't intend to use it, sir.'

Carson swore in his head, cursing Ducky and his damn

misguided principles. The man had earned five separate decorations for tending to and retrieving wounded men under horrendous fire, and he had been stripped of them all, one by one, because he refused to kill and refused to lie about it.

The whole company was focused now on Stanhope.

'What's your name, trooper?'

'Sir, Private Drake, sir,' Ducky replied with the cool, slight smile that Carson knew he would still be wearing when they put him up against a wall.

'Private Drake,' Stanhope considered, 'I do believe you may be the only sane man here.' And with that, he turned on his heel and carried on down the line. Carson was shocked still for a moment and then followed after. He checked on Reeve, but the commissar was looking off at another unit marching past. Ducky had got away with it. How could one man be so damn lucky?

Stanhope's review of Booth and his third platoon passed with as few incidents. By the time Stanhope finished the inspection and dismissed the men, Carson had grown more suspicious. Perhaps the major had not wished to condemn a popular man in front of his comrades. If he truly was a coward, then he would just send the notification to Reeve and he would do the rest. But in that instance, Carson might be able to placate him. He walked with him back to his room.

'I'll have a new weapon issued to Private Drake and ensure he holds onto it.'

'Do not bother on my account,' Stanhope replied indifferently. 'I meant what I said.'

Carson was surprised; perhaps Stanhope would not be a disappointment as a commanding officer after all.

'I only hope the commissar feels the same way as you do, major.'

Stanhope passed through the wide portal back into

the barracks. 'I wouldn't concern myself with Reeve. He wasn't there to stand judgement over your men. He was there to stand judgement over me.'

'What makes you think that?'

Stanhope gave a thin smile. 'Because he's following me.'

Carson could not hide his look of disbelief.

'It's true,' Stanhope continued. 'Every time I'm transferred to a new regiment, there he is. For four years now, from the 99th to the 263rd to the 371st to here.'

'I've never heard of such a thing. Why would he being doing that?'

'Honestly, lieutenant, I don't know. We've never so much as exchanged pleasantries. I can only imagine that he has some hook into me and is waiting to reel me in.'

Carson regarded Stanhope. He knew of his record; he knew he had been a hero once, but his best days were years past. No amount of official gratitude, no goodwill for such endeavours, no matter how glorious, would hold a commissar back from his duty.

'So Reeve was there to judge you,' Carson said sceptically. 'Do you think you passed?'

'You mean was I acquitted? Well, I suppose we will see. By tomorrow dawn, if I'm up against a wall, then we'll assume not,' he turned to Carson. 'By the way, I'll be engaged much of the day. If orders come through, just carry them out. Don't worry about getting my say so. I'll check in with you before the evening.'

'Shall I assign one of the men as your steward or would you prefer to pick one yourself?'

Stanhope opened the door, revealing little of the dark room beyond. He stepped in, making it clear that he did not wish Carson to follow. 'That won't be necessary, lieutenant. You can keep your fighting men in the fighting line. I can shine my own boots and button my own jacket.'

Carson was surprised again. Having a personal steward or batman was not simply a commander's perk, it was the only practical thing. Even the most fastidious procedural directives acknowledged it was better to have commanders spend their time commanding their men, rather than buffing their gear.

'You *are* a major.' Again, the 'sir' stuck on the tip of his tongue and travelled no further.

'Yes, lieutenant, but a major what?'

'What?' Carson said, confused.

Stanhope raised his eyebrows, but did not continue the thought.

'Very well,' he concluded as the door closed. 'You can have one man bring me any messages or orders first thing in the morning. That is all.'

THEY WERE GETTING close, Arbulaster felt. They were getting very close. The crew of the *Brydon* were making their final preparations to release the DOV. The landing site was ready, he had approved the schedule to ferry the troops and armour across afterwards in order of priority to complete the deployment of the DOV and ensure its security. The pathfinders had not seen any orks in the vicinity, but if there were any his advance guard would be in position long before they could pull together a force of any size. He just needed a few more hours without interruption from that hectoring governor and they would be done.

'Excuse me, sir,' Major Brooce interrupted him. 'Commissar Reeve would like to speak with you.'

The commissar's name poured ice-water on Arbulaster's irritation. 'The commissar?' he said. 'Very well. Very well.'

'Shall I send him in, sir?'

Arbulaster glanced around at the mess in the control

centre caused by days of feverish activity and at the number of men nearby who would doubtless overhear every word.

'No. No need. Take over here, Brooce, and send some-one to tell him I'll meet him outside my study,' Arbulaster decided. 'Do emphasise *outside*, will you Brooce?'

'I will, sir.'

Brooce sent off one of the troopers and Arbulaster strode off to his study. As he went he took the opportunity to straighten his uniform surreptitiously. You didn't give these fanatical black-coat bastards an inch if you could avoid it. You never knew what they were going to choose to care about from one day to the next.

Arbulaster fastened the clip on his high collar just as he arrived at his door. Reeve wasn't there yet, so he would have a few moments to ensure that he left nothing out that might catch the commissar's interest. He walked in.

'Thank you for seeing me, colonel,' Commissar Reeve greeted him from beside his desk.

Arbulaster swore silently in his head. 'Of course, commissar.'

The commissar did not walk to meet him, he merely stood where he was. He had obviously been a big man in his youth, but that had clearly been decades ago. He was old and, as he had aged, his body had shrivelled back in on itself.

Arbulaster walked up to the desk, but Reeve's position prevented him from going around and sitting in his chair. It was yet another of the petty power-plays that were so endemic amongst the Emperor's political officers.

Arbulaster refused to be thrown off-guard, or to sit down in the visitor's chair, which would allow Reeve to sit in his position behind the desk. Instead, he stayed on his feet. He stopped in front of Reeve, but did not salute. Brimlocks did not salute commissars unless they had assumed the responsibility of a line officer.

'You wished to speak with me?'

Reeve did not respond at once. He merely stared at the colonel as though with a single glance he could see every lapse in judgement Arbulaster had ever made. But Arbulaster was not unnerved by it. If Reeve thought that he could be intimidated by a look, he was sorely mistaken. Arbulaster had survived five different commissars in the course of the crusade; he knew they bled red just like any other man.

At length, Reeve finally opened his mouth. Each time he did so, Arbulaster half-expected to hear a death-rattle, but Reeve's voice was clear and smooth.

'I was observing the inspections this morning and I happened to see your Valkyrie flyers. One flyer in particular.'

Arbulaster had no doubt which one he was referring to.

'Tell me, colonel,' Reeve continued, 'who is responsible for the condition of those craft?'

The Valkyries were the Navy's craft, and each one was the pilot's responsibility. Arbulaster knew that, and he knew that Reeve knew that as well. He knew that neither was the right answer.

'I am responsible for the condition of that craft,' Arbulaster replied; he had played this game before.

'Then you are responsible for that vandalism to it?'

This was the reason that Reeve had pulled him away from their imminent deployment on Tswaing? He lowered his opinion of the man another notch.

'They're devotional images, commissar. The pilot, you understand, is most devout.' Devout, yes, Arbulaster thought to himself, it was simply that his devotion was to the flyer rather than the saints.

'They are obscene, colonel. A single devotional image is all that is allowed. We cannot have the Emperor's blessed fighting craft appearing like some tattooed merchant crewman. They will be removed.'

So this was the kind of commissar that Reeve was, Arbulaster considered. A petty obsessive who would commend a man for taking a breach, then have him flogged for having his boots dirty. Or perhaps it was simply another power-play to enforce his will over his line officer from the start. Either way, Reeve would have to learn that he was not dealing with some wan subaltern; even commissars had their place, and their place was not to impede the fighting effectiveness of his regiment with their righteous whimsy.

'I will see to the necessary arrangements, commissar,' Arbulaster replied, 'as soon as it is possible. At present, you appreciate, we are approaching a critical juncture.'

'I appreciate it entirely, colonel. You are a busy man, I understand.' Arbulaster hoped for a moment that that might have been it. Of course, it wasn't. 'So I have made my contribution to sharing your workload and have attended to this matter personally. I have given orders for the crew to be issued with the necessary equipment, the pilot especially. I think it rather fitting that he should remedy the damage he has caused. Unless,' Reeve paused and fixed Arbulaster with his sunken gaze, 'you have any objection?'

He didn't. Zdzisław would have a fit, but if he was going to fire off and snap Reeve's withered old neck then so much the better.

'No objection. Do as you see fit.'

'Excellent. The colonel of my last regiment often had objections. I am glad it will not be the case with us,' Reeve said. Arbulaster noticed that, at the mention of the old colonel, the commissar's hand had gone to one of the skulls upon his coat and he was stroking it a fraction.

'Nine hundred and eighty-nine, colonel. In case you were counting.'

Arbulaster snapped his eyes up. In that instant he felt a touch of chill. 'An impressive record,' he managed to say. Reeve merely nodded and then took his leave, leaving Arbulaster alone. The man had killed nearly a thousand men, nearly as many men as he had left in his whole regiment. He'd killed more Imperial troopers than probably any single individual foe they had faced. In the Emperor's name, what kind of madman was he?

As much as Arbulaster regretted it, Zdzisław would have to be on his own. Arbulaster had permitted such customisation in the past. The regiment was a thousand strong, but those thousand were what was left of a million Brimlock troopers, across fifty regiments, who had begun the Ellinor Crusade. He knew that to survive such a journey took its toll upon the mind as well as the body. He understood his men, and where it did not disrupt the regiment he had made allowances. He allowed for the totems, the trophies, the lucky bullet cases, the dubious relics; he allowed for Captain Drum, his bizarre garb and the vox-amplifiers he had fitted on his tank to blast out battle anthems; he allowed for Captain Gomery and Mister Emmett; he even allowed for Lancer Diver and his immodest post-battle displays. Arbulaster would tut and shake his head, but after all this time, he didn't care what a man wore, or didn't wear, so long as he was back in his uniform and ready to march before sun-up the next day.

He had seen other officers try to fight such things in their regiments, try to enforce uniformity in the face of the inevitable insanity that gripped any man after a lifetime of war. Those officers who attempted to keep the appearance of complete normality in their regiments were driven mad themselves. Mad, or up against a wall

before the black-coats or their own men. Well, Arbulaster was not going to let either of those happen to him.
He was not going to fall now, and certainly not at the
hands of Commissar Reeve.

He returned to the control centre and released his fear
as frustration over the vox with the *Brydon*. The Navymen
there picked up their pace and, an hour later, four days
after the 11th paraded through the streets of Voorheid,
the *Brydon* launched the DOV, the giant outpost vehicle,
with its drop-cradle towards the chosen site.

The DOV left a burning streak through the sky as it
entered the atmosphere. Then, as it approached the
surface, the drop-cradle's thrusters ignited and the stag-
gering force they generated slowed the DOV's descent,
vaporising the vegetation beneath it and allowing the
vehicle to settle in place. Only a few minutes later, the
first Valkyries swooped in, delivering their cargo of men
to defend the DOV and deploy it into a Brimlock outpost, a full base of operations for their expedition on
Tswaing. The campaign proper had begun.

CHAPTER SIX

Brimlock outpost DOV-A, Tswaing, Voor
pacification Stage 1 Day 7

CARSON CAUGHT SIGHT of the ork war-party as it crashed through the jungle. The orks had the scent of their quarry in their nostrils now and were chasing it hard to run it to ground. Their prize was still a dozen paces ahead of them. It was big, bigger even than the orks, though its own skin was pale. It ran like a bull, head down, arms pumping, smashing the smaller branches in its path into splinters. But it was slowing, tiring, and the orks pressed after it all the harder.

It managed to reach the base of one of the giant trees and collapsed there a second, chest heaving. It glanced to either side, but then it heard the war-cries behind. It turned and stood at bay. It reached down onto the ground, like a wrestler preparing to charge, and roared its defiance at its pursuers.

The orks paused a moment, catching their own breath, relishing the imminent kill. They readied the clubs, stones and spears they carried. The ork in the lead, wearing a headdress of teeth and fur, raised a bone sharpened into a pick and led his warriors in a mighty bellow of their own in reply.

Got you, Carson thought, and he pulled his trigger. The las-bolt from the heavy pistol struck the ork right in its gaping maw. Its eyes bulged wide as the back of its mouth and the top of its spine were incinerated in a flash. It dropped its bone and clutched feebly at its throat as it fell, not a mark on it.

The jungle trail erupted with light as a volley of las-fire burst from the undergrowth. The fire was focused, with three or more shots hitting the closest orks, incinerating their faces, throats and the side of their heads. An autocannon opened up, its shots whipping through the foliage like angry insects. Those struck tumbled to the ground; the rest of the orks, caught by surprise, wavered a moment, unsure which way to face. There was a second volley, and a half-dozen more ork bodies hit the dirt. Inexperienced troops, caught so completely off-guard, would break. They would dash for cover directly away from the fire and thus expose themselves to the second line of ambushers placed to strafe fire down the length of the other side of the trail. Veterans would never have allowed themselves to clump together so, they would strike back along the route they had come, even while their comrades behind them would strike forwards looking to flank their attackers.

Orks, being orks, just charged straight down your throat. Even as the third volley lashed out, the orks were ploughing into the jungle towards their unseen adversaries. Ahead of them, shapes in grey uniforms, stained brown with dirt, started to rise from the ground to run. The orks bellowed again, hacking and slashing at the undergrowth as their attackers ran from their charge. For an instant it looked as though they had broken out through the ambush, and it was at that instant that the second line, stationed behind the first and not on the other side of the trail, opened fire.

The Brimlocks of the first line ran, one hand on their hot lasguns, the other holding down their tanna-stained helmets. No one needed to remind them to keep low as the las-fire flashed over their heads at the orks running after them. The second line shot twice more, as those of the first line dove into their firing positions and whirled around, ready to add their fire. But the orks' charge had been shattered and the few of them that reached the second line were impaled by a half-dozen bayonets even as they raised their clubs to strike.

'Hold your fire!' The order echoed across the line.

The last ork stumbled away. Even orks could sometimes be made to see the sense of living to fight another day. There, in front of it, however, stood the great white bull-monster that the war-party had chased into the killing ground. The monster swung a huge branch and smacked the ork off its feet.

The ork crumpled, unconscious, and fell into the leafy undergrowth. Across the rest of the jungle there was a moment of silence as the survivors drew breath, waiting to see if it truly was the end, or whether another threat was to emerge.

'Good job, Frn'k,' Carson called. The bull-monster, an ogryn with a corporal stripe tattooed on his arm, nodded and picked up the ork at its feet. He slung it over his shoulder, then turned and gave Carson a crude salute.

'Now keep it safe,' Carson continued. 'That one's for the colonel, special delivery!'

There was a smattering of laughter from the jungle and, one by one, K Company began to emerge from between the trees.

'Section leaders, count up and clean up. Booth, take

a squad up-trail, look out for any stragglers. We've got what we came for. I don't want any surprises.'

Carson rolled over and sat up. He unstrapped his helmet and shook out his dirty blond hair. A caterpillar dropped into the mud, righted itself, and crawled away.

'Sorry for the inconvenience, I'm sure,' he muttered. He then rested his hand on his thigh and lowered his head. 'Come on. Come on,' he said to himself. He did not move. 'All right.'

He twisted around to check on the men. Booth's platoon had already disappeared up the trail. Carson thought it unlikely that they would be disturbed, however. The company had been scouting the jungle for two hours already and this was the only band of orks they'd encountered. Red had distributed cremator-packs to the men and they were torching the bodies. Frn'k the ogryn had instinctively returned to Corporal Gardner and was trying to carry both the ork and Gardner's heavy autocannon at the same time, while Gardner patiently tried to get Frn'k to drop the ork.

Carson noticed that Red was coming over to him. The company's colour-sergeant carried his lasgun in his off-hand, while in his right he wielded 'Old Contemptible' his iron-black mace. It was an anachronistic weapon to wield on the battlefield, to be sure, but one that had proved its worth, in raids such as this, where prisoners needed to be taken.

Carson did not know why they had been sent out to bring in a prisoner. The order had come to him from Major Roussell, straight from the colonel, so he could not argue against it. Perhaps it was simply habit, just as his men knew exactly how to set up the ambush without specific orders. Habit formed by many repetitions.

But there was nothing that the commissar's interrogators would get from the ork that Carson had not already

learnt from killing its kin. He looked at the leader he had
shot as a cremator turned it to ash. Its body was under-
developed and its skin was light, not nearly as tough as
the fully-matured orks he had fought in space. It was no
survivor of the rok's crash; it was a new-spawn. No matter how few orks had survived the impact, their kind was
now growing within the dirt of Voor.

Red was closing on him quickly. Carson turned away
and placed one of his pistols in his lap, so that it might
appear as though he was correcting some fault. Red
would not believe it, though; Carson's pair of heavy
pistols had not misfired as long as he'd had them. They
were beautiful pieces: each one had a rorschbone stock,
customised to fit regular Guard power-packs, a sculpted
antique lock and breech, and finely-etched patterns
down their barrels – wings on one, vines on the other.
But their true beauty was on the inside. There, embedded
within, was a glistening power-amplifier that made his
shots twice as deadly as a regular lasgun. These pistols
had made him what he was today. They had to take
some of the blame at least.

Carson felt, rather than heard, the colour-sergeant
standing over him. One expected such a big, blustering
NCO to stomp around, smacking the earth with every
step, but Red could be as silent as a breath, as many
drowsy sentries on both sides had learnt to their cost.

'Red,' Carson pre-empted. 'What's the bill?'

'One injured, sah. Corporal Marble.'

'How bad?'

'Put his foot on some bug-hill. Twisted his ankle and
split his lip. Ducky's taking a look at him. He'll get him
walking.'

'Good.' Carson surreptitiously tested his leg again. Still
nothing. He played for time. 'Remind me to put Frn'k up
for a commendation when we get back to Dova.'

'A commendation, sah?'

'You don't think he deserves one?'

'Of course, sah. Just think he'll prefer a day's extra rations over a sheet of paper he can't eat.'

'Good point. Let's do that. And let's see if we can't get his commendation on some kind of rice-paper as well. Then he can have his cake and eat it,' he said, chuckling half-heartedly. He looked up at the fearsome colour-sergeant's stone expression and thought better of it.

A flicker of movement in the corner of his eye caused Carson to twist again to look back at the rest of the company. Mouse was there, moving quickly from body to body ahead of the cremators, checking them for anything of value.

Red saw him as well. 'Private Chaffey, get your miserable self back to your squad!' he shouted.

Mouse snatched up guiltily from the body he was inspecting. With a second's defiance, he triggered the cremator before scampering away. Carson sighed.

'I do wish you'd give up on him, Red.'

'He's a parasite, sah.'

Yes, Carson reflected, Mouse was. But on Mespots, he had traded for the promethium that prevented the company dying in the desert; and on Kam Daka, it had been he who had bribed the tribesmen to allow them past the rebels' positions. But then again on Azzabar, the wrath of the eldar had come down on their outpost for days, until Red happened upon the large jewels that Mouse had looted from their warriors' armour. Carson had torn a strip off the private after that. Red had made it plain that he wanted him handed over to the black-coats, but Carson had refused. There were no extra points in war for playing by the book. As much as Red detested him, Mouse was a resource and Carson would keep him as long as his worth outweighed the risk.

Red was watching him intently now, waiting for him to give the order to move on. Carson tried his leg again. Still nothing, but he had run out of excuses.

'Do me a favour, Red. Keep the men occupied for a few minutes.'

'Ah, right you are, sah.' Red twitched his moustache and pursed his lips in concern. 'Shall I get Ducky up here for you as well, sah?'

'No, no,' Carson waved him away. 'A couple of minutes, that's all I need. Then I'll be right as rain.'

'Yes, sah.' Red gave a crisp salute and turned back to the company. 'Right, you shockers, peg your ears back and listen up!'

COLONEL ARBULASTER AND Major Brooce walked through the construction site of the regiment's forward base. All around them, troopers were stripped to their shirtsleeves, hefting, carrying, assembling and digging. Just half a day before, this part of the jungle had been indistinguishable from any other of the hundreds of miles around them; then in the grey dawn the Brimlocks had arrived. The down-blast of the drop-cradle's engines had scorched and flattened the vegetation beneath it. It had landed, released itself from the DOV it held and then launched again, creating an even wider circle of devastation around it. The Navy had done their part, now it was down to the Imperial Guard.

The DOV, or Deployable Outpost Vessel to give it its full name, was an integral part of a Brimlock campaign. No matter to what part of the galaxy a regiment might be sent, no matter what xenos world they might find themselves upon, the DOVs provided the Brimlocks with secure forward strongholds. Arbulaster had a great respect for them. It was from them that the 11th had fought off the eldar at Azzabar, from them they had beaten back the Tarellian dog-soldiers at Takht, and from them they had stamped down upon the uprising at Kam Daka, even though they had been outnumbered by over a hundred to one. And now this DOV was rising from the jungle.

The external wall had been the first thing to be assembled and put in place. The regiment's sappers in their worker-Sentinels had dragged the cornerstone blocks into place and drove them into the ground to provide a firm base. They'd installed the sentry guns on their tops, and supervised the men as they carried the armour plates from the DOV to create the wall. As the last section was welded into place, Arbulaster had felt a great surge of relief flow through him. The inside of the walls was a familiar place of safety. It was a little piece of Brimlock carved out far from home.

Everything was going to schedule and Arbulaster had not heard another peep from Commissar Reeve. He was in an expansive and generous mood.

'Do you know what makes the Brimlocks the greatest of the Imperial Guard?' he asked Brooce as they walked past the salient being erected for the landing pad.

'Yes, sir.' Brooce replied.

'It's because– What?' Arbulaster broke off mid-sentence.

'Sorry, sir. Did you want to answer that one yourself?'

Arbulaster harrumphed. 'No, I was... Don't horse around, Brooce. I was going to say–' Arbulaster caught Brooce's temperate, long-serving expression. 'Very well. Very well. What were you going to say?'

'I thought you wanted me to say 'the men', sir.'

'The men! Marguerite's breath, it's not the men!' Arbulaster exclaimed, then heard a sudden silence as the noise of the work on the salient suddenly halted. He turned and met the questioning stare of the dozen men on the scaffolding.

'Well?' he demanded of them. 'Did your beard call a break? No? Then get back to it.'

The men returned to their jobs and Arbulaster returned to Brooce. 'You really think that that pile of rookery droppings is what makes Brimlock great? You remember home don'tcha? You remember recruitment? You think any of those pale-skinned nambies with muscles like suet could be the match of a Catachan, or a Cadian, or a Finreht Highlander?'

'No, sir.' Brooce snapped back obediently.

Arbulaster led him over towards where the medicae and the officers' wives were establishing the base hospital.

'It's not the men. They are what they are. Pack of grumbling old women…'

'Yes, sir.'

And now Arbulaster noticed that a couple of the old wives were giving him the evil eye. He tipped his helmet to them and led Brooce back to the central bastion.

'Not that I mind a bit of grumbling, Brooce. I'll let you into a little secret, a little command insight for when you have a regiment of your own. When your men are grumbling, you know everything's as it should be.'

'Really, sir?'

'Oh yes. You've got nothing to fear from a grumbling soldier. They build up hot air and it's just them releasing it. No, it's when they stop grumbling that you've got to worry. Because when a soldier stops grumbling about his lot, it means he's planning to do something about it! And when soldiers take action into their own hands, Brooce, it invariably ends up with someone up against a wall. Either them or you. You know, if that tight-rod Carmichael had allowed some honest Brimlock grumbling, then that whole debacle with the Sixty-Seventh might never have happened.

'We might be the greatest complainers in the Guard; that would be no surprise,' Arbulaster continued. 'But no, we're not the largest, we're not the fastest or the toughest out there. What makes the Brimlocks the greatest of the Imperial Guard is this!'

Arbulaster encompassed the entire base with a single grand sweep of his arm.

'Building! We build, and we're the best damn builders in the Guard. These other regiments, they take a place, they move on, a year later they find they've got to take it back again. Not us. What we take, we hold. You come back a hundred, a thousand years, and what we built will still be there, ready for us to defend. And *that* is what makes us the greatest.'

'Very profound, sir.'

Arbulaster shot his second a look, but Brooce maintained his imperturbable expression.

'Sir,' Brooce glanced at his chronometer. 'You asked me to remind you when–'

'Is that the time? Throne, yes, yes, let's see what we're up against.' Arbulaster hastened back the way they'd come. The gate lowered at their approach and a squad of sentries joined the officers as they went out onto the scorched plain. There the Valkyries stood on their temporary landing field. The flyers were being refuelled by Trojans carrying promethium tanks and Zdzisław was giving his pilots their final briefing. Arbulaster and Brooce stood a distance away, while they concluded.

Arbulaster noticed that their blue flight-suits were covered in flecks of paint and recalled then that they had spent the entire previous day painting over the ostentatious devotional images and battle art on their craft at Commissar Reeve's instruction. He looked over again at the four Valkyries sitting in the midday sun, looking just as they had when they were first rolled off the assembly line, each one indistinguishable from the rest.

'Was there anything you wanted, colonel?' Arbulaster turned at the sound of the familiar, artificial voice and nearly gasped at the sight of him.

'No, no...' Arbulaster muttered, fighting the urge to recoil. He had never had a problem with Zdzisław's injuries before. To him they were merely the mark of a determined warrior. And yet today, for some reason, he found them gruesome. Nothing had changed physically, yet there was a cold, dead look in Zdzisław's one natural eye. For the first time, Arbulaster realised that this was not a living man before him but rather an animated corpse. 'Just to say, good luck, the Emperor protects.'

'Thank you.'

Arbulaster tried to make the best of the unfortunate situation, as was his way when his own self-interest prevented him from doing anything to change it. 'She looks good out there, doesn't she?' He motioned to what he thought was Zdzisław's craft. 'All the ladies love a new coat once in a while, eh?'

Zdzisław didn't reply. Instead, he walked away, flight helmet in hand.

'Commissar Reeve–' Brooce interjected.

'Yes, he has a lot to answer for,' Arbulaster muttered.

'–is here, sir.'

Arbulaster felt the silence behind him. 'Afternoon, commissar.'

'Yes, it is,' Reeve replied. Zdzisław stopped by the Valkyrie's nose and made to hold out a hand to touch it, to caress it as he had done before each flight hundreds of times before. But then he dropped it, as if there were no point and stepped perfunctorily up onto the ladder.

Colonel Arbulaster, who had seen villages and crops put to the flame, who had seen fathers and mothers blown apart going to their children's aid, who had seen men forced to shoot their comrades caught on razor-wire, still found his heart quickening a fraction as he watched Zdzisław haul himself, without ceremony, into the cockpit of his Valkyrie and pull the canopy down.

'I should have had him flogged,' Reeve said suddenly, 'but there seemed little left of him that would feel it, and the Navy can be so precious about their pilots. Still, an example should have been made.'

'Of course, commissar,' Arbulaster found himself agreeing. The rest of his words were lost as the engines of the Valkyries ignited and Zdzisław led his flight into the sky to get the regiment's first proper look at their enemy.

CHAPTER SEVEN

ARBULASTER HAD HAD the company commanders gather on the shooting deck. It was close to the top of the bastion, with only the vox tower and the flagpole flying the Brimlock colours above it. It was designed to give a commanding view of the area, whether for sniping the enemy or the local wildlife. Here on Voor, though, all it gave was a commanding view of the limitless green that stretched off to the horizon in every direction. Armies of orks might be encircling the outpost and an observer wouldn't have an inkling.

As he had requested, his officers were already assembled by the time he, Brooce and Reeve arrived. Most of them had been taking their ease in the canvas chairs, but they shot bolt upright as soon as he entered.

'Stand easy,' he told them, quickly scanning the room. All his company commanders were there, with one exception for which he was most grateful: Major Stanhope. He saw the Voorjer girl, Van Am, standing apart from the rest, wearing the same unimpressed look she seemed to have every time Arbulaster met her.

'Afternoon, gentlemen,' Arbulaster began. 'I don't believe we've met en masse before. I hope you've been using the time to get to know the new arrivals.'

There was a respectful chorus of agreement that Arbulaster had long ago learnt meant that they hadn't so much as said a word to them.

'Good,' he said firmly. 'Captain Ledbetter here is joining us with the two companies of horse left from the Fifty-Sixth and Lieutenant Mulberry has already been doing great work taking charge of our sappers. Captains Ingoldsby, Tyrwhitt and Wymondham will be reporting to Major Brooce who commands the line companies and lastly Major Stanhope, who unfortunately has other duties and cannot be with us, will be under Major Roussell who commands the light.

'To you new bugs, I hope you will have already made yourselves known to Captain Drum, who commands our armoured detachment, and Major Rosa, our artillery. If you wish to avoid having your troops either run over or shelled I recommend you keep on good terms with both of them.'

There was a chorus of polite laughter and the veterans exchanged nods of acknowledgement with the newcomers, both sides assessing their relative positions. Arbulaster ignored the wisp of tension in the air and double-checked his own officers. The dark-skinned giant Colquhoun was staying quiet in the corner next to the diminutive red-haired Fergus. Gomery had fortunately not brought Mister Emmett on this occasion, the plump and smiling Rosa for once was not snacking, and Drum, the spindly clean-shaven tank commander, had mercifully confined his war-paint to a discreet white line across his nose and cheeks on this occasion. Roussell appeared sober, but was still stealing glances at Van Am. She had noticed and shifted her stance. Her long coat gaped open and Roussell's eyes flicked down to glance at what might be revealed, only to see a heavy machete on her hip and a holstered autopistol behind it.

Arbulaster sensed Reeve make his presence felt beside him.

'And, of course, we all recognise our new officer of the Emperor, Commissar Reeve.'

Reeve paused a moment before addressing them.

'Ranks and privileges are not my interest, only the fortitude and vigour by which His servants enact His will. There is only one authority on this world, and that is His.'

There was certainly no laughter, nods or glances after that.

Breaking the silence, Arbulaster strode over to the grand table in the centre of the room. He keyed in a few strokes and the surface flickered and came to life, displaying a topographical map of the area. Two icons appeared there: the first, the familiar red and black roundel of the 11th; the second, a leering green-etched orkish glyph. He allowed his officers a minute or so to peer over the map.

'This,' Arbulaster continued, pointing to the roundel with a stylus, 'is here. DOV-A, or Dova as the men call it.'

He moved the stylus to the green glyph. 'This is the ork rok. I'm told its original Crusade Command designation was 692 *Brutal Fury*. Brooce?'

Arbulaster took a half-step back to allow his second to talk them through the specifics and the speculation. He had long ago learned that it was good command to do so. Brooce had a chance to act outside his shadow, and he had a chance to watch his officers and not be observed himself.

Brooce began: 'We have only been able to acquire limited information on the rok so far. From the size of the crater, however, we estimate that the rok did not strike the planet at full speed, rather that it must have slowed before it hit. Either some kind of re-entry engines or something more... alien. That, and the interference the rok is still generating, leads us to presume that some or all of its point defences may still be operating. We expect to acquire more detail shortly. Squadron Commander Zdzisław is leading a flight of Valkyries to the crater in order to reconnoitre for any defences or other activity. He shall feed those images straight back to this room for our consideration. Major Roussell? What's the current status of the other matter?'

The languid commander of the light companies shifted closer to a respectful stance. 'Received a message just before you arrived, major. We've caught one of the beasts and are hauling it in for the commissar's interrogation, prior to our own... dissection.'

'Good,' Brooce replied crisply. 'Pass on my commendation to Lieutenant Carson.'

Roussell shifted again, this time in discomfort at Brooce's implicit criticism that he had not led the raiding party himself. Arbulaster suppressed a smile and contented himself with a slight twitch of his eyebrow. The petty antagonism between his two infantry commanders was well-known and had kept him amused for half a decade now. One needed to find these little diversions in a life of boredom, violence and horror, and both officers were careful enough not to commit the colonel's cardinal sin of 'affecting the regiment'. Brooce had a point though, Arbulaster reflected; Roussell had become lazy, spending so much time resting on his former glories that the other officers joked that his backside looked like it had been awarded the Imperial

Laurel. If Carson hadn't killed the wrong man all those years ago, Arbulaster would have put him in Roussell's place right now.

'Dova base, Dova base, this is Valkyrie G for Galaxy.' The robotic words crackled over the speaker on the shooting deck.

Brooce activated the transmitter. 'G for Galaxy, this is Dova base. Go ahead.'

'Valkyrie flight holding at aquila five. Ready to descend. Request clearance for mission.'

'Commander,' Arbulaster spoke up. 'This is the colonel. Any trace of the interference at that height?'

'Negative, colonel. I expect interference once we go below aquila two.'

'And how low do you think until you can get a clear picture through that cloud?'

'Below five hundred, colonel.'

'Understood. You are cleared for mission, commander. Good luck.'

HIGH ABOVE THE ork rok, Zdzisław acknowledged the colonel. He looked out into the white cloud, pressing up against the cockpit and hiding the rest of the Valkyries from view. He switched the vox to call out to them.

'Valkyrie flight, this is G for Galaxy, acknowledge and confirm vox-net is active.'

'Leader, this is D Doctrine, acknowledged and confirmed.'

'Leader, this is P Pius, acknowledged and confirmed.'

'Leader, this is T Terra, it's all bang on here!'

The pilot's enthusiasm made Zdzisław smile, with what little of his natural face remained. It was the first time he'd smiled in the last two days. He knew that his Valkyrie was the same bird as he'd always flown. He wasn't so befuddled that he thought a simple lick of paint would stop her being who she was. It didn't, it had just made her hate him.

He checked that all was well with his co-pilot sitting behind him. They had left the other crew back at Dova to save weight.

'It's all buttoned up, skipper. Ready when you are.'

'Link the vox-net with Dova and confirm Dova receiving.'

'Linked,' the co-pilot replied and then heard Dova confirm. Now, if one of the Valkyries could get a picture, even if it was embroiled in the interference, it would be retransmitted from the other flyers so it would appear back at Dova. With that, they were ready.

'Valkyrie flight, I'm descending. Hello, D for Doctrine, are you there?'

The voice of Zdzisław's second, Lieutenant Plant, crackled through: 'Here, leader.'

'Stand by to take over if I lose contact.'

'Okay, leader, good luck.'

Zdzisław powered back the throttle. The whine of his bird's engines quietened and she started to descend. He brought up the display from the nose-picter, pointed straight down. There was nothing to see yet but more cloud, getting darker and darker as they dropped. He called out his height as they went. He felt the first tug at his controls as they hit twenty-five hundred metres. There had been a vain hope, voiced during planning, that perhaps the interference would not extend directly above the rok, but Zdzisław had not given it credence. To his mind, this interference that jostled his flyer in the sky could only be one of two things: first, a defence mechanism, designed for use in space, to disrupt assault boats and boarding actions, which given that orks adored the chance to carve their enemies apart in person seemed unlikely; or second, a by-product of whatever had functioned to slow the rok's fall as it plummeted towards the surface of Voor. In neither situation would it make sense for it only to project out and not above as well.

Nineteen hundred metres and Zdzisław felt the invisible force from this ork machine kick his bird to one side. He burned the jets for a moment to stabilise and then throttled back again. She hated him for this. First he had allowed that commissar to bully him into painting over her decorations, stripping her of all she had done, and now he was forcing her down to be pummelled by these ork ghosts in the air.

Seventeen hundred metres and the Valkyrie was slewed to one side. Zdzisław yanked the stick back around to compensate, but she bucked and protested beneath him.

Sixteen hundred metres and the ghosts tried to spin her; Zdzisław turned the nozzle adjusters and overrode the equalisation to steady her with a burst.

Fifteen hundred metres and Zdzisław was thrown near out of his metal body as the bird flipped under him. Alarms rang, the co-pilot swore and the cockpit display lit up with a battery of red lights, as the engine thrust that had been fighting gravity to keep them up was now accelerating them ever faster down. The numbers on the altimeter blurred and Zdzisław desperately twisted the nozzle control. Then the ghosts struck anew, and the bird lurched to one side and flipped again. Zdzisław shoved forwards on the throttle and the angry engines roared. Zdzisław tipped the bird's nose down and away from the rok and powered clear as quickly as possible.

His heart was thudding, someone was yelling in his ear, his co-pilot was heaving behind him.

'This is G Galaxy responding.'

'Leader!' It was Plant on D Doctrine. 'Confirm condition.'

'Operational at this time. The old girl gave me a bit

of a fight. We'll check to see if anything's shaken loose
and return to aquila five.'

'Glad to have you back, leader. Are you clear?'

'Clear.'

'This is D Doctrine, beginning descent.'

'**Acknowledged, D Doctrine. Watch for the daemons
at fifteen hundred.**'

'Will do, leader. Going down.'

'**Okay, D Doctrine. Better luck.**'

But D Doctrine did not have better luck. The ghosts
came for him in force at twenty-one hundred and by
eighteen hundred he was boosting clear. P Pius came in
on a different vector and made it to sixteen hundred,
before nearly stalling his engines and dropping a hundred metres as a dead weight. Zdzisław heard the shaking
in the pilot's voice as he recovered.

All the pilots could hear the growing impatience in the
signals from Dova as T Terra began his descent. T Terra
was determined and he rode his Valkyrie all the way down
to thirteen hundred. Zdzisław watched on T Terra's nose-
picter through the vox-net, as the clouds below him went
from a white to a dirty grey, hoping against hope that he
had been wrong in his estimate of how low the cloud
descended. At eleven hundred T Terra was swatted from
the sky, and he went spiralling away from the crater-site.
His vox went out but the picter stayed transmitting and
Zdzisław, the other pilots and Dova watched in horror as
T Terra fell below cloud cover five miles from the crater
and they saw the jungle much too close beneath. They
were helpless as the Valkyrie continued to spiral out of
control as the green canopy raced up towards it. But then
flames burst around the picter as T Terra's engines fired
at full blast and the fall slowed and stopped.

'Sorry, leader, bit of a close shave there,' the officers
back at Dova heard T Terra report back.

'Quite a show,' Arbulaster muttered. The images from the Valkyrie's picter had been fed back and displayed across the entire table. As T Terra fell, every officer in the room was falling with him. None of them had looked away as it happened, but now the moment had passed, a few dared to step back, take a draught from their drinks or glance out at the calmer jungle outside their own windows. Reeve, of course, was unmoved; he looked almost bored. Van Am also, Arbulaster noticed, appeared unaffected, rather she was staring at him, waiting to see what he would do.

'Brooce,' Arbulaster said quietly. 'Get me a private line to Zdzisław.'

'Yes, sir.' Brooce configured a handset and passed it over.

'Zdzisław here.'

'Commander Zdzisław, it's the colonel.' Arbulaster stepped away from the other officers.

'Yes, colonel.'

'Is that it then?' he asked curtly. 'You said five hundred metres. None of you even came close! Are you just going to keep throwing yourselves in until you run out of fuel or do you bluebells have any better ideas?'

There was a long pause at the other end of the line, and Arbulaster for once considered that he might have overdone it. These were Navymen, not his Brimlocks, and if they decided to fly off, well, he could request they be court-martialled, but that would be of precious little use to him here and now.

'There may be another possibility…'

Arbulaster heard him out, considered the risk and approved it. He stepped back to the table, which had returned to its tactical view, displaying the positions of the flight of Valkyries as they moved into position for their next attempt.

Zdzisław's plan was to descend not one at a time, but all four Valkyries together. If whatever was generating the interference had limited capacity then it might be possible to overwhelm it. The danger, though, was clear. For best effect, the four Valkyries would have to descend close together, targeting the interference at a single point. But with such limited control, if one should strike another then both craft would be lost. Arbulaster, though, with his officers, Reeve and Van Am all watching, felt he had no choice. He would trust Zdzisław and his pilots to keep themselves safe.

To test Zdzisław's theory, he and D Doctrine descended as a pair. Zdzisław started getting buffeted at twenty-two hundred, but coaxed his bird down to thirteen hundred before aborting. D Doctrine, however, had a smoother ride. Only once Zdzisław pulled back, did the ghosts attack him with a fury. He made it down to eight hundred metres and Arbulaster willed the details of the crater to appear on the table showing D Doctrine's picter, to get the picture now and have this damned mission finished already. But eight hundred was still too high. D Doctrine was rolled, flipped twice and spun before the pilot finally managed to break away. Arbulaster stopped himself from tugging at his moustache in annoyance, but the theory, at least, had been proved. Now nothing remained but to try it out for real.

Zdzisław watched the icon for D Doctrine edge across his viewer until it settled in position. The four Valkyries were formed up in a spiral to reduce the chance of collision, and facing out so that if any of them hit their engine-burn they would head out rather than in. They were at the closest quarters, yet would be utterly reliant on their instruments. It all made tactical sense, but the formation gave Zdzisław the eerie feeling of four warriors standing back-to-back, making their last stand. The other pilots called in ready. He gave the order.

'Valkyrie flight. Descend.'

He kept his eye glued on the spacing between his flyers. In mid-air collisions, you could not rely on conscious thought, they happened too quickly; you only had instinct and you had to pray that your instinct was right otherwise you were simply dead. At twenty-five hundred, right on cue, P Pius reported the first twitch. Zdzisław acknowledged, there was little else he could do. By twenty hundred he could see P Pius's engines firing as the pilot tried to compensate for the buffeting, T Terra had felt the first knock, but Zdzisław, in the third position above, was still flying smooth. At sixteen-fifty, P Pius's icon suddenly swivelled in its place on Zdzisław's display and the pilot's terrified scream burst over the vox as his flyer was spun. He hit his thrusters and powered clear. Then T Terra started reporting the ghosts' attack. The close call during his previous run had not dampened his enthusiasm.

'I'm going to make it this time, leader!'

'Hold formation as best as you can.'

'I'm going to make it!' Then he swore violently at his bird over the vox as he wrestled it down. At ten hundred the ghosts pummelled him hard and he was thrown across the sky, but he was ready for it and flicked the engines around and regained control.

'Crossing eight hundred!' he said triumphantly over the vox. Zdzisław could hear the Valkyrie's distress in the background. 'Activating picter!'

Back at Dova, the officers looked down at the table as the cloudy image appeared there. Still not close enough.

Suddenly, T Terra shouted and Zdzisław's proximity alarms shrilled. The ghosts had struck the flyer hard in the nose and it flipped back. The safety distance between the two flyers vanished in a split-second and Zdzisław's instinctively powered forwards. It was the right choice. T Terra grazed the back of his tail, spinning end-to-end. Only as it passed did Zdzisław hear the pilot's warning. D Doctrine heard it as well and hit his engines the same as his leader. For D Doctrine, however, the instinct was wrong. The screen at Dova flashed white as T Terra's nose-picter pointed up to the sky. For an instant, they saw the shadow of another Valkyrie racing towards them. Then the screen went black.

Inverted, T Terra had collided with the other flyer, the two armoured undersides smashing against each other. D Doctrine's hull structure held, but the flyer was knocked clear of the spiral and the ghosts came for it.

'D Doctrine. Aborting! Aborting!' Arbulaster heard the pilot shout.

'Commander Zdzisław, report!' Arbulaster demanded of the blank screen, but there was no reply.

'Report, damn you,' Arbulaster urged again, and this time he was answered.

'This is–' and then the transmission was interrupted by the howling of the air through a breached cabin.

'Repeat that.'

The voice, faint over the rushing air, responded. 'This is T Terra! Aborting! Aborting!'

'G Galaxy,' Brooce interrupted firmly, 'report your status.'

As if in response, the screen flickered back to life and Zdzisław's artificial voice resounded over them.

'**Crossing five hundred.**'

For the first time, through the cloud, they could see the details of the ground below. The image was shaken and blurred but it was there and Zdzisław was still going.

'**Four-fifty.**'

'Excellent work, commander,' Arbulaster said with relief.

'**Four hundred**,' was Zdzisław's only response.

The view of the crater was clear now and the officers clustered around closely. The orks were there. The crater was pock-marked with dark splotches, huts and other primitive buildings, which made up the burgeoning settlement around the rok.

'**Three-fifty**.'

'That's enough, commander. Abort,' Arbulaster ordered. Zdzisław did not respond. 'Can he hear us, Brooce?'

'Acknowledge, G Galaxy,' Brooce said clearly into the vox.

'**Three hundred**.'

'Respond, G–' Brooce began again.

'**Aborting**,' Zdzisław replied, but the ground below kept coming closer. '**She's fighting me**.'

The rok skewed from the screen as Zdzisław tried to steer the flyer away.

'**She won't, she's not–**' he began. They had crossed two hundred now.

'Pull out, commander!' Arbulaster instructed, and at the same time, they could hear the co-pilot start shouting at him to do the same.

One hundred, and now the officers around the table stood back from the sight, as if it were them falling towards the ground.

'**Engines stalled**,' Zdzisław said, even now his toneless voice not wavering. '**Come on, girl. Come on**.'

'**Forgi–**' Arbulaster heard, and then the vox went silent and the screen went blank.

There was silence on the shooting deck. The officers stayed fixed on the black screen, unwilling for a moment to raise their heads and catch another's eyes. Then the table lit up again. The cogitator had pieced together the imagery from the Valkyries' picters into a single plan. As they watched, it began running its identification routines, highlighting the likely nature of the shapes the images had captured.

'There it is,' Arbulaster breathed. There were the orks. There was a settlement. It was indisputably defended and fortified. But here it was, all laid out before them.

The room crackled as the vox-net reactivated. This time, though, it was not the mechanical, yet so human voice of Zdzisław.

'This is Flight Lieutenant Plant in D Doctrine requesting permission to recover G Galaxy.'

Arbulaster cleared the roughness in his throat. 'This is the colonel. Is G Galaxy within the interference radius?' he asked, though they all knew the answer. They had all seen it happen before them.

There was silence on the vox-net for a few seconds, then: 'Yes, it is, colonel, but we're willing–'

'Then your request is denied, flight lieutenant. Valkyrie flight is to return to Dova at once. Objective has been accomplished.'

'Colonel,' Plant began again, 'please reconsider, we are–'

'Brooce, cut the vox-net,' Arbulaster interrupted, and Plant's words died in mid-air.

Now, Arbulaster looked around at each of his officers.

'Here we are then,' he told them. 'Here is the face of the enemy and here are my orders. We will proceed here, we will annihilate them and then we will be done. Gentlemen, you all have work ahead of you. Get to it and make it happen.'

His officers all concurred and Arbulaster watched them as they began to plan the offensive. There was one man there he did not regard, however; the man who had no role in their planning and who excused himself shortly after. That man was Commissar Reeve.

CHAPTER EIGHT

Jungle Trail, Tswaing, Voor pacification
Stage 1 Day 17

'KAY-VEE!' STANHOPE HEARD the shout as the whine of the lascutter shut off. 'Kay-Vee!'

At the front of the column, the beard shouted again, as the ancient tree he had cut through groaned and shifted a fraction to one side. 'Kay-Vee!'

The tree, slowly at first but gathering speed, fell to one side, as stiff as a well-trained trooper passing out during parade. Stanhope watched the men fall upon it with their machetes and hatchets, stripping it of its leaves and branches, so that it might be hauled out of the column's path.

Kay-Vee, Stanhope remembered. It meant 'Beware'. Cadets for the Brimlock officer corps learned it in their first weeks at schola and they took such phrases with them on their regiments' journeys through the galaxy. Words once whispered after lights-out to warn their bunk-fellows of an approaching magister were shouted loud as the enemy's shells fell on them, or terrible monsters burst through flimsy walls and tore men apart.

That fraction, that tiny fraction of cadets who survived to return to Brimlock as colour-guard and perhaps become magisters themselves, brought new words back with them. Exotic, mysterious words that laced their speech and fired the imaginations of the cadets of the next generation. Most did not catch on, some took a grip but then were forgotten with the changing fashion, but the best became so deeply ingrained, that within a few years they were as traditional to Brimlock as Saint Marguerite herself.

Such development was not limited solely to words. Tanna itself was a Valhallan beverage brought, so the story went, to Brimlock by a returning officer of a colour-guard, who had fought alongside the ice warriors. So too were the fell-cutters. The first auxilia recruits from the tribute world Marguerite were not intended to be soldiers at all, only labourers. They had been unarmed, except for some local chopping blades called falcatas, which a regimental commander had purchased for them so they could cut back the woods around his camp. Yet when that regiment was ambushed by the enemy and surrounded, far from safety, the margoes had gone to their rescue and assaulted the foe's positions with only their blades, allowing the regiment to break out and escape. None of the margoes had survived their sacrifice, but that commander took the blades and their story to their home. After that, Brimlock never recruited the men of Marguerite as labourers again. They were only ever raised as soldiers, issued with lasguns and flak armour, and carrying those same chopping blades that had brought their people such honour. And so the fell-cutters were born.

The Imperium valued Brimlock solely for its industry: its skill at making guns, the men to fire them and the vehicles in which they could be transported. But truly what was great about Brimlock was that its regiments went and found the best the galaxy had to offer, brought it home, distilled it and then spread the result with the next generation.

The best the galaxy had to offer, and sometimes the worst as well. Stanhope felt the need again. His fingers shook a little as he eased them into the small slit in his jacket. He took something from its hiding place and slipped it into his mouth, as he pretended to mop his brow. Then he relaxed and went back to watching the jungle, as it slowly retreated before the might of the Imperial Guard.

CARSON WALKED DOWN the line of his men. They all had the equipment contents of their packs laid out in front of them on their groundsheets: lasguns, pistols, spare power packs, fragmentation grenades, smoke grenades, bayonets, ration cans, canteens, cremators, toilet articles, mess kits, fire-lighters, medicae treatments and more. It was an oft-repeated witticism amongst the armoured fist companies that the light infantry carried the most and travelled the slowest. There was an element of truth in it; while the other companies could rely on their Chimera transports to carry their heavy gear, a light company were most often deployed in terrain where the Chimeras could not operate, so anything they needed they had to carry themselves. Still, it did not mean they had to become beasts of burden and, as he went down the line, Carson tapped those extraneous items that would weigh his men down and make them less effective on the raid he was about to lead.

It had been ten days since the Valkyrie flight over the crater. Ten days since Commander Zdzisław went down. Though he had been a Navy man, he had been attached to the 11th as long as anyone could remember. But, as ever, there was no time for mourning or regrets. The images of the crater showed exactly what the colonel had expected. The ork survivors had established a fortified position around the rok, and that meant he would not risk sending his infantry in unsupported, they would have to get their tanks there, and that meant cutting a path through the jungle.

The beard, Mulberry, had reckoned it would take five or six days to cross the fifty miles from Dova to the crater. Now, ten days later, the crater still loomed in the distance, taunting them. Van Am had been right. It hadn't been the trees, they fell quickly enough to the lascutters and plasma fire; it had been the ground. It was relatively flat around Dova, but as they tore the jungle away further in, the beards found the terrain a mess of rocky slopes, sudden valleys and concealed pits. Even the tree roots themselves were stretched out across the surface, the oldest ones as tough as stone. The largest were as thick as a man was tall and had to be cut through to allow the tanks and trucks to pass. The advance continued, with little for Carson's company to do but stand and watch the jungle, guarding the beards from an ork attack that had yet to emerge.

Carson did not know what game the orks were playing. If he had been in their position, he would have been harassing the column ever since it left Dova. The colonel knew how exposed they were and was taking every precaution to ensure they were not surprised. Infantry patrols constantly circled the head of the column, and Drum's tanks and Rosa's heavy artillery stayed close at hand. But Carson had fought orks before, and knew that they did not shy from a fight, even when their enemy was ready for it.

To relieve the tedium, Carson asked for and was granted permission to lead raids far further from the column, deeper into the jungle ahead. He had no short-age of volunteers for his raids from the men either, as the beards were a dab hand at roping in any man standing idle. The prospect of scouting into the unknown, and maybe biting it from an ork or a jungle beast, became far more appealing after one had spent a day trying to push a Leman Russ battle tank up a debris-strewn slope. All of his own company stood up and, as soon as word got around, the men from other companies started putting themselves forward as well.

Carson accepted as many as he thought the company captains might allow; he knew he had an imposing repu-tation amongst them, but he was still a second lieutenant and that rank would only ever allow him so much lib-erty. His own company captain, or rather major, had the rank but did not appear inclined to do anything with it.

The first day after he had taken command, Stanhope had spent 'engaged.' Carson had assumed that Stan-hope was involved in Arbulaster's planning sessions, but Mouse reported back at the end of the day that the major hadn't left his room. Then Carson thought that perhaps Stanhope was looking to ease the transition for him, to allow him to continue to command as he had done before, until the campaign proper began. But then the morning came when the regiment was due to march, and a message came that Carson should retain command.

Stanhope appeared before they left, his uniform stripped down so that, aside from the fell-cutter, he appeared almost as a regular private. Carson had inquired about his dress and Stanhope had curtly replied that reg-ulations permitted officers to remove identifying rank markings as required where enemy snipers were sus-pected to be operating. If Stanhope's face had not been deathly serious, Carson would have laughed in it. It was true, the regulation was there, but their enemy were orks, who fought only with blood-curdling charges, deafening roars and noisy guns. After that, Carson thought Stanhope might simply be cripplingly paranoid, but that was not the truth either.

It was on the fourth day, when Mouse told Carson what he had noticed about the plants Stanhope kept in his room, that Carson realised the truth. Stanhope had surrendered. He had given up. Not to the enemy, but to the war. He was a leader who no longer wished to command. He was an officer who did not want to give orders, or have others look to him for them. He was a soldier who had no interest in living; yet one's service to the Guard was for life, and the Brimlock mindset did not allow the self-curtailment of that term.

When first Carson realised, he had been annoyed at having such an officer foisted upon him. Then he had been sympathetic. Then he had appreciated the advantages in having a commander who wished to be nothing more than a private soldier. The company had Stanhope's name upon it, but it stayed Carson's in all but that name and he did not have to struggle with another Blunder to keep it. That appreciation had lasted three days before, as is the way with all humankind when given what they want but not what they need, his mood had soured back into irritation. What gave Stanhope the right? Carson asked himself. Why was he allowed to call it quits, to surrender his duty, when all around him were expected to uphold theirs?

Carson's patrol was ready. He had chosen second platoon to come with him today and the men sat, packed and loaded. Van Am and a half-dozen of her Voorjer scouts were coming as well. He had consulted her before undertaking his first long patrol and she had told him that if he planned to find his way back at all, then he should ask her to go with him. And so he had. In truth, the Voorjers had limited knowledge of this area; it was a tiny part of a vast jungle that the colonists had barely scratched. But her scouts, hunters mainly, could move quietly enough and Van Am was determined to maintain her worth and so took every opportunity to be of use, from identifying the less pleasant fauna to demonstrating the crampons the Voorjers used to climb trees, pick fruit and get their bearings.

Van Am wandered over to him, her hunting rifle carried in the crook of her arm.

'Are we waiting for the major?'

Carson saw Mouse approaching and directed Van Am towards him. Mouse presented himself to his lieutenant and saluted.

'What's the word?' Carson asked, knowing what the answer would be.

'Major Stanhope sends his compliments, sir, and entrusts you with command of the company for the day.'

Carson nodded perfunctorily, then rose and swung his pack over his shoulders.

'Any reply, sir?'

'Tell him…' Carson started, his irritation catching his tongue. Then he paused for a moment and took a breath. 'You know what to say, Mouse. Tell him the usual.'

With that, Carson called his men to their feet and Van Am and her voorjers led them into the jungle.

THE COMMAND SALAMANDER vehicle hit another of the beards' makeshift ramps and the jolt very nearly made Brooce bite through his tongue.

'Have a care, Parker,' he admonished his adjutant at the wheel.

'Sorry, sir,' the driver replied without thinking, his focus on the circumnavigation of the barricades and the men constructing them ahead. Brooce looked out the side at the troopers as they dug and cursed, and then looked over to his passenger.

'It appears as if the transit camp is well on its way, sir. Once we're through the rest of the trees it should be close enough to act as a launching point for the main attack.'

Arbulaster glanced over in the direction Brooce was indicating with little interest. He then returned to looking out his own window. He'd been nursing this mood for days now, ever since the Valkyrie went down over the crater. He'd been acting very oddly as well. After the senior officers had had their fill of analysing Zdzisław's pictures and retired, Arbulaster had asked Brooce to gather the service dockets for all the men in the regiment. Brooce offered to have them summarised if the colonel could give him an idea of what he was looking for, but Arbulaster waved him away, saying that he had no fear of bumph.

Two days later, Brooce had delivered a half-dozen boxes full of records to his quarters. The colonel had spent the next three evenings dining in private, poring over the dockets. On the fourth morning he told Brooce to remove the boxes and instead compile for him all correspondence related to Carson's company since the last campaign. He then went out on inspection. Brooce went to accompany him, but he said he wanted to keep it informal this time around. Brooce had the correspondence ready by that evening and handed it over to the colonel anticipating some kind of explanation. There was none.

Two days after that, Arbulaster asked Brooce to convene a field advancement panel to consider any and all proposed promotions, decorations or commendations. The promotions at least would only be temporary, subject to consideration and confirmation by Crusade

Command, but he'd said plainly that they shouldn't go into battle with gaps in the command structure.

When the findings of the panel were issued, Brooce went through them, hoping for some clue as to what had obsessed his colonel. There was only one matter relating to that company, the approval of the application to commend one ogryn called Frn'k. And it was that commendation that Brooce now held in his hand as they bumped along the track towards the head of the trail.

Brooce was not the kind of man who worried. If he was a worrier then ten years with the 11th's officer corps and six years as Arbulaster's second-in-command would have finished him off long ago. No, Brooce was not a man raised to worry. He was a man raised to be *concerned*, however, and such behaviour from his colonel in the midst of a campaign had him more concerned than he had ever been.

Whatever it was, Zdzisław's death was the spur. It had triggered something in the colonel's mind which had caused him to divert his attention from the ongoing operation and led him on this peculiar quest. Brooce knew it was down to him to say something. It was his duty, both as his second and his fellow officer. Arbulaster might be putting not only the operation but his own life in great danger if Reeve grew suspicious. Brooce had been able to deflect the commissar over the last few days, but Reeve would act on little more than suspicion if he decided that Arbulaster was not fit to command. The hundreds of little skulls upon Reeve's coat were ostentatious, but effective, and Brooce had the unerring feeling that they watched him whenever he was in Reeve's company.

He had to say something, but he could not just come out with it. Brimlock men, and their women as well perhaps, simply did not discuss such things. When, during the invasion of Gandamak, Major-General Macnaughten learnt that a column of camp followers had been ambushed by a tribe of treacherous allies and that his wife and children were dead, they gave him a gun and an armoured division to wipe that tribe from the face of the planet. No one had tried to talk to him about his feelings!

'Have you had a moment to review the notification for the Navy, sir?' Brooce decided to open with. 'Over their loss?'

Arbulaster looked over and focused on his second, his brow furrowed in puzzlement.

'What's that?'

'Over the loss of Commander Zdzisław and his flight officer?'

'Oh,' Arbulaster remembered. 'No, not yet.'

Brooce continued: 'I tried to be circumspect with the wording. After all, we don't know what we might find when we reach the site. He might still be alive.'

Arbulaster dismissed the thought out of hand. 'He crashed ten days ago, right in the heart of them. If he hadn't died then, he would have done so by now.'

Now for the plunge. 'Yes, sir. And I've made it clear in the notification the importance of the mission and that he understood and accepted the risks. There certainly shouldn't be any blame attached to the regiment or to your command, sir.'

That last sentence caught Arbulaster's attention. 'Me? Why should anyone blame me?'

It was not the reply Brooce had expected. 'I'm saying there certainly shouldn't be any blame attached to you and that the notification makes that clear…'

'It wasn't my fault, major,' Arbulaster said without a hint of doubt. 'Zdzisław said it himself, the Valkyrie was fighting him. It doesn't matter if you believe in that clap-trap or not. *He* believed, and his confidence was shot.

That's what killed him, and I know exactly who's to blame for that.'

He caught sight of something on the side of the track.

'Pull her up here, Parker,' he ordered the driver and stood up out of the Salamander.

'Commissar!'

Reeve, who was watching the beards supervising the men, turned and regarded the colonel. Arbulaster carried on.

'We are presenting some of the commendations tonight, commissar. There is one where your attendance would be much appreciated.'

Reeve said nothing, as he always did when he did not consider that a response was required. Arbulaster was undeterred.

'It is an ogryn, very dedicated. You know how they especially venerate those of your position. If you were there, I do believe it would be ten times as inspirational as if I presented it alone. Will you attend?'

Reeve considered it for a moment.

'This is Ogryn Frn'k attached to Major Stanhope's company?'

'That's correct.'

'I accept, colonel. I have some other business with that company. I will attend.'

'Glad to hear it.' Arbulaster couldn't care less as to Reeve's reason; getting the commissar there was all that was important. 'Tonight then, commissar. At the new transit camp.' He tapped the driver's helmet and sat back down as they powered off to the head of the column.

CARSON'S PATROL ADVANCED quietly through the jungle. The going was relatively easy. Unlike the jungle areas close to the coastal settlements, which had once been cleared by the colonists but which now had grown back as an impenetrable mesh of thorn thickets and under-brush, this jungle was old. The battle for supremacy had been won long ago by the great trees whose canopy blotted the light from the ground and thereby suppressed the growth of any competition. There was no grass, no flowers; all that covered the ground was a thick carpet of dead leaves. The only other plant-life that prospered were the parasites: the creepers, vines and mosses that drew their life from others. In the half-lit gloom and deep shadow, the trunks of the giants stood like pillars in a dark and limitless cathedral. In such a place, the men needed no reminding to stay silent and so their progress was accompanied only by the crackle of the dead leaves underfoot.

Van Am held her hunting rifle ready in both hands. They were pushing further forwards today than they ever had done before. Their target was the great ring of grassland that stretched five or six miles from the crater. When the rok had impacted, super-heated fragments of it fell on the jungle, starting wildfires in every direction. On her first expedition, she had discovered the crater surrounded by a blackened plain of charred vegetation. The Valkyrie pilots had reported that that plain was now green. Arbulaster had considered this a significant boon, allowing his tanks to cross the final stretch in a day. Carson, though, wanted to ensure that it was just grass and fireweed and nothing more pernicious that would delay the column even further.

The jungle was quiet. Quieter than Van Am had ever known it. Her grandmother had sent her to Tswaing fifteen years before, to 'prepare her' as she had cryptically pronounced. But the young Van Am found the isolated Tswaing settlement little better than a prison. It was surrounded by the jungle and tree branches encroached over the settlement's walls. The jungle appeared to her a gloomy and dangerous place, very different to the wide plains of the farms near Voorheid where she had spent her earliest years. It held that same sense of oppression that her grandmother claimed the first colonists had been trying to escape. The young Van Am endured her exile with little grace, paying scant attention to what her keepers tried to teach her of survival there. Her uncooperative attitude only shifted after one of her guardians finally lost his temper and let slip that her grandmother would be granting her all her land in Tswaing, thousands of acres, the settlement included, when she turned fourteen.

It shocked her. The sudden sense of ownership, of responsibility, struck her hard. On Frisia, scarcely any usable land existed outside of that possessed by the Imperial government. The rights and deeds over what little there was were a source of immense pride to a family and were vigorously defended. Even on Voor, only some of the colonists, those who had worked off their indentured service to the Imperium, were allowed to own the land they worked. The rank of landholder was treated with dignity and respect. To have a chance at it so young… Van Am was determined to prove herself worthy of it. When she travelled out into the jungle again, the trees and animals no longer felt like her gaolers, rather she saw them as her wards. They were savage, yes, even deadly, but she knew that if they should kill her it would only be because she had not learnt them well enough.

But now she could sense the sickness of her land. The alien chill caused by the clouds overhead was slowly killing the plants. As the plants died, so did the creatures. Even on her first expedition to the rok the jungle was still full of the sounds of life. Now it was quiet. There were only the orks and the Guardsmen, trespassers both.

She saw a slight commotion at the head of the platoon

and they halted. One of the Voorjer scouts approached to report to the command section, and she and Carson went to the front of the platoon to see for themselves. Another party had stopped there at some point before. Orks were not subtle creatures and the evidence of their residence was easy to see: the carpet of leaves had been kicked aside where they had walked, they had clumsily felled a tree for wood to start their fires, and they had left the bones of the creature they had cooked and eaten in the embers.

Carson ordered the platoon to deploy from its file to encircle the area. The men split and advanced cautiously on either side, Forjaz taking his section to the left, Corporal Marble taking his to the right. Only once they were in place did Carson lead the command section forwards to investigate.

The lieutenant had made an impression on Van Am. The other Brimlock officers she had encountered were exactly as her grandmother had predicted: hide-bound, crude and old. They were all old, even the troopers. They were veterans, to be sure, but as far as Van Am could tell that just meant that they had learned one way of warfare and stuck to it. Even when they did patrol, they stayed close to the path, their link back to Dova, back to warfare they understood. They felt secure there and, in thinking so, they automatically considered everything outside to be hostile, everything including the jungle itself. They spooked themselves believing that the orks were phantoms, able to move through the terrain with ease, without making a sound.

Carson was the only one of them who had shown he thought differently. While the others clutched their lasguns tight, keeping them ready to fire in an instant, Carson kept his pistols holstered. He walked through the jungle with none of the others' instinctive fear. He knew that the truth, as the patrol now saw before them, was very different. It was the orks who were on the alien world. The jungle was even more unfamiliar to them than it was for the Guardsmen. Carson appreciated what Van Am had tried to tell the rest: the jungle was not against them, the jungle was neutral.

As Carson went to look at the remains of the creature, Van Am examined the tracks. 'A few dozen, their path is curving back towards the crater. Not orks though.'

'No,' Carson replied. 'But it's something they brought with them. Look at this.'

She went over.

'Do you know what this is?' He pointed at the remains of the carcass. She looked at it and scowled in disgust. The body was squat, bulbous, without arms; but the face, the face was almost human.

'No. What is it?'

Carson picked up one of the bones, broken in two to drain the marrow. 'A walking larder. They follow the orks, eating anything that moves, and then the orks eat them.'

He looked down the trail for a moment. Van Am watched his face while he thought, the slight deepening of the lines on his brow, the intensity of his gaze, the sudden focus when he made his decision.

'We follow them, but we stay off their path,' he said and began dictating the new marching order. His men obeyed his commands quickly. Van Am saw that they did not obey him out of fear or obligation to his rank, rather because they did not want to disappoint him. She could understand why; the lieutenant cast an aura of confidence about him. He knew as little as she did as to what lay ahead, yet as he gave his orders, she could believe that he had planned it all from the beginning.

'Holder?'

Van Am blinked. 'Yes?'

'Are you all right?'

She swung her rifle barrel up to grip it with her other hand. 'Perfectly fine.'

They moved out cautiously at first, but quickened their pace as they progressed and did not encounter the enemy. After a few minutes they saw a mound of leavings on the trail; they were pungent, warm and very fresh. Spurred on, Carson and Van Am closed the distance up to the head of the column. Suddenly, one of the men in the lead made a frantic signal and dropped. In the split second it took Van Am to realise what he was doing, the other Guardsmen had all flattened themselves to the ground and she felt Carson tug at the side of her trousers to bring her down as well. They lay there, utterly still, for a long minute, waiting to see some sign of whatever had excited the scout. Nothing. Carson rose to his haunches and ghosted forwards. He reached the front of the patrol; it was the trooper they called Blanks. Carson made a gesture with his hand and Blanks replied in kind. She watched the silent conversation until finally Carson nodded and motioned her to join them.

Ahead of them was their quarry. There were not a few dozen but sixty at least of the orkish herd animals. Their features, which had appeared merely freakish on the corpse, were grotesque upon the live examples. They were bunched together, butting and biting at each other in bad temper. A dozen gretchin armed with poles and spears prodded them to keep them marshalled together, and at their rear was the largest ork Van Am had ever seen. It pulled the remains of an unfortunate jungle creature from the jaws of the herd and flicked its whip. The loud crack urged the gretchin to shove the herd forwards down the trail and it moved with a great cacophony of screeches, growls and snaps. The ork did not care about being quiet. It felt secure, confident, as though it were the master of this place.

Van Am was ready to put a shot through its head to demonstrate how wrong it was, but Carson gave no move towards an attack. Instead, he was looking ahead, at the line of grey light now visible through the trees and the curve of the slope of the crater beyond. They were nearly at the edge.

They shadowed the ork and his herd the rest of the distance until finally it emerged from the trees. There, back on familiar ground, the herd beasts picked up speed and waddled away on their two legs. The ork cracked the whip again and the gretchin went careering after them to stop them dispersing. The patrol reached the edge of the treeline and looked out.

The green expanses the Valkyrie pilots had seen were not grasslands but miles and miles of lichen and mould carpeting the ground. The few trees that still remained were covered with the black and yellow fungi eating away at them. Hardened mushrooms with wide umbrellas were still low to the ground, but were growing quickly to take the drying trees' place. Their thick stalks were covered with their smaller cousins, sticking out like flints. Others grew in clusters, like sickly-coloured flowers, while still more littered the ground, their appearance varying from crystal-latticed eggs to piles of leavings. The perverted landscape flowed all the way to the rise of the crater in the distance, and from that crater the leering orkish glyph carved from stone looked over its lands with pride.

For Van Am, it was a monstrous vision, a living bruise on her jungle. She finally began to understand that she could not merely kill these xenos, she would have to burn her planet to be rid of them.

CHAPTER NINE

CARSON'S COMPANY HAD slotted into the lines of men marching back from the head of the path to the new site of the transit camp. Although Drum's tanks and Ledbetter's cavalry were able to return to the greater safety of Dova each night, the infantry needed to be housed closer to the front. So, as well as carving a path through the jungle, the overworked beards had also constructed the transit camps, clearing nearly twenty acres of jungle around the path for the fort and the dead ground surrounding it. Every few days, all work at the front halted as the beards moved the fort a half-day's march up the trail to the next area they had cleared. The whole process took an immense amount of effort across such terrain and it slowed down the overall advance, but it was steady and it was secure.

As the company marched into the camp that the colonel had designated Fort Eliza, after his wife, the beards in their construction Sentinels were hurrying to place the last sections of the wall behind the glacis and trench dug around the camp. The skies were growing black. The ever-present clouds blocked the light of the setting sun and so day rapidly turned to night. Only at the line of the horizon could hints of orange and red be seen through the cracks in the darkening grey.

Red led the men to the tent cluster where they were billeted. Forjaz and Booth came around with the evening rations and the men groaned at the sight of them. Officially the company had been 'rested' during the day and so their lot had been drawn to be the first on sentry duty. They had half an hour to cook their rations as best they could before they took their posts to stand watch, as the other companies took their time to eat in the central mess. The men grumbled as usual but without much rancour. At least, once they were done, they could have an uninterrupted night's sleep. And the men of second platoon were additionally fortunate because Mouse, having been excused the patrol, had had a full day to get up to his usual business and knew the wisdom in being generous. He had acquired cheese, pudding, fruit and pastries and, having eaten his fill already, handed the rest around.

'Crumpet?' he said, offering it to the circle.

'Yes, muffin?' Ducky said from the other side of him.

Mouse turned around. 'What's that?'

'Oh sorry,' Ducky continued, taking it. 'I thought we were trying out new pet names for each other.'

Mouse shook his head at the medic's antics and moved on to Marble. 'Anything for you?'

Marble, nicknamed such because of eldar gun-gems he'd picked up 'for research purposes' on Azzabar and managed to sneak past Commissariat inspectors by hiding them internally, was busy re-rigging his lasgun yet again.

'Do you have a micro-energy regulator?' he said without looking up. 'It's still overloading when you ride the pull too long.'

'How about a scone?'

Marble looked at him, exasperated, then glanced back at the scone, took it, and went back to his task. Mouse carried on round to Gardner.

'What about you, corporal? Got a few day-old loaves here that might be good for Trouble.'

Gardner looked them over. 'Where'd they come from?'

Mouse sighed. 'Why'd you ask that, corp? They ain't got a name on 'em.'

Gardner frowned for a moment, but then took the sack and headed off over to the corner where Frn'k was sitting. The ogryn ate separately to the rest of the company so he wasn't tempted to take their food and they weren't nauseated by his smell. Mouse finished distributing his haul to the rest of the platoon. Blanks sat a small distance from the rest of them, feeling neither welcomed nor excluded. It was time to change that, he decided. He approached Mouse.

'So, where'd they come from?' he asked.

'You as well, Blanks?' Mouse narrowed his eyes. 'Funny, I know you don't remember anything, but I didn't take you as the sort to stick by the law.'

Blanks regarded Mouse carefully, then picked out a piece of cheese and took a bite from it. 'I think you're right,' he said, and smiled. Mouse chuckled at that and, with that small gesture, there was an opening.

'I tell you,' Mouse began. 'Sticking by the law doesn't say anything about you. Down in the rookeries, there ain't laws. None that matter. That's where you learn what you're willing to do and what you ain't.'

'Is that where you started?'

'It's where I'd still be if I hadn't volunteered.'

'You're not a conscript?'

'What are you talking about?' Mouse exclaimed. 'None of us are. We're all volunteers.'

'That's right,' Ducky added. 'Brimlock is very strict on that. They'll only conscript you if you're not smart enough to volunteer.'

'We all had the choice,' Mouse continued. 'The choice to starve, the choice to get locked up, to have your back whipped on the factory lines or catch your death working the outside of the dirigibles.'

Ducky perked up. 'A man offered to sell me a dirigible once, but it turned out to be a lot of hot air.'

Blanks ignored him. 'Maybe you'll see it differently when you go back.'

'Go back?' Mouse exclaimed. 'None of us are going back. One-way ticket when you join the Guard. They'll fork out to lug you halfway across the galaxy, but they won't for a return trip.'

'Apart from their favourites,' Ducky amended.

'Apart from them. Room for a few to go back with the colours. The clinkers, you know, the ones with the medals, to found the next Eleventh.'

'The officers?' Blanks said.

'A few of 'em,' Mouse said. 'The colonel, of course, and anywhere he goes he'll take Brooce with him. The Rooster's already been promised a place; he won it after Mespots. Drum's too barmy. Rosa wouldn't fit. The new one, Ledbetter, he's a good bet, they like to take a tin belly with 'em. Some of the sergeants as well, 'cos you need a few who actually know the end of a lasgun. Red'd be top of the list, I'd wager.'

'Won't be Forjaz,' Ducky said. 'He's got so many kids in tow it'd be quicker to bring Brimlock to us.'

'Will they take Carson?' Blanks asked.

'Well, he killed the wrong man, didn't he. They can't

take him.' Mouse shrugged and carried on. 'Would you head back, Ducky? If they gave you the chance?'

'They're not going to offer it to someone like me.'

'Yeah, but just saying if they did?'

The half-smirk that Ducky perpetually wore dropped away. 'Go back to being a street cutter in the rookeries? All that ails you cured, thrice the price, no guarantees, no questions asked? Sewing up the cuts on drunks, picking out arbitrator buck-shot from the arse-cheeks of part-time anarchists? Lightening the load of women in trouble in a rat-infested flophouse? No, not again. Never again.'

Ducky looked around the circle. 'I'm here. It's a new colony. They'll need medicae and they won't care where they've come from or what they've done, and they won't ask you to kill, and everyone you save is going back to a life, not going back into the grinder. I'm staying.'

The circle was silent for a few seconds before finally Blanks took the lead. 'So, you're going to settle down here and find some pretty Voorjer nurse to bat her eye-lashes at you and learn at the feet of the master?'

'I think I'll leave devoorjing the local girls to the lieu-tenant,' Ducky languidly replied, his half-smirk once more in its rightful place.

The circle cackled loudly with salacious glee and envy. For all that the striking young woman leading the Voor-jer scouts had remained hard-nosed and resolute in front of the senior officers, her focus on their lieutenant whilst out on expedition had been obvious to the company's old hands.

'She won't get anywhere sniffing around him,' Marble said, closing his lasgun up and joining them. 'None of the others ever have. He doesn't do anything.'

'Oh, I bet he does. He's just picky I bet,' Mouse coun-tered. 'If I was an officer and I looked like him, I'd be picky I tell you.'

'If you were an officer and looked like him,' Blanks said, 'you'd help yourself as much as you liked.'

Ducky interjected. 'If Mouse was an officer, Emperor help the rest of us.'

The circle laughed again, but their smiles froze as Forjaz pounded up to them. 'Look lively! Look lively!' he shouted. 'The brass are coming. Up! Up!'

The laughter stopped instantly as the men ditched their rations and sprang to their feet, groping for jackets, clasps, laces and buttons. Forjaz told Mouse to run off and get the lieutenant.

'What does the bleeding colonel want with us?' Mouse muttered.

'I must've forgot to inquire when I showed him into the parlour!' Forjaz bit back. 'And it's not just the colonel, it's the new black-coat too.'

If Forjaz thought his men were moving fast before, then they suddenly jumped up a few notches. Within a few breaths, the men of second platoon were in a rough formation. Forjaz smacked them into crisp lines and took his place to the side, just as the brass appeared from between the tents. They were chatting jovially between each other or, more accurately, Forjaz realised, the colonel and Major Brooce were chatting amicably while the commissar walked, unengaged, beside them.

The colonel came to a stop a metre away from Forjaz and looked at him expectantly. Forjaz took a step forwards and whipped off a crisp salute: 'Sergeant Forjaz, sir. Second Platoon, K Company.'

Arbulaster returned the salute. 'Excellent, sergeant. Stand your men easy, I hear you've pulled the short straw and are up on first watch?'

'That's right, sir.'

'I'll not take up too much of your time then. Now,' he turned to the platoon lined up beside the fire, 'which one of you men is Ogryn Frn'k?'

The ogryn stood in line towering a metre above every other man. Forjaz's eyes flicked to the colonel's face, but his expression had no trace of anything but honest curiosity. Forjaz gave a nod to Gardner and Gardner discreetly elbowed Frn'k in the thigh. The ogryn looked down puzzled at his friend for a moment and, at Gardner's gestures, slowly raised his hand.

'Excellent!' Arbulaster said without a trace of sarcasm. 'If he could step forwards and... er...' He gestured at Gardner, 'If his friend wouldn't mind helping him along.'

Gardner led Frn'k to the front of the platoon, still uncertain as to what was going on. They were quite a pair, Arbulaster reflected. He did not know which of them looked more savage: the shambling ogre or the brute of a corporal who had covered himself in trophies made from the detritus of war. Once they were still, and the ogryn was at a semblance of attention, Arbulaster motioned to Brooce who passed over a sheet of paper.

'I have here,' Arbulaster announced, 'a commendation for Ogryn Frn'k, currently attached to the Brimlock 11th, K Company, 2nd Platoon. To whit, that on 058.660.M41 Corporal Frn'k carried out an individual act of heroism by which he led a group of enemy warriors into a prepared position and subsequently did single-handedly capture a vital prisoner. As this was in direct face of the enemy and at great personal risk to himself, his actions are worthy of commendation.'

Arbulaster handed the paper to the ogryn who took it carefully between his thumb and forefinger.

'Try not to eat it, there's a good man,' Arbulaster said as he patted the ogryn on the chest. 'Commissar? A few words?'

Arbulaster stepped away and beckoned to Reeve. The commissar came forwards, each step accompanied by the chink of his kill-studs striking together. Forjaz felt himself push his chest out even further. He did not dare look Reeve straight in the eye. No soldier ever benefited from a commissar's attention, all one could hope for was to be forgotten as quickly as possible. And so he looked past Reeve and thereby had a perfect view of the expression on Gardner's face as Reeve stepped into the light to address the platoon. In a brief second, Forjaz watched Gardner go from shock, to anger, then pale to terror.

'Major Stanhope,' Reeve declared as the officer appeared at the edge of the gathering. 'You are just in time.'

Forjaz glanced over at Stanhope. He was standing bolt upright, but Forjaz could tell he was on it again and wasn't about to intervene.

'Blessed are the small minds,' Reeve began, 'for they are easily filled with faith. This ogryn here, less than human but no less a servant of the Emperor, is an example to this regiment. Though today we have commended his actions alone, I have faith that all of you here are equal to his dedication.'

Forjaz did not hear the commissar's words, his only concern was Gardner. He was deathly white and looked ready to pass out. Forjaz wanted to get him out of there at once, but he did not dare draw the commissar's attention.

'And with that faith in my heart,' Reeve continued, 'I deliver to you a gift.' Reeve held his hand up. From behind the tent came two soldiers that Forjaz didn't recognise. They carried another between them, tied and bound, struggling. As they came closer, though, Forjaz realised it wasn't a man, it was an ork.

The two soldiers dumped the ork in front of the platoon. 'That very prisoner which has brought us here today.'

The ork was bound head to foot, yet it squirmed and slithered along the ground, trying to break free of the bindings. The platoon broke from its ranks, those closest retreating, those at the ends lapping around so as to have the ork encircled. Forjaz took the opportunity to step up and shove Gardner into Frn'k and push them both back towards the tents. Marble, who was never without his jerry-rigged lasrifle, raised it to shoot the ork dead.

'Hold!' Reeve ordered him, and Marble held. Reeve stepped across the circle, ignoring the ork, and held out his hand. 'I commend you on your keenness, soldier, but this one is not for you.'

At Reeve's insistent look, Marble unstrapped the lasrifle and handed it over to him. Reeve took it and held it out to the man next to him. Ducky picked it up, not knowing what was happening.

'Private Drake, I understand that the Emperor has never granted you the opportunity to rid the galaxy of one of his foes. That will change now. You will kill this animal that lies before us and join the rest of your fellows as one of His defenders.'

Reeve stepped away. 'Back, all of you. Give him room. We do not wish this night to end in accidental tragedy.'

The rest of the platoon did as they were ordered. Ducky, the focus of their attention, looked aghast.

'No, no,' he said, almost stammering, to Reeve, 'it's not my place. Frn'k took him, it should be his... honour.'

'The ogryn has already received his honour,' Reeve replied. 'This one is yours.'

'I can't take it for the whole platoon, we should draw lots.'

But the scarred and wizened Reeve would not budge, 'You have been chosen, private. I insist. It is an order.'

Ducky looked at the ork on the ground. It looked up at him, its xenos face twisted in anger and hatred. Its life was dedicated to destruction and death. It would be a mercy, a kindness to the entire galaxy to end it. But then, the decision that Ducky had made so long ago not to kill had never been about the enemy. Xenos or human, it did not matter. His duty to his god and to the Guard did not matter. It had only ever been about how he could live with himself in this damned universe.

'No,' Ducky decided. 'I won't.' He lowered the lasrifle.

'You're refusing a direct order?'

'Yes,' Ducky said and the platoon held its collective breath, knowing he was about to die.

'That is unacceptable.' Reeve pulled his pistol from his coat and fired straight into Marble's leg. Marble howled in pain and collapsed, clutching at the burn.

Forjaz instinctively took a step forwards, but saw Reeve's pistol pointed at him. 'Hold your position, sergeant, or your life will be forfeit.'

Reeve whirled the pistol back to point at Marble. 'Kill the animal, Private Drake, or my next shot will be to the head.'

But Ducky was already pointing the lasrifle at Reeve. 'So will mine, you black-hearted parasite. Leave us alone.'

Reeve's cold gaze locked with Ducky's furious glare. Forjaz looked desperately to the colonel to intervene, but Arbulaster merely looked on with a sombre expression. No one else dared move. No one wished to aid the commissar, no one dared oppose him. No one but Ducky, whose finger was trembling with rage around the trigger.

Reeve was unfazed. He was outnumbered and surrounded, and yet he had them all in the palm of his hand. He lowered his pistol slowly.

'If you wish to kill me, private,' he said, taking a step towards him, 'you had best hope to do so with your first shot. For if you do not, then I will have you and every other man of this platoon ended. And I will take my time in doing so. It will be slow and there will be pain, and only when they have scratched their throats raw with their screams will they be granted the mercy of death. Or, private, you will follow my orders and this will all be over.'

Ducky felt his hands shake wildly. Reeve would do it too. He would have them all killed for the slightest reason, and Ducky had just given him that.

The ork on the ground was bucking and snarling, ignorant that its fate was being decided. Ducky ignored it, his world full only of the grey eyes and the scornful expression on the commissar's sunken, ancient face. He raised the rifle to his shoulder to reduce the shaking, his eyes watered as he squinted down the barrel at his target in the middle of Reeve's forehead.

'Just do it!' Marble shouted.

For a split second, Ducky stopped shaking and stood perfectly still. Then he swept the rifle down towards the ork. He shoved the butt down and pulled the barrel in, back towards himself, as though about to club the xenos to death. And then he pushed the trigger. The lasrifle fired, then sparked and exploded. Ducky fell in silence his face a mass of burns and blood, his uniform burning from the misfire.

'What in the Emperor's name is going on here?' Carson appeared, Mouse trailing behind.

Reeve, for the first time surprised and unsure what to do, retreated. He stepped away and strode off into the darkness with the two Guardsmen he had brought. Carson did not wait an instant. He drew one of his pistols and shot the ork clean through the head as Forjaz and the rest of second platoon scrambled to save Ducky's life.

'WELL,' ARBULASTER COMMENTED to Brooce as they boarded a Valkyrie to fly them back to Dova. 'I think that went far better than expected, don't you?'

Brooce did not know how to begin to frame a reply.

Fortunately, the colonel did not need one.

'Did you see his face, Brooce? Did you see it?'

'Who? The commissar's?'

'Not him! The other one. Oh, it doesn't matter.' He activated the intra-vox. 'We're all on board, Plant. Up, up and away!'

CHAPTER TEN

CARSON WATCHED THE medicae try to patch Ducky's face back together again. He had been standing there for two hours already, but the surgeons were still working. They had no one else to attend to aside from Corporal Marble and a private who was laid up after a mishap with a las-cutter. Carson had not even known that the colonel was here. He had been giving his report to Major Roussell when he had heard the news. By the time the platoon had taken Ducky to the medicae tent, none of the senior officers who had caused the disruption could be seen.

Carson ordered Red to get them to their sentry posts. They would be early but it would be better to spread them out and give them a sense of purpose. At the very least, none of them would be falling asleep at their posts tonight. He held back Forjaz and got the story from him, then went inside. Stanhope was already there, watching the surgeons work.

'Seems like you weren't the only one Reeve was interested in after all,' Carson said.

There was no response.

'Where were you?' he continued.

Stanhope said nothing. He just stood there like a ghost, a presence without substance.

Carson went over to talk to Marble. He had needed little attention beyond a bandage for his las-burn. He was distraught, over Ducky rather than his rifle. Ducky, he said, must have ridden the trigger too long and overcharged it. He kept on swearing that he hadn't known that when he told him to shoot the ork. Carson forgave him, though he knew it wasn't his place to do so. Even so, Marble took comfort from it.

Carson stayed there until he realised the sentry shift was nearly done. The company found him waiting for them at their tent cluster. The hours in the dark had not done much to cool their tempers and several of them wore murderous expressions.

'Listen close all of you,' he said quietly. 'There's nothing about this that isn't rotten. Rotten to the core. But Ducky has shown us the way. No matter how that circumstance came to be, when it came down to it he put the company first and himself second.'

He heard the men shift uneasily. He carried on.

'Now, as likely as not, there'll be a battle tomorrow. Maybe our last one. Think on that and get some sleep.'

The company fell out and retired to their tents. He stopped Gardner, though, and pulled him over.

'I understand you have something to tell me, corporal.'

'No, sir,' Gardner answered stiffly, but Carson could see the murderous intent in his demeanour.

'Yes, you damn well do. This Reeve character, who is he? How do you know him?'

'I don't–'

'Don't lie to me, corporal,' Carson hissed. 'You're worse at it than your big friend. Forjaz saw you. You recognised him. So you tell me, why's he got my company in his sights?'

'That I don't know, sir. Honestly, I don't. But I have seen him before,' Gardner replied with menace.

'When?' Carson urged.

'At Cawnpore.'

'He was on the Execution Boards?' Carson said, incredulous.

'Yes, sir.'

'The one that ordered your brother…'

'Yes, sir. They didn't tell us the names, and he didn't wear that coat of his, but I wouldn't forget his face.'

'I understand.' The man was committed, Carson could tell. There was no way to deter him, only to stop him heading out this night and deflect him down a more favourable path. He shook the corporal fiercely. 'Now listen, there'll most likely be a battle tomorrow. Maybe our last one.'

'Yes, sir.'

'A great battle. A lot of confusion. A lot of death. Think on that,' Carson felt his meaning could not have been more clear. 'Now get some sleep.'

AFTER THAT, CARSON took his own advice and retired for the night. His sleep was restless, though, filled with the stories he had heard of the Cawnpore Execution Boards. They hadn't just taken the mutineers out and put them up against a wall, they had ordered them tied, spread-eagled, across the mouths of Basilisks. When the artillery fired, so he had been told, there was nothing left of the men except their arms, still tied to the cannons, and their blackened heads, which would roll to the ground. At which point the barrels would be lowered and the next mutineers strapped on. He had seen men die in worse ways on the battlefield, but to do that to your own kind… The image plagued his dreams, first seeing his men strapped on and fired through and then the arrival of his turn. As he was raised up and he looked down the barrel he could see the officer about to give the order to fire. It was Stanhope.

'Lieutenant? Are you awake? Have you heard the news?'

Carson cracked an eye open. Someone was inside his tent. Someone who was reaching for him. As his mind struggled from sleep his body reacted. He grabbed out with one hand, struck cloth, gripped tight. His other hand already held the bayonet he kept by his side. He yanked the shape down and rolled on top of it.

'It's me! Wait! Wait!' the shape whispered in a panic as it felt the sharp point of the bayonet at its throat.

Carson's mind awoke and found the firm body of Van Am tensed beneath him.

'M'sorry,' Carson muttered and took the knife away. He then coughed in surprise as Van Am punched him in the kidney.

'Damnation, you could have killed me,' she muttered, flustered. Carson rolled off and made to sit up, but found he couldn't.

'What are you doing here?'

'You haven't heard?'

Carson ordered his body to stand. It refused. 'Heard what?'

'The attack. It's going to be tomorrow.'

'Tomorrow? Well, we thought that might happen, didn't we.'

'You didn't know for sure? They said the word had gone out to all the company commanders.'

'Then it would have gone to Stanhope, wouldn't it?' He started to lever himself up just using his arms.

She sensed his effort beside her. 'What's wrong?'

'Nothing,' he said with a grimace. He felt her sit up beside him, felt her cool hands on his shoulder, on his arm. He gave up the struggle and allowed himself to fall back on his bed.

'What are you doing here?' he asked her again.

She rolled onto her side. Carson felt her body pressing into his, the heat of her flesh burning his own. Her scent flooded his nostrils, the mixture of the familiar sweat and dirt that all bodies acquire after two weeks in the field and beneath that the heady essence of the female. He could not see her in the darkness, but he knew she was above him, looking down at him, her hair falling around her face, grazing his cheek.

He felt nothing.

He felt her lean in and he put his hand up against her chest to stop her. Her hand encircled his wrist and tried to push it aside, but he held firm.

'Truly?'

He nodded and then realised that she could not see him in the darkness. 'I'm afraid so.'

She retreated, sitting back on her knees. 'So,' she said after a moment's silence, 'is it just me, or is it all those like me?'

Carson knew what she was implying. 'No, I'm not that way either.'

'Then what way are you?'

'I'm just...' He cleared his throat. 'I'm simply not in the game.'

He could tell that that answer had not satisfied her.

'I think it would be better if you–'

'Don't send me away,' she whispered softly. 'Don't send me away. There must be a dozen pairs of eyes who saw me come in here, and they'll be watching us still. If you send me away so quickly... What will they think of me if they saw I could not interest you even a little?'

'If your reputation is your concern, I'm surprised you came here at all.'

Van Am flashed from anxiety to amusement. 'Perhaps, lieutenant, you and I have different ideas as to what I wish my reputation to be.'

He had no argument to that, but merely let the uncomfortable silence linger.

'How is your man? Your medic?'

'Blind,' Carson answered curtly.

'You weren't there. And even if you were, what would you have done?'

'I'd have done something. He was one of my company. I would have done something.'

'If you had tried to stop it, Reeve would have just had you shot. And then shot Ducky as well.'

'Reeve?' he spat. 'Commissars are human like the rest of us. They bleed and they die. I've seen them. There's nothing special about them, nothing that we don't create in our own minds.'

'Do not be so sure,' she replied thoughtfully. 'My grandmother and the rest, they came here to be free of men such as him. To live free of Imperial dogma, to worship the Emperor, but to do it in their own way. To have lives of choice, not of blind suppression. And they found here... and we have had a century of freedom before men like Reeve have come chasing after us again.'

She was talking of the commissar, but Carson could tell it was not him alone she resented. It was all of them.

'A century, yes, before the galaxy caught up. And then your grandmother called for help.'

Van Am grew defensive at that. 'Don't make light of her decision. It was an impossible one, but she had to make it. And we will have to carry the consequences.'

Carson felt the sudden coolness form between them.

He had not wanted Van Am here, but he did not want her to leave carrying hatred for him. He reached out and took hold of her arm gently. 'You should know, she made the right choice.'

Van Am covered his hand with her own and held it a moment, then moved away.

'I think that should be time enough,' she decided, sitting up.

'Now it is *you* not considering *my* reputation,' he said, trying to lighten the mood.

She laughed at that, quietly but freely.

'Such a shame.' He felt her hand, cooler now than it was before, on his temple and tracing up into his hair. 'You're beautiful, Laurence.'

'Perhaps. In my day.'

'No. You are more so now than you could have been back then. Your men, they all love you. They'd give their lives for you. Maybe that's it? How can one woman compare when you have a whole company who adores you.'

He did not reply, and she knew he would not be drawn further. She sighed one last time.

'Would it really be so bad? Just two trails crossing in the dark. We may die tomorrow. And even if we don't, after you take the crater, I will go back to my farms and you will go back to your stars.'

Carson shook his head.

'No,' he replied, 'we won't be leaving.'

'No?'

'You really do not understand who we're fighting, do you. The orks, they are not like any other foe you can imagine. You cannot just kill them once. Their spores float around them, they're in the air. You can go through every jungle on this planet, you can shoot every one of them that lives, burn their bodies, and in a few years this place will be teeming again. Voor has not been attacked, it's been infested, and you and your militia will never be enough.

'On every world the crusade has encountered with this menace we have left a garrison, sometimes one regiment, sometimes two, sometimes more, all for that very purpose. Whether we take the rok tomorrow or not, we're here for good.'

'I see,' Van Am said quietly. 'I must go. I hope your man recovers.'

'Thank you.'

She paused a moment. 'If you had been there, if you could, would you really have stopped Reeve? Even if it meant...'

Carson did not hesitate. 'Yes.'

Van Am turned to leave, but stopped suddenly as she saw a group of torches flash by. Men were running outside, quiet but urgent, all over the camp. One of them burst into the tent beside Carson's and woke the officer sleeping within. Carson heard a mumble of voices, and then a sharp exclamation cut through the night air: 'Attack! The orks are attacking!'

Carson tried to jump up, but his body collapsed beneath him. He swore and cursed. Not now. Not now!

Van Am stepped to help him, but then stopped short. 'I'll get Red, I'll get one of your men.'

'No!' Carson demanded. 'Help me up.'

'But you don't want them to see–'

'I don't give a damn how it looks. My men need me! Help me up!'

CORPORAL DENNETT STOOD sentry on the fire-step of the fort wall and watched the darkness. He had little choice; there was nothing else to look at. The camp behind him was shuttered, the external floodlights were extinguished, any torches inside the tents were on a low-light, and the hopeful light from the moon and stars was smothered by clouds of dirt and ash. Without his noctocle he would not be able to see his own hand before his face. As it was, even with the small noctocle strapped over one eye, he had to strain to make out the detail beyond the walls. There was the ditch the beards had ploughed, the shallow glacis they had constructed with the spoil; beyond that were the stumps of the trees that had been lasered down so as to create a dead ground around the fort.

Beyond those were the ghosts of the trees which had been allowed to stay standing, the barest lines of their trunks and branches visible through the noctocle. Dennett counted himself lucky to have caught sight of the orks at all. He watched them now as they crept towards the wooden walls. They appeared to be having no trouble navigating in the blackness.

Dennett had fought orks before, he knew them to be tougher, stronger, more resilient than men. It seemed to Dennett that the same was true for most of the xenos races that the crusade had encountered. Each one outstripped men in some capacity: the eldar with their speed and their technology, the orks with their numbers and their savagery, the Karthadasim and the bewildering array of spined, horned, bestial mercenaries in their employ. And yet they had all been defeated by armies of men; men, who Dennett knew to be little more than weak, pink, fragile, with little granted by nature be it in defence or attack. How had they done it?

Through the noctocle Dennett could see that some of the orks were grouped together, holding aloft crude ladders made from the giant trunks and branches from the trees. A few hours earlier, those same logs the orks now carried had been felled by the beards. There must be some irony in that, Dennett reflected, but he doubted that either side would appreciate it. When he had fought the orks before, he had been one of the 74th, one of Ingertoll's Ironsides. It had been they who had spearheaded the last strike against the Waaagh, had boarded the rok when it had been in space, had laid the explosives to cripple its engines and send it spiralling into the sun. Few of the 74th had survived. Those few believed they had succeeded. Those who had passed since had at least been spared this, the sight of the orkish taint upon another world.

Dennett heard a whisper from the man beside him and passed it along. The first of the orks were closer now, approaching the glacis. If he had not seen them by now, though, he most certainly would have heard them. They believed they were being stealthy, but they were young, little more than new-spawns. For all the fighting instincts that orkoids were spawned with, there were many lessons you only learned through experience. And sometimes the price you had to pay for that lesson was your life. There was probably some irony there as well, Dennett mused.

'Fire!'

The volley of las-fire flashed along the length of the fort walls, illuminating the shocked orks for an instant before it burned into their flesh. They yelled in pain and surprise; some bodies dropped, others stumbled. Dennett had targeted one of the ladder carriers at the front. He had gone for the face, hoping for a kill-shot, but the ork had swayed a fraction just before the volley and the shot had struck the side of its temple instead. Dennett saw the shot hit, saw the ork's head flick to one side as the shot scorched into it, saw it roar then shake itself and continue on. Dennett cursed. He had been tempted to go for the kill. He should have known better. He shifted his aim down and went for the legs.

'Free fire!' The order came just a second later from the officer a few yards away.

Dennett heard the whine of his lasgun as it finished its cycle and fired again. This time the ork, who had started to charge, stumbled. It lost its grip upon the ram and brought its two kin behind it down as well. The ram lurched and swung out of control. Better, Dennett judged.

The floods burst on, transfixing the orks with light for the moment it took for their red eyes to adjust. Dennett's noctocle flared in his eye like a starburst before it cleared, shutting down automatically before it overloaded. He saw clearly now the sheer numbers of the wave of enemies about to break against them. The orks, blinded, surprised and confused, did what they always did when confronted with the unexpected: they charged, some of them even dropping their siege tools, so gripped were they by the instinct to rush forwards. They charged up the glacis towards the wall, waving their blades high in the air, thinking the slope would take them straight up to the walls, and then they tumbled down into the trench, pushed forwards by those behind, striking their kin as they flailed for purchase. Dennett heard their cries of alarm beneath him and then the plaintive blows as they vainly tried to chop through the thick trunks of the base of the wall.

'Grenades!' the order came down.

These ork whelps may have sprung from the ground born for war, but Dennett and all the other Brimlocks had lived it these last twenty years. The whelps had thought to try to take the 11th unawares. But Dennett and the other sentries had seen them coming even before they reached the dead ground, had alerted their officers who had roused the camp and readied the platoons that were now pouring fire into the outclassed besiegers. All the while the misguided orks slowly crept forwards, still believing that the advantage was theirs. It was time, Dennett thought with relish as he reached for a fragmentation bomb, to teach these newest pustules of the orkoid galactic pox the difference between instinct and experience, between savagery and soldiery.

Dennett activated the bomb, held it those crucial few seconds to ensure there would be no time for the foe to throw it back, and then tossed it down into the trench.

CARSON HEARD THE distinctive crack of the frag grenades as he struggled from his tent, his arm locked around Van Am and trusting her to take his weight. They staggered over to where his company was already formed up. Standing orders for such night flaps as these were for only those companies closest to a wall to respond to the attack.

He knew he must look ridiculous, reporting for duty, half-dressed, his arm slung over a woman. None of his men said anything and, to their credit, most did not think anything either. Red instantly came over and helped lower him to the ground. There were no orders, not that he could move out even if he were ordered to. Stanhope had turned out, looking almost as ridiculous, still dressed as a common trooper. He could see Carson's predicament, but took no steps to take command. After what had happened earlier that night, Carson would not have let him anyway. Damn him, Carson thought, he'd ride to battle strapped onto Frn'k's back before he'd let that man near his company. He just had to pray that his body responded before Major Roussell found a use for him.

CHAPTER ELEVEN

Fort Eliza, Tswaing, Voor pacification
Stage 1 Day 18

THE ORK ATTACK was in chaos. The trench hidden between the glacis and the fort wall was filled now with their dead. Those who survived the murderous shrapnel of the fragmentation grenades found themselves trapped there, having ditched their rams and ladders in the confusion of the Brimlocks' fire. A few of them started trying to climb back up the glacis to go back and retrieve them, and they were easy targets for the troopers' guns. The rest were left to hack desperately at the wall itself, trying to heave apart the wooden posts. Then the autocannons in the closest corner tower opened up and swept down the entire length of the trench, blowing both the dead and the living apart without discrimination.

For a few moments then there was relative peace. There was no sound from the trench aside from the high-pitched growls of a few squig pets, either mourning or eating their masters. Dennett lowered his hot lasgun. Behind him, the camp was still rising, officers were sending back for orders, sergeants were yelling men into their ranks. Dennett heard a horse whinny as an alarmed trooper pulled too tightly on its reins, and then the rumble of engines as the beards awoke their Sentinels. He heard some of his fellow troopers ask if that was it. One of them suggested that it had just been a raid to test their defences and steal from them an hour's sleep. Another that the orks had seen how their first wave had been slaughtered, and had then tired of the fight.

From the darkness beyond the dead ground, a single horn sounded. First one, then another, then dozens. A light, a torch, flared amongst the trees. It split into two, then four, then dozens, then hundreds to either side as each ork warrior lit its torch from that of its neighbour, until the arc of fire stretched across the width of the jungle horizon.

Dennett heard the thudding steps of another company of troopers as they ran up onto the wall and took up firing positions alongside them. He heard the autocannon crews in the towers call for more ammunition and the profanity uttered by the trooper who had proposed that the orks might have tired of the fight. Dennett leaned forwards again, sighted his gun and stroked his Ironsides insignia once more. An ork could no more tire of war than a man could tire of his own breath. They could only be killed, all of them, and that was exactly what Dennett intended to do.

'HOW MANY OF them are there?' Major Roussell asked again, as he prowled around inside the tent at the centre of the camp.

'Looks like at least a thousand,' Captain Gomery replied again.

'How many more might there be?' Roussell asked again.

'We don't know,' Gomery replied again.

Roussell stopped suddenly, the conversation was going in circles.

'Are they attacking just the west wall?' he asked.

'So far.'

'Are they going to attack the other walls?'

'We don't know,' Gomery replied again.

'Why not?'

'Well, we can't see into the jungle and the rok is still fouling up the auspexes.'

'Well what use is that?' Roussell exploded.

Captain Gomery bridled a bit. He wasn't some lagging corporal Roussell could bawl out at the drop of a hat. He was an officer, and almost as senior as Roussell. He'd been a leader most of his life and even back at the cadet schola on Brimlock it had been he who'd captained the field game squad to a nearly unbeaten season, not Roussell. Gomery secretly suspected that if it hadn't been for Arbulaster's disapproval of Mister Emmett, then he would have been promoted above Roussell a long time ago. He certainly wouldn't be here waiting for orders while Roussell paced up and down like a ratling trying to decide on his dinner.

'Have we got through to Dova yet?' Roussell cast about.

'I don't know–' Gomery started.

'Then go and find out!'

Gomery stared, piqued, at Roussell for a moment, then picked up Mister Emmett, tucked him under his arm and strode outside.

ROUSSELL WATCHED GOMERY depart with not a little relief. The man had been trying to oust him from his seniority for three years now, ever since the 92nd had been decimated crossing the Katee River on Ordan and the survivors had been folded into the 11th. He'd never let up about his nearly unbeaten season as team captain in his last year at schola either, as though prancing up and down a field and kicking a ball had anything to do with an officer's competency to lead men into battle. Even now he still carried a ball around him wherever he went, painted to look like a face with white daubs for its eyes, nose and mouth.

Roussell had no idea who the real Mister Emmett was, or even if there ever was one, but he praised the Emperor for him because that was all the colonel needed to see to ensure that Captain Gomery was never going to be promoted again.

Roussell knew that, as the senior officer, he was in charge, but he had been left here practically alone. The only other major up at the fort with him was the artillery commander, Major Rosa, and you couldn't trust an officer whose idea of a day's work was to sit down with paper and pencil and a cogitator in order to work out how to hit something five miles away. That wasn't proper officering. The colonel and Brooce had gone back to Dova, so had Drum and his tanks. The orks weren't supposed to be attacking them at night when they were battened down safely in their fort. Why now and not during the day when they dispersed along the trail and it was Arbulaster or Brooce who would have to put their reputation on the line?

Brooce had it in for him; he had been trying to oust him from his seniority for ten years now, ever since the 371st had been the first to go in on Mespots and the survivors were folded into the 11th. In fact, Roussell wouldn't have put it past Brooce to have set him up, leaving him in command when he knew an attack was coming, so as to blacken his eye. Roussell had served the entire crusade, he had won over a dozen victories in the first ten years, he had a chest-full of clink, his place in the colour-guard had been guaranteed even then, and he had steered clear of all disgrace since. But it would all be for nothing if a costly debacle could be pinned on him here at the last!

But the battle was going well, too well. The orks' first attack had been beaten back without loss by Captain Wymondham's company on the west wall. Tyrwhitt's company, as the closest company encamped, had automatically moved up to the wall to add their firepower. The remainder of the line companies were either on the other walls watching out for flanking attacks or were forming up as a ready reserve in the centre of the camp. Rosa's mortars were deploying and in a few minutes would be dropping ranging shots on the ork's horde. Everyone was doing exactly what they should be... despite the fact that he had not issued a single order yet!

It was a nightmare! If they won the battle without him issuing a single order then he would look a fool, as though he had slept through the whole thing. But as everyone was doing exactly what they should be doing and everything was going splendidly, any order he did give would be to get someone to do something that they shouldn't be doing and he would look like an idiot. Worse, if everything then stopped going splendidly, it would be his order that would get blamed for turning the tide against them. And if he issued an order to order everyone to do exactly what they were already doing he would look like an incompetent who didn't know what his troops were already doing. And if he issued an order to order everyone to *continue* doing what they were already doing he would draw even more attention to the fact that they had all been doing exactly what they should be doing without any orders from him! He was trapped. Utterly trapped.

Another runner came into the tent looking for orders,

his helmet and uniform both stained brown.

'Lieutenant Carson sends his apologies, sir, and requests orders for his company.'

Roussell eyed the runner suspiciously. He wasn't a young man, but then none of them were. He was heavy-set with a powerful frame, his skin mottled and scarred, though his stare was as wide-eyed as a child's. But if he came looking for orders he had come to the wrong place.

'What's your name, trooper?'

'Private Stones, sir.'

'Don't know you. Where's the second lieutenant?' Roussell stressed the 'second'. Too many people, officers and men alike, seemed to forget Carson's proper rank. Carson, Roussell knew, was another one who would have ousted him from his seniority if he could. Then he could have both the light companies to himself. But he'd killed the wrong man and he was never getting out from under that.

'He's indisposed, sir.'

'You mean he's in that Voorjer trollop.' Roussell mocked Carson's success with her because he'd had none himself. 'Tell him he can stay there! *Stanhope's* company stays in reserve. They shall not engage until and unless they receive orders to do so.'

He swept away from the man, dismissing him. But Blanks didn't leave.

'And if attacked, he should still not engage?'

Roussell tried to peer down at the private; however, he found it difficult to peer down at the taller man. 'Are you trying to be smart, man?'

'No, sir. Merely trying to understand your orders fully. Sir.' Blanks replied. Roussell did not miss the slight lengthening of the pause.

'Of course he should engage!' Roussell snapped back. Carson wasn't going to get the chance to have his men stand passively by as they got hacked apart and then blame it on his orders! 'He should do exactly as he should do at all times until ordered otherwise.'

'Is that an order?'

'Most definitely not!' Roussell fumed.

'Understood, sir,' Blanks left. Roussell would have called him up on failing to salute an officer if he had not then been distracted by Gomery walking back in, still carrying Mister Emmett.

'Signals in touch with Dova. They're waking the colonel; they'll patch it through here.'

'Excellent.' Roussell started stalking again impatiently. Soon someone else would be giving the orders and it would be their reputation on the line and not his. He noticed Gomery was staring at him.

'What is it?' he demanded.

'Orders for my company?'

'Yes, of course.' Roussell considered for a moment as he prowled. 'First, though, the orks.'

'Yes?' Gomery asked impatiently.

'How many of them are there?'

THOUSANDS OF THEM. That's how many there seemed to be to Dennett as he pulled his gun's trigger, listened to it whine as the power cycled back and then pulled the trigger again. His shoulder ached and his cheek was burning from being pressed against the overheating gun, but he continued to fire as quickly as he could.

The las-shots poured from the top of the wall like bolts from the heavens, but their effect was far less impressive. The ork was tough; a single lasgun shot, more often than not, would scorch its hide but not bring it down. The troopers had to hit their targets two or three times in succession to get the kill. Dennett himself had hit one ork five times in a row; each time the ork lurched, but then shrugged off the injury, before the sixth shot made it tumble.

Tyrwhitt's troopers had already mounted the wall and were adding their own fire, but as fast as they all shot, it wasn't enough to hold the horde back. The orks had swarmed across the dead ground and the glacis, and as soon as they had reached the trench they had lobbed their torches up into the blinding light of the floods and onto the wall. Some were thrown too short and rebounded off the ramparts back onto the heads of the orks in the trench, but the rest sailed high, slow enough for a man to dodge normally, but not when crammed onto a firing-step, pressed up close with fellows either side.

The torches smacked home onto Brimlock helmets, and troopers all along the wall jerked away from the flames, believing themselves to be alight. They shouted in alarm and stepped back from the step, dropping their guns and batting at themselves. The men either side of them stopped firing as well to aid them or to defend themselves against their fellows' wild flailing. The las-fire lessened and the orks bellowed in triumph and hoisted up their makeshift ladders again.

The officers shouted at their men to keep shooting; the sergeants stepped up behind them, smacking the panicking men and hauling them back to their posts, kicking the torches off the back of the walls for the next company coming up in reserve to douse. The autocannons in the high towers continued to spray their fire, unable to miss the mass of ork warriors beneath them, but it was not enough. Even as the singed troopers picked their lasguns up again, the ladders were thumping onto the ramparts.

'WE'RE TO STAY put?' Carson questioned Blanks. He could stand on his own again and Van Am had returned to her Voorjer scouts.

'Unless attacked,' Blanks replied.

Carson turned to the assembled company. His eyes flicked briefly to Stanhope, but the major was simply staring over to the west, lost in some personal reverie. Carson drew his breath and opened his mouth to give his orders, but whatever he was going to say was lost in the explosion.

'FIX BAYONETS!' CAPTAIN Wymondham had shouted a few minutes before as he fired his pistol into the face of a climbing ork. They were crawling all over the wall now. The autocannons had targeted the base of the tree-trunk ladders where the orks had bunched together and swept them clean, but there were too many ladders and not enough guns.

The orks dropped their weapons and used the logs as though they were ramps, charging up on all fours like apes. The troopers concentrated their fire on those at the front, the orks' bodies erupting with the red shot as they cartwheeled off the trunk-ladders, dying in mid-air. But then the troopers faced agonising seconds, while their guns recycled and the ork behind the first kept charging on. That ork got two metres more before the red shot lashed out again, and the one behind it got one metre further.

The orks bought each step with lives, but they were willing to spend them, until finally they were close enough to leap from the end of the ladder and cannonball into the knot of humans ranged against them, smacking them aside.

Dennett halted his fire and grabbed his bayonet. He ducked down, brought his lasgun back, swore as he burned his fingers on the barrel and slotted the bayonet home. A thick green hand slammed down on the rampart right by his face. Dennett snapped his head up and looked straight into the red burning eyes of an ork who had climbed up the sheer wall. It shouted unintelligibly into his face and let go of one of its handholds to grab him, catching the lip of his helmet. Dennett tried to rip it off, but the chinstrap had caught and wouldn't come free. He hauled himself away from the wall and the ork held on tight, dragging itself over the rampart.

Gun and bayonet lost, Dennett fell down the earth slope behind the fire-step and the ork rolled with him, both of them punching, scratching and kicking at the other with all the strength they could muster. Its barks and grunts filled his ears, its pungent fungoid smell invaded his nose.

They hit the ground tangled together, the ork pressing down upon him. It heaved and Dennett felt his throat tighten, and then a sudden release as his chinstrap broke and the ork ripped the helmet from his head. The xenos monster towered over him in the night and gripped the helmet with both hands, ready to smash it down on Dennett's head and break his skull apart. Dennett scrabbled in the dirt behind his back for anything to defend himself with, but he was too slow and the ork hammered down with a cry of victory.

Dennett clenched his eyes shut as the ork's cry turned into one of outrage as it found itself plucked from the ground and lifted effortlessly into the air.

Dennett looked and there above him stood another monster, this one standing twice the height even of an ork and made of cold, grey steel. The Sentinel held the struggling ork aloft in its hydraulic claw and, without missing a step, the beard at the controls activated the las-cutter and sliced the ork to pieces. Dennett shielded himself from the rain of cleanly cut segments of ork.

All around him, the Sentinels of the support company were climbing the earth slope up to the ramparts. The troopers fighting on the walls made way to give them room. The Sentinels ignored the orks already on the ramparts, instead making straight for their targets: the log-ladders. One Sentinel was not quick enough, and an ork leapt onto its cockpit. The beard inside fired his pistol, but the ork held on and wrapped its hands over the man's head and crunched. The Sentinel overbalanced and fell forwards, smacking down on the log-ladder and knocking it from the wall.

The rest of the Sentinels took a grip on the logs but did not push them off; rather they pulled and dragged them over the wall and into the fort. The climbing orks clung on as their ladders were launched forwards, but the Sentinels merely twisted their grip to turn the logs upside down and wiped the orks off like a gentleman using a boot-scraper.

Dennett scrabbled back up the slope. Everywhere men were cheering, and he found himself cheering as well. The orks remaining on the ramparts were outnumbered and swiftly skewered by the merciless Brimlocks. Dennett found his gun, the unused bayonet still in its socket, and took his place again on the fire-step amongst his jubilant fellows.

He looked out onto the floodlit dead ground, now fully deserving its name as it lay carpeted with ork corpses, and the furious ork warriors cutting hand-holds into the wall. He raised his gun once again to pick them off and so did not see the shape in the darkness beyond the floodlights. He heard the boom, however, and looked up just in time to see the giant comet of fire burning towards him.

ROUSSELL DID NOT hear the sound of the mega-bombard firing, but he did hear the explosion that cracked the western wall and reverberated throughout the camp.

And when he heard it, he muttered his thanks to the Emperor. Finally, all was not going to plan.

Arbulaster's angry, flustered voice erupted on the vox in front of him.

'What the throne is going on up there?'

Roussell replied crisply. 'We're under assault, colonel. Several thousand attackers. We're coming under heavy fire. All companies are in defending positions. Transmitting details now and awaiting your orders.'

Roussell breathed a quiet sigh of relief. Back at Dova, the colonel would be receiving all the data he needed so as to decide what actions were best. The battle was finally out of his hands.

CHAPTER TWELVE

CARSON ARRIVED TO find the western wall still burning. The bodies of a half-dozen troopers littered the earth slope at the point of impact. Their platoon-mates were tumbling down either side of them in disarray, Captain Wymondham calling uselessly after them from the ramparts, his company dissolving around him. Carson heard the explosion again from beyond the walls and Wymondham was plucked from where he stood and thrown in a flaming arc through the air. The survivors around him rolled down the slope to extinguish themselves and then kept running.

The wall had held so far, Carson saw, but that wouldn't matter if there was no one left defending it.

'Stop 'em, Red,' he ordered, pointing at the fleeing men. 'Booth, take the north section up to the tower. Forjaz, you're with me.'

Carson led Forjaz and second platoon up the slope, his thrice-cursed legs pumping hard. An ork appeared, hauling itself up over the wall. Carson drew his pistol and snap-fired as he ran. The heavy shot burned through the xenos's face and caused its brain to explode inside its skull. Another ork appeared. Carson flicked his hand and his other pistol was there, firing. The second xenos met the same fate as the first.

Second platoon crashed into the top of the wall and threw the climbing orks back. Frn'k bounded up, snapping an ork's neck and knocking it off the ramparts with a smack of his hand. Then he suddenly dropped down onto his hands and knees and the autocannon strapped to his back was in the perfect position to fire down the length of the wall. Gardner, following right behind him, was there ready to pull the trigger, and he and his ogryn cackled with glee as the climbing orks fell from their tenuous fingerholds and scrambled for cover.

Further along the wall, Tyrwhitt's men were holding their footing against the attack. Carson snatched a glance over the wall at the dead ground. This assault had been too light and he quickly saw why; it had consisted only of those orks who had survived the previous waves and had been caught in the trench below. The next wave proper was holding its position beyond the range of the floodlights. They were waiting for a breach.

As if at their request, the mega-bombard fired again. Carson ducked instinctively, but this shot went wide, striking further down the wall, incinerating in an instant half a squad from one of Tyrwhitt's platoons and the dozen orks climbing up at them.

With that bombard, it would be deadly to stay where they were. The orks could pound them with impunity, and until their main force attacked, his men could do nothing but sit there. Better to send second platoon back to the rest of the company at the bottom of the earth slope; a few observers in the towers could give them warning enough to get up to the ramparts.

'Message incoming from Major Roussell,' Peel, his vox-officer, started. Carson took the proffered handset and held it to his ear. The voice of Major Roussell crackled back at him.

'--- *All companies --- Defend the western wall --- No retreat --- Hold the wall at all costs --- Order direct from the colonel --- Stay on the wall ---*'

Direct from the colonel? Carson swore under his breath. The colonel was nearly forty miles away, why in the blazes was Roussell deferring to him? And why were they piling the men onto the wall like ducks on a shooting range?

'That's it. I'm going to take it out,' one of the platoon announced a few paces away. Carson looked back. It was Blanks, and he was already strapping on a noctocle he had taken from a dead corporal and readying to move out. He wasn't going to ask permission.

'You bleeding well stay in line, trooper, or I'll have your guts on the end of my poker,' Forjaz ordered him.

Blanks stopped, suddenly confused, though only for an instant.

'Yes… yes, sergeant.'

'What did you say?' Carson pushed his way over to him.

'I'm sorry, lieutenant,' Blanks corrected himself. 'I only meant to say that I volunteer…'

Carson grabbed his arm. 'You think you can do it?'

Blanks looked up at him. 'Yes. I do.'

Carson looked at the man. No one should be volunteering to do such a task, certainly not on their own, and yet, even crouched here behind the ramparts waiting to be blown to oblivion, this new man to his company had such an air of confidence about him that Carson actually believed he could.

'What do you need?'

'Just a permission slip, lieutenant, in case an officer stops me.'

'Mouse!' Carson shouted, and the trooper scurried across. 'Give Blanks one of my absence slips.'

'Sir!' Mouse claimed. 'You know I don't keep any–'

'Don't bull me, trooper,' Carson told him and Mouse reluctantly reached inside his coat.

'Forjaz,' Carson continued, 'you go with him. Watch his back.'

Forjaz was speechless for a moment. Surely, he thought, the lieutenant knew it was suicide. Feeling Carson's stare upon him, however, the hard-bitten sergeant muttered 'Yes, sir' with a shaky voice.

'I'll be quicker on my own, lieutenant,' Blanks said, taking the plas-sheet that Mouse produced.

'I'm not sending a man out there on his own. That's not how we do things,' Carson replied. And I don't know you, he mentally added. Maybe you are what you seem and maybe you're not, but either way I'm not letting you run wild.

Carson watched the two men hasten towards the gate in the southern wall. He doubted Blanks would succeed, but Forjaz would keep his head. Forjaz would come back alive and most likely bring Blanks with him.

'Incoming!'

Even though they were already crouched behind the ramparts, the platoon ducked instinctively at the sound of the mega-bombard. This time, however, the explosion was followed by the sound they all dreaded to hear; from further down the wall the shout began:

'Breach! Breach!'

FORJAZ PAUSED A moment when he heard the shout, but Blanks did not. He knew what his mission was. There were nearly a thousand men in Fort Eliza, more than enough to defend a breach so long as their officers kept their heads. Given time, however, that mega-bombard could make a dozen more like it. That was the real threat and so Blanks kept running, and Forjaz cursed and hurried after him.

THE BREACH WASN'T fatal. The shot from the mega-bombard had struck the glacis and deflected up, striking the wall there, a quarter of the way up. It had smacked into the wall and the earth behind, but it had not shattered and instead rolled back into the trench, crushing the orks floundering there. With the top half of the wall caved in, the shot formed a giant stepping-stone over the barrier and into the fort.

It wasn't much, but for the ork warriors who had been forced to wait in the darkness beyond the dead ground, even such a crack was encouragement enough.

'Red! Red!' Carson called as the orks roared in slavering anticipation. Red, bless his flaring nostrils and scarlet face, was there.

'Ready, sah!' the colour-sergeant acknowledged. 'Right, you shockers, after me!'

Red no longer commanded only first platoon. He had bawled, shoved and bullied sixty more men from the late Wymondham's company into line. Now, at their head, Red manoeuvred them like a giant stopper to plug the breach. The construction Sentinels moved ahead of them, carrying empty crates, spars and drums to fill the gap.

Gardner opened fire out over the dead ground again. Carson looked and saw the horde plunging towards them, the light of the floods casting their green skins grey. This was it. Gardner's weapon and the other autocannons firing along the wall barely scratched it; the mortar shells that Rosa's men were now lobbing into their midst were not enough. If the western wall was to be held, then it would be with only lasgun and bayonet.

MAJOR ROUSSELL HEARD the news of the breach. Established procedure in the instance of a breach was to construct a second line; however, adhering to established procedures was not a cast-iron defence in a court-martial. Following a direct order, on the other hand, was. Guard officers were not excused the use of their initiative in the pursuit of victory, but orders were inviolable. And so Major Roussell used his initiative and relayed the news to the increasingly exasperated Arbulaster and waited for orders.

'GRENADES!' CARSON COMMANDED. The orks were racing for the breach now. For all their bulk they had a surprising turn of speed. Each one of them was running at full pelt, but even in such a mass, they were not stumbling or tripping over each other. Their base, unerring warrior instinct kept their charge intact, and they were going to beat Red's scratch company to the breach. They shoved their weapons between their teeth and, dropping onto all fours, they bounded up the impromptu ramp made by the bombard shot and launched themselves at Tyrwhitt's defenders.

The orks, however, would not beat the Sentinels. The beards at the controls manoeuvred the striding engines of war up the incline with the ease of long experience. Now the orks had committed their full force, Carson's men and the Sentinels would only have to hold their attack for a few minutes until the companies still held in reserve all around the camp could come up. Then any ork that made it through the breach would be met by hundreds of lasguns.

Carson heard another squawking on the vox, but did not care to hear Roussell exhorting them still further. But the beards in the sentinels had listened. They paused a moment and then, with the same expertise with which they had advanced, they swung their walkers around and marched back down again.

Carson could not believe his eyes. He looked in askance at his vox-trooper, but he was already staring back towards the camp; in every corner the reserve companies had halted as well. Then, following a chorus of new orders, they too turned to retreat.

'What's that idiot done?'

'YES, MAJOR, FOLLOW established procedures if you are not certain the breached wall can be saved,' Colonel Arbulaster repeated over the vox, while the sounds of the Valkyries lifting-off could be heard in the background.

'And the companies still engaged on the wall, colonel? Can you just confirm?' Roussell queried.

'Is your secondary defence line already established?' Arbulaster's voice seared with sarcasm.

'No, colonel,' Roussell reported conscientiously.

'Then they'll have to buy you the damn time then, won't they.'

'HOLD POSITION, SIR,' the vox-trooper replied. His voice had not quivered, but Carson could see that beneath the brim of his Guard-issue helmet the man's face had paled.

Carson felt the blood thundering in his ears. Roussell was hanging every man at the wall out to dry. Carson was going to kill him, if he didn't die here first.

BLANKS FLEW THROUGH the darkness. He and Forjaz had run over to the southern wall, ignoring the flood of men who streamed past them towards the breach, and dropped down the other side of the main gate onto the hard track beyond. With the orks focused on the new partial breach in the western wall, speed was more important than stealth.

They had dashed down the track, almost as though they were fleeing the battle, until they were outside the range of the floodlights. There they had switched to the noctocles and looped up into the woods and around to where Blanks was certain he had spotted the ork mega-bombard.

As they went, Blanks could see the glowing outlines of the trees and the morass of tangled undergrowth through the noctocle. It was difficult terrain even in the day; at night, at a run, it should have been nigh impossible, and yet every time he put down his foot it found somewhere firm, every time he stretched out his hand it grasped solid wood to steady his step.

Behind him, he heard Forjaz breathing hard at the exertion, but he had barely broken a sweat. A tree had fallen across his path; he leapt and vaulted across it. He did not know how his body knew to do such things, it just did. Maybe this is what he had been in his old regiment: a runner, a messenger, someone who might deliver the vital ammunition to the gun team, the spare part to the broken-down tank, or return the critically wounded man to the medicae.

He saw the outline of the ork on the other side of the tree trunk just before he crashed into it. They both went down in a tangle of limbs. Blanks felt his elbow strike the beast's throat, then found his bayonet in his hand plunging into its eye. He pulled it free, rolled to his feet and flung it hard in front of him. The other ork made a bubbling noise as it sank to its knees, Blanks's bayonet embedded in its neck. It was only then that his instincts stopped firing and his thoughts caught up.

'You're a violent bastard, aren't you,' Forjaz said from atop the fallen trunk, regaining his breath.

'You need to stop?' Blanks asked.

'No,' Forjaz bit back, but his heaving chest said otherwise.

Blanks stepped warily over to the gurgling xenos, watching its eerie green outline through the noctocle. Its eyes were fixed, but its arm was still flapping a fraction. Its brain was trying to send signals to its arm to pull the weapon free from its neck, but its arm no longer understood the brain's instructions. It hadn't been like this at the ambush; there he had been in the third line, the orks had been shapes through the trees and then scorched corpses on the ground. He had seen them alive and dead, but he had not watched them die.

He trod down on the arm to stop it moving, twisted the bayonet and cut it free through the flesh, opening the ork's throat. It slumped, dead, into the undergrowth.

'Rearguard, do you think?' Blanks asked.

'Unlikely.' Forjaz sat on the trunk and pushed himself off, his breathing still heavy. 'They're new-spawns. Whelps. They were probably doing the same as us. Trying to sneak around the back.'

'Orks sneak? I thought they only went straight for you.'

Forjaz stared at the trooper. 'Of course they sneak! You never fought them before?'

'I don't remember.'

'Perfect,' Forjaz spat.

Ahead of them, the woods lit up as the mega-bombard fired again.

THE SHOT FLEW across the same path as the last. The wall exploded, throwing fragments of wood, earth and pieces of both the orkish attackers and Tyrwhitt's defenders up into the air. As the shower of blood, flesh and dirt fell to the ground Carson saw the yawning gap that had now been created, as though the orkish gods had swung an almighty hammer and smashed their way through.

'Get the breach! Get the breach!' Carson bellowed to his platoon, but the orks were already there. They were ugly, snorting animals, daubed with war-paint decorating their bodies with the symbols of their gods, wielding clubs and cudgels hewn from the jungle trees, and picks and axes made from sharpened spars and rocks. They roared with bloodlust as they charged forwards over the trench of their dead and into the fort.

'First rank, fire!'

The orks at the front were sliced to pieces by the criss-crossing las lines.

'Second rank, fire!' It was Red. As soon as he had realised that he would lose the race to the breach he had formed the survivors of Wymondham's company up within the camp itself. Now he was calling out the ranks as quickly as he could, disciplining the fire against the cycle time of the lasguns to work them at their utmost effectiveness. Against a human foe it might have been enough, but orks were not human.

'Gardner!' he shouted to the corporal still blazing away on the autocannon that Frn'k had braced against his shoulder. 'Redeploy!'

Gardner released his trigger and smacked the ogryn on the side of the head.

'Trouble, we move! Quick march!' The ogryn grunted and then heaved both the autocannon and Gardner bodily into the air. When they reached the rest of second platoon, Frn'k simply dropped to one knee, holding the gun like a bazooka, and Gardner was firing in an instant.

The platoon poured their fire down onto the endless ranks of orks streaming inside. Even as some of the orks turned to meet the threat, the toughest of the first wave, screaming and scarred, reached the ranks of Red's company, only to be pierced by the tips of the troopers' bayonets.

But the orks did not feel pain as men did. Each attacker had to be crippled or killed to halt them and, even impaled, they still clawed at the troopers. Red's company lost their firing routine, as their line crumbled into a brutal close combat they could not win. Red launched himself forwards, swinging 'Old Contemptible' high to bring it crashing down on ork heads. Carson flicked his pistols up to help him, but one of his troopers blocked his shot.

'Get out of the way!' he snarled, but the trooper was already moving, running down the slope towards the melee, drawing a heavy, curved blade as he went. It was Stanhope. He was not yelling; he was deathly silent, his energy entirely focused. He reached the combat just as Red fell back, face crumpled by an ork fist. The ork grabbed the sergeant by the arm to finish him off and Stanhope whirled the fell-cutter in his grip and brought it down.

The fearsome reputation of the fell-cutter, and the margoes who wielded them, was well-deserved. Though it looked like a sword, its use bore little relation to the swift, slender blades that Brimlock officers and cavalrymen carried, which were designed to thrust at their opponents; the fell-cutter's sole purpose was to cut, and that it achieved with great effect.

Stanhope's first blow chopped straight through the arm holding Red and carried on going, slicing the cap off the ork's knee. Even as it fell back, the beast behind it grabbed straight for Stanhope who spun and drove the blade into its stomach, its curve sliding it up behind the ribs. Stanhope shoved it away, pulled the sword out and, bringing it round like a windmill's sail, chopped the ork's head in two.

Carson adjusted his aim and blew out the brains of the third ork about to swing a stone axe down upon the major's back. Stanhope did not notice, he only kept on fighting.

The volleys of fire began haltingly again as the foremost orks reeled back for a moment. Stanhope fought through the beams, miraculously untouched by his own side, but Carson knew this moment's brilliant madness could not last.

A few orks had stepped back, but that was nothing against the tide behind them pushing them further in, and the orks redoubled their charge.

The mega-bombard fired again and struck the southern tower and Tyrwhitt's heavy weapon crews firing there.

'Sir!' Gardner called as he continued to fire. 'Need more ammo!'

Carson heard the sound in the wind, the screech that would turn into a deathly roar as though now the planet was coming for them. Any retreat under these conditions would turn into a rout as the orks launched themselves upon them, but he had no other hope.

'Message from Valkyrie flight, sir,' the aide reported to Major Roussell. 'They're incoming, requesting targeting instructions.'

'Targeting?' Roussell declared. 'There's an ork horde outside our walls and they want us to tell them where they are? Tell them to look out their damn windows.'

'They're coming in rather fast, sir. If they have to fly-past first to recce then it will delay–'

'Yes, yes, very well.' Roussell gritted his teeth in annoyance, yet he could not allow any evidence that he had been negligent in his duties. 'Give them the coordinates

of the breach. The orks will have taken it by now, they'll
be massed there. They can fire free.'

'Yes, sir.'

CROUCHING LOW IN the dark undergrowth, Blanks
watched the mega-bombard being reloaded. Its crew
of dozens of gretchin swarmed across its surface, trying
to hoist a new shot into its wide gaping mouth. One
of them slipped and fell inside, leaving the others to
burst into hoots of laughter, curtailed by one of the
ork overseers cracking its whip. The defences around
the mega-bombard were exactly as Forjaz had feared.
Formidable. Aside from the overseers, nearly fifty ork
warriors stood close at hand. These were not the thin-
ner, smaller new-spawns they had fought before; these
were fully matured. Even hunched over they were as
tall as men, the muscles of their arms as thick as a
man's torso. At their head was an even larger ork carrying a stone hammer and adorned in armour made of
bent metal rings. It was obviously enjoying the carnage
the mega-bombard was inflicting.

'That's him, that's the warboss,' Forjaz muttered, lying
beside Blanks. 'I don't know what your plan is, but if you
think you're going to pull some one-man-army bollocks
and try to storm it with just the two of us, I'll shoot you
myself.'

'Understood,' Blanks replied. In truth, he did not know
what his plan was. He hadn't had a plan even when he
volunteered, he hadn't been thinking; it'd been instinct.
The mega-bombard was the primary threat, it had to be
destroyed. He could not destroy it from a distance, and
so he had to get closer. It had all been obvious to him at
the time, but now he was here he found himself reaching for knowledge in parts of his mind and finding them
empty. But then he heard the sound of the wind, and

that was when he stopped thinking and started letting his instincts rule his actions.

'Give me the hand-vox,' he told Forjaz.

'Who're you going to call?' he asked, mockingly, as he handed it over.

But Blanks wasn't going to call anyone. Instead, he tore open one of the panels and went to work.

Forjaz shook his head. 'It doesn't matter. They're never going to risk sending another lot out here.'

Blanks sealed the panel, then took off his helmet and secured the hand-vox into the lining inside. He stood up and hurled his helmet into the branches of the trees above the mega-bombard.

'What the–' Forjaz began. 'Unless you've been stashing atomics that's not going to do–'

'Run!'

The helmet hit the branches and dropped onto the ground. With their natural thieving instinct, three of the gretchin sprang from the gun to grab it. The biggest of them smacked aside the other two, scooped it up and proudly planted the helmet on its head. As it jeered in triumph, the mega-bombard and the entire jungle around it exploded in fire.

CHAPTER THIRTEEN

CORPORAL GARDNER CLICKED the last catch of the autocannon into place and wiped the grease off his hands with a rag. He was putting the gun back to bed. It'd had a busy night. It had held the breach until the Valkyries had screeched down from above the black clouds. They annihilated the mega-bombard and everything around it in their first run and then set about the main body of the ork force still piling into the breach.

The sudden attack from the air, coupled with the stubborn defence by the four companies that had stayed on the wall, had been enough to break the assault. The orks streamed away, back across the dead ground, into the cover of the trees. Gardner had carried on firing until the last body he could see stopped twitching.

Even though the orks had gone, the companies remained at their posts. It was only after Major Roussell was finally convinced that the wall had been held that he ordered the reserve companies forward. There was to be no pursuit into the dark, unfamiliar jungle, of course, but they took control of the dead ground to burn the carpet of ork bodies that lay there. The soldiers of these companies, who had sat out the battle waiting on the second line, at least had the decency to look embarrassed as they passed the bloodied defenders of the western wall.

Carson's company was stood down and the men returned to their tents for the second time that night, but this time few could return to sleep. Instead, each man followed their individual rituals to calm themselves from the fire of battle: Frn'k ate, Mouse prayed, Booth drank the spirits from which he otherwise abstained, Prosser wept quietly, and Red collected up the property of the men who had died. Gardner stripped and cleaned his gun and planned how to kill Commissar Reeve.

He had killed an officer before, Captain Blunder, though in that instance it had been an accident. All it had been was a simple salute, but that salute had given the sniper his target. Gardner had been lucky to have been under the scope of a marksman experienced enough to wait and pick his target, and then go to ground rather than blaze away to scrag a couple more before being picked off himself.

The incident had taught him that the best weapon to use against one of your own was the enemy. He could imagine how it might easily be done to another of his unit; when fighting such xenos monsters as the crusade had encountered one depended so greatly on the support of those beside them that, should one of them delay even a second it might make the difference between life and death.

But killing a commissar in such a manner was harder. Those commissars who chose to lead from the front did not last as long as Reeve had. He would stay close to the colonel and Gardner could not rely on the enemy to kill him there. He would have to do it himself.

Even the thought of murdering a commissar was treason; worse, heresy, for they were the representatives of the Emperor's will. Should a Commissariat interrogator pluck that thought from Gardner's mind they would execute him for that alone. Such draconian measures were designed to instil terror, to ensure that a commissar's personage be treated as inviolable by any and all who might question him. Gardner, however, found it liberating. If the punishment for the thought of the sin is no greater than the punishment for the sin itself, then there was nothing to be lost in its completion. He had thought it as soon as he recognised Reeve's face the evening before. All that remained was the action.

He would keep it simple. Simple worked. He would just walk up to him and then, with a single las-blast, there would be justice: justice for his brother and the hundreds others like him who were condemned after Cawnpore. He'd already filched a pistol for it. Couldn't use a lasgun, no; it would be too obvious to hold. Reeve would be on his guard as soon as he saw it. But a pistol, he could just reach inside his uniform as though he were delivering a message.

He zipped the autocannon back into its cover and stepped around the slumbering hillock of Frn'k whose lips were still smattered with food. He and Frn'k had been together for four years, since they had both joined the 11th after Charasia, and they had fought side by side ever since. But Gardner would not wake him up for this. He would not understand. In many ways ogryns were monsters, but in others they were children. They venerated commissars second only to the Emperor. Even after Frn'k saw what Reeve did to Ducky and Marble he still could not comprehend what had happened. He thought it some horrible mistake. He would not understand why

Reeve deserved to die; he would only get in the way.

Gardner stepped out of the tent, the pistol a reassuring weight beneath his armour. Reeve was here, Gardner could feel it. Mouse had told him that one of the Valkyries, instead of returning to Dova, had landed inside the camp. It had to be the colonel, come to inspect the battle-site and tear a strip off Roussell, and if the colonel was here, then Reeve would be here too.

He walked through the camp, taking his time. Hurrying would draw the attentions of others. He reached the major's tent in the centre. There were two sentries at the entrance and so Gardner held back, lingering in the darkness. Officers were definitely inside talking. He could wait. His stood and watched for a few minutes then he casually reached under his chest armour as though to scratch and stroked the hilt of the pistol.

'What are you doing here?' a voice said behind him.

Gardner felt his breath catch. He turned quickly to see Carson standing there. Carson saw the moment's guilt in Gardner's face and the hand disappearing under his armour. He pressed against it and felt the object beneath. With a savage tug, he pulled Gardner's hand free and yanked the pistol loose. He looked at it for a moment and then regarded the corporal once more.

'He's not there,' Carson said at last. 'Reeve's still with the colonel at Dova.'

'What's that, sir?' Gardner replied dumbly.

Carson grabbed him by the collar, dragged him into the lee of a wares container and shoved him against the side.

'I told you to wait.'

Gardner grimaced. 'How can I? How can I when we could bite it any second? We nearly died tonight. You, me, all of us. If I die and he lives…' He let his bitterness hang in the cool night air.

Carson had had enough. First, Marble and Ducky, then Van Am, then the attack and Roussell's idiocy, his patience was worn out.

'You sorry, selfish, son of a bitch!' he whispered furiously. 'You shoot him here? Now? They'll take it out on the rest of us! I haven't carried this company for ten years, just for you to get every one of them put up against a wall!'

Gardner was no wilting violet, but he was still taken aback. Carson had never spoken to him, or to any other man in the company, in such a manner.

'Sir?'

'Shut your mouth! Listen to me. They know about your brother. If they don't already, they'll find out when he bites it. If Reeve dies then they're going to come for you, and through you they'll get us.'

'They won't–'

'They will. So when he dies you need to be nowhere near him.'

Gardner pushed himself free of Carson's grip. 'If I can't go near him, how am I going to kill him?'

'You're not. We are.'

Gardner hesitated.

'This is one of those sacrifices, corporal, that has to be made for the men one serves beside. You and I, we both understand that.'

Gardner nodded and did not resist as Carson led him out and pushed him away in the other direction. Carson watched him for a few moments to make sure he went and then doubled back, tucking the confiscated pistol away in his own jacket, ready for the real fight.

'I HAVE NO trouble *hearing* your answers, pilot, I have trouble understanding them,' Roussell reiterated. 'What do you mean when you say that it just "popped up" on your targeting auspex?'

'Exactly what I said, major,' Flight Lieutenant Plant, who was not accustomed to being addressed so sneeringly, replied. 'The location of the orkoid war engine appeared as a priority target as we were beginning our first run and we altered our attack accordingly. I presumed that it was someone here on the ground who had tagged it.'

As the flight lieutenant spoke, Roussell noticed Carson slip in through the door. He ignored him; Roussell had deliberately invited only the company commanders to ensure that Carson did not attend, and yet the man had come anyway. Still, he did not want to have the further interruption of having a spat trying to get him out, he was having trouble enough with this debriefing as it was.

It should have been straightforward enough. Roussell considered that it was quite clear that he had been responsible for the victory, he just wasn't certain how. In past actions of a similar nature, he'd found it prudent to deliver the formal debriefing to his subordinates as soon as possible, to ensure that they were all aware of the official record and knew not to contradict it in their individual filings. Here he had been, all set to grant a measure of credit to the Valkyrie pilots for their assistance in chasing the orks away after the success of his plan to contest and defend the breach, when this dim-witted bluebell unveiled the mystery of the targeting coordinates. Roussell would not have cared, but if the pilot was going to file it to the colonel then the colonel was going to quiz him, and if he didn't have an answer he'd look an idiot.

'I have always encouraged my sub-commanders to exercise their initiative in battle,' Roussell said smoothly. 'I'm sure that there were several units who were placed and could have advised as to coordinates. Major Rosa?'

The podgy artillery officer woke from his doze with a

start. 'Your observers would have been in place to "tag"' – Roussell's tone made clear his disdain for Navy slang – 'this war engine, would they not?'

Rosa readjusted his spectacles. 'Yes, well, perhaps. But I must admit that with our heavier pieces back at Dova we were focusing on the ground outside the walls and the, er, softer targets there.'

'You misunderstand, major,' the flight lieutenant interrupted, not inclined to make life easy for Roussell. 'To be clear for the record, we were not voxed with coordinates; it was a Navy signal direct from the target.'

'That was us,' Carson announced. 'Two of my men, Sergeant Forjaz and Private Stones, volunteered to make a flanking excursion and take down the bombard. They transmitted the signal from its location.'

A look of concern crossed the flight lieutenant's face. 'Did they survive the attack?'

Carson turned to him. 'Both men reported back a short time ago, alive and uninjured.'

'They're to be commended. They were just in time, we were only just able to divert from our initial–' the flight lieutenant began, relieved, but Roussell interrupted, clearing his throat loudly. He wanted to shut up the Navy pilot before the topic of the first targets arose again. Now he knew that Carson had held the breach, he thought it wiser not to make the lieutenant aware that he had given that position as the original target. It would be an excuse for Carson to finally call him out and kill him as he'd done so many others.

'If that's all accounted for then? Let the record show the commendable actions taken by these two men who were under Major Stanhope's command.' There, Roussell thought, the matter was closed and he was safe.

* * *

'SOME OF YOUR time?' Carson caught Stanhope as Roussell dismissed the assemblage. 'In private?'

Stanhope nodded wearily and led the way to his tent. 'I'll put a note in my filing,' Stanhope began as they went, 'to ensure that the colonel has an accurate account of who authorised the attack on the bombard and who led the company at the breach.'

'Do not trouble yourself, major,' Carson replied offhand. 'The colonel and Major Brooce are perceptive men. They will discern the truth.'

'Still, for the record—'

'Do you really think that I care what the record says about me?'

Stanhope paused for a moment and regarded him. 'No, I do not.' They walked a way further and Stanhope began again. 'This man Stones is something of a mystery. Boosting the signal of a hand-vox is one thing, but setting it to transmit a Navy targeting sign is quite another.'

He noticed that then, Carson thought. He must not be on it at the moment. He was actually trying to be friendly. Collegiate. Obviously he thought that fighting side by side at the breach had drawn them together, that the two of them might actually confer and share command of the company. He was deluded, but Carson would hold his tongue until they were in private.

'More than that, even,' Carson said, keeping his tone even, 'if you had heard Forjaz's report.'

Stanhope heard the touch of censure in the lieutenant's words. He had not been there to hear Forjaz's report; he had not even known whether the two men had survived or not until Carson announced it. He suspected he knew what Carson wished to talk to him about. He had witnessed it, they all had. It was not the way things should be done, but Stanhope was not going to hang him for it.

'Your relations with the governor's granddaughter are

of no interest to me,' he said as he entered the tent, 'if that is your concern. Your appearance together at the call to battle was... unfortunate, but I'm sure that you will be more discreet in the future.'

It was then that Carson decided to let Stanhope really have it.

'I don't want to talk about Stones. I don't want to talk about Van Am. I want to talk about Ducky.'

'Private Drake? What about him?'

'What in damnation were you doing?'

'What do you mean?'

'You know what I mean: when you stood there and watched as Reeve shot two of my men.'

'Take care as to your tone, lieutenant.'

'I'll take whatever tone I please with you, you washed up, clapped-out, pitiful excuse for an officer. What gives you the right? Eh? What gives you the right to sit out the rest of the crusade? To stand and watch while men of mine are crippled, not by the enemy, but by their own side? If this is how you treated your own men, no wonder they got murdered. Do it to your own command, but why did you have to come and take–'

Carson felt the side of his face explode. He stumbled back, blinking in surprise. He focused and saw Stanhope standing there, fist still outstretched, knuckles white. Stanhope stood stock still for a moment. He had shocked himself with the punch; it was as if it had come from another person. It was that instant of delay before Stanhope's fighting instincts kicked in that prevented Carson being knocked to the ground in seconds.

Stanhope swung again, more deliberate, this time putting his weight behind it. Carson deflected it and tried to grab the arm, but Stanhope was still moving forwards and tried to ram his temple into Carson's nose. Carson twisted his face out of the way and Stanhope's crude head-butt smacked into his ear. Blessed Marguerite! Carson thought, he hadn't taken the aloof Stanhope to be such a dirty fighter.

The sudden panic lent extra urgency to Carson's muscles. He grabbed the major around the head and punched him in the side of the neck, then felt the pain in his side as Stanhope tried to hit him in the kidney. Stanhope tried to yank free of the lieutenant's grip, but Carson brought his other arm around, grasped hold of Stanhope's hair and brought his leg up to protect his own groin and knee Stanhope in the face. Stanhope, with a rabid strength Carson hadn't suspected he had, shoved them both forwards. With Carson off-balance, the two of them fell back, Carson's knee raised, his foot pressing into Stanhope's stomach. He kicked hard and Stanhope was fairly launched back across the tent and stumbled to the ground. He grabbed the side of his bed to steady himself and readied for another attack when he saw the pistol in Carson's hand.

The two officers held position for a few moments, both of them panting for breath.

'I wondered what it was going to take to get you to fight,' Carson said finally.

'Go ahead,' Stanhope snarled. 'That's what you like, isn't it? I'm not so addled that I don't know your reputation, lieutenant. How many duels have you fought? How many men, how many imperial officers have you murdered with those guns? More than any single one of the enemy. More than Reeve even?'

Carson's expression froze. 'Don't you dare compare me to him.'

'You're right. Reeve kills men because he thinks that's his job. You kill because you enjoy it. I saw it in you yesterday with Reeve's ork. I can see it in you now. What would you have done? What would you have done if you had been there sooner? You couldn't have done anything.'

'I'd have stopped it.'

'No, you couldn't. You're a second lieutenant and second lieutenants can do damn all. Twenty years, Carson, twenty years of fighting; your men love you, your commanders trust you, so why have you never been promoted to a rank where you can make a difference? It's because when Ellinor's fat fool of a son picked a fight with you, you wouldn't walk away. And when he told you a time and a place, you met him there. And when his shot just creased your shoulder, you didn't disarm him, you didn't injure him, you shot him through the heart. People said you were proud. You're not proud. You're sick. You kill because you like it, but you killed the wrong man. And that's why you couldn't save your precious Private Drake last night.'

Carson felt it now, he felt the urge come on him. His mind knew that this was lunacy, that he'd get put against a wall, but his blood did not care. All it could feel was the power, the power of having another life completely at its mercy, a hugely complex organism and the unique identity that it had developed which could be snuffed out by the slightest move from him. It disgusted his mind, but his blood called out for it. His whole body tensed with the effort of the struggle. But then his body betrayed him.

Very slowly, Carson toppled backwards. His pistol fell from his hand and thumped onto the ground. Every muscle was clenched and shaking and he could not release it.

Stanhope stepped towards him and saw the rictus on his face. 'Carson?'

'Get...' he managed through clenched teeth, '...Red.'

CHAPTER FOURTEEN

RED EMERGED FROM Stanhope's tent, his normally severe face softened a touch.

'Is he up?' Stanhope asked crisply.

'He's moving, sir. He's not on his feet yet.'

'What's wrong with him?'

Red looked away. 'It's not exactly my place, sir. I'm afraid you'll have to ask the lieutenant.'

But Stanhope did not relent. 'I'm asking *you*, colour-sergeant. In fact, I am *ordering* you.'

Red snapped to attention, standing stiff enough to support the whole of Dova, and Stanhope saw defiance blaze in him.

'Axomitic gas,' Carson said from the flap of Stanhope's tent. He was in his shirt-sleeves and swaying, but he was upright. 'And if you have any questions, Mister Stanhope, I'd be obliged if you directed them to me.'

Red saluted quickly and disappeared, most unsettled at being caught between the two officers, and at the rebellious streak that had emerged in him. Stanhope let him go and followed Carson inside.

'You can walk again?'

Carson half-sat, half-collapsed on the bed. 'I find your presence irritating, Stanhope, but not permanently debilitating.' He gathered his jacket and slowly started to put it on. Stanhope waited for the explanation.

'There's little to it. It was a Kartha booby-trap, the second week on Kandhar. We got out quickly, but I wasn't quick enough.'

'We were told axomitic gas was instantly fatal.'

'No, it takes a few seconds. Time enough to use the auto-injector. Did it never strike you as odd?' Carson asked. 'We were given myecyclone to inject ourselves with if we were exposed to a gas that was supposed to kill you in a split second?'

Stanhope nodded gently. 'It doesn't normally pay to question orders.'

'It doesn't pay to follow them blindly either, does it? You know that.'

Stanhope straightened up, disliking the lieutenant's inference. 'And so the myecyclone didn't work, is that it?'

'No, it worked alright. It's the cure that's killing me,' Carson said.

Stanhope did not know what to say to that. 'Only the Guard could issue a remedy that does exactly what the poison does, only takes longer to do it,' Carson continued. 'And it won't be clean; anyone who's ever lost all control of the lower half of their body can tell you that it isn't clean. It's happening more often, each time is longer, spreading further, and soon it will be permanent.'

'How long do you have?'

Carson pulled his jacket on and started fastening the buttons. 'Of use? Not long. The medicae said that when it reached this stage, it wouldn't be long. Until I'm finished completely? They couldn't say.'

He stood up off the bed and faced Stanhope eye-to-eye. 'So now I know your little secret and you know mine. Both of them. I imagine you're thinking right at this moment whether you should have me removed from command. I think you could. But I think you won't. Because then you would have to run the company, you'd have to be here for these men. And here is the last place you want to be. You need me and we don't need you.'

Carson walked out, leaving Stanhope alone. Stanhope breathed hard, stamped his foot and looked up to the canvas above him and the clouds and the stars above those. Carson was wrong about one thing. The company did need him. They needed to know that there was someone there, not to replace the lieutenant, but to succeed him.

But Carson was right about him. Stanhope unbuckled his sword from his belt and sat down and began to twist off the base of the hilt, revealing a small compartment. He took a dry leaf from inside and put it in his mouth. He did not wish to be here. The men of the company needed someone, but it did not need to be him.

IN THE SILENCE of the morning the sentries at the fort's gate heard the rumble of a convoy approaching them from the east. They voxed the news to Major Roussell and he hurried over. Finally, it was Captain Drum's armour, and as pleased as Roussell was to add the armoured company to the garrison, he was even more keen to rub Drum's face in the victory he had missed.

Hard as Roussell found it to imagine, the flamboyant tank commander fought not to garner personal glory but for the sheer thrill of riding his tank into combat. Why on earth would any sane man want to do that? The answer, of course, was that Drum wasn't sane, he was howling mad. Roussell had never understood the crazy fool, and certainly did not understand why the colonel overlooked the man's eccentricities. He disliked him intensely as a result. And it didn't help that a population of the wives and widows thought Drum's ridiculous, tightly-cut costumes rather dashing and paid him a good deal more attention on his arrival than they had ever done Roussell.

The pitch of the rumble rose as the vehicles got closer and Roussell waited for the first of them to emerge around the curve of the track leading to the fort. Nothing appeared, and then the rumble was overshadowed by the whoosh of a Valkyrie coming in low, ready to land.

'COLONEL!' ROUSSELL ACKNOWLEDGED Arbulaster and saluted rather briskly. He'd had to run from the gate to the landing area and was not best pleased about it.

'Major.' Arbulaster returned the salute with equal discourtesy.

'Captain Drum has not yet arrived, sir. I do believe he may have taken a wrong turn on the way here,' Roussell reported with satisfaction. 'I'm not sure if he may have missed some instruction during one of his wardrobe changes...'

'Unlikely, major,' Arbulaster replied without humour. After an entire night of authorising every single action Roussell took, including lavatorial demands, he was quite sick of the sound of him. It was a pity really, he had once been a rather talented and highly courageous infantry commander, but over-quick promotion and the assurance of a place in the colour-guard had curbed his audacity and he had shrivelled into paranoid mediocrity.

'Captain Drum is on his way to the start point. As you should be, major, if you intend the infantry to play any kind of role in taking the crater.'

'The attack... It's still going ahead today?' Roussell was a little astonished.

'Of course it is,' Arbulaster replied. 'What did you expect, major? A few weeks R&R to recover from missing a night's sleep?'

'No, of course not,' Roussell started, mortified.

'They're on the run and we can hit them hard. They've played right into our hands.' Arbulaster laid a comradely hand on Roussell's shoulder. 'We didn't want them bolt-holed in their rok up there. No! We wanted to get them out, have a stab at us where we're ready for them in a rok of our own. And they broke themselves on it.'

'Yes, I–'

'After all, why do you think I put you out here in the first place?'

ARBULASTER'S INTENTION IN ordering the infantry into fortified positions at night had had nothing to do with luring the orks into an attack, but if there was credit to be had he intended to grab his fair share before Roussell had the lot.

At Roussell's insistence he briefly inspected the breach, sombrely looked over the bodies of the men as they were buried in the trench and finally ordered the walls they had died defending be brought down.

It might have appeared a trifle heartless, but Arbulaster was past caring about a few troopers. His message was clear. Fort Eliza had served its purpose and kept them safe for a night; now their entire force was going to be thrown against the ork rok and he wanted none of his men being tempted to retreat from the field to hole up back here. It was to be all or nothing for them, as it was for him as well.

* * *

THE BRIMLOCK 11TH sat on the ground watching the beards cut through the trunk of the last tree in their path.

'Kay-Vee!' The call went up, though every man there was already aware. The tree toppled to one side and the seated men raised a ragged cheer. Lieutenant Mulberry pivoted his Sentinel to face them and then leaned the cockpit forwards in imitation of a bow. The sarcastic cheer was replaced by a ripple of genuine laughter, which in turn dissipated before the angry bawling of the regiment's sergeants.

'On your feet! On your feet! In your sections! In your sections! Ready march!'

Drum's tank men rose to their engines and Ledbetter's horses whinnied and stomped the ground.

'ONE MOMENT.' The colonel's voice cut through it all. He stood upon Drum's tank using its vox-amplifiers.

'IN HIS NAME.'

The cavalry dipped their lance points and the men lowered their heads.

'THE EMPEROR EXPECTS EACH MAN TO GIVE HIS STRENGTH, HIS SPIRIT, HIS ALL, AS HE GAVE FOR US.'

The colonel made the sign of the aquila; most men followed, a jaded few did not.

'FOR DEATH IN HIS SERVICE IS NO END, FOR THOSE THAT FALL SHALL LIVE ON IN HIS LIGHT.'

Those with faith in the crowd nodded along; it was the truth, they'd always been told so.

'NOW, MEN OF BRIMLOCK, RAISE YOUR VOICES. FOR MARGUERITE, FOR THE CRUSADE, PURGE THE XENOS! DESTROY THEM ALL! TO ARMS! TO WAR! THE EMPEROR CALLS! FOR THE EMPEROR!'

'FOR THE EMPEROR!' the regiment swore.

The cavalry raised their lances and the bugler called the advance. The tanks growled back to life and eased forwards into the lichen, Drum standing proud upon the lead tank, dressed in the brocaded jacket of an ancient

Brimlock cavalryman. Rosa and the heavy artillery rolled out next, the Griffon mortar vehicles following in the tracks of the tanks. Finally, the infantry companies fell in, Roussell first leading the two light companies, behind him Brooce commanding the line, and by his side the command section flew the regiment's colours high.

Beneath those colours marched the Brimlock 11th, the mind of each man plagued with the fear that they would die here, at the last. The mind of each man but one. One lieutenant, whose thoughts were not focused on his own death, but on the death of Commissar Reeve. Today that death, he swore, was guaranteed.

CHAPTER FIFTEEN

Fungal plain, Tswaing, Voor pacification
Stage 1 Day 18

KILLING A MAN on a battlefield, even a man on your own side, was simple. Hundreds of men, sometimes thousands, died on every single one. Killing a man universally loathed and despised was even easier.

Killing a commissar, supposedly a direct representative of the authority of the God-Emperor of Terra, was very different. Their daily meat and wine was to be hated and despised. No one even remotely careless or sloppy ever made it to wearing the black coat and the skull insignia of the Commissariat. Commissars had the inherent authority to execute immediately and without explanation any trooper or officer who they suspected of cowardice, incompetence, treachery or taint, as judged solely by themselves. Some armies, some entire campaigns, had been saved as a result of quick and terminal action taken by a commissar to remove swiftly from the command structure any who had been infected with fear, madness or disease. But mostly they contented themselves with ruling troopers and officers alike with an iron fist in an iron glove, exacting terrible punishments for the slightest infractions that caught their attention.

Carson considered that conspiring to kill one of their number might just attract that kind of attention. He could not simply walk up to Reeve and shoot him. Even if he did not mind dying himself, the revenge would be taken out on his men as well. Therefore, the attack would have to be untraceable, completely deniable, and it would have to succeed first time, or his entire company might as well line up against a wall and save the firing squads the trouble.

They were setting a quick pace, quicker by a fraction than the rest of the regiment. The column was beginning to stretch out. These fungus fields were bizarre. Many of the orkoid fungi shared properties with the fully formed orks themselves. Some were the same colour, others even had knots and growths that resembled ork heads and muscles. This was no longer a trek through a jungle on Voor, this was an invasion of the skin of a single giant organism, whose many natural defences were ranged against them.

He could hear the whoops of Ledbetter's cavalry ahead. Many of the ork survivors of their assault the night before had stumbled back to the fungus jungle and dispersed, scavenging for food and water, and a place to finally rest. They were awoken now by the rumbling of Brimlock tanks and struggled from shelter to find horsemen all around them, firing las-shots into them at near point-blank range.

The column's progress was fast, faster than even Arbulaster had expected. The ground was soft underfoot. It was made up of the ash of the trees that had once been there, the trees that had burned when the rok had struck. And on top of that ash now grew the bizarre array of fungus that sustained the orkoid species. The few stumps that remained were so riddled with these parasitic growths that they crumbled easily before the shells of the armoured company. The treads of the tanks and the hooves of the cavalry's horses found easy purchase in the ground-mould, but kicked up such a cloud of spores that the infantry following behind were covered. Arbulaster gave the armoured company permission to open their throttles, and they surged ahead.

The ork resistance was non-existent, in any case. Everywhere they were running, and the cavalry was harrying at their heels, and now amongst them came the tanks of Captain Drum, straight towards the crest of the crater that hid their last objective.

On top of the leading tank, Drum stood and sang in sheer pleasure. He hadn't engaged the vox-casters yet and the sound was lost beneath the bellows of the machine-spirits. The orks, with their clubs and spears, scattered before the engines of forty-first millennium warfare. Drum stood tall, outside of the protection of the armoured turret, and rode the vehicle as though it were a giant shield and he was some ancient chieftain being borne into battle.

Captain Ledbetter galloped back towards him, running to ground a confused ork who had broken in the wrong direction. Ledbetter leaned forwards in his saddle as he swept his chainsword down and hewed through the ork's back. It dropped, its spine severed, and Ledbetter tugged his reins as his horse instinctively swerved away from the falling body.

Drum doffed his tricorne hat and waved it at the horse dragoon as he circled, about to return to his squadron. Ledbetter pointedly ignored him, but Drum did not care. He was happy. He was more than that; he was ecstatic. He was not quite sure when he had gone mad, he was not even certain he was mad at all. He had been born literally by the side of the production line in a factory on Brimlock, his mother one of thousands of menial servers who laboured in that one plant alone. He was raised by her side, watching the manufactorum adepts assemble the revered engines of war, and here he was, having gone from crewman, to officer, to commander, to captain through this crusade, riding such a beast and leading his armoured company into the fight on a far-distant world. What a life it was compared to that which he would have lived had he stayed on the production lines. What a life the Guard had given him!

Drum swept back his cape, raised one knee-high boot and stomped twice on his tank's turret.

'Aiken, clear the path!'

'Aye, sir,' the reply came from his gunner. The turret rotated a fraction to target a knot of hardened fungus stalks and Drum whooped as it roared. He began to sing again.

Ledbetter ducked a fraction in his saddle as the tank's cannon fired and silently cursed his instinct. Even his horse had had that trained out of him. Was he not even this animal's equal? He spurred it forwards from the advancing line of tanks and revved his chainsword to clear it of the ork's remains.

Ahead of him, the rest of his squadron were chasing the band of orks they had roused. As Ledbetter watched, he saw one of the beasts trip and roll. The lancer who had been after it was taken by surprise, stabbed and missed. His horse broke its step to avoid getting its legs entangled and galloped on with the rest. The fortunate ork rose unscathed and then launched itself upon one of the squadron's stragglers, caught the man's leg and managed to rip him from the saddle. It raised a meaty fist to smash in the back of the prone lancer's head and

Ledbetter sliced its arm through at the elbow. The ork did not even have time to howl in pain before Ledbetter's back-cut mutilated its face.

A good kill, Ledbetter considered, as he watched the fallen lancer clamber wretchedly to his feet. But it would not be enough. Not enough to be selected as one of the colour-guard. He had already failed it twice, the first time with the 74th when it was dissolved after Mespots and a second time with the 56th just a few weeks ago. He had been so certain that time, but no, the regiment's commissar had vetoed him and his colonel had not cared enough to fight. Now he had to prove himself again, in just these last few days, or he would never return to Brimlock and prove to his family what he had become.

But there! There on the hills before them was a challenge that would burn his name onto the list for the colour-guard.

THE ORKS WEREN'T running away. They were running *towards*.

A warband had appeared over the rim of the crater and had marched halfway down the slope on the other side. Their presence had formed a rallying point for the orks running from the Guard out of the fungus jungle. They scrambled up the slope, up off the more level ground where the cavalry dominated, and joined the warband's ranks. That single ork warchief suddenly found himself commanding not one, but two, three, then five warbands' strength as more and more of the scattered orks sensed the growing concentration of power and instinctively flocked in its direction.

The cavalry chasing the stragglers now found themselves being assailed by rocks, clubs and spears hurled by the ork line. Carson saw a single horse stumble and toss its rider. The rest of his squadron instantly broke off their pursuit and circled back, protecting their fellow with fire from their pistols while he remounted, before they all withdrew together. It was a tiny victory for the orks, but it was enough to provoke bellows of mocking hoots and chanting directed at the horsemen's fast-retreating backs.

'FINALLY, BROOCE,' ARBULASTER commented, standing in the open hatch of the Salamander, 'the orks are showin' a bit of backbone.'

'About time, colonel.'

'Damn right. Not going to do them any good, though,' he chuckled. 'Soon as Ledbetter gets himself out of there, our ill-tuned Drum will have a field day.' Arbulaster adjusted the focus on his monocular a fraction. 'Vox the captain. Tell him to pick his targets. Break 'em as quick as he can, hammer straight through. We're not stopping for a few orks today.'

'BLOODY IDIOTS,' MOUSE exclaimed. 'Don't they clock what those tank cannon are gonna do to 'em?'

'Not if they've never seen tanks before,' Blanks said.

'They're gonna get *murdered*,' Mouse said, with no small degree of relish at the prospect of a swift, crushing victory that he would not even have to fight in. Now the armoured company had gone forwards, the light companies had taken its place in the vanguard. Second platoon had an excellent view of the tanks churning over the moss-covered ground towards the orks on the slope, but Blanks had noticed something wrong.

'Look at that!' Blanks pointed. 'The cavalry!'

ARBULASTER HAD SEEN it as well. Ledbetter was not leading the cavalry back, they were reforming to charge.

'Blessed Marguerite! Is every single one of my officers mad?' He whipped the monocular away and grasped his vox-officer. 'Get me Captain Ledbetter now!'

The vox-officer tried. 'Sir, there's no reply, sir. Maybe it's the interference…'

'My copper-bottomed arse, it is. I can see him from here! Get him! Get anyone to stop that charge!'

But the vox-officer of Ledbetter's command squad did not respond. Arbulaster could only watch, half-incoherent with rage, half-gripped with the irrational fear that these orks, after killing the cavalry, would somehow drive the rest of the column back and be the end of him.

Ledbetter's cavalry were going to die. The slope began gently but then skewed upwards. No horse would be able to climb it straight; the charge would founder and then the ork mobs would jump down amongst them and tear them apart. Yet none of this seemed to deter the steady lines of grey and gold horsemen on their steeds. They spurred their mounts quickly from the trot to the canter to the gallop with little delay, their explosive lances held firmly upright, ready to let their points drop at the last moment. They hit the base of the slope and began to climb, the horses slowing despite their riders' urging. The line of orks now had no fear for they too instinctively saw how the attack would stall. But then another rider entered the scene, and his mount was far more formidable.

'Don't you ever! Don't you ever!' Drum called, hunched down on the back of his metal monster, as its thundering engine powered it forwards and it slewed into the path of the charge. For a moment, Drum's crazy stunt worked and the horsemen began to slow. But then the cavalry's bugle sounded again and booted heels dug into horses' flanks. Ledbetter's veterans knew how to deal with an unexpected obstacle in their path. The cavalry ranks split, going left and right to flow around the tank before them. Their orders were clear, they knew this might be their last chance at glory, and they were not stopping for anything.

Drum sprang to his feet on the tank's hull, his cape flowing in the wind and kicked the turret twice.

'Sing for me, my beauty. Sing!' he shouted and his battle cannon fired at the cavalry's front rank.

The shell was aimed short, but that barely lessened the impact. The case of the shell exploded in the face of the horsemen and, in an instant, three of them, man and horse together, were little more than bloodied ruins that tumbled and somersaulted to the ground. The mounts of those either side stumbled and fell, tossing their riders, already dying from the overheated shell fragments that had struck them.

The cavalry's horses were desensitised to the sounds of war, but nothing could have kept them calm in the face of such a thunderclap and they broke their gallop, whinnied and reared in alarm at the carnage, the men upon them no less stunned at what had happened. Even those horsemen distant from where the cannon had struck gaped in astonishment, then outrage, and pulled their horses up.

The cavalry's charge was over, the lancers wheeled away to the side or halted in shock. Unmoved at the destruction he had caused, Drum braced himself on his tank's turret as it turned upon the orks above him, delightedly hooting at the spectacle he had given them. They did not realise that that was just a taste of what was about to happen to them. Drum saw the rest of his command move into line beside him, drawing into close range. He gave the signal and his tank rocked savagely as it and the other nine war engines of the armoured company fired. He did not wait to see the results. Instead, he thumbed the control for the vox-amps upon his hull and called out:

'On! On! On!'

The armoured company struck the base of the hill and their tanks appeared to rear up like giant metal mounts in order to climb. The orks' javelins and other thrown weapons clattered harmlessly off their thick armour. As soon as the tanks' front ends landed, their battle cannon fired. At such short range, they could barely miss and huge chunks were blown out of the ork warband. As the cannons fired, the heavy bolters mounted in the tanks' hulls opened up as well, firing explosive bolts at the crumbling ork line. Surprised by these strange weapons, the orks followed their instincts and charged at the tanks and struck them with their clubs and cleavers. The tank drivers barely noticed the slight loss of grip as the ork warriors tripped or were caught beneath their tracks.

Their victory was already, literally, crushing. But as the tanks moved up, the legendary orkish endurance kicked in. Those who appeared dead or crumpled into the earth began to pick themselves up and try to jump on the tanks from behind. The only force who could take the crater, as well, was the infantry. Carson's company was the closest and they hurried to keep in contact with the tanks. For all the destruction caused, the survivors were maddened nearly to a frenzy, and so Carson's men had to take them down hard.

'On! On! On!' Carson shouted to his men as they stumbled up towards the crater rim. He fired his pistol at one of the ork warriors clinging onto the outside of a Leman Russ and trying to batter its way through the armour of its hull with a heavy stone. His shot hit the creature in its side, but it ignored it, entirely focused on the slight dent it was making in the tank's side. Carson paused for a split second to aim and then incinerated the side of its head with his next shot. He cursed silently at his slip; he could not afford to be distracted now, here, in the middle of the fight. He had to get his men through this first and then he could deal with Reeve.

'Stay in close, you dogs!' Red lambasted the men again. His face was more crimson than ever, having to both shout and run, but he had to keep up with the charging tank beside them. The whole company did. It was the only way this haphazard assault would succeed.

Carson fired a shot, killed another enemy, then spun his pistol back into his holster. In battle, he tried to keep his hands free as much as he could. It was an old habit, one he had picked up after Red had dragged him from that foxhole on Torrans in his very first battle. He was fast enough that, if he needed his gun, it would be in his grasp in an instant; but if he kept hold of it he thought like a trooper again, worried only for his own position, concerned only for his next shot. Without it, he could see the whole battle. Without it, he thought like an officer. He had been a third lieutenant back on Torrans, Red a regular sergeant. He could never have believed they would survive this long.

STANHOPE CLAMBERED UP the slope, sweating like a pig. It was not the exertion, it was far worse. He instinctively touched the hollowed out hilt of his sword. He had discovered it was empty that morning. He was out. He had thought back, trying to sift the real memories from the haze of the previous night, but he only checked it when he used it, and using it blotted out the memories before. That was the point of it after all, to dull the mind and live solely in the present.

He struggled to piece it together. It had been after Carson had collapsed, he remembered that, and he remembered the explanation as well. He remembered his hand going to the hilt then... Had there only been one left then? Had he taken more in those final few hours of the night? The tiny pocket in the lining of his jacket was empty as well, as was the cut in his cuffs. How could he have taken them all?

Whatever the cause was, he was stuck with the outcome. It had been long enough since any regiment had allowed him into full battle, and now he was going in completely cold. The sweating was not even the physical withdrawal; it was far too soon for that. It was just the knowledge that he would be without until they returned to Dova. Forget the battle, that knowledge alone terrified him enough.

It made everything harder. The slope was steeper, his lasgun heavier, the fabric of his uniform rougher against his skin. The air bit harder in his lungs, and when he blinked the lids scraped over his eyes.

He crested the hill and before him there lay the rok. He had seen the images that Zdzisław had provided for them at the cost of his love and his life, but plans and layouts were nothing in comparison to the sight before him.

The crater, which appeared a mere pockmark upon the surface of Tswaing from above, swept in a smooth curve a kilometre either side of the impact point. At the centre itself, the orks had dug down. Driven by Emperor only knew what impulse, they had excavated a massive pit, until, digging deeper and deeper, they had reached the rok that had failed to brake in time. The dirt they shifted had been dropped in a heap of spoil. That first heap had mounted higher and higher, and, as they had tunnelled deeper, they were forced to shift the spoil to four more mounds, one roughly in each direction of the compass.

The top of each mound had been made into a rudimentary fortress. They were littered with collections of crude log walls and xenos icon-towers. There was little to distinguish between them, but Stanhope found his mind automatically supplying the objective codes that the colonel had assigned with his usual inimitable style: Chard and Drumhead, the two furthest forts on the far side of the crater; Bitterleaf, the largest spoil-heap right on the edge of the pit; Endive behind it, overlooking Bitterleaf's right, and the closest and smallest, to Bitterleaf's left, appropriately labelled Acorn. It was there that his company would attack.

That morning, while the beards cleared the final stretch of road and the men sat idle, chatting over tanna, Stanhope had been one of the senior officers who had stuffed themselves into the cramped compartment of the command Salamander to hear Arbulaster's plan of attack.

The fortifications on top of the spoil-heaps were the key to the rok, he had said. If the 11th could take them and hold them, then Rosa's artillery could call down its barrages on any part of the crater with pinpoint accuracy. Conversely, if they were not taken, the regiment would have to fight its way through the cluttered dirt paths of the ork settlement with its flanks constantly endangered. The spoil-forts had to be taken, sooner or later, and in his mind there was never any doubt that it must be sooner. He knew that by the time they crossed the fungus jungle they would have only half a day to defeat the rok's defenders so utterly as to make counter-attack impossible. If they did not, then the regiment would have to endure yet another night assault, and this one with the regiment right in the enemy's heart.

Arbulaster's plan, therefore, was straightforward, fast and brutal. It was in the best traditions of the Brimlock Dragoons, or at least that was what Ledbetter had announced as the details were unveiled.

NOON WAS LONG past, but the sun was still high in the sky. Not that the orks inhabiting the crater knew what the sun was. None of them had ever even seen it. All they knew was that the thick cloud permanently over their heads sometimes filled with a grey light and sometimes didn't. Theirs had been a chaotic morning. The warboss had led away two thousand of their warriors the day before to kill this new group of pink-skinned aliens who were marching towards their domain. The warboss had yet to return, though some of the warriors had reappeared. The warboss's second had had them brought to him, and they told him of the attack, of the sudden burning light that had sprung from the aliens' walls, the scramble over the ditch that blocked their path and the death they found there, and finally the fire from the sky that had erupted all around them.

The warboss's second was confused; the aliens still lived and the warboss had not returned. This was not victory. Defeat was not something that he understood. The Stone Smashas did not suffer defeat; defeat was what they inflicted on the other ork tribes that eked out a primitive existence beyond the crater. The Stone Smashas knew only victory, which was why it was they who controlled the crater and the riches they had unearthed from the pit.

Given a day, the baser instincts of the warboss's second would have reasserted themselves. He would have realised that while a single ork still lived there could be no defeat, only a continuation of the fight. He would have realised that the warboss was dead, killed in the first Valkyrie attack upon the cannon, and would smack the heads of his challengers together, take control of the Stone Smashas and lead them against the aliens once more. Given a day. That day, however, was a luxury that Arbulaster did not allow.

Just as with their fellows who'd been surprised in the fungal plain, the first warning many of the orks had was the rumble of Imperial engines. They stopped in the middle of their daily tasks and looked up to the crater rim and saw the outlines of the Brimlock tanks emerge over the crest.

For many armies, many species, that would have been the end. Their units were dispersed across the crater and beyond. Their leader was missing and no one had stepped in to replace him. They were surprised, unprepared, and under attack by metal beasts that none of them had ever encountered before. Some armies would have broken and run, others would have withdrawn to their last defences in confusion looking for their units, looking for their commanders, looking for some kind of instruction. Orks being orks, however, took hold of their weapons, looked to the largest warrior in their midst to lead them, and then followed their instincts: they charged.

CHAPTER SIXTEEN

Impact Crater, Tswaing, Voor pacification
Stage 1 Day 18

'FIRST RANK, FIRE! Second rank, fire!' The orders rolled out again, timed to perfection from long experience. Carson's men held a tight line, each man no more than a pace away from his fellow beside him. Van Am and her Voorjer scouts did the same, tacking onto the end of the line and picking their shots in their own time. The orks had little to throw back at them and so there was no need to seek cover. The troopers knew it was far better to stay close to their comrades and concentrate their fire. The tank beside them thundered as it fired its main cannon. Down the slope, a knot of orks disappeared in a bloody cloud of spores kicked up by the shell's explosion.

The cloud dispersed and the orks' latest push against them dissipated. Carson was not yet concerned. This first wave of tiny, ragtag bands was little threat while his men held the crater rim. Each one would emerge from the edge of the settlement on the slope below, bellow, stomp and roar. Then they would try to climb up to reach their enemies and the Brimlock fire would send them tumbling back down again.

Gradually, though, the orks were learning. The small groups stopped trying to rush up the slope on their own. Instead they waited for more and more of their fellows to join them before beginning another attack. Each assault left ork bodies in the dirt, yet each assault was stronger than the last. That was the way it always was with orks, Carson knew; if they did not win at once they simply wore you down, keeping you under continual pressure, exhausting ammunition, fuel and men. All you could do was pray that when their final assault came you still had the strength to withstand it.

The shouts and calls of the orks echoed up to the soldiers. More warriors had filtered in from the rest of the settlement and they were once more psyching themselves up to throw themselves headlong into the Brimlock guns. Then, from somewhere beside Carson, a single voice began to sing. For once it was not Captain Drum, rather it was Private Heal. He began to sing an ancient song of his home, from one of the far-flung continents of Brimlock. It told of war, of victory, of defiance and death; of ordinary men facing the extraordinary. Heal finished the first stanza and was about to launch into the second when another voice rose above his:

'Private Heal! Shut your gob, you appalling shocker! We fight in silence until told otherwise. You understand me?'

'Yes, colour!'

'Shut it!'

The men of Brimlock needed no war-cries to scare the enemy; they needed no shouted oaths to bolster their courage. They were not animals or xenos filth. They fought as professionals, in disciplined silence, punctuated only by the crisp commands of their officers. When their wild and wailing foes charged they found themselves facing a grey line as still as death, and that shook them all the more.

As if in concurrence, another tank commander chanced a shot at long-distance into a cluster of orks, and their own belligerent hooting transformed into cries of alarm. It would delay them a few minutes more.

Carson looked behind him, down the slope they had climbed. Laid out below he could see the shape of the attack forming. On the column's right, Brooce and Deverril's companies were embarked in their Chimera transports and had turned sharply at the base of the crater. While the orks' attention was focused on the troopers at the rim, these mechanised dragoon companies were flanked almost a quarter of the way around the crater's circumference in order to strike for Endive, hoping to catch it undefended. In the centre, Arbulaster was massing three companies for the main attack on Bitterleaf. Fergus and Gomery's companies were just breaking ranks to start their climb, clambering over the lines of dead orks that Drum's tanks had crushed. Ahead of them, Arbulaster had given command of the main assault to Roussell, and Carson could see the distinctive, leonine major struggling up the slope at the head of his troops.

Carson mentally urged him on. The sooner he arrived to hold the rim, the sooner Carson could redeploy to assault his company's objective: Acorn. The sooner they could launch their assault, the fewer orks they would have to deal with and the faster Carson could capture it. The faster Carson could capture Acorn, the more time he would have to pursue his other, personal, objective.

Roussell finally approached the crest. He looked less than content, and it was not merely physical exertion or the sight of the Voorjer woman standing a few paces away from Carson that was souring his mood. The colonel was taking no chances with the dogmatic major and had attached himself to Roussell's personal squad for the assault upon Bitterleaf.

Roussell could not object – it was supposed to be an honour after all – but all of the officer corps recognised it for what it was. A slap in the face. An indictment of his failure to lead during the raid the night before. A removal from the decision-making process.

In a way, this was exactly what Roussell had wished for; no matter what transpired in the battle, no liability would be placed upon him. The heroics of his early career would survive untarnished by any reversal in this final battle, and if he survived, his place in the colourguard was secure. However, Carson could see that there was just enough pride left in Roussell for him to resent his relegation.

The only resentment that Carson had felt as the colonel announced that particular deployment this morning was that he'd had to hide his elation. Where the colonels went, so too did their commissars. Later on, Carson wanted no one to recall any reaction from him at the opportunity the colonel had given him to kill Reeve.

'Major,' Carson announced briskly over the renewed sound of las-fire from his men.

Roussell halted, out of breath and unable to speak as his men moved past him and into position. He glowered at the second lieutenant standing in front of him, hands clasped calmly behind his back.

'I transfer defence of this position to you, sir, as per the execution of the colonel's battle-plan,' Carson said, throwing in a salute to annoy him further. 'The crest is yours.'

Roussell opened his mouth to speak, but whatever he

said was lost beneath another booming shot from the tank's battle cannon. Carson smiled thinly at Roussell's frustration and then he and Van Am turned sharply away. He saw that the ork attack had been broken again. That was the shortest yet; obviously they had decided that a frontal assault was not for them. Carson could see the growing mass of orks still amongst the settlement buildings stretching to either side as their instincts told them to strike the flanks. And on one of those flanks stood Acorn. Now it was to be a race.

'Company!' he called. 'Advance Quick! On me!'

STANHOPE'S SWEATING HAD nothing to do with terror now, it was pure exertion. All his strength was focused on keeping his legs pumping. Right foot down, push up, left foot down, push up. Up, up, up. That was the only direction that mattered. He had already tightened the strap on his sword belt to stop it flapping at his waist as he ran. Now he shouldered his gun so he could lean forwards and scrabble at the earth with his hands as well.

The men around him were doing the same. They all knew that speed was paramount. Less experienced men would have needed to be bellowed at and whipped by their sergeants to get them to make such an assault. These, however, were veterans; their sergeants could save their breath. For all the bellyaching and trouble such veterans gave on- and off-duty, when it came to a battle, when the margin between life and death was a split second hesitation or the wavering of an inch, their caution for their own safety was as scant as a body's concern at losing a few cells. The unit, the platoon, the company, was everything, and the unit was safest if it reached the summit of Acorn first. And so the troopers all ran as hard as they could. And Stanhope was amongst them.

The battle cannon fired again behind them. Stanhope

was too busy to duck, but the shells were fired high any-way, as high as they possibly could be to avoid hitting the climbing troopers. They struck the topmost battle-ments, blowing apart a wall segment of sharpened stakes and toppling one of the xenos icon-towers. A shower of dirt and debris covered the leading infantry. That was too close, Stanhope decided; that should be their last shot.

He pushed on up, gaining a lead on the other troop-ers. A broken stake-wall was in his path. Rather than losing ground by trying to go around, he pulled himself up through the hole the battle cannon had made, past the corpses of the orks that had taken cover behind it. The tanks had reduced the defences on the nearest face of Acorn to splinters, but their fire could not reach over the curve of the slope. Once they reached the flat top of Acorn, it would be the men who'd have to push through the ork defenders, take the fort and hold it.

The top of Acorn was only a few yards away now and Stanhope broke his step to pull out his fell-cutter. He realised that he had come to the head of the attack; he would be the first one over the top. For a second, his mind went back to a very different battlefield, one where he had given the orders, yet others had had to pay the price. But this was not Cawnpore, and here no one had been foolish enough to look for his orders again. This would be an appropriate way to finally end it.

He took the final few steps and an ork warrior erupted from the hidden ground above, bellowing in his face. Stanhope had no breath to reply in kind. Instead, his strength fed his fell-cutter. It swung to meet the ork's cudgel, blocked it, and sliced right through. Stanhope instinctively jerked away as the severed end of the ork's weapon flew past his ear. Irritated, the ork punched out, its fist still holding the stub of its cudgel.

The fist struck the side of Stanhope's helmet. The ork

hadn't been able to get its full weight behind it, but still it left his head ringing. He stepped back, found little purchase on the slope and nearly stumbled. His guard was down and the ork readied for its finishing blow. Then it yelped in pain. A trooper beside Stanhope had speared it with his bayonet. The ork grabbed for the gun, but the trooper had already withdrawn the weapon and was stabbing into the xenos's face. The bayonet punched against the hard bone above the ork's nose and was deflected to the side into the eye-socket. The point went through the ork's red eye and into its brain beyond before the trooper pulled it out again.

Stanhope saw the ork reel away, clutching its face. Someone shouted an order behind him and a well-aimed Voorjer bullet turned the other side of its face into a blackened mess. The trooper who had come to his rescue turned back to him.

'Find your bloody feet, troop!' Blanks shouted in his face. Stanhope already had and, hauling the ork corpse aside, surged on beside him.

The volley from Van Am and her Voorjers, and Sergeant Booth and third platoon, had cleared away the orks lying in wait to spring upon the climbing Guardsmen. Behind Stanhope, second platoon was following in its path, while to his left Red was at the fore of first platoon, staving in the back of an injured ork's head with 'Old Contemptible', as Carson's pistols flashed in his hands, killing still more of the xenos.

Stanhope looked only ahead of him. Through the struts of the icon-towers he saw the orks they had raced there boil up over the other side. Blanks paused, snap-shooting and slicing through the knee of one of them, and Stanhope took the lead again.

Red was shouting something about forming a firing line, but it was too late for Stanhope. He was already charging. His body was protesting at further ill-treatment, but his mind demanded more and his muscles provided. He angled himself at the closest ork and raised the fell-cutter, still unbloodied, above his head. An ork at speed was as powerful as a bull, but in its inexperience it had expended its energy hurrying up the backside of Acorn and found it had little left to give.

It drew back its cleaver, telegraphing its downward swing. Stanhope brought the fell-cutter down, not forwards but backwards, spinning it around like a windmill's sails. He sidestepped the ork's blow and brought the heavy blade up in an uppercut against its undefended belly. The ork arched its body back and Stanhope's blade cut through air until it caught the underside of the ork's chin and sliced its face in two. Stanhope shoulder-charged the flailing ork and knocked it to the ground.

All around him, the lines of green and grey were colliding, the bellowing ork warriors swinging their weapons and the silent Brimlocks firing their rifles at point-blank range, before lunging in with their bayonets. Even though the Imperium had arms that could devastate continents, its victory here would once again be gained by its exhausted soldiers grappling toe to toe with its foes.

Las-shots, bayonets and cleavers struck home, and as the orks fell so did men, as the luck of twenty-year veterans finally deserted them. The rest fought on, knowing flight to be more deadly than combat, clustering in small groups of men who were closer than brothers. Zezé impaled an ork with a thrust, but it just reached out, gripping the barrel, and ripped the blade clear. Repton came in alongside and plunged his own weapon into its now exposed armpit, holding it steady like a fish on a hook for one critical moment so that Heal's shot blew straight through its head. While another warrior was distracted trying to grab the elusive Mouse, Forjaz kicked out its knee, stunned it with a second blow as it stumbled, and opened it up for Mouse to get the kill.

Stanhope swung again at the warriors who opposed him; heavy, cutting swings that severed heads and limbs. The smallest tricks sufficed to mislead many of his tough, yet inexperienced opponents, and those who worked past his guard encountered Blanks by his side, striking throats, eyes and tendons, deadlier even with his small blade than Stanhope was with his sword.

Suddenly, a volley of las-shots cut across the melee. First platoon was firing. Fragmentation grenades flew overhead, exploding amongst the orks. The surprised ork warriors reeled back for a few moments to counter this new threat.

Stanhope thrust his sword down to finish off the ork at his feet and nearly collapsed. It had been less than a minute since he had crossed over the top of Acorn, yet already he felt the fury of the initial assault had dissipated. He caught himself before he fell and willed himself on, but this time his body refused, wasted from the apathy and abuse he had inflicted upon himself over the years.

As his strength went, another part of his mind took hold. It was the officer he had suppressed for three years. The officer scolded him worse than Blanks had done. It ranted at him for leading such an unsupported charge. The excuse that he had not given anyone orders rang hollow in his head; he had led and they had followed. They were his responsibility whether he acknowledged it or not, and he'd had to be saved again. Red and first platoon were pushing forwards, Forjaz was trying to haul second platoon back to link up with them and form a single line that could repel the stream of the orks that were still climbing. That should be you, the officer in his mind berated him. It should be you pulling them back into order, dressing the line, detaching a force to flank...

That thought caught in his head, and he was struck by a horrible suspicion. A suspicion confirmed when, beneath the sounds of the volley fire from first and now second platoons, he heard new sounds of combat from the right. He stumbled over and thumped against a log barricade for support. Booth and third platoon were not following directly behind; Carson had thought of everything. Instead, they were climbing around the summit of Acorn, aiming to strike at the vulnerable flank of climbing orks and prevent them reinforcing the top.

The success of Stanhope's wild charge, however, had pushed the orks back too quickly. They too were skirting around the summit to try and surround the platoons on the top. Now one of those forces was about to slam straight into Booth and third platoon.

Booth, a great moustachioed sergeant, with an attitude chiselled from the same block as Red, led from the front and so was the first one of third platoon to see the danger. He acted at once. He knew that, with his men undeployed, strung out in column, clutching to the slope behind him, they would come off worse once the orks got within reach. He abandoned his attack and ordered his men to climb up, straight up, to the comparative safety of the other platoons at the top. The orks saw their enemy break and run and climbed after them, only for their leader to reel back, flesh blackened from las-fire. The orks looked in the direction of the shots to see Sergeant Booth balanced coolly on the slope, lasgun in hand.

'You greenskins keep your hands off my lads,' he muttered and fired again as the orks turned their attention from the fleeing troopers and directed it solely at him.

On top of Acorn, Stanhope pounded back to second

platoon where the distinctive shape of an ogryn carrying an autocannon was crouching. 'Gardner!' he ordered. 'Redeploy!'

Gardner glanced at him, confused, but did not release the trigger.

'Redeploy, corporal!' Stanhope demanded. Gardner shook his head as though he couldn't hear.

'Hold the line!' The shout came from Forjaz, who was striding over.

Stanhope had no time to argue. The instant the auto-cannon burst finished he smacked Frn'k on the side of the head. 'Trouble, we move! Quick march!' Stanhope shouted.

Frn'k, half-deafened by the fire over his head, felt the blow, made out the words and responded as his brother had trained him. Gardner yelped as Frn'k heaved him and the hot autocannon into the air, but the ogryn had already spotted Stanhope pointing where he should go.

Gardner swore blue murder for the few seconds that he was carried along, but as soon as Frn'k deposited him where Stanhope had indicated he saw what the major wanted from him. The orks climbing after third platoon did not know what an autocannon was, but they learned quickly as Gardner sighted down the steep slope and pressed the trigger. The orks had no cover and nowhere to run, and Gardner blew them off the slope without hesitation, methodically cutting across them, adjusting his aim as he fired to catch them all.

The men of third platoon raised a ragged cheer as they saw the carnage Gardner created and they climbed up to form behind him. All but a group of four of them, who started climbing down to recover Booth's body.

'Third platoon,' Stanhope ordered. 'Form on me!'

'Third platoon,' Carson countermanded, as he approached. 'Form on me!'

The troopers of third platoon knew who their true commander was and looked to Carson for orders.

'Form line here! Fire in your own time! Push 'em back!' Carson rattled out and third platoon obeyed. 'Gardner! Redeploy!' he continued, and Stanhope watched as, with first and second platoons advancing over the summit, Carson led third platoon to seize the far side of the top of Acorn and cast the orks down.

Less than a minute after they had taken it, Gardner was pouring autocannon fire straight down the throats of the orks still trying to reinforce the annihilated defenders at the top. First and second platoons took up supporting positions, and Carson voxed and ran the company's pennant up the side of an orkish icon-tower. The message went back. Acorn was taken. The main attack could begin.

CHAPTER SEVENTEEN

THE SOUNDS OF the regiment's main column starting to move into the edges of the settlement towards Bitterleaf echoed up to Carson on Acorn, but he did not have time yet to focus on that battle. He'd seen Stanhope staring at him as well, but he didn't have time for him either. Instead, he was on the vox, ordering his support weapons to be brought up and his wounded and dead taken down.

Another benefit of attacking first was that the medicae were standing idle until your wounded came in. They got the best care they could out in a place such as this. A shame it wouldn't be enough for Booth. Carson hadn't been able to spare more than a glance at the body, but even from that he could see that Booth had not died easily. Blessed Marguerite, let Booth and the others he had lost in taking Acorn be the last he should ever lose. At least Booth had no family back at Dova that would need to be told. Carson wasn't sure how he could face Forjaz's wife and children if he died.

He told himself that they were not a factor in the decision he'd made. Why he was going to take Red with him and not Forjaz. He'd known Red the longest, had fought beside him more times than he could remember, he had a level of trust with Red that he didn't share with any other under his command. Still, it made it damn convenient why Forjaz should be the one left behind.

At that moment, the husband and father himself appeared and reported in.

'All the men are digging in, sir. The Voorjer lot as well,' he said. 'The 'skins won't shove us off.'

'Good. Well done, sergeant. Now, you know what Red and I are about?'

'Yes, sir. No problem with it at all, sir,' Forjaz carried on, unbidden.

'Thank you,' Carson replied. 'Command of the company is yours then until we return. If Rosa brings his mortars up here, make room for them, but if he tries to bring a Griffon tell him that it'll have to be his men to shove it up here. Don't take anyone off the defences. Especially not Gardner. You understand?'

'Yes, sir.'

'Don't even let him out of your sight.'

'I understand, sir.' And he did. This wasn't the first time they'd had to do this after all. 'And what about the major, sir?'

'What about him?'

'If you want me to look after him–' Forjaz began, the dark intent in his voice unmistakable. Carson cut him off.

'That will not be necessary, sergeant,' Carson said formally. 'This is our last time, the last time for the whole regiment. We've done our job today. We're done and he's done. He's no danger to us. Leave him be.'

'And if he tries giving orders again?'

'The men know who to follow, sergeant, just make sure he doesn't see us leave.'

Carson left Forjaz to engage the major while he went off to meet Red. There was small chance that Stanhope wouldn't notice his absence eventually, but he would not be able to prove anything. And, as sharp as he appeared today, everyone knew that his word could not be taken seriously. He could safely ignore him.

One person he could not ignore, however, blocked his path.

'Lieutenant,' she said.

'Holder,' he replied.

'Where are you going?' she asked.

'Reconnoitre. I'm taking a small squad out of the fort. Vital part of a static defence.'

Carson watched her reaction. She let a half-smile play on her lips to show that she wasn't fooled; but then, Carson reasoned, she was on their side, after all.

'Good hunting,' was all she said, and let him go.

Carson stepped beyond the battlements on the quiet south side of Acorn. Red was already waiting for him there in the shadow of a stake-wall.

'You have it?' Carson asked.

Red held it up.

'You have any problems with Mouse?'

Red's grim features turned even grimmer at the mention of the company rogue.

'He said it cost him more money than expected, sah.'

Carson was not bothered. 'I'll settle up with him tonight,' he said, and then saw a trace of pride emerge in his colour-sergeant.

'I may have dissuaded him already, sah.'

Carson did not want to ask, and so didn't. He inclined

his head and the two of them started down Acorn and on their circular path towards Bitterleaf.

THE FIRST ASSAULT on Bitterleaf began within half an hour of the fall of Acorn. By that time, Brooce on the far right was already reporting multiple mechanical breakdowns amongst his Chimeras with a resulting delay of the attack on Endive. Drum's tanks were suffering as well, and only two-thirds of armoured company were ultimately to lead the drive and clear the way through the settlement.

The ramshackle ork buildings, constructed from a mix of wood, mud and the more rigid fungi, proved little obstacle to tanks, however; they simply flattened and outright demolished whatever was in their path. The warriors of the Stone Smashas who were still milling in the settlement had nothing to oppose them and so could only hammer on the tanks' hulls as they drove past. On those few occasions that tanks became wedged, the Stone Smashas emerged from the sides with heavy hammers and picks to try and bash them open, but Roussell's infantry following close behind drove them off far enough for the vehicles' battle cannons and close-quarter weaponry to be effective.

As the individual Stone Smasha bands found their instincts failing them, they looked for direction, and flocked to Bitterleaf where they saw the banner of the warboss flying. The warboss, of course, was not there, but his second had finally decided to seize leadership of the tribe and had chosen to make his stand there.

As it happened, there was more to Bitterleaf than it merely being the largest of the spoil-heaps. The Stone Smashas, in excavating the rok, had discovered huge cannons embedded on its surface. Most of these had been destroyed on impact, but a few of the smallest ones still appeared operational.

When first they had been found, none of the orks had known what they were. Most ignored them or tried to break them down to create more of the metal weapons that gave the Stone Smashas the edge over their rivals. Some, however, didn't. In the days that followed, these orks drifted towards the cannon, obsessed with them to a fanatical degree. The other orks ignored them mostly, but left them food so that they could continue to tinker. The watershed day came when one of them, having been drawn deep inside the rok, emerged with a large hunk of metal which it proceeded to put in the nearest cannon's barrel before pulling a lever it had found.

The resulting explosion wiped out the ork and all those who had crowded around him, but it fired the interest of a legion more who sought to be able to repeat such explosions and direct them against the enemy.

The smallest of these cannons to be recovered from the rok became known as the mega-bombard. It was light enough to be dragged with the Stone Smasha warriors to obliterate any of the other tribes that opposed them. The other three were larger and so were left on Bitterleaf to deter any from trying to take the valuable crater from its rightful owners.

The strangeness of their shapes, mixed in amongst the icon-towers and defences on Bitterleaf, along with the incongruity of such savages having such a level of technology, caused the Brimlock officers poring over the recording from Zdzisław's Valkyrie to misidentify them, believing them to be makeshift cranes or counterweights used in digging out the pit.

And so when the tanks of the armoured company, who had hitherto been invulnerable to the primitive ork weapons, saw the first one fire at them as they approached Bitterleaf they were, somewhat understandably, surprised.

'BLESSED MOTHER MARGUERITE!' Drum exclaimed, breaking off his latest rendition. The mega-cannon shot appeared like a meteorite burning through the atmosphere towards them. It struck short, ploughing through a line of ork hovels before finally coming to rest. Drum watched the dwellings catch fire. He had two choices: advance and gamble that his tanks could destroy that cannon with their own, or retreat and gamble that they could escape its range and keep their hides. He activated his vehicle's vox and screwed the dial to transmit to his company.

'Men of steel, slow and fire! Ork guns are only good for grabbing our attention,' he signed off with a smirk. If there was just a single gun, his tanks could take it, if the orks themselves didn't drop a shell and blow it up first!

But before the armoured company could respond, the rest of the Stone Smasha's battery had their say. The second mega-cannon fired from amongst the structures on Bitterleaf, sending its shot high and scattering a squad of Roussell's company following up behind. The third one, through fluke or skill, struck just in front of the armoured company's line. The tanks were driving close together so as to clear the path and so, as the shot barrelled into the left-most tank, it clipped its neighbour as well. The stricken tank was crushed by the fireball, whilst the other blew off its tread and ground to a halt.

The remainder of the tanks fired their turret-weapons, the shots grouped around the site of the first mega-cannon. The shells flew true, but impacted against the maze of scaffolding and other constructs on the top of Bitterleaf.

Drum had seen enough. He did not care how the orks had managed it, but he had lost a third of his active force without scratching the enemy. He flicked the vox on again.

'Armoured company, turnabout and retreat! Repeat, turnabout and retreat!'

'Scratch that order,' the colonel's voice crackled over the vox. 'Captain Drum, your company is to reverse only. All armoured units acknowledge. Reverse only. Don't let these xenos filth see your backs.'

Drum twisted the vox to the private channel as he heard his tank commanders acknowledge the colonel's orders.

'Colonel, if we only reverse we'll be as slow as–'

'I comprehend the difference, captain,' Arbulaster replied. 'Do recall that I am out here as well. I have three companies of infantry here who are all now sprinting for their lives. The orks will counter-attack now they see us retreating and we cannot abandon them. Acknowledged?'

'Acknowledged, sir,' Drum agreed and turned his battle-hymn vox-amplifiers to maximum in the hopes that the noise itself would keep the orks at bay.

'THE ARMOUR, SAH. It's retreating,' Red called.

'What?' Carson replied and leaned up to see. They were both hunched in the lee of an ork hut, covered by the shadow of another icon-tower bearing a leering orkish glyph. They'd spent twenty minutes carefully working their way across the settlement, hiding and scurrying through cover, to reach close enough to Bitterleaf's slope to be ready when Arbulaster's Salamander disgorged its passengers, and now the whole damn force was in retreat!

Red knew the obvious course of action – retreat with the rest of them – but he could also see that certain mood in the lieutenant: that strange determination which had destroyed his career and threatened his life over the years.

'We can't keep going back and forth, we'll be spotted. They'll be back here, Red. The colonel will be back here.'

As would the orks, Red knew.

THE ORKS CAME, as both the colonel and the colour-sergeant knew they would. They had fallen back before the tanks' irresistible advance and now emerged from the side-streets around Bitterleaf to snap at their heels. The heavy bolters affixed to the tanks' hulls opened up, firing their explosive bolt shells into the most enthusiastic of their pursuers, whilst the tanks' turret guns swivelled to keep pelting Bitterleaf.

Their slow speed allowed their gunners to place their shots carefully, but unfortunately the same was true for the orks manning the mega-cannon. Most shots still flew wild, but a few landed too close. With shells of such size, even a near miss could cripple a vehicle and two more tanks were disabled, one even knocked onto its side by the force of the explosion. Both tanks were abandoned by their crews before their pursuers overwhelmed them.

The second mega-cannon demonstrated the danger-ous temper of such war machines when operated by creatures working on programmed instinct rather than knowledge. An ill-handled shell detonated as it went into the weapon's barrel and made a new crater in the side of the spoil-fort. The third mega-cannon proved deadly, however. Another tank had swerved beside the one the cannon had immobilised with its first shot in order to rescue its crew. The mega-cannon's operators barely nudged it a fraction of a degree and fired again. The hapless crew running to safety suddenly dived away as the shot impacted, but the rescuers could not escape as the massive shell struck them dead-on. The sound

of Drum's battle-hymns cut off as he and his crew were
obliterated.

ARBULASTER SAW THE icon representing Drum's tank
flash and fade out on the hologram display inside the
Salamander. He felt Reeve's gaze bore into him from
where the commissar sat, on the other side of the cabin.
He resisted the urge to order the driver to turnabout
and speed away. He could do nothing that smacked of
cowardice, or even of hesitation. Reeve was looking for
an excuse, any excuse, to prove that Arbulaster had failed.

'An unidentified threat.' Arbulaster addressed his words
to no one in particular, but they were meant for Reeve to
hear. 'A minor set-back only. We will swiftly counter.'

He opened a new vox-line. 'Major Rosa, acknowledge.'

'Here, colonel.' Even over the vox, it sounded as though
the rotund major was unwrapping another ration bar.

'Do you have your firing solution?'

'We are offering it to the cogitator-spirits now, colonel.'

'Keep this channel open. Confirm when ready to fire.'

'Acknowledged,' Rosa replied.

It would take Rosa a minute or so to confirm. Arbulaster looked down at the hologram. The three infantry
companies were out of the confines of the settlement,
out of immediate danger. The armoured company had
chewed up the orks that had tried to counter-attack, but
at a cost. Only one tank was still functional. Of the rest,
all but two could be recovered and repaired, but for the
objective of the push on Bitterleaf the armoured company was operationally eliminated. Arbulaster glanced
at Reeve, sitting calmly, dressed in that ridiculous
skull-robe he wore, no longer even looking at the map
between them but looking only at him. He'd already
made his decision, Arbulaster realised. Reeve was going
to kill him. He was going to kill him today.

'Fire ready, colonel,' Major Rosa's voice crackled back over the vox.

Arbulaster stepped out of the dark interior of the Salamander, taking the vox handset, and onto the open deck. He wanted to see this in person.

'Fire. Fire!'

Major Rosa relayed the command to his Griffons, self-propelled heavy mortars with short, snub barrels large enough for a man to fit down them, and in each one the officer in charge gave the order to fire.

Arbulaster peered hard at the Griffons on the crest of the crater behind him. He did not expect to see much evidence of their firing, but hoped to see something just the same. The tell-tale smudge of smoke above each one was enough to inform him that their barrage was underway. He turned round to Bitterleaf, counting down the seconds he had estimated for the rounds to fly up, turn over and come crashing back down. He reached zero and a series of small, but visible detonations wracked the top of Bitterleaf. Inside the Griffons the crews would be watching for their strike, making minute adjustments before beginning their well-drilled routines to reload and fire, reload and fire, as fast as humanly possible.

Beyond Bitterleaf, Arbulaster fancied he started to see tiny strands of light on Endive. He went back inside the Salamander and confirmed that Brooce and Deverril were finally assaulting that fort. Brooce reported in that their opposition, as anticipated, was light. The bulk of the orks had bunched around Bitterleaf and Bitterleaf, Arbulaster reflected, was about to have the sky fall down upon it.

THE MORTAR ROUNDS fell upon the spoil-fort without respite. For a full half-hour, Carson and Red watched from their hiding place in the icon-tower where they had gone to ground. They said little to one another; Red knew that the lieutenant did not need reminding of how exposed they were.

They were hundreds of yards ahead of the Brimlock line and just as likely to be struck by their own side as the enemy, as no one knew they were there. Carson held the rifle close. It was not a lasrifle, and certainly not of Brimlock design. He could not use a las-weapon to kill Reeve: the effect would be unmistakable and worse, sharp eyes would spot his position. So Carson had asked Mouse to procure this, and Mouse had acquired it from one of the Voorjer scouts, no questions asked.

Had the Voorjer known what Carson intended to do with it, he may have been more cautious, for Carson was going to implicate him and his comrades in the death of an Imperial commissar. But Carson knew that Arbulaster had no love for Reeve and would not investigate too thoroughly. He hadn't for Blunder after all. All he needed was a convincing story as to why a Voorjer bullet might have struck Reeve, and Van Am had, unsuspectingly, given it straight to him. These were the same rifles that the first expedition had carried to the rok and had been lost there. Unlike the lasguns, the orks had already captured several Voorjer rifles, and that would be story enough.

The two of them watched the remaining megacannons as they were abandoned by their crews and then destroyed by the mortar rounds. The first toppled over forwards, ploughing through the defences in front of it before it crashed to a halt at the bottom of the spoil-heap. The second's ammunition detonated, scything the area around it clear of all other structures and life, leaving a scorched bald patch as the only evidence of its existence.

Bitterleaf was ready for a second assault, but still the

Griffons fired, adjusting their aim to a target behind the fort where the orks must have believed they were safe. Ledbetter's cavalry had appeared just as the Griffons began their firing, but they had held themselves apart from the rest of the regiment, refusing to acknowledge any orders they were sent or budge from their position.

As the full hour approached, Carson was suddenly struck by doubt. What was the colonel doing? The light was already dimming; he had to advance. He had to take Bitterleaf and then the rest of the crater before night fell.

What the colonel was doing was waiting for the orks' natural instincts to resurface. They had been forced from Acorn and Endive, Bitterleaf was no longer defensible, and they had lost their mega-cannon. Other races would have withdrawn to their final bastions at Chard and Drumhead, held there, and used the night to slip away. But orks were not like other races. When no other options presented themselves, orks, being orks, simply charged.

This was the Stone Smashas' last gasp. Their leaders had finally marshalled all the forces they could and were throwing them all into the fight. The green tide poured from the pit behind Bitterleaf, growing as it spread, and absorbed the smaller warbands that had scattered throughout the settlement. It emerged as one giant pincer, the orks avoiding the flattened trail left by the armoured company and advancing as far as they could using the settlement for cover. On the Brimlock right, the orks ignored the troops quietly holding Endive in favour of the large mass of enemy deployed in front of the hated Griffons. Arbulaster saw the threat and formed up four of his infantry companies. On the Brimlock left, the orks would have to run straight past the defences on Acorn and so he allocated only a single company, Gomery's, and also, puzzlingly, himself to defend that flank.

'What in damnation's name?' Carson exclaimed as

he saw the command Salamander lead Gomery's company into the shadow of Acorn. He and Red desperately shuffled around in their hiding place to turn their firing position around.

'Do you still have the range?' Red asked.

In all honesty, Carson didn't know. He looked down the sight, recalibrating for the distance.

'I believe I can,' he said finally, slowly shifting to cover the Salamander's advance. That was true; he could make the shot, given enough time. The time he had, though, was only as long as it took Gardner to realise the golden opportunity Arbulaster was offering him.

GARDNER PULLED THE trigger and his target blew back, knocking down its fellow warriors climbing behind. The orks' pincer focused first on Acorn and, for the second time that day the orks tried to scale a contested slope. Carson's men had responded with full force, cutting down the first wave with ease. Now the second had to clamber over their dying fellows. They bellowed their defiance to no avail. For all their determination, their savagery, they simply could not scale the slope with such firepower ranged against them.

'Trouble! Feed me!' Gardner bellowed over the cannon-fire. The change in sound of the ammunition feeding in from its can told Gardner he was running low.

'Grab another can!' he yelled and the ogryn obediently turned around to pick up another. Gardner squeezed off another few rounds and then released the trigger to give the cannon a few moments to cool.

The light was fading fast and the shapes of the orks were increasingly indistinct against the churned up fungus that covered the crater's floor. Gardner saw Gomery's company coming around the base of Acorn, ready to deliver the final blow and roll the orks back for good.

Gardner watched as the captain unslung his pack and removed Mister Emmett. Gomery held the ball out from his body and looked up, judging the distance. He took three quick steps and then hoofed it high into the air. The small ball with a crude face painted on went flying into the orkish horde.

'Bully!' he shouted to his men. 'Get after him! Points for the first man to touch him down!'

His men cheered and advanced behind their captain. One of them would find Mister Emmett, one of them always did. All of Gomery's men knew he was mad; he was still team captain, playing games back at schola. They had learned, though, that a mad officer who looked after them as his team-mates was far better than any sane one who treated them as so much human ammunition, so at times such as these they allowed his madness to infect them all.

Frn'k, with the care of a conscientious child, placed the new can beside the autocannon. Gardner got ready to fire off the last burst of the old can, when his attention was distracted. Advancing alongside Gomery's men was Arbulaster's Salamander, and inside it would be the colonel, and beside him would be Reeve.

'HE'S SEEN THEM, sah,' Red reported as he watched Gardner through his monocular. Carson cursed silently again. Arbulaster's command squad was still inside their Salamander; he could see nothing of Reeve at all.

'TAKE US UP as close as you can, Parker,' Arbulaster ordered the driver. The hull-gunner was already firing his heavy bolter into the ork lines. The driver came to a halt on the near side of Gomery's company, which was still advancing quickly. Arbulaster checked his pistol and power sword and made to exit.

'Are you egressing?' Reeve queried. His voice carried no intonation, but Arbulaster sensed a note of fear underneath.

'Of course, commissar,' Arbulaster replied. 'We leave counting cartons to the staff officers at Crusade Command. Regimental-level officers should lead from the front. Guard doctrine, is it not?'

'It is,' Reeve replied, but Arbulaster would not let it go at that.

'Will you be remaining within the Salamander?' he asked, all politeness.

'I will not,' Reeve said and gathered himself to leave.

'Very good,' Arbulaster replied. He climbed out of the Salamander's cabin and jumped down from its tailboard. He did not show it, but inside he was as sick now as he had been when he took his first command. There was nothing more he could do except rely on others. He glanced at Carson's company firing from the slope of Acorn; they had the perfect angle on his squad, he could give them no better opportunity. Now all he could do was get out of their way.

'Forward!' he cried, and ran as hard as he could.

THIS WAS IT, Carson knew, as he saw first the colonel and then the rest of his command squad pile out of the Salamander. He saw a flash of a bone-covered cloak and tried to track it, but Reeve had already landed on the other side of the vehicle. His shot was blocked.

GARDNER WATCHED REEVE stand up after his landing. He was right there in front of him. All he had to do was move his gun a fraction, just a few inches and he would have his brother's killer in his sights.

'Trouble! Another can!' Frn'k had been idolising the commissar ever since he'd given him that commendation, and Gardner did not want him to see this.

Frn'k was confused and held up the can he already had.

'Another one! Get another one!' Gardner ordered and the ogryn dutifully turned around to pick up another. Reeve was striding away now, going after the colonel's command squad, which had surged ahead after Gomery. Gardner fired off three rounds at the orks and then, not daring even to blink, slid his aim those vital few inches.

CARSON SAW REEVE'S peaked cap appear over the tracks of the Salamander. He was coming forwards. Another second and he would have him. Another second. Then Carson's vision blurred as the Salamander accelerated away. Reeve was completely exposed. Carson nudged his sight back a fraction and pulled the trigger.

GARDNER PULLED THE trigger.

ALONGSIDE GOMERY'S COMPANY, Arbulaster suddenly heard a voice on the vox-channel blare with news that almost made him collapse in relief.

'The commissar is down!'

It was Ledbetter. His cavalry had finally decided to intervene and now were galloping around the side of Acorn to where Reeve had fallen. Arbulaster fired another couple of shots at the beaten orks and looked back. It took him a few seconds in the poor light to identify the crumpled stormcoat on the ground.

He flagged down the Salamander and climbed onto the tailboard. 'Parker! We have to go back for the commissar. Make certain he's retrieved.' And if he was still living, Arbulaster added mentally, make certain he wasn't for much longer.

* * *

'GOOD SHOT, SAH. You hit him!' Red shouted.

Carson's breath was caught in his lungs. 'No, I didn't.'

He had not seen his shot impact, but a lifetime of marksmanship told Carson he had missed.

'Blessed Marguerite,' he whispered, tossing the Voorjer rifle to one side and then turning to Red.

'It's nearly dark enough now. Let's get back before Forjaz has kittens.'

I'VE HIT HIM, Gardner thought as he saw the coat collapse in on itself. I've done it. The words were all that ran through his mind. His body retained enough sense to push the autocannon back towards the retreating orks and then he felt the familiar large presence beside him.

"Nuvver can?' Frn'k asked and laid the second can down beside the first.

'Reload,' Gardner said, and realised his voice was breaking because his mouth was so dry. He licked his lips. 'Reload!' he said louder, and he reached to release the empty can while Frn'k held the new one in place.

Gardner let his hands work automatically. He had never thought about what he would do afterwards. Some vestigial belief-form had led him to expect that the Emperor's retribution for assaulting one of his servants would be instant. That the clouds would roll back and he would be scourged from the earth as a traitor. Had anyone even noticed?

The colonel certainly had, Gardner saw as he triggered the autocannon at the orks once more. His Salamander was returning, Arbulaster standing on the tailboard, but before he arrived the fallen coat was surrounded by horses. Ledbetter's cavalry. Gardner watched as the colonel disembarked and marched up to them. Ledbetter trotted out to meet him and a furious argument erupted between them. Meanwhile, his cavalrymen were carefully lifting Reeve's form up, ready to lay it out over one of their saddles. Ledbetter turned his horse from the colonel and, at an order, the cavalry trotted away, leaving Arbulaster alone and infuriated even as all around him his forces won his final victory.

CHAPTER EIGHTEEN

Objective Bitterleaf, Tswaing, Voor pacification
Stage 1 Day 18

COLONEL ARBULASTER STOOD on the Salamander's hull and looked out from the top of Bitterleaf. It was fully dark now, but the crater was theirs. The last spoil-fort had been captured and his men were dragging the ork bodies into piles to burn.

It was another victory, it was to be his last victory. He should have been proud, triumphant, perhaps even a little saddened that his time leading the regiment was nearly at an end. That was what the men expected, and so that was the show he was putting on. In truth, he felt nothing like. His head was stuffed, his blood was pounding in his ears, he couldn't breathe and he could barely see. A single thought echoed in his head: get away. Get away from the battlefield, get out of the crater, get back to Dova.

Reeve had been dealt with, but that damnable pious fool Ledbetter had taken him away. A load of nonsense about having no trust in his command, some rot that he had ordered Drum to fire on Ledbetter's cavalry so as to stop them charging. The vox records bore him out, of course, but one could never convince the fanatics in the cavalry of anything they did not wish to believe. Ledbetter felt aggrieved, and when he saw Reeve fall, his mind concocted all sorts of conspiracies, so much so that he had removed his men entirely from the Brimlock camp and trusted only his own medicae to treat Reeve.

And that was how Arbulaster had learned that Reeve still lived. He was wounded, of course, perhaps mortally. Arbulaster hoped so, for short of leading a direct assault on Ledbetter's company and wiping them from the planet, he had no other ideas on how to reach the commissar.

Arbulaster had made sure to cover himself, though. He'd had Lieutenant Mulberry quietly poke around the site where Reeve had fallen. Arbulaster expected Mulberry to come back with nothing so he could safely attribute the incident to 'general enemy fire', and indeed Mulberry found it difficult to discern the different weapon impacts given the number of times that piece of ground had been fought over that day.

Working under the lights from his Sentinels, however, Mulberry had made an intriguing discovery: a Voorjer bullet embedded in the slope of Acorn close to where Reeve had been standing. Mulberry looked at the angle and determined it had to have come from inside the settlement. As all of the Voorjers had been on top of Acorn, none of them could have made that shot.

Mulberry mentioned it to the colonel out of tangential interest only. In his opinion, no bullet fired from a Voorjer rifle could have travelled through a man and that far into the bank behind him. He soon found, however, that the colonel was of a different opinion, and soon a portion of Mulberry's findings were documented, alongside accounts from a variety of different amenable troopers attesting to the fact that they had come under fire from ork marksmen wielding captured Voorjer rifles. Whether Reeve died under Ledbetter's care or not, Arbulaster would have the final say as to what had happened to him.

Arbulaster felt how close he was, to the end, to the finish line, but he wouldn't be safe until he was back behind Dova's walls. Back there, he was protected, in control of everything around him. Out here, every single second he thought he would hear the shot, the explosion, the whistle in the air that would kill him. He could not bear being out here another moment. He wanted to run, but he couldn't. He had to stand there upon that tank and shine proud over his troops, because that was what was expected.

His hands were shaking, and so he gripped them together as tight as a vice behind his back. He couldn't stop his eyes blinking and so he tilted his head so they were hidden below the brim of his helmet. He felt his knee begin to twitch; he was going to fall off this damn tank and break his neck if he wasn't careful, and wouldn't that be a fine way to go!

'Did you need something, sir?' Parker spoke up.

'Get off with you,' he shouted back to him. He kept his voice gruff so as to prevent it cracking. 'Give me a moment's peace.'

His staff obediently left him to it, no doubt believing that their colonel had been momentarily gripped by some nostalgic emotion. That would have been acceptable; ah the old boy's got a heart after all, they might say. Let them think that, Arbulaster thought, far better that than the truth.

He turned around, taking immense care not to lose his balance, and clambered down off the back of the tank. His knee gave out midway and he landed heavily in the dirt. There, in the small space between the Salamander's tracks, he realised he was hidden from view. He collapsed onto his backside and tore open his collar and top-buttons with his shaking hands. He gasped in shallow breaths of the fuel-tainted air, panting like some first-day dispatch runner. He hugged his knees into his chest and buried his face between them while he desperately tried to regain his control.

Don't let them see me this way, was all Arbulaster could think. Don't let them see who I really am.

Gradually, his breathing slowed. The worst of it had passed. He pulled himself back to his feet and started to straighten himself up again. It had been less than a minute, but each second had been like an agonising hour fearing that he might be discovered. He brushed off the dirt from his uniform and turned the corner around the tank track and back towards the regiment. Not a moment too soon, as he saw his second stepping carefully across the slope towards him.

'Brooce!' Arbulaster called to the major. His second had done well this day, grabbing not only Endive, but leading his troops back to crush the orks' other pincer, catching them from behind as they threw themselves at the four companies Arbulaster had deployed to protect that flank. He had no hesitation in leaving Brooce in command.

'Yes, sir?'

'Call one of the Valkyries in. I need to get back to Dova, start the ball rolling on the next phase. And I should get in touch with our men back at the capital. I don't know where that female's granddaughter has disappeared to, she might have heard something. If word gets back to that female about what's next before we're ready, might get a bit sticky.'

Arbulaster saw the look on his second's face. He had been talking too quickly; Brooce could tell something was wrong. He needed to cover himself, make as though everything was to plan. He forced himself to give the major a hearty smile. 'Plus, I've got a little surprise for the men when they get back. Just need to do the last prep. Little reward for them.'

'Oh?' Brooce said, happily surprised. 'Good show, sir. I'm sure that'll do just the job. What've you got?'

Arbulaster tapped his nose.

'Ah, I see,' Brooce said. 'I'll keep the old flap buttoned.'

Arbulaster had nothing, of course, but he would have a few days to concoct some return celebration once he was back in safety behind the walls of Dova.

'I'll have Parker take me over the rim and meet the Valkyrie on the other side. Don't want to take any chances of frizzing another.'

'Actually, sir, that's what I was coming to tell you, there's one already inbound. It's the Navy crews, they're requesting permission to form a search party and go after Zdzisław.'

'Fine, fine,' Arbulaster brushed it off without thinking. 'They'll just have to wait until the Valkyrie has dropped me off to come back.'

'Very good, sir.' Brooce saluted and turned on his heel. Arbulaster paused for a moment and then stopped him.

'Wait, major.' Brooce halted and turned back. Arbulaster sighed heavily. 'Zdzisław pranged his bird on the far side of the crater. It's an hour's march at least. We can't have a bunch of bluebells stumbling around out there in the dark. Hold them here for the night. Then send 'em out with one of the light companies in the morning. Keep a picket around that pit tonight and then root out anything left inside tomorrow and get everything sewn up. Day after you head back to Dova. Understood?'

'Yes, sir,' Brooce nodded.

'Good. Oh, and Brooce?'

'Yes, sir?'

'Don't tell the bluebells the change in plan 'til I'm in the air.'

And with that, Arbulaster felt the fog in his head clear, his chest release, and the air pour into his lungs. He knew he shouldn't be leaving, but he didn't care. For twenty years he had stood in the fire, held firm in the face of bullets, bombing raids, berserkers and terror machines. He had seen his men diced into confetti by xenos weapons, or filleted from the inside even as they stood before him, and his only reaction had been to stand up and lead the charge. Twenty years of war in the Emperor's name. Well, this last one He owed him.

'To Booth. No better sergeant to protect you from your officers,' Heal toasted.

'To Booth!' the other troopers around the fire toasted and drank. It was a muted celebration. Nothing to do with the dead. There were always dead, even with victory. It had everything to do with their camp being on the edge of Bitterleaf and with them having marched across a jungle and fought two battles in a single day with barely an hour's rest.

For Carson and Red, however, their fatigue would have to wait. Once the casualty list was exhausted they wandered off together.

'The story's gone well around the regiment, sah,' Red reported.

'And the troopers believe it?'

'Not about the ork marksmen, no. They all think the Voorjers somehow pulled it off.'

Carson considered it. 'Are Van Am and her men in any danger? They've not stopped with us as they've done before. They're keeping a very low profile wherever they are.'

'Not from the troopers, sah. They'd give 'em a parade if they could. They're saying that all Reeve had in his pockets were more of them little skull-trophies, for all the troopers he was planning to shoot on the way back.'

'What about Gardner?' Carson asked. 'Does he know?'

'He knows of it. Doesn't believe it though.'

'I've told Forjaz to keep a close eye on him. Closer than he did on Acorn. You do the same, Red. If he looks the least bit twitchy, bring me in to talk to him again.'

'Right you are, sah. Let's just hope the tin bellies don't go digging around themselves.'

Carson looked about the different campfires checking for someone. He should be out, but would he be over here? A slight commotion over on the right told Carson he was.

'Come on, Red. Let's get it straight from the horse's mouth.'

They crossed through the camp until they had caught up with their target.

'Lance-Corporal Diver,' Carson hailed him.

'Yoo halloo, lieutenant,' Diver hailed him back. He sat on his horse, lance in hand, not a stitch of clothing on him. He did it after every battle. Something about cleansing himself or some such thing. The cavalry always considered themselves the best, the most pious, of all the Brimlock units and, as such, developed all sorts of strange ideas about sin and salvation. Lancer Diver's was a unique peccadillo even for them.

'I'm concerned, lance-corporal, about the health of dear Commissar Reeve.'

Diver shook his head sadly. 'Aren't we all. Aren't we all.'

'Do you know how he is faring?'

Diver considered it. 'He's being monitored carefully. Whatever struck him has buried itself too deep to be extracted without worsening the damage. I don't think he's woken up yet.'

Carson relaxed a fraction. 'Should we not be sending him back to Dova?'

'Oh, no,' Diver said, shaking his head and placing his lance across his thighs. 'The captain, that is Captain Ledbetter, will not let him out of his sight. After all, if the colonel tried to kill him once, he might well try again.'

'The colonel?' Carson said, surprised.

'Oh, yes. Why, who else could have ordered Drum to try to kill our captain and so leave the commissar without protectors?' Diver said gleefully, pressing his bare heels into his mount's flanks to spur him to walk on. 'We don't know the how, but we certainly know the who. Take care and keep your pecker up!'

So, Ledbetter was determined to demonstrate some kind of connection with the colonel. That meant he would have to keep Reeve away from the regiment until he recovered, if he ever did.

'It sounds very promising,' he said, turning to Red. 'Thank you for your help today. It worked out well enough in the end.'

'So long as Chaffey doesn't open his mouth, sah,' Red scowled. 'Or have it loosened for him.'

'Why don't you call him Mouse? Everybody else does.'

'That's cos he's not a mouse, sah. He's a rat.'

'Quite a collection we've built up, eh, Red? A mouse, a marble, a blank slate and one solid piece of Trouble.'

Red grunted noncommittally.

Carson, relieved, and feeling the effect of the toasting liquor and his tiredness, was gripped by a fit of whimsy. 'What do the men call me?'

'Don't know, sah,' Red said, closed off.

'Yes you do.'

'Wouldn't like to say, sah.'

'I am telling you to,' Carson pressed.

'Not my place, sah.'

'I am making it your place.'

'It's Dead-Eye, sah. Cos you're a fine marksman.'

'I am, but that's not what they call me.'

'It's Crackshot, sah.'

'No it isn't.'

'It's Two Guns, sah,' Red said, his imagination running short.

'Really, colour, you are trying my patience. Now this is a direct order, what do they call me?'

'Well…' Red said with a type of anguish Carson had never seen on his face. 'You know how your first name is Laurence, sir?'

'Yes… Is that it? Is it Larry? Laurie? It's not Loll is it? I had enough of that when I was a boy. It's not one of those?'

'No, sir. It's Florence.'

'Florence… Florence? Florence!' Carson laughed loudly. 'Excellent! How exceptional. From now on you must call me Florence as well.'

'I'd prefer not to, sir. Out of respect.'

'Red, I'll never doubt the respect you have for me.'

'Thank you, sir. But I didn't mean you, sir. My wife's name was Florence.'

Carson suddenly felt the warm glow of the liquor recede.

'Your wife?'

'Yes, sir. Florence Elsie Towser.'

'I didn't even know you were married. She wasn't one of the wives who came with us?'

'No, sir.'

'You said her name *was*… She had… she'd already passed into the Emperor's light?'

'Oh no, sir. She was as right as rain when I volunteered.'

'Then why did you say…'

'Well, she must be dead now, sah,' Red commented. 'It's been twenty years for us, but with all the time we've spent travelling… system to system, through the warp and all… It's been a lot longer for them. They're all dead, aren't they?

'But it's what you sign up for, isn't it, sah,' Red continued. 'They tell you up front, you'll never go home. And even if you did, even if you got picked as one of the colour-guard and they sent you back express all the way, it'd be the place you started, but it wouldn't be home.'

'So you left without her?'

'Had to. There was nothing else for it. No honest work in the rookeries, and I could never turn my hand to thieving. So there it was. "Starve, steal or soldier", that's what they say in the rookeries. It's even on the recruiting posters now. So I chose soldiering. And I've not done badly by it. It's kept me fed. Kept me warm. And I know that every week she was alive, my Florence went up to the recruiting base and she was given my pay.

'And then this came. Back on Kandhar, back when we got on board ship to come here, I got a message from the Munitorum. My account.'

Carson took the paper and looked at the figure at the bottom.

'Well, Red, you've got quite a surplus here.'

'I know. And that's how I know she's dead.'

'I…' Carson started and then stopped. 'I don't know what to say. I'm sorry.'

'Thank you, sah. Now, sah, if you'll excuse me.'

'Of course,' Carson said and let him leave. Carson stayed put for a while, then left to track down Van Am.

* * *

Major Brooce stared thoughtfully at the piece of paper in his hand as he sat in the signallers' tent. It was the communiqué back to Crusade Command, notifying them of the victory. Arbulaster had, for the first time, left him in charge of it. It was a simple enough task, but as a message that might be read direct to the First Lord High General, and possibly repeated across the sector by the Voice of Liberation, commanding officers tended to be quite jealous about the responsibility. Still, Brooce had had plenty enough examples to copy and now it was finished, all but for one detail.

'Good evening, sir.'

Brooce looked up and saw Lieutenant Mulberry. 'Oh, good evening, lieutenant.'

'Just here with requisition orders,' Mulberry said conversationally, taking a puff from his long clay pipe. 'Going to need quite a bit of oomph if we're going to bury that thing tomorrow.'

'Good,' Brooce replied without interest.

'If you don't mind me saying, sir, you look like a man with a problem, sir. Care to run it by me? We've got a good head for solutions, us beards.'

Brooce regarded the cheerful lieutenant. If it had been the colonel sitting here rather than him, Brooce doubted Mulberry would have tried to be so familiar; and if Mulberry had tried, the colonel would have sent him away sharpish with a flea in his ear. Brooce was about to do the same when he had a sudden change of heart. Did he really wish to model his way of command after the colonel's in every single way? Brooce had seen his face before he left, had seen the agitation, the hint of terror in it. But he had not wished to share it even with those closest to him and, whatever it was, it had led him running back to Dova.

Brooce knew he himself was to be one of the

colour-guard, he knew the colonel needed someone to
return with him to confirm all his adventures and the
heroic role he had played in them. After he was done
with that, Brooce wanted a regiment of his own, to build
a reputation of his own. He had immense respect for the
colonel and gratitude for all he had done; he simply did
not want to end up like him, isolated and gnawed away
by something inside. With that in mind, he turned the
paper over to the lieutenant.

'For immediate dispatch, Crusade Command, Ellinor
Crusade,' Mulberry read. 'On 072660M41, the Brimlock
11th Regiment (Consolidated), under the command of
Colonel Arbulaster PC VL OSV, engaged with a size-
able orkoid force numbering several thousand warriors
at _____ on the Imperial planet of Voor. Despite being
greatly outnumbered, the Brimlock attack was pressed
home at close range and with determination and coolness in the face of fierce resistance. After several hours'
fighting, the enemy force was annihilated and the regiment took full control over their fortified base in the
name of the Emperor, of Brimlock and of the Ellinor
Crusade. Praise the Emperor, all glory to His name.'

'It's very good, sir,' Mulberry concluded, handing the
paper back. 'Just the one detail left.'

'The name of the battle.'

'Is it that important, sir?' The lieutenant took the
opportunity to sit.

'Of course it's important. How many battles do you
remember that didn't have a name?'

Mulberry thought about it. 'Well, none come to mind.'

'Quite. And you normally just name it after the nearest
town or landmark or the like, but this entire continent
has barely been scratched. There are no towns, no settlements; we don't even have names for the mountains.'

'What about the name of the rok: *Brutal Fury*?'

Brooce stared at him. 'Much as I respect the fine, talented strategists at Crusade Command, they can get rather excitable when it comes to nomenclature.'

'Why not just the battle of the crater then?'

Brooce considered it. 'Needs to be a bit more specific.'

'Orks Crater? Orks Rift? Ork Gulch?' Mulberry started to reel off.

Brooce stared at him. 'Don't be facetious, Mulberry.' The lieutenant managed a look of contrition. 'No, it needs a proper name. I wonder where that Voorjer girl is?'

'Ah, I might be of use there,' Mulberry exclaimed, jumping up. 'I spent quite a bit of time with her on the path from Dova, to try and get her help filling in my map.' He pulled a folded sheet of laminate from his uniform and laid it out. 'She had a lot of local names for places hereabouts... How close does it have to be?'

'Not very,' Brooce admitted. 'You know of the Battle of Defiance, of course?'

'Oh, of course,' Mulberry nodded, 'Lord Ferresley's greatest victory, it's compulsory study.'

'Ever wonder why it was named after a town that was over fifty miles from the actual site of the battle?'

Mulberry searched his schola education. 'I thought it was because that was the place he spent the night after the battle.'

'Yes, but why did he spend the night there? It was so he could name the battle after it rather than any of those towns with Vostroyan names nearby. He would rather have been hanged than split the credit with the Vostroyan commander.'

'Is that true, sir?'

'Oh yes, he told me so himself. Lord Ferresley had an undoubted ability to win battles, it's true. But even that was outstripped by his ability to win the credit afterwards. So what's the closest?'

Mulberry arched his thumb and forefinger across the map, measuring the distances. 'Looks like either *Bronkhorstspruit* or *Schuinshoogte,*' he announced.

'Anything a little less… foreign?' Brooce ventured.

'These mountains here, they're very close by, she had a name for those. That would be perfect.'

Brooce read the map, and then read it again to be sure he had read it right the first time.

'I think she might have been having some fun with you there, lieutenant. Would you care to read it?'

'Beeg Nokkers? What's funny about that?'

Brooce stared at him harder this time, but Mulberry appeared completely innocent. 'I'd prefer not to have a name that will provoke guffaws in every cadet studying the regimental history.'

Mulberry still appeared confused, so Brooce peered closely at the map.

'What's this one?'

Mulberry looked where the major was pointing. 'That's just a cabin they put there on one of their climbing expeditions. It's just a shack really. There are no people there.'

'High Point.'

'Or high place. It's not a name, it's just a description.'

Brooce was already marking it down on the communiqué, however. He handed it over to the signaller who started the transmission to Dova, which would then be redirected off-planet and to Crusade Command. Mulberry saw the look of satisfaction on Brooce's face.

'Thank you, lieutenant,' Brooce said as he left. 'I do believe it's all downhill from here.'

INTERLUDE

Orkoid birthing sac, Tswaing, 659.M41 – One year prior to the Battle of Highpoint

THE CREATURE THAT would become the ork known as Choppa shifted in his birthing-sac. He was uncomfortable. Confined. It had never felt this way before. He had always felt safe and protected inside it, but now he felt cramped, constrained. The sac had shrunk, or maybe it was his body that had grown bigger. Either way, he wanted out.

His nails had not yet toughened, but still he managed to use them to score a groove on the inside. He dug his fingers into the groove and pulled it apart. After a moment's resistance, the sac tore and split apart. Choppa felt a new sensation, that of loose earth between his fingers. It crumbled as he grasped at it; he had never felt anything crumble before. He liked it. He tried the taste of it, then felt the muscles of his face grimace and scowl. The taste he did not like and he spat it out. He was angry now. He had never experienced it before, but he recognised the sense of power he felt with it.

He grabbed the soil in front of him and started shovelling great handfuls of it. He did not know what was before him, but he knew that his future was out; there was nothing left back inside for him. He felt his fingers break out of the earth, and he reached up until there was nothing more to grasp. He pushed with his other hand, shuffled forwards and straightened his spine to shove his head through as well.

He felt a chill on his hand, outside the soil. Something moved past it; something light, just brushing over his skin. He felt his mouth and throat reverberate into a growl. He tried to speak but more soil fell into his mouth. He spat again, as hard as he could this time, and pushed himself up with all his might. The top of his head broke out. He felt the air sweep over his hairless scalp and around his pointed ears. He pushed again and he felt his face scrape free. He opened his red eyes and saw for the first time.

There was a figure there. He was facing in Choppa's direction, but he didn't see him. Choppa saw that the figure was in light while he was in darkness. Choppa looked up and saw the twisted gills of a blackened toadstool casting shade where he emerged. The figure looked his way and Choppa held still. He knew it was bad to be seen. The figure pulled something from the ground, turned and walked off. When he was out of sight Choppa moved again. He pulled himself entirely free, pushing the canopy of the toadstool out of his way and stretching out to his full height. The figure was larger than him, he could tell. That meant he was small. That meant he didn't have power. He was not safe. He must find more strength to protect himself. He looked in the direction the figure had gone and then in the direction he had come from. It was a simple choice. He took his first step after the figure.

His steps were halting at first as he swayed and staggered, grabbing at the fungus growths around him to keep him steady. His balance came to him quickly, however, and then he could walk with more confidence. He could see the figure ahead of him now. He saw him bend down and pull something from the ground. He straightened up, looked closely at what he held in his hand, then pulled a small object from around his neck and blew into it. Choppa heard the noise. The figure was calling others to him. Perhaps he had seen Choppa, perhaps he had let him follow after him so as to bring him to these others. Others would be coming here and Choppa knew that would be bad. He knew he was weak. If he faced others then he would have to be strong.

He took a step back and lowered himself behind a thorny stalk. He put his weight on it as he crouched and felt it bend a fraction at the base. Its roots were loose in the soil. It was weak as well. He went on again, interested, then pulled, and it came free in his hands. Choppa gripped it tightly. This was strong. He was strong now and so had nothing to fear. He rose and left his hiding place behind. The figure blew on his object again and stood there waiting. Choppa walked up behind him and, as the figure turned, swung his weapon hard down on his head.

His enemy's head jerked away at the blow. The enemy whirled around and snarled and Choppa struck him again. The enemy stumbled this time and Choppa went after him to strike him once more. This time, however, he raised his arm and so Choppa's blow struck that and not the head. The enemy's other hand curled into a ball and struck Choppa in his body. Choppa felt pain for the first time. It made him even more angry, and from that anger he felt even more power flow.

Choppa took a step back; the enemy did as well.

Choppa noticed that where he had struck the enemy's head a liquid had spread from the wound. He felt his own midriff where he had felt the pain. There was no liquid there. That meant he was winning. He saw the enemy reach down to his leg. He had a weapon as well. Choppa swung again, but this time not for the head; rather, he struck at the enemy's knee. The enemy howled and fell over. Choppa stood over the fallen enemy for a moment. Did that mean that he had won, he asked himself? His anger had the answer and he struck the enemy once more, twice more, a dozen times more until his face was covered by the liquid. Now Choppa knew he had won.

His enemy no longer moved and Choppa took his time studying the body. Then he looked at his own. It was only then that he realised that he and his enemy looked the same. Choppa found it curious, but it did not concern him greatly. The shape of things did not matter to him nearly as much as what was strong and what was weak. And he had proved himself the stronger here. The enemy's weapon intrigued him, though. He pulled it from its strap upon the body. It resembled the stalk he himself carried, but it was bigger, its surface was harder, it did not bend no matter how hard Choppa twisted it. It was stronger.

He tossed the stalk away and took the enemy's weapon as his own. It was then that he realised he was being watched. Another creature, this one like his enemy but far smaller, was looking at him. Was this one of the others that his enemy had called? Without hesitation, Choppa turned in the small one's direction.

The small one darted away from him into the shadows beneath the tall fungus canopy and Choppa chased after him. The creature scampered through knots and tendrils attempting to escape, but Choppa merely knocked them aside and his longer strides quickly brought him close.

Then the small one ran out from the cover and into a clearing. There were more creatures here. These did not resemble anything that Choppa had seen before. Their bodies were bulbous and they had no arms, merely large mouths that they were using to chomp up the shoots and knobs of fungus at their feet. The small one scurried through their midst, leaping nimbly away when their mouths snapped at him.

Choppa followed, but as he approached they all turned on him. He used his weapon and struck the first of them in between its eyes. It keeled over and the rest of its kind flew into a panic and jumped away in every direction. Choppa thought of continuing after the small one, but now the animal carcass at his feet caught his interest. He was feeling weak again, but this time the weakness was not in his arms but in his centre. He felt hollow, drained.

Instinctively, he put his hand upon the carcass's flank and tore a wodge of meat from it. The meat and his hand were covered in the liquid, but this time it did not feel like victory. Instead, he had another impulse. He shoved the meat into his mouth and tried to chew and swallow at the same time. He choked and coughed and nearly spat it out, but this taste he liked. He chewed for a while first this time and only then tried to swallow. Each piece sliding down his gullet filled his centre with its warmth. This was good.

While he was eating he saw that the small one had returned and was watching him again from a greater distance. Choppa thought of chasing him, but he was enjoying the meat too much to bother. The small one was gone by the time he'd finished. His head felt heavy now and so he returned to the blackened toadstool from whence he had emerged and dug himself back into his hole to sleep.

Choppa slept and rested, and then dug himself up

once more. It did not take long before he saw the small one again. He chased after him and again he led him to where the meat-beasts were. For the first few days, the two of them followed the same pattern and the small one left him while he ate, but on the fourth day he stayed. That day, once Choppa had eaten his fill, the small one approached and took a bite of the remains. Once he had swallowed it, he stood before Choppa, pressed his tiny hand to his pigeon chest and said something:

'Nabkeri,' he said.

Choppa looked at him blankly. He repeated himself, but Choppa did not know what he meant. He walked away as though disappointed, but then he looked back and beckoned for Choppa to come with him. Choppa was no longer hungry, but he did not tire as he had before after eating, and so he followed.

Nabkeri led him a distance, further from his hole than he had ever been. He finally brought him to the edge of another clearing. In this clearing there were mounds. Not fungus mounds, but shapes made of the earth. Choppa saw gaps in them and realised that they were hollow inside. Creatures that looked like his enemy, that looked like him, were sitting around and walking amongst them. Nabkeri pointed at them.

'Boyz,' he said. Then he pointed at Choppa.

'Boyz,' he repeated, gesturing emphatically. Choppa did not respond. Nabkeri set out towards the village and wanted Choppa to come as well, but he refused. He could see that there were many of them, and only one of him. These boyz together were strong, far stronger than he, and so he would not face them. Instead he disappeared back into the lands he knew.

Over the days that followed, however, he returned to the village many times to watch these boyz. He told himself at first he did so in order to determine how to beat them, but as he watched them more and more he realised that there was another yearning he felt inside of him besides anger, hunger and fatigue. He wanted to be amongst them and yet he denied himself the company he desired.

That changed the day that Nabkeri appeared before him, telling him to follow. This time Nabkeri took him neither to the meat-beasts, which Choppa could now find himself, nor to the village, but to somewhere, something, else.

Choppa and Nabkeri watched the new-spawned ork struggle along the ground. Its knee was turned inwards at an unhealthy angle and so it could not find its footing. It was weak. Choppa would need no weapons for this. He advanced towards it, preparing for the kill. The new-spawn pushed itself up from the ground as it saw Choppa approach and then scrambled backwards in fear. Choppa caught it with ease and tossed it onto its back. It flailed with its hands to keep its attacker at bay, but Choppa knocked them aside and took a grip around its neck, readying to rip its throat out. Suddenly, there was a flurry of movement in front of him and he felt tiny scratches on his face. Nabkeri was attacking him. Choppa grunted in indignation and swatted the gretchin away with his free hand. Nabkeri dodged away and started to screech.

'No kill! No kill! No kill!'

Choppa turned back to the new-spawn in his grasp who was trying unsuccessfully to pull Choppa's fingers away. Choppa readied to make the kill when Nabkeri flew at him again.

'No kill da boyz! Boss no kill da boyz!'

Choppa paused, comprehension beginning to seep into his well-insulated brain. Nabkeri now turned his attention to the new-spawn, scratching its face.

'Da boss! Da boss!' Nabkeri shouted at the new-spawn and pointed a tiny green finger at Choppa. The new-spawn mewled in pain at the treatment, but eventually Nabkeri began to get through to it.

'Da boss... Da boss...' the new-spawn began to say along.

'Da boyz,' Nabkeri said, pointing at the new-spawn, then pointed at Choppa. 'Da boss!'

'Da boss,' the new-spawn agreed, and Nabkeri batted at Choppa to have him stand up off the new recruit. Choppa did so and, as he did, Nabkeri's demeanour shifted abruptly. The frantic peace-maker switched in a flash to the cautious horse-trader. Nabkeri walked around the prone greenskin, checking everything about it. He peered in its ears, pinched at its skin, prodded at its paltry belly. He rolled back its upper lip to check its teeth and the new-spawn snapped at him only to receive an irate scolding from the gretchin before he returned to his inspection. Nabkeri finally focused on the new-spawn's knee as his particular concern. He probed it thoughtfully and then brought Choppa over.

'Dok it,' he said.

Choppa did not understand.

'Dok it! Dok it!' Nabkeri began to rant, and he mimed what he meant. Choppa followed what he thought the gretchin was demonstrating, took a hold on the knee and the calf, and then wrenched and twisted as hard as he could. The new-spawn howled this time, but Nabkeri was ready. He grabbed a certain piece of fungus from his belt and jammed it into the new-spawn's mouth. It bit down and swallowed, and then it stopped shouting. The look on its face showed it was still in pain, but it could no longer make a noise. Nabkeri returned to Choppa and seemed pleased with what the ork had done. Choppa dropped the leg and the new-spawn rolled onto its side.

Choppa understood what Nabkeri had done, but he did not yet understand why the gretchin had bothered. The new-spawn was weak. The weak got killed. If one happened upon someone stronger than you, you found something that made you stronger still and then you killed them. He wandered off to find another meat-beast and then return to watch the village.

NABKERI FOUND HIM a few days later and took him back to the new-spawn. It was walking properly now and it was stronger. Nabkeri had obviously been showing it where the meat-beasts were, for it had killed one of them and was beginning to eat. Choppa emerged, ready to fight for it, but as soon as the new-spawn saw him he ducked his head subserviently and moved aside, allowing Choppa to eat first. Choppa did so, eyeing the new-spawn suspiciously and left nothing for him.

When he had finished, Nabkeri had them both follow him and took them to a new place where Choppa saw the largest meat-beast he had ever seen. As they approached, this one did not flee, but rather pawed the ground with its three-toed foot and lowered its head to charge. Choppa and the new-spawn threw themselves to either side out of the way of its attack. The meat-beast turned to chase after Choppa, but then found the new-spawn clinging onto its back. It spun around to try to shake the new-spawn off and Choppa launched himself at it. The two of them together brought it to the ground and got the kill. Once again the new-spawn let Choppa eat first, but this time Choppa only ate a fraction and then allowed the new-spawn to eat the rest.

Once more a new concept was diffusing into Choppa's mind. He had thought that a weapon could only be something inanimate, a rock or a club, something he could hold. But a weapon could be another creature as well. Having others made him stronger, but only if they were under his control.

Off to one side, Nabkeri grinned in satisfaction as he saw Choppa motion for the new-spawn to follow him, then he knuckled over to the carcass and started to chew fast before the other scavengers arrived.

With Nabkeri's help, Choppa added a dozen more new-spawns to his burgeoning warband. Many of them, he found, emerged close to where he had done and then later, nearabouts to where he had killed his first enemy. The same process worked on each. He would prove his strength to them by besting them in combat. Then, as soon as he had his hand around their throats, he would demand they recognise him as boss. Hunting together, they could take any meat-beast they wished, but Choppa knew a far greater challenge awaited them. He returned to the village often to count the number of warriors they had, and each time he did so he realised that, even with his warband, together they were still weak.

The time came when one of the new-spawns came running up to Choppa. There were so many new-spawns now that Choppa had found himself having to create names to tell them apart. The first new-spawn he called Badrukken after his knee, then there was Noshgobber after his appetite and increasing girth, Gruffdreggen after his destructive tendencies and so forth. He needed no name to refer to himself, of course, and to the rest he was always simply Da boss.

This one he'd called Krumpkopperd for the great smack to the head Choppa had had to use to subdue him when they first fought. Krumpkopperd had news. He'd seen more boyz, the boyz from the village. A whole bunch of them were coming out together.

Choppa's first thought was that they knew about him. They knew he was growing stronger and so had set out to finish him off before he could threaten them. Well, he would not wait to be attacked. He would find them first. Krumpkopperd had seen them heading towards one of the meat-beast clearings and so Choppa gathered the new-spawns together and went after them.

They tracked them down not far from the clearing. They were moving quietly and carefully, but they were on Choppa's home turf and his new-spawns merged amongst the shadows cast by the toadstool canopies. It was not all the village boyz, only about the same number as Choppa had new-spawns. It was good enough, though, and Choppa was about to give the signal to attack when he noticed that Nabkeri was amongst their gretchin slaves. As though he could sense his gaze, Nabkeri stared straight at where Choppa was concealed and shook his head, making a motion for patience.

Choppa was ready for battle, but still he paused. Nabkeri was amongst them, and that meant he was an enemy, and yet Nabkeri was still helping him. So perhaps one could pretend to be an enemy and yet still be a friend. Choppa found this thought too confusing. Instead he and his new-spawns followed the village boyz to the clearing and watched them catch the meat-beasts. They used spears and nets, but Choppa saw they were still not as good as he and his new-spawns were at catching the meat-beasts. He took pleasure in that.

The village boyz ran after the meat-beasts for some time before they had finally caught all they wished. Some they had killed, others they had tethered and were dragging away. The gretchin scampered behind the tethered meat-beasts, trying to prod them forwards and avoid their sharp tails. The village boyz and their trophies gathered themselves together and then started back. They were going slower, Choppa realised, they were laden down and tired now. One or two of them were even sporting injuries incurred from the meat-beasts. They were weaker than they had been before. Now was the time to strike.

As the party approached the path where Choppa was waiting, Nabkeri suddenly jumped onto the largest meat-beast's back and bit it hard between its eyes. The meat-beast went mad, bucking and tearing at its leash. The other gretchin swarmed over it, while Nabkeri slipped down and bit through the meat-beast's leash. Its bucking turned into full-fledged spasms as it found itself free and it spun to try to knock the gretchin away. The village boyz turned to see the commotion and that was the moment that Choppa bellowed the charge.

The fight was over quickly. The village boyz were distracted, several had waded amongst the meat-beasts to try to restore order and found themselves set upon as the attack drove the meat-beasts to even greater frenzy. Choppa caught one off-guard and brained it. The rest of his new-spawns launched themselves at the defenders, two on each one, fending away the village boyz' blows and taking their legs out from under them. Once they were on the ground they quickly fell victim to the new-spawns' kicks.

Choppa knocked the last one down himself as it threw off the wounded meat-beast that had made a bloody ruin of its chest. Once the ork was on the ground, Choppa grabbed it round the throat and started once more demanding recognition as boss. This one, however, kept on fighting and would not relent, scrabbling for Choppa's face, looking for purchase. Shocked at this, Choppa automatically dug in his nails, pulled and ripped the village boy's throat clean out. These boyz would not acknowledge him; they would not make him stronger.

He took his club and smashed in the brains of fully half their number before the remainder hastened to make signs of subservience. Choppa was unconvinced, now deeply suspicious of these orks. They each bore a mark, a blue circle, around their chin. It made them different from his new-spawns, separate from them. They would never be his weapon and that made them his enemy. He raised his club and slew the rest as they squirmed on the ground, held down by the new-spawns.

Choppa slew them all bar the last, who Nabkeri made to protect as he had done when they had first encountered Badrukken. This last one was the smallest, but it did not wear the same mark as the rest. Perhaps, Choppa reasoned, it could be his weapon after all. Solemnly, he slapped the last one's head up, gripped its throat and said the incantation. The last one, wide-eyed, agreed quickly, but Choppa held it firm until its babbling stopped and it started repeating the word as slowly and deliberately as he did. He told the new-spawns to equip themselves with the clubs, nets and sharpened poles that the village boyz had dropped and, as he did so, he gave his latest recruit a name: Mugkileen.

Choppa wasted no time. When he had killed his first enemy, no one had come looking for it, but these enemies were taking food. The other village boyz would be expecting them to return and would come looking for them soon. With these warriors dead, their numbers were fewer, they were weak, and they would not yet expect his attack.

He led his small warband with its latest recruit straight to the spot from where he watched the village. Choppa was right; a few of the village boyz were outside of their mounds, but they were lying idle, leaving their weapons scattered around. Choppa did not announce their attack, but rather ran straight in without speaking. The bizarre spectacle caught the village boyz off-guard and they leaned up and stared at the sight rather than instantly

reaching for their weapons. Choppa managed to knock
one of them aside before they saw the rest of his new-
spawns charging silently after him and realised they were
under attack. Badrukken had chosen himself a spear and
ran one of the village boyz through while it struggled
to its feet. Badrukken held it in place while Noshgobber caved its head in with a rock. Gruffdreggen threw
a net over a fumbling village boy just as the hunters
had thrown them over the meat-beasts. With his enemy
entangled, he gave it a crack on the knee to knock it to
the ground and then set about hammering it with his
club.

Those village boyz outside were nearly overwhelmed,
but a couple of them were faster and managed to lay a
hand on their weapons before they were assailed. The
noise of the combat attracted more of the village boyz
from inside the mounds and Choppa quickly ordered
his new-spawns to the entrances so as to block others
emerging from behind. A scream of agony to one side
told him that they had not all been successful.

Choppa looked up from the village boy he was bludg-
eoning to see Krumpkopperd fall away, his shoulder
sliced from the rest of his torso. The severed limb, still
holding its spear, lay on the ground as the new-spawn
looked down at the gaping hole in his body and then
slowly collapsed.

Behind him stood the largest ork that Choppa had ever
seen. It stood more upright, nearly a half a metre taller
than Choppa. It had not only a blue circle on its chin,
but also a far larger one emblazoned across its chest and
its belly. It wore necklaces and bracelets made of greenskin teeth. It was the boss of the village boyz and it held
in its hands a weapon that Choppa had coveted from
the moment he had first laid eyes upon it. It was over
a metre long, its shaft was not made from some tough

fungus crop but from stout wood, and it had a blade of metal. The only weapon of such kind to exist in all of Choppa's world. Choppa had seen him many times as he watched the village, each time anticipating the time when it would come to fight him.

The village boss hefted his weapon and caught Choppa's eye. Choppa returned the challenge and turned to face him. The other combats around them fizzled out and fell quiet as all of the orks focused on the fight between the two champions. Choppa raised his club and, for the first time, hollered a battle-cry as he flung it straight at the boss. Surprised, the boss swung his weapon and batted the missile to the side with a hefty, satisfied swipe. His opponent's desperate strike had failed and he had disarmed himself in the process. The fight, he believed, was practically over, but Choppa had not finished.

Even as the club was leaving his hand, Choppa was leaning forwards. As the boss shifted his focus to the club, Choppa started to run. He sprang and barrelled into the boss as he circled the weapon back and smashed them both to the ground. Choppa scrabbled at the boss's face as he tried to defend himself and hang onto the weapon caught between them. He tried to lever it free, but Choppa held his weight down upon it. The boss howled in agony as Choppa plunged his jagged fingernails in and released his grip to press his hands into his face. Choppa jumped to his feet, gathering the blade and then buried it in the boss's chest and cut off his screams. Then the screams began again as the victorious new-spawns set about their opponents and the massacre began.

CHOPPA'S WARBAND KILLED those who were marked, sparing those few who were not on condition of their fealty to their new boss. The new-spawns ransacked the mounds for items, taking more weapons, food, necklaces of teeth, and anything else that caught their eye. The village and the fungus fields around it were the entire world to Choppa and now he had proved that he was the strongest of them all.

Once they had finished with their looting, Choppa gathered them up and led them back to where they had come from. Nabkeri appeared before him again, incensed with anger. He tried to drag Choppa back to the village, but Choppa was not interested in returning. He had defeated the enemies who were there and brought back more warriors for his warband. There was nothing in the village for him; he had taken all he desired: the metal weapon that was now his. Nabkeri threw up his hands and left him. He gathered together the gretchin who had been left masterless and, with them, he himself occupied the mounds.

Despite his earlier inclination, Choppa found himself returning to the village often. He felt a sense of ownership there, it was a prize for which he had fought and won. Those of his warriors who had come from the village, Mugkileen and the few others, had also returned to the village and had begun to order the gretchin about, much to Nabkeri's annoyance. Watching Mugkileen, Choppa began to understand the purpose of the mounds. They were warmer at night and when the weather turned cold, and when it rained they were better cover than a mushroom cap. The carcasses of the meat-beasts his warband killed could be better protected there against the predations of the carnivore squigs than out in the open or buried in the ground, too. He also discovered more newspawns emerging, many of them appearing first around the fringes of the village.

Bit by bit, Choppa and his warband centred their world around the mounds, wordlessly reasserting his authority over Mugkileen and ensuring that all the new-spawns swore fealty to him. Choppa did not forget how Badrukken and many of his first new-spawns had appeared where he had killed his first enemy and so led regular hunting patrols searching not only for meat-beasts but also for more new-spawns to bring back.

Even with the names, Choppa found himself beginning to get confused between those new-spawns who had sworn themselves to him. He recalled the blue mark used by the old boss and decided he could do something similar. He discovered within one of the mounds a squig creature which excreted the blue colouring, but he did not wish to use the same mark, the mark of a loser. Instead, Nabkeri showed him one that excreted red. Choppa used that to devise his own symbol, a single straight line, a 'blood stripe' as it came to be called, down his warriors' foreheads and one of their cheeks. The only orks that did not wear it after a few days were those few new-spawns who Choppa had yet to get round to making declare him boss, and Choppa himself. He needed no mark to tell him who he was.

CHAPTER NINETEEN

Impact Crater, Tswaing, Voor pacification
Stage 1 Day 18

TWO HOURS AFTER the Battle of Highpoint concluded deep night had descended. In the air Colonel Arbulaster was aboard his Valkyrie with the lights of Dova in sight. In the crater Major Brooce was showing the frustrated Navy pilots to a fire where they would have to wait until morning. And out in the dark, an entirely more determined searcher caught his first glimpse of the site where Zdzisław went down.

The low-hanging clouds blocked almost all the light from the moons, but they reflected a little from the pyres back in the crater. No one else would have dared venture out in such darkness, but it was enough for Mouse.

The colonel wasn't the only one looking towards his future. Mouse was the same. He had slipped away from the regiment as soon as he could, while the men were still dispersed dragging the ork bodies to the pyres. There was always the same confusion after a battle as the dead were counted, the injured tended to, equipment salvaged, and each man gave thanks to have survived the day. For Mouse, however, the battle was merely the preamble; his true work began now. For where others looked upon a battlefield with pride, sadness or disgust, he saw each battlefield as a field of harvested crops, ready to be gathered in.

This one, though, had not been promising. Not a great number of men had died, and they'd had their friends standing by them to recover their valuables. The Brimlock casualties had been concentrated within the crater, which was now under a watchful guard. The ork dead, well, they carried only their weapons and a few bone trinkets good only as novelties. Their bodies were already burning. The victory had been too easy. When the victory was too easy the regiment stayed in good order, casualties were accounted for quickly and Mouse went hungry. The hard-fought battles, where the foe had retreated but the regiments were too exhausted to take control of the field, the fast-moving fights where companies were redeployed as soon as the last enemy fell and small knots of soldiers were caught out of position and overwhelmed, those were the battlefields where Mouse ate.

He was not a thief. He was very clear about that. There had been thieves, to be sure, in the 11th. The ones who were brazen, or stupid, were quickly shot or hanged. Even the ones who were smarter, more careful, still fell foul of their comrades' unofficial retribution. Some of them survived it, some of them didn't. Because it didn't matter how sly you were about it, soldiers always knew. And none of them, even if they were doing it themselves, wanted a thief about.

So Mouse was most definitely not a thief. He knew where the line was and he knew not to cross it. He would endure being called many things, but never thief. He was a scavenger, a reclaimer, a recycler. He took only from the dead, and kept their items amongst the living. He was a vital part of the regimental ecology.

He had learned other rules as well. Never take anything you do not know how to sell. Never try to take anything you can't carry yourself. And, if it's an officer who left a wife, you make sure she gets her fair share. He had learnt that last one in a particularly painful manner at the hands of the widow Murdoc and the sharp end of a scalpel blade that she had used to threaten his sensitive area.

That incident had turned out to have its compensations, however. After the next battle, when he returned certain items back to the new widows, whilst some of them ignored him and some of them spat at him, others were painfully grateful to have anything of their husbands back. They came to accept his little service, expect it even. The wives of the living officers protected him, knowing they might have to rely on it themselves one dark day, and with them came the tacit protection of their officer husbands. He realised he had security in his other endeavours and so his business thrived.

These orks had been very poor. Other orks they had fought during the crusade had been more rewarding. Nothing they made themselves, of course, but things they had looted. Eldar were the best. Everything they carried was a thing of beauty. Even a pistol carried by one of their lowliest troopers was gilded and patterned to be a work of art. Their armour was encrusted with jewels of the richest colours and deepest purity.

That had been a glorious campaign, for Mouse at least. The Brimlock casualties had been horrendous; none of the sandy towns of Azzabar were safe. The eldar attacked with the desert wind, haughty, elemental, but as Mouse discovered, mortal. He remembered his excitement when he first got his hands on one of their bodies. A large jewel on the centre of its breastplate would have made Mouse enough on its own to bribe his way out of the Guard for good. But then they were besieged, and the eldar suddenly quit their hit-and-run tactics and cut them off from any support.

It was a stand-off, which the company would ultimately lose. Red, when he discovered Mouse's jewel stash, had tried to break it by tossing the lot of them out into the desert. Of even greater annoyance to Mouse was that it appeared to have worked. The next morning the jewels were gone and so were the eldar. Red had tried to have him put up against a wall for that one, only Carson had been able to calm him down.

Mouse brought his attention back to the moment and started stalking through the crash-site. He saw Zdzisław's body, looking as inhuman as ever, and crept over to it. Personal effects, cash, sentimental jewellery, they were all worth something, either to Mouse or Zdzisław's next of kin.

Mouse leaned over the body, deftly removing a neck-cord, a ring and some kind of spare part, either for the Valkyrie or for Zdzisław himself. A heavy hand landed on his shoulder.

'Got you, you little rat.'

Mouse nearly jumped out of his skin.

'Red! Sarge! Colour!' he gasped. 'Don't do that to me.'

'I'm going to do a lot worse to you, private. This time you're going to be shot.'

'What? Why? I just went to have a crap. I must have got lost on me way back. You can't shoot a man for that?'

'I can shoot him for desertion, for dereliction and for attempted theft, I can.'

'Theft? Theft? I was only reaching to check to see if he was still breathing.'

'Wiggle all you like, Chaffey. You won't get out this

time. The campaign is done. The lieutenant's got no more use for you any more.'

Mouse switched to a different tack. 'Then maybe other people might have a use for me *about* the lieutenant.'

That proved to be a mistake, Mouse realised, as Red smacked him hard on the Valkyrie's fuselage. 'I was hoping you were going to say that, you piece of filth. The lieutenant won't shirk from having to deal with rats like you.'

Then Red stopped talking and released his grip on the front of Mouse's uniform. Mouse looked up, half-expecting to be kicked down again and, when it didn't happen, he wondered what had inspired the sudden change of heart.

What had inspired it was the ork warband standing all around them.

'I UNDERSTAND YOU'RE looking for me, lieutenant,' Van Am said, meeting him in the darkness.

Carson paused a moment as he saw the coolness in her eyes. 'Holder,' he replied.

There was silence between them, until Carson finally ventured: 'There are rumours going around the regiment regarding the injury to Commissar Reeve.'

'We've heard them. A Voorjer bullet from a Voorjer gun. It is natural to assume a Voorjer would be shooting.'

'I know it's not true.'

'I think, lieutenant, you can trust us to know the truth of which Imperial officers we have shot and when. We have reason, in short, to make a habit of it.'

'Don't be such a fool, girl,' Carson chided her.

'And yet the next time we meet you will be trying to kill me and I will be trying to kill you.' Carson began to reply, but Van Am cut him off. 'Don't deny it, don't even try.'

'You don't have to fight us.'

'Yes, we do.'

'The garrison is–'

'The garrison doesn't concern me any more. It's the ones who'll come now you're here: the missionaries and the witch-finders, then the administrators and the quotas, then the arbitrators and the laws. Your laws. Your society. Not ours.'

'That doesn't have to be, but if you resist, we won't have a choice.'

'You'll never have the choice. You're an owned man, lieutenant. You all are. The Guard purchased you with food and protection and a uniform and a gun. You don't have any choices.'

'Then that is just the price you pay.'

'For you to defend us?'

'No, for living. On this world, in this system, in this galaxy, in this time. The Imperium is the price you pay to live as a human.'

'No one lives in the Imperium, lieutenant. They only exist.'

There was silence between them. She knew that whatever might have been would never come to pass, but she was willing to tease out these last few moments of his company.

'You're leaving tonight, aren't you?' Carson guessed.

'I'll do you a favour, lieutenant,' Van Am replied. 'I won't tell you. Then all you have to do is walk away, and you won't have to choose whether to betray me to your superiors, or betray them for me.'

BY THE NEXT morning it was noted that Van Am and her Voorjers had disappeared from camp. The pickets had been lax, distracted by the celebrations behind them, and the Voorjers had slipped away into the night. They could not be spotted on the trail back to Dova and so it was assumed that they had headed through the jungle towards the coast. Carson understood why they had gone, but it wouldn't matter. It would take them a week at least to get to the sea. By then, Voorheid would be in the Guard's hands. She was going to fight, Carson knew, but she wasn't going to win.

What regret he felt, however, was instantly forgotten when Forjaz brought him the news that two of his men were missing.

IT DID NOT take Carson long to guess where Mouse and Red had gone. Whilst it was not unknown for two soldiers to disappear on some joint enterprise, he could imagine no unlikelier bedfellows than the two of them. Red must have gone after Mouse, and there was only one place in the area that would have appealed to the light-fingered scavenger. Carson applied instantly to Major Brooce for permission to lead a search party out to the Valkyrie's crash-site, but when he arrived he found he was already half an hour too late.

'I'm sorry, lieutenant,' Brooce told him, 'but I need your men here to scour whatever taint of the orks remain down in that pit. The Navymen left at first light to go and recover their dead, though; we will inform them of the circumstances and ask them to keep their eyes peeled.'

'Major,' Carson exclaimed, 'Those bluebells couldn't spot a trail any more than you or I could navigate a battle-ship. Roussell can burn out the orks, let my men and I–'

'Major Roussell,' Brooce interrupted, 'already volunteered to provide the escort for the expedition. Personally.'

The realisation seized Carson instantly. 'So Roussell and his lap-dogs,' Carson's voice rose in frustration, 'baby-sit the bluebells while my company has to risk their skins again!'

Carson's anger was attracting the attention of Brooce's own troopers standing nearby. He gave them a quick glance to show them that he was still in control of the situation and, as he did so, caught sight of another officer striding up towards him.

'Major,' Stanhope launched in at once, 'I'm afraid I have to report that two of my men are missing.'

Before Brooce even had a chance to open his mouth, Carson turned upon the newcomer with fury.

'They're not *your* men, Stanhope, they're mine! My company! My men! So do me a good service and butt out!'

'Lieutenant!' Brooce warned sharply. Stanhope, surprised by the outburst, had retreated a step in the face of Carson's glare. 'Lieutenant Carson!' Brooce said again and Carson turned back to him. 'Yours is not the only other company risking its skin today, we will all be going down there to clear the place out. Major Roussell–'

'Is a damned coward,' Carson said, but Brooce maintained his tone.

'–has the rank and the seniority. And his own expedition is by no means without peril. We will communicate the circumstances to him and he will investigate as far as he is able.'

Carson drew breath to reply, but now it was his turn to be cut off.

'Stand down, lieutenant,' Stanhope ordered and before Carson could object continued on to Brooce. 'Major, I agree with you completely. With your permission, I will take responsibility to communicate the circumstances to Major Roussell and the naval expedition.'

Brooce raised his eyebrow at the request. 'That's hardly necessary, major, we have vox-officers here.'

'Major, these are my men, I must insist.'

Brooce shook his head, but he replied. 'Very well, you have my permission.'

'Thank you, major.' Stanhope then turned to Carson, and Brooce himself felt a chill from the cold look in the lieutenant's eyes. 'Lieutenant Carson, I hereby order you to proceed to the naval expedition headed for the Valkyrie's crash-site and communicate our circumstances to Major Roussell in person, and then assist in searching for the missing men as appropriate. Do you understand?'

Carson did, but he did not believe it. He could only stare at Stanhope.

'Major Stanhope,' Brooce spoke up, 'simply arrange for the message to be transmitted to Major Roussell. It is entirely unnecessary to send the lieutenant out in person.'

'However, major,' Stanhope countered, 'such a communication might be intercepted by the enemy. If Mouse and Red are still alive and undetected, informing the enemy of their existence and their approximate location might put them at far greater risk.'

'Intercepted by the enemy?' Brooce said, incredulous. 'The only communication devices these savages use are the two rocks they bang together!'

'Nevertheless, I think you will find that it is a generally acceptable concern and, given that this is now my responsibility, I am justified in my orders.'

Brooce exhaled sharply in irritation but complied. 'Very well, major. It is your responsibility.'

Brooce, having exhausted his patience and the time he could spare concerning a mere two men that morning, said nothing more and moved off to deal with one of the other dozen urgent issues requiring his attention. As he went, Carson stepped over to Stanhope and eyed him up and down. The major appeared quite different this morning. He still wore the same unexceptional uniform of an ordinary trooper and, like all the rest of them, had two days' stubble on his face, but he appeared sharper, he stood straight, he was in focus.

'I'm obliged to you,' Carson told him simply.

Stanhope nodded a fraction. 'Go and find your men.'

CARSON GATHERED UP Forjaz, who had remained standing beside his tent. He needed someone to watch his back out there and Forjaz was probably the closest to Red in the company, besides Carson himself. Five minutes after that, he'd requisitioned a Chimera transport and a driver from one of Captain Deverril's armoured fist squads. Neither Stanhope nor Brooce had authorised it, but Deverril had given him what he wanted almost before he could tell him why.

The driver began his prayer to the Chimera's machine-spirit, but then caught the look on Carson's face and condensed the remaining twenty benedictory verses into a single command, slammed the ignition control and brought the engine roaring to life.

They quickly found the tracks of the naval expedition, heading straight in the direction of the crash-site. Roussell had a half-hour head start, yet Carson directed the driver onto a different route. Carson knew he could not afford to catch up with the expedition directly. Roussell could, and most likely would, just accept the message and order him straight back again. He had to get around them, and ahead. Until Roussell saw him, he was free.

Carson, looking out the Chimera's open hatch, peered intently past the strange, bulbous landscape of lichen, thorny toadstools and less recognisable types of fungi. At this hour just the day before he had been confronted with this weird xenos world for the first time; now he was already used to it and ignored the vivid colours and strange shapes, searching only for the dull grey of Brimlock uniforms.

INTERLUDE

STANHOPE SAT IN the darkness and waited for his men to come and kill him. He sat on his bed and cradled the distress ticker in his arms as he watched the messages appear, one by one, which told him his fellows were dead.

The orders had come through the day before. There was a black-out on all but the most critical communications. All commanding officers were to take personal charge of the signals room in each barrack. The doors were to be barred and no men were to be allowed in there under any circumstances. Command was desperate to contain the unrest, reasoning that news of one regiment's turn would spur the others to action.

Command was correct, but their orders were far too late. Hacher's network was perfectly able to transmit their messages wherever they wished. All it did was allow them free rein and seal the officers off away from their men.

The orders were pointless, but Stanhope had to follow them anyway. He had moved his bunk into the signals room so he could spend the night there. He did not bother to bar the door. He was the one Brimlock officer in the regiment; if his men wanted him dead then a single door would not stop them.

He had lain down, but could not sleep. He had kept his uniform on; if they came for him he refused to die in a night-shirt. He had paced back and forth across the small chamber. He tried standing still, but he found himself stamping his foot in agitation. All across the barracks his margoes were talking, arguing, making the decision that would either condemn him or condemn themselves.

He was desperate to go to them. Six times throughout the night, he took a hold of the door to leave and go to his men and hash it out with them. Emperor damn him, he agreed with them! He did not want to move against his own, but those were the orders and orders had to be obeyed!

There could be no latitude, no room for discretion in this matter. If there was then this entire campaign, the entire crusade would fall apart under self-questioning and hesitation. He had his orders and he had given them to his men. He could not go to them now and negotiate them. He had been their commanding officer for seven years; they either trusted him as he trusted his superiors, or his rank was trash. He had to wait.

He had tried to activate the vox, but all the lines were dead. All the other equipment had been deactivated as well. His only companion was the distress ticker.

The ticker served a single function. If a particular code was not entered at certain times each day, it sent a powerful signal to every other ticker and then melted itself down. It was the last resort if every other means of communication had failed. He had never even seen a message appear on it before. Each signal was short, carrying as little information as possible to avoid aiding the enemy. Its only use was if you knew the context.

There was no doubt in Stanhope's mind as to the context at present. Every message was a regiment that had mutinied. Every message was a signal that the men had killed their commander. The check-time had come and he had entered his code, then he had lifted the ticker from the desk and gone to sit on the bed and wait for the numbers to appear.

Minutes went past and then the ticker started to hammer and the first digits appeared:

203076

That was the 452nd under Colonel Exton. Stanhope didn't know him. The ticker hammered again:

583139

That was the 731st under Colonel Edmunds. Stanhope had met him once at a formal. Stanhope had met him, his woman and his young children. He prayed silently for them.

557096

That was the 1109th. Another auxilia regiment, but not from Marguerite, from Icena. He swore, he and Major King had taken their commands at the same time. He had known the man for years.

100120

Stanhope could not believe his eyes. That was the 47th under the fearsome Colonel Terrace. Every officer knew him, he had commanded the 47th ever since Brimlock. His men could not have turned against him. It must be a mistake. If his regiment could turn then any of them could.

The numbers kept appearing, but Stanhope could not keep looking. He put the ticker down on the bed and wrapped his blanket around it to try to silence it. He could not pull it off the wall, as it would send its own signal. He put his head in his hands and waited for the hammering of the ticker to be replaced by a hammering at his door.

The alarm on his chronometer sounded. It was reveille. In a few minutes his men were supposed to be lined up outside in the courtyard where he was supposed to read them the orders of the day. The men wouldn't have to burst in. He had to go to them.

Stanhope clambered to his feet. Aside from his bed, he had brought nothing else from his quarters. He had no toiletries and no new uniform to replace the one he had spent the night in. He rubbed his face to hide the moisture that had appeared on his cheeks and straightened himself as best he could.

The only weapon he had with him was his regular sidearm, a standard issue laspistol. He left it off. It wouldn't make any difference anyhow. He caught his breath and exhaled and inhaled. Then he opened the door and stepped out.

The light of the dawn hid the courtyard from him. He blinked and shaded his eyes with his hand. His men were already there. They stood in silence, not in their ranks but in a loose arc around his door. They stared at him.

Stanhope fought down the urge to fight for breath. He did not dare say a word. Instead, he stepped forwards and looked for his second-in-command, Sub Pagedar.

A couple of the margoes stood to one side and there he was. He had fought by Stanhope's side for seven years. They had not been commander and second, Stanhope had never treated their relationship as such. They had been partners and together they had led the regiment to greatness. But now, Stanhope had led them here.

Pagedar stepped forwards. He carried no weapon but the heavy blade by his side. Stanhope kept his head high and forced his eyes to stay open. Even now, Stanhope did not blame him. He was doing what his men willed. They had made their decision, but Stanhope could not stand aside.

Pagedar took a grip on the hilt of his fell-cutter and, with practised ease, drew it smoothly, high into the air.

CHAPTER TWENTY

Impact Crater, Tswaing, Voor pacification
Stage 1 Day 19

WITH ROUSSELL AND Carson away on their errands, Brooce commenced with the main objective of the day: the destruction of the rok and the burial of this last remnant of the Waaagh that had interrupted the Ellinor Crusade. Mulberry and his sappers took charge once more, just as they had done so many times before in this expedition. Their squads descended into the vertical pit the orks had dug, in order to ascertain the best detonation locations, both at the bottom of the pit and within the warrens drilled through the rok at the bottom. Mulberry knew that Brooce did not care for economy or style, he just wanted it done in a day. He split his sappers into as many teams as possible and sent them in, while Brooce provided a platoon of Guardsmen for each for protection.

Brooce kept Carson's company out of the expedition, and so they were given the duty of burning the many ork bodies left in the crater. While his men felt slighted, the other companies looked at them with envy. They dropped down into the earth with flamers, grenades and explosive charges, expecting one final harrowing close-quarter battle.

Their expectations turned out to be incorrect. The orks, when they had retreated, had gone away from the crater and into the fungus. None of them had decided to make a fruitless last stand at the bottom of a hole. When the men of these companies emerged, and while their sappers gathered furiously comparing notes, they shared stories of what they had seen: the entire rok had become one great mausoleum, dead orks, real orks, none of these new-spawn whelps, lay in every chamber. Their exploration of the rok revealed nothing more than what the first Voorjer expedition had seen. Endless caverns of desiccated bodies, fully grown orks carrying guns and grenades, equipped with crude bionics and with hangars full of war machines that had been reduced to scrap in the impact. The original reports to Crusade Command had been wrong. No one had survived the crash. Every single ork that the 11th had faced and killed had grown here in the soil of Voor.

When the sappers were ready again, the platoons followed them back in, making half-hearted complaints about the chill and gloom down there, but in truth relieved not to have to endure the heavy, noxious task. It was after they had descended again that Stanhope approached Blanks.

'Private Stones?'

'Yes, major?'

'Walk with me a while,' Stanhope offered. Blanks dumped the corpse he had been dragging and went with him.

'You did well yesterday,' Stanhope began. 'Quick, decisive, perfect instincts. It reminded me of how an officer should be.'

'I'm just newly assigned,' Blanks replied guardedly, not knowing where Stanhope was heading with this line of conversation.

'Not just newly assigned. New to everything, isn't that right? Clean slate. Mind a blank. And yet you fight as though you were born to it. You give orders as though you're used to having them obeyed. You can size up a tactical situation in an instant. And you haven't called me or any other officer 'sir'. You're a man with a mystery about him.'

Blanks considered it.

'Then I suppose that makes us even then,' he replied.

Stanhope looked at him, puzzled.

'Your private soldier's uniform?' Blanks explained. 'That sword you wear? You like people to know there's a mystery about you as well.'

Stanhope looked out across the crater. 'There's no mystery about me, Blanks. Everybody knows my story. You just have to ask them.'

'Well, I never did.'

Stanhope paused for a few moments. 'Were you at Cawnpore, Blanks?'

'I don't know.'

'Of course you don't. Well, I was. I was there for the fighting. I was there for the mutinies. I was there for what came afterwards. This sword,' Stanhope reached down to the fell-cutter on his hip, 'I was given this sword there. I was given it by the most honourable man I've ever known. He was a margo. You know what a margo is?'

'The Brimlock auxiliaries from Marguerite.'

'Hah,' Stanhope gave a hollow laugh. 'I believe if I asked every trooper in the regiment, I would receive no politer description than that.'

Blanks shrugged as if to say that others' opinions were no reflection on his.

'We "discovered" them on their world,' Stanhope described. 'Emperor knows how long ago, perhaps before the Imperium found us even. Once we'd taken it we renamed it after our saint, then we took their men to fight in our wars. And you know the strangest thing? If there was one here, and you asked him how he felt about that, you know what he would say? He would say he was grateful for all we men of Brimlock had done for him. It's so strange. We hold the fell-cutters in this mixture of fear, awe and contempt as well. And yet all they feel towards us is gratitude.'

Blanks stayed quiet. Stanhope had decided to take him into his confidence and did not need prompting.

'That was my regiment,' Stanhope continued. 'The 1201st. I was a captain in the 33rd when they offered it to me. Not only my majority, but the command of a regiment of my own to boot. My fellows in the 33rd said I was mad. They told me that no one comes back from the auxilia; I'd be stuck there, branded a "margo officer", I'd never make it back to the line. I didn't care. I just wanted to command. They'd be my regiment, the 1201st, Stanhope's Own…'

Again he paused as the memories came back to him. 'They were mine for seven years and they were the greatest, the most glorious, of my life. We blazed a trail across half a dozen planets. The fell-cutters were known before us, they were legend, but we were the ones that made the legend live again. For the troopers who fought beside us, a fell-cutter was no longer a story, a fable; they were flesh and blood creatures to fear when they opposed you and be thankful for when they were your allies.

'I wonder if that was the reason why we were sent to Cawnpore. As if one legend might defeat another,' he continued, his tone darkening. 'Cawnpore was a mess. It was a fortress world, a whole planet of dug-outs, traps and ambushes. A whole planet designed to bleed an army of men. But Crusade Command, Ellinor himself, decided he wanted it. He wanted it because it was so infamous. If he could take that planet from the Karthadasim, he thought, then a half-dozen of their allied worlds would surrender. They'd see how much punishment his armies could take and yet still emerge victorious. The assault force certainly demonstrated the punishment. They fell short at the victory.

'A dozen Brimlock regiments went in to reinforce them. Two dozen went in after that to reinforce the first batch of reinforcements. The Brimlock general wanted the prize, wanted so badly to please Ellinor, that he threw every single regiment he could pressure, bargain or bribe from the others into that poisonous place.

'Eventually, he got his victory, but when we dragged the Kartha defenders into the light we were appalled at how few of them there were. And when the number of casualties it had taken to win was counted, even Ellinor baulked at the cost. Needless to say the Karthadasim's allies were not overawed. Ellinor cancelled his inspection of the troops there, aborted the campaign decoration that was being designed, sent orders to switch us all to different warzones as quickly as we could be ferried away.

'The transport shuttles came to evacuate the first regiment due to leave. It was the 67th under Colonel Carmichael. But before Carmichael left, he had one last piece of business. On the final day of the pacification, one of his majors had refused to order his men to charge over a minefield. The pacification was almost over. Everyone knew it. The whole attack would have been irrelevant.

'Carmichael, though, would not listen. Right or wrong, his orders were to be obeyed. He lined up a firing squad, three men drawn by lot from each of that major's platoons, the very men he'd saved, and Carmichael gave them the order to fire.

'The men did nothing. Carmichael told them then that he would have them all shot if they refused to fire and ordered them again. They still refused. And then the major, standing there against the wall, shouted the order himself. And *that* order, the men obeyed and the major died.

'Carmichael would not let it rest, however. He had been defied. He ordered a platoon to round up the firing squad and put them under arrest, ready for execution. The first platoon he ordered refused to do it, and so did the next. Every platoon in his regiment refused to arrest the men of the firing squad.

Carmichael found he had run out of men and so he fled to the Brimlock general. He labelled it a mutiny and called in the storm troopers. The storm troopers went in to destroy the 67th, but found their barracks deserted. They'd fled. Some had gone out into Cawnpore, into the defence-systems and tunnels they had learned so well; the rest went to ground in other units, finding sympathetic Guardsmen and even officers. So many regiments were there, so many men had been lost, they found it easy to switch identities and conceal their past.

'The storm troopers went hunting for those of the 67th who had stayed together, but there weren't enough of them to cover the ground. The Brimlock general ordered the rest of us to be brought in, our redeployments delayed to squash this hint of rebellion. None of us wanted to find them, though, and so we obediently stumbled around the planet, to all intents deaf, dumb and blind.

'But then the rumour went around that the 67th had established some kind of free-port where the Imperium had no authority and any Guardsman who came to them would be free of his duty to the Emperor. Men started disappearing from the regiments. More rumours went around that the 67th had discovered a Kartha-dasim treasure trove, the wealth of an empire that all the defences of Cawnpore had been designed to protect. It was a lie, but it was what so many Guardsmen wanted to hear. We heard the name of the ringleader. Hacher, his name was, though that itself was another fake. There was no Hacher in the 67th or any other any regiment on Cawnpore.'

'It's a verb,' Blanks suddenly spoke up. 'It's from a Karthadasim word.'

'What does it mean?' Stanhope asked.

'To chop, to cut to pieces.'

Stanhope nodded and then continued. 'He was the coordinator of the 67th, obviously, a pseudonym to pro-tect whomever was leading them. But the name became more than just a cover. Hacher became a ghost. A spectre. Whenever men went missing, Hacher had taken them. Whenever Chimeras broke down, Hacher had sabotaged them. He was a spirit, a joke, a traitor, a hero all at once.

'The inevitable happened. One of the 67th turned and exposed much of their network, including the location of their free-port. We were finally going to turn our guns on our own. We were marched to our preparation posi-tions and then readied ourselves for the worst. Hacher knew we were there. Whatever he could do to stop us, he'd do it that night, everything he could destroy, every man he could take, every regiment he could turn.

'The next morning I came out for inspection. That was when you found out how badly you were hit, how many men had slipped away during the night. Some of the other regiments hadn't reported in at all. The men had mutinied, killed their officers and gone to join Hacher and his cause.

'My men didn't even waver. They came out. All of them. Every man. Even the injured, even the bed-ridden came out, leaning on their comrades, some of them were even carried. But they wanted to be there. They wanted to be counted. They wanted me to know they were loyal. I was so proud of them that day. The most senior margo amongst them, Sub Pagedar, he had known I had stayed awake that night and told me that he was full of shame that I ever doubted them. He stood at their head and he drew his sword and he handed it to me. He took an oath then that the sword would be mine until he and his men had proved that they would never side against me as long as the Emperor and Saint Marguerite gave them breath.

'We went out to battle. I had just received our orders. Because of Hacher's infiltrators, every piece of information regarding the battle-plan was kept separate. None of us had any idea what the regiments around us were doing, where they would be. We only had to pray that the general in command knew what he was doing.

'I sent my regiment in at the preordained time. The orders specified that I myself should hold back and keep passing reports to the general's staff. My men were to attack without relenting. I knew we would be one of the first in; it was so early in the day. I thought they needed me to stay back so I could spot weaknesses in the enemy positions, that they needed my men to make the crack for other regiments to move up and exploit. It turned out that all the general needed from my men was for them to die.

'Every defender knew we were the fell-cutters, every defender knew to fear us. Every gun they had was turned on us. My fell-cutters surged into the killing-ground because I told them that the other regiments would be advancing after. But there were no regiments behind us.

It was when I saw the storm troopers burn in from high altitude that I realised what our role was. We were the diversion. I tried to order my men back, tried to get them away, but they kept on advancing. They were fell-cutters, no hesitation, no retreat. That was what had made them such a good decoy.

'I was still stood there, rooted to the spot, when the extraction team came and got me.'

Stanhope went quiet and Blanks ventured a question.

'And why had the general kept you back?'

Stanhope looked up into the clouds. 'I asked him that, when he voxed around all the regimental officers to give his congratulations. He told me he hadn't thought about it much, that maybe it was because he didn't think that a Brimlock officer should die amongst a pack of margoes.'

'And Hacher?'

'The storm troopers got him. That's what the general said. The whole place was kept closed off after the fight, so who knows? A person named Hacher had made himself the figurehead of the mutiny, and therefore he had to be killed. But who knows if he ever really existed? Maybe he did, maybe he didn't. Maybe there was a dozen of them all using a single name to try and create a new legend. Perhaps that was why the general and Ellinor tried so hard to scratch every last memory of Cawnpore from the crusade.

'After that, I thought I had been through it all. It had been the worst for me, but for everyone else the real horror came after. Hacher was gone, the free-port was buried, but what about all those other regiments who had refused to attack? Who had been driven to capture or kill their leaders? How many more were guilty and how many more were there to be punished?'

* * *

THE ENGINE WAS drowning. The same detritus and spores churned up by the tanks in their charge to the crater, that had choked the infantrymen struggling behind, were now congesting those same engines. Forjaz had tired of swearing at it and was now working alongside the driver, who was up to his armpits clearing out the fungus while Carson kept watch.

There was nothing he could do. Short of abandoning the Chimera entirely and ordering them to proceed on foot, which would slow them even further and rob them of the transport's defences, there was nothing he could do. Nothing but stand there and watch and listen as the others worked around him.

Was this what it was going to be like, he wondered, when the myecyclone finally took hold and didn't let go? Just to watch? Just to listen? Just to receive and never to act? If it was, then it was no life for him. He would end it himself if no enemy could. If Reeve still lived then he could take him along with him. Just reach out to him, hold him close and pull the pin from a grenade in his pocket. If only he could be sure that, being denied their culprit, his avengers wouldn't extract their due from his men.

They were all that was left to him. Red had said it right, the night before. Twenty years of fighting, but how many more had passed for those back home. The dating of events in a galaxy where every inhabited world was a tiny speck in an ocean of darkness would always be susceptible to local practicalities. What do the workers on one world care that another world has twenty-four hours in a day if they have twenty-six? To them, a day will be when their morning begins and their night ends. Their years turn upon their seasons and their crops, not upon the rotation of a far-distant planet around a far-distant star. The communiqués from Crusade Command were of no benefit as they referenced everything from the year the Ellinor Crusade began. They said twenty years had passed, but what was that back on Brimlock? Was it the same? Five more? Ten more? Fifty? A hundred?

Crusade Command would never tell you, it wasn't in their interests. They wanted their common men to feel connected, wanted them to feel as though the world they fought for was still the one they had left. Crusade Command would not want them to know how isolated they were, and Carson wagered that the men did not wish to know either. They knew they would never go home, but that did not mean they did not draw strength from knowing that *their* home and those they left behind were still out there.

They're all dead, aren't they. Those were Red's words. And that meant that his men, indeed this whole regiment, were more than the survivors of an army; they were the survivors of an entire generation. He would not give up a single one of them, and he would damn any who thought to leave them.

The engine spluttered back to life with an oath from Forjaz and an alleluia from the driver. It didn't matter, though, Carson knew. They were going to be too late.

STANHOPE FINALLY CONCLUDED his tale and he and Blanks returned to the rest of the men.

'Why did you tell me that?' Blanks asked as they walked.

'Because I wanted you to know. I wanted you to understand why I am the way I am. Yesterday, you followed me up Acorn. You were watching out for me. That's right, isn't it?' Stanhope stopped and regarded him carefully, the hard features, the heavy brow, coupled with the incongruous innocent stare he had.

'Yes, I was. And I am.'

'I want to be able to trust you. And the first step in that is you being able to trust me.'

'Thank you,' Blanks replied; he did not know what else to say.

'Good,' Stanhope said and started walking again, but Blanks stopped him.

'In that spirit, major, perhaps there is something I should tell you.'

Stanhope turned back to him. The innocence in his gaze was gone.

'I took them.'

'What?'

'That stuff you use. Those leaves. I took them and destroyed them.'

Stanhope gaped slightly. 'When?'

Blanks shrugged. 'Does it matter?'

'Then why?' Stanhope demanded.

Blanks contemplated it for a second. 'Because I would never allow a soldier under my command to go into battle whilst intoxicated.'

'I'm not under your command!' Stanhope declared.

'You're certainly not under your own,' Blanks countered and continued before Stanhope could protest further. 'I'm watching out for you, major, in every way. You want to trust me, then this is part of it. The rest of them, Carson, the colonel, they want you out of your head so you'll cause them no trouble. They want you passive. I do not.'

CARSON'S CHIMERA HAD finally made it to Zdzisław's crash-site and, Marguerite be praised, Roussell and the naval party were nowhere to be seen. He could only assume that they had been struck by even worse mechanical breakdowns than he had.

Even though Zdzisław had crashed more than a week

previously, the crash-site still had an air of immediacy about it. His and his co-pilot's bodies were still bound within their harnesses. The ground was still stained where the vehicle's fluids had poured out. It was only if you looked closely that you could see the rugged algae trying to forge new life on the detritus closest to the ground.

Carson did examine it carefully and he found what he was looking for. The impression of a ring that had been removed, and pockets opened that would normally be closed. The body had been looted by an expert and, as Carson believed that an ork after the ring would have more likely yanked off the entire finger or even arm, the looter had been a human.

Now he knew Mouse had been here, he could guess that Red had been there as well. He looked through the ground. There were ork footprints everywhere. The tracks crossed and criss-crossed and were blurred and smudged where a struggle had taken place. Then they had headed off. Carson looked in that direction and was ready to return to his Chimera when finally Roussell and the naval party hove into view.

A HALF-HOUR LATER the news flashed back to the Brimlock camp on Bitterleaf. Second Lieutenant Carson had been placed under arrest. The charge: the assault and attempted murder of Major Roussell.

CHAPTER TWENTY-ONE

Impact Crater, Tswaing, Voor pacification
Stage 1 Day 19

'THIS IS AN outrage,' Carson stated again as he sat in the sealed-off rear compartment of a Chimera.

'I have made a note of your feelings on the subject already, lieutenant,' Brooce said a trifle wearily.

'Then let me out of here so that I may return to my men,' Carson said in a stern tone that attracted a look of pique from Brooce.

'I can't do that.'

'Yes, you can,' Carson shot back with even greater irritation. 'You have the authority.'

'Yes, you're right' Brooce agreed, testily. 'I could release you; however, I choose not to do so. And do you know why I'm choosing not to do so?'

Carson knew exactly why. 'It's because, even though you know he's a coward and a liar, you won't tell Roussell that you think his charges are a pile of stinking–'

'You're wrong, lieutenant,' Brooce cut him off. 'It's because of your reputation.'

'My reputation? As what? A damn good officer? One of the best in this whole regiment?'

'It is your reputation as a killer.' Brooce snapped. 'A killer of your fellow officers. How many has it been?'

'I don't know what you're talking about.'

'All your duelling "partners"?'

'They were private matters of honour, and how are you, Roussell or the colonel in any position to judge me on those?'

'Captain Blundell?'

'He was killed by the enemy,' Carson asserted.

'An alarming majority of the commanders you dislike succumb to uncommonly accurate enemy fire. Much as Reeve did yesterday.'

'How is the poor commissar?' Carson asked with mock concern.

'If I were you, lieutenant, I would not show too much interest in Commissar Reeve's well-being. It may be misconstrued. Sometimes I wonder if that was why the colonel gave you Stanhope in the first place. What spared him?'

Carson did not reply.

'Let me lay it out for you, Carson. Tell me what you think. This man, this officer of such reputation, who is also known to own a fierce loyalty to his men, is hot on the pursuit of two he has lost. He's then told by a senior officer he despises that he may not continue because there is need of his vehicle. Roussell is adamant that, when he gave you that order, you started to pull one of your pistols on him.'

'I think that if I'd wanted him dead, he wouldn't have even seen me pull my weapon,' Carson snarled. 'He'd be laid out in the fungus with a smoking hole in his chest.'

Brooce shook his head sadly. 'You don't understand, Carson. It's sentiments such as those that has every other officer in this regiment running scared. You know it. You enjoy it. Lording it over them, while you're still only a second lieutenant. I've already hauled Deverril over the coals this morning for letting you go with the Chimera in the first place. They all think you're out to kill them. Because it's only if they're all dead that you'll ever command more than a paltry company.

'I can't release you, Carson,' Brooce continued, 'because every officer in this regiment who dislikes you thinks you did it. And even the ones you count as your friends think you *could* have done it.'

Carson couldn't bear to look at Brooce any more. 'So, I'm to be sacrificed on the altar of general suspicion.'

'Not at all,' Brooce replied. 'As soon as we get back to Dova, the colonel will perform his investigation, have a word with Roussell and the charges will be dropped. A misunderstanding. After all, he has need of good officers for the next phase. Especially officers who perhaps have the attention of Voorjers close to their governor. Don't treat it as an arrest, Carson, rather a comfortable taxi ride home.'

Brooce was not going to budge. Carson could see him making plans for the future, and part of those plans would be to demonstrate that he could control 'wild' officers like him. 'Very well, but I have a price.'

'This is not a negotiation, lieutenant, but go ahead anyway.'

'At least send another party out. My men, if you can't spare any others. Give them the rest of the day to find out what happened.'

Brooce considered his response carefully. 'Colour-Sergeant Towser is a sad loss, and my wife has spoken very highly of Private Chaffey, but it is out of the question. Every single vehicle is being overhauled to cope with these damn spores so it will be ready to function

tomorrow. I'm afraid, lieutenant, there it is. Do you
really expect you'd find them alive in any case?'

MOUSE LOOKED DOWN out of his cage as the latest ork
warband arrived at the encampment. It was the third
one to appear that morning alone, and this one was a
big one, several hundred strong. Their chieftain, his skin
daubed blue with paint, a bone stuck through his nose
and his hair tied in a topknot, marched at their head. He
was a full head taller than his bodyguards either side,
who shoved aside any lesser ork foolish enough to be
standing in their chieftain's path. His warriors further
behind him betrayed their discomfort, however, and
they kept clustered together, eyeing the other warbands
with great distrust.

Mouse had realised that, just a few days before, these
warbands would have been at each other's throats on the
battlefield. Today, though, Mouse had counted orks from
at least four major tribes: the blue faces, the ones with
black war-paint around their eyes, those who draped
themselves only in bones and had brought a giant squig-
beast with them and, the most numerous, those with a
red stripe down across one eye.

Even within these main divisions there were dozens of
different warband variations, markings in yellow, black,
white, red, blue, green and any other colour they could
extract from the strange squig creatures and the fungus
that grew wherever they travelled. Like the blue-faces,
they did not mix or mingle, but sat in their groups, ready
at a moment's notice to hurl themselves at one of the
other warbands. The orkish lust for battle was a powerful
drive indeed.

Whatever was holding them back, Mouse concluded,
must be even greater.

Nothing was going to restrain the blue-face chieftain,

however. He headed straight for the entrenched den at the centre of the encampment. Bodyguards from all the other tribes already stood clustered around it, but they stepped aside as he passed and disappeared inside.

Capture was not a facet of war given much attention in Guard induction. Command knew that the vast majority of opponents viewed captives as good only for enslavement or consumption. The captured Guardsman, if not killed out of hand, most probably faced either torture and sacrifice in the name of dark gods, or being shackled to some xenos engine to endure the most bone-crushing conditions until the last ounce of life was wrung from him.

Guard doctrine, therefore, had only one straightforward instruction in case of capture by the enemy: die quickly. Mouse considered, not for the first time, that a slavish adherence to Guard doctrine was not the right course for him. They had kept him alive for some reason. That must mean they wanted something from him. That meant that he must have something they wanted, and having something they wanted meant that he could bargain. If he could bargain then he could stay alive. It was as simple as that.

Things were not so simple for the fellow occupant of his cage. Mouse at first thought that Red would not survive. He was bleeding a lot, but then head wounds always did. The thought struck Mouse then, that it might be better if he did die. If the orks had just wanted them for food they would have killed them back at the Valkyrie. They obviously wanted them for a purpose. Whatever it was, Mouse knew that Red would resist; it was just the type of man he was, and he would expect Mouse to do the same. He wouldn't understand that it was their chance to survive. Mouse could do it. Mouse could make it. He could provide whatever they wanted from him yet hold back enough to ensure they kept him alive. He could do it, but only on his own, and so he willed the blood to pour quicker from the colour-sergeant's head.

'Just get on and die, old man,' Mouse whispered.

There was a commotion around the den. One of the red stripes had come out and fixed its gaze on Mouse. It started over towards him and a half-dozen more red stripes fell in behind it.

Mouse felt himself freeze. He could only think of fleeing, but there was nowhere to go. He looked down at Red slumped on the cage floor. He grabbed his arm and started shouting in his ear.

'Wake up! Wake up! Wake up! Wake up!'

Red began to stir as the red-stripe warriors lifted open the cage door and then yanked on the leashes tied around the Guardsmen's necks. They pulled Mouse out and then slammed the cage door shut behind him. Making no attempt to lead him, one of the red stripes simply picked him up in the air and started back to the den. He was carried into the dark inside and dropped onto the dirt like a sack. He coughed and spluttered at such treatment, then curled up tight into a ball, protecting himself, fearing an attack at any moment.

When twenty seconds passed and none came, he carefully stole a glance around him. In the murky light, he saw that he was surrounded by orks. They were watching him silently, a few with a trace of xenos interest, the rest with a bland expression of disinterest. The ork in the centre was the largest. It wore no war-paint whatsoever and carried only an almighty metal cleaver. It prodded Mouse with a heavy jab from the handle of the cleaver and Mouse scrabbled to his feet, yelping in protest.

A low grumble rose from the circle. Mouse retreated a couple of steps, then sprung around as he sensed the orks behind him. He spun a few more times, trying to keep them all in his line of sight. He felt a solid, slightly spongy, hand carefully take his. He turned and saw that one of the orks was holding his left hand, appearing fascinated by it. Mouse backed away a step, but the ork followed, its step betraying a slight limp. Mouse let it explore his hand and it turned it round and peered at it all the closer. Then it took a grip with its second hand on Mouse's pinkie finger and, with a swift thrust, yanked it back.

Mouse screamed in pain and dragged his hand away from the ork's clutches, cradling it in his arms. Another low grumble reverberated around the circle.

'Listen! Listen!' Mouse blathered. 'You don't have to hurt me. Just tell me what you want! Maybe, maybe, we can work something out?'

The orks watched him as he spoke, but as soon as he finished they all turned back to the largest of their number. The red stripe who had carried him in there stepped into the circle. It held Mouse's lasgun above its head. It looked to the big ork and the big ork nodded. The red stripe held out the lasgun and gave it to Mouse, and the other orks started watching him again.

Mouse was confused. This was not how he expected it would go. He held the lasgun limply in his hand. The big ork, who must be the warboss, Mouse realised, said something to him and pointed at the red stripe. Mouse didn't understand. The warboss repeated itself, stomping its cleaver for emphasis, and pointing at the red stripe even more emphatically. A third grumble started around the circle, but the red stripe suddenly launched itself at Mouse, bawling at him. Mouse instinctively fired and the beam of red light exploded in the small space. The red stripe fell growling to the floor. The other orks in the circle were interested now and all went to reach for the lasgun. Mouse whirled it at them, this way and that.

He had a gun, he could get out of there. All he needed was to...

A thorny hand from behind him wrenched it from his grasp and then started passing it around the others.

'Smak!' the warboss declared, and the others paused and slowly passed the gun over to him. The red stripe picked itself up off the floor, hand clasped over the lasburn on its side. It dragged itself across to the warboss and then presented its injury. The warboss stared at it, and then stared at the gun. It hooked a finger around the trigger and pulled in careful imitation of Mouse. The red beam flashed and a part of the roof of the den began to smoulder. Again there was a chorus of interest from the others.

The warboss turned around. Behind him, Mouse saw a banner pole shoved into the ground. On its head was a totem, another sculpted orkish glyph. The warboss raised the lasgun up towards the totem, almost as though it was an offering to the gods. The totem glowed a dull red and Mouse sniffed the distinctive acrid smell of burning tech-equipment. The warboss turned back to the circle, pulled the trigger again and this time nothing happened. It tried it a second, then a third time. Still nothing. It looked around the circle, and this time the orks all made a sound of near agreement. The warboss held up the lasgun and then crumpled it in its single massive hand.

'Waa-Choppa,' it said. 'Na Choppa!' And it let the pieces fall to the ground.

A Valkyrie flew in Mulberry's munitions. They were loaded into Chimeras and ferried to the pit. Brooce left the troopers long enough for the sappers to lay their charges and then, after a very careful count to ensure all men were present and correct, Mulberry pushed the detonator. In an instant, the efforts of the Stone Smashas to unearth the falling star that had brought their kind to this place were annulled. Likewise, the interference that had protected that filthy cradle of xenos life was finally silenced.

It was not over. It could never be over with the orks. The whole continent was infected. It would have to be watched. The Voorjers would not be enough; it would require the veterans of the Brimlock 11th and then, in a few years, it would be the turn of their children, then their grandchildren, and then their great-grandchildren after that. And, eventually, perhaps there would be sufficient manpower to raise a whole new regiment: a regiment of scouts and ork-hunters that could proudly add their strength to the Brimlock auxilia. Whether the Voorjers appreciated it or not, the Imperial Guard was here to stay.

Should the Voorjers not appreciate it, not welcome the imposition of a permanent armed force on their world that would inevitably evolve into the planet's new dominant faction, then the Brimlock 11th would have to assert their rightful position over these separatists at the point of the sword.

That was the next phase. Arbulaster knew it. Brooce knew it. Carson had guessed it, and so had Van Am. The generous Imperium had finally granted their loyal Brimlock soldiers their prize; they just had to take it first.

THE BRIMLOCK COLUMN broke camp an hour after dawn the next day. The most seriously wounded, aside from Commissar Reeve who had remained the guest of the betrayed Captain Ledbetter, had been airlifted by Valkyrie back to Dova. The stable wounded were given berths in Chimeras co-opted from their regular duty to act as ambulances. They headed out first, along with the pitiful remnants of the armoured company, while

Mulberry and his sappers strode ahead of them in their construction Sentinels to ensure the trail was clear.

One Chimera that did not find itself transporting the wounded contained only a single passenger, with three guards. Major Roussell was rigid in his implementation of Guard doctrine regarding the captivity of Second Lieutenant Carson. Roussell did not want him marching with his former company, he did not want his men to even see him, and so he locked him away in a Chimera which drove alongside Roussell's own company in the centre of the column. Carson's company were banished to the far rearguard where, Roussell considered, with some luck they might never even make it back.

Most of the Brimlock 11th, however, cared nothing for the enmity between Roussell and Carson. They were finally at liberty to think of the future. They had survived where so many million men had not. They had paid their service to the Emperor and now they could live for all those they had lost. The jungle, which had first appeared to them as a nightmare of gloom and danger, would now be remembered as the setting for a great victory, and when Private Heal began to hum, he found he could do so uninterrupted, for there was no colour-sergeant there to quiet him. For almost all of them, Voor would become a home for them and the families they would raise, and they would have years of comfort and plenty to offset the two decades of hardship and horror that they had endured.

If there was any justice in the galaxy.

LANCE-CORPORAL BOWLER SAT in the turret gunner's position inside his Chimera and watched the jungle go past. He did not think much about the future. He knew it would contain pretty much the same as the past. He was a Brimlock Dragoon through and through; he didn't want out, he wanted to stay in. He was in a lot better position than some of the poor souls they were carrying. Two arms, two legs and one protruding organ was what Bowler had managed to keep hold of all these years. It didn't matter how old or decrepit he got, he figured, so long as he could still sit in this chair, point the multi-laser and pull the trigger.

The Guard had given him a lot. 'Starve, steal or soldier' the poster outside the rookeries had said. Well, he had tried the first two and found that the last option had let him live far better and far longer than running with the rook-gangs.

He knew the driver, Baker, sitting beside him, felt the same way. They'd done well by each other, and planned to stick to it even after this. Bowler and Baker, there had been a few jokes about that when they were first assigned together back in the 371st. It didn't help, either, that their commanding officer was Brooce. A few fists had to be thrown before the other crews realised that there really was no humour to be made from the coincidence.

The 371st, now there had been a proper Brimlock regiment, before they were consolidated at least. Every company had its Chimeras, the whole regiment was an armoured fist, fast, hard-hitting, none of these pathetic foot-sloggers slowing everyone down. They were called the Brimlock Dragoons after all, not the Brimlock Draggers–

'Fire!' Baker shouted suddenly. Acting on instinct, Bowler's trigger finger twitched, before he held it back.

'What?' he wanted to know, but Baker was busy grabbing the vox.

'Chimera one-zero to Chimera zero-five. Tabor, you're on fire!'

Bowler twisted to see. It was true, there was the unmistakeable red glow of flames coming from the underside of the Chimera ahead. The driver tried to swerve off the trail, but ran out of room before he could fully make it off. Baker swerved the other way, voxing the rest of the transports to hold position and calling Mulberry's Sentinels back.

Bowler pulled out the extinguisher, cracked the hatch and shimmied out onto the dirt. He ran over to blast the flames before they could reach the fuel tanks while Baker went to open the back hatch and evacuate the wounded. Bowler gave the fire a full burst; it dimmed for a few moments and then grew wilder. He hammered on the side of the driver's cabin.

'Tabor, get your arse out here!'

Tabor appeared, eyes wide, at the window.

'Fire,' he said.

'I know that,' Bowler ranted. 'Get out and help!'

'You're on fire,' he said.

'No, *you're* on fire,' Bowler replied.

'No...' Tabor repeated. 'You're... *on fire!*'

Bowler felt the heat on his forehead, went to touch his helmet and burned his hand on his targeter. He dropped the extinguisher, yanked off his smouldering helmet, turned around, and threw it to the ground. He swore violently, looked up, and saw a burst of flame coming from under his Chimera.

'God-Emperor,' he whispered. Tabor was trying to fight his fire, but it was useless.

'The wounded!' Bowler shouted at him as he grabbed the extinguisher he'd discarded. 'Get the wounded out!'

Bowler ran back to the rear hatch of his own Chimera. He pulled it open and got a face-full of smoke. The wounded pushed past him, dragging each other out of the burning vehicle. He looked back down the column for help, but the first half-dozen Chimeras were in the same way, their crews desperately trying to battle the flames.

He looked ahead and saw something that would haunt him for the remaining few moments of his life: a Sentinel, still tottering back to respond to the distress call, burning in a column of fire with Mulberry's blackened corpse still stock upright at the controls.

In the jungle, Choppa lowered his totem and the red light that glowed from it faded. Its job done, Choppa raised his cleaver and roared the charge.

CHAPTER TWENTY-TWO

*Ambush site, Jungle Trail, Tswaing, Voor
pacification Stage 1 Day 20*

THE NEWS CAME through garbled over the vox-receiver.
Major Roussell's comms officer tried to make sense of it,
but Roussell grabbed the receiver off him and listened
himself. The column was under attack. The Chimeras
at the head had been halted and immobilised in some
manner; the jerry-rigged tanks were being attacked by
blue-faced orks shoving explosive spores and nests of
hornet-like creatures into hatches and through vision
slits. A substantial number of orks with black war-paint
around their eyes had appeared and were attacking
Brooce's company. Orders were for all companies to
advance and engage as fast as they could.

Roussell passed the orders on to his men and saw
them all grip their weapons a little tighter. It had been
too early to think of the future after all. The orks of Tswaing had one last trick up their sleeves, it seemed. Ahead
of them, Roussell saw Ingoldsby's company advance to
the quick. Then it was Colquhoun's turn, but before any

of his men took another step Colquhoun ordered his company to halt. No sooner had he done so, than Fergus, behind him, did likewise.

Unwilling to push his troops past, Roussell went ahead himself. He strode quickly along the length of Fergus's company and discovered the two captains there.

'What, in Marguerite's name, is the hold-up?' Roussell demanded. 'The column's under attack!'

'Quiet!' Fergus shot back. Neither of them looked round at him; they both had their heads lowered as though listening to the earth. They were a mismatched pair: the black giant and his scarlet dwarf was how their men referred to them as they were often seen together. Only ever out of earshot, though; Colquhoun habitually carried an antiquated heavy halberd with which he ostentatiously cut his enemies into pieces, while the diminutive, red-haired Fergus became a raving berserker in battle, capable of any act of savagery. The terror they inspired, in their own men as much as the enemy, was a secret delight to them both, and each one constantly sought to outperform the other.

It was perhaps this that influenced Roussell not to continue to rant at the two captains from a distance, but to cross over to discover what had caught their attention.

'Yer think so?' Fergus asked his fellow captain quietly.

'For certain,' Colquhoun replied.

'What?' Roussell demanded.

The two captains broke their quiet conversation. Both rose and started shouting orders to their men.

'Sergeants! Get the men in line!'

'Weapons ready!'

'Bayonets! Bayonets! Fix bayonets!'

The sergeants picked up the call and the two companies, driven by the urgency in their captains' voices, snapped to obey. Roussell felt a moment of panic.

'Firm up yer men, major,' Fergus told him. 'They're coming from the south.'

For a split-second Roussell wanted to demand the proper respect from this captain who thought to give him orders, but then he heard the noise, the rumbling from the depths of the jungle, which turned his blood cold.

He hastened back to his men. The urgency of the preparations being taken by the men ahead had unnerved them, but Roussell had previously impressed upon them his disfavour for anticipation of his orders and so they stayed motionless. Roussell cursed them for the caution that he had formerly required from them.

'Get in line!' he bawled at them. 'Ready weapons! Fix bayonets!' His men scrambled gratefully to obey.

Behind his company, he saw Gomery's men quickly follow suit and, behind them, Rosa's Griffons halt in confusion. The chain reaction flowed down the length of the Brimlock column as each man swiftly took the lasgun from his shoulder, slammed his bayonet into its socket and turned to his right to put himself in line. There was no fumbling for magazines as no veteran carried his gun unloaded, but a score of men cursed dumping their heavier weapons on transports so as to save themselves the labour of man-handling them back to Dova.

It would be a matter of just a few minutes for every man to be ready and in position to create a wall of fire and steel facing towards the jungle to the south. It was a few minutes that the Brimlocks did not have.

The distant rumble had grown louder, closer. It grew into a continuous rolling thunder that shook the vines and the leaves. The sergeants were already cautioning men to hold. Whatever its cause, it sounded to each as though it might be their doom. It wasn't fair, they thought, it wasn't just. They had survived their final battle; that was it, they were done. They couldn't die *here*, on the way *home*. The Emperor surely wouldn't allow it.

Animals burst from the jungle, wailing creatures disturbed from their homes and fleeing what was coming after. Lasguns flashed down the column as edgy troopers fired, incinerating the refugees even as they scuttled.

The thunder grew deafening and Roussell glanced behind him, to the jungle on the north side of the track, which appeared identical to the jungle to the south. Not a single gun was pointing in that direction and with the echo from the trees, the sound of the thunder bounced at him from every side.

'God-Emperor,' he muttered to himself, 'let Colquhoun be right.'

Colquhoun was.

'Blessed Marguerite, what are those?' Roussell gasped as the jungle on the south side exploded with creatures. His sergeants did not concern themselves with such questions, only the response.

'FIRE!'

Readied or not, every man brought his weapon up and pulled the trigger. Hundreds of las-shots burned into their raging, wild-eyed attackers, burning the foremost. Those behind stumbled over the blackened corpses, but continued rolling towards the firing Guardsmen; living, angry balls of teeth and claws.

They were not orks. This was not a charge. It was a stampede.

A thousand, two thousand, squig-beasts were being driven into the column, bursting from the shadow of the jungle only a few dozen metres away. Some racing, some bounding, all maddened, tearing into anything that stood in their way. The Brimlock firing discipline collapsed at once, the shouts of sergeants lost beneath the bellowing of the squig-beasts.

Ingoldsby's company, ahead of Colquhoun and Fergus, was caught mid-step, hastening to reach the fighting at the head of the column. The men were taken completely by surprise. The closest whirled to face the new threat too late and the squig-beasts leapt upon them, biting through limbs and tearing through the flesh of those that fell with the wicked claws upon their feet. Those men on the far side of the column could only hear guttural snorts, rips and the screams of their fellows. Their sergeants instinctively shouted to hold, but there were no mere words that could make them stand. They stumbled back and then broke and ran into the cover of the jungle to the north, the squig-beasts trumpeting with relief as the human barrier before them disintegrated.

Fergus and Colquhoun's men fared better, firing a blinding rain of light. Every man fired as quickly as he could, but in their desperation the rigorous routines that had been drilled into them began to fade, and shots began to be snatched too early, before guns had fully recycled. Inhibitors installed years before by Brimlock gunsmiths prevented early discharges and frustrated troopers had to grab at their triggers a second time to fire. Those who had stripped their inhibitors out could fire as fast as their finger could grip, but their rapid shots singed the squig-beasts' flesh instead of bringing them down.

Troopers tried throwing grenades: some short-timed them and so they detonated as they landed, blowing chunks from the squig-beasts; others, in their hurry, did not bother and a few grenades struck the raging squigs and bounced back, cutting down creature and Guardsman alike. The luckless Private Schafe tossed his grenade at the squig leaping high over the bayonet wall to devour him. The grenade flew into the squig's gaping mouth which then closed over his head, teeth chomping down on his torso, before detonating, killing the unfortunate trooper and covering his comrades nearby in a shower of their mixed internals.

Everywhere Roussell looked, the line was starting to buckle. The squig-beasts were dying in their hundreds, but those behind were hemmed in by others either side and so could only continue to throw themselves forwards. Even as they were struck, their bodies smashed into the Guardsmen, crushing some, distracting others, causing gaps in the fields of fire that the next wave could then pour through. Ingoldsby's company had disappeared entirely from view. Fergus and Colquhoun's men were scrabbling, keeping the squigs away at the points of their bayonets. Colquhoun was trying to clear his flank on his own with great sweeps of his halberd knocking the squig-beasts off to the side.

The vox in Roussell's ear was a cacophony of unintelligible orders, oaths and screams. He tried to contact Brooce for instruction, but it was useless. His company faced collapse; the sheer pressure of the stampede smashing against it would break it. He would lose his company and he had no orders to protect him. One way or another it was the end of him. But then somewhere inside, the young officer who, ten years before, had dragged his isolated company for months through the horrors of the mud-valleys of Mespots to earn his place in the colour-guard emerged.

'Company! Form on your section!' He threw the order into the maelstrom. Nothing happened. He stomped down his line, hauling the men of the back row into tighter groups, who in turn hauled in close the men in the rows in front of them. A straight line was not strong enough to withstand the force of the enemy's blow. Instead, he pulled them into deeper pockets until finally the last remaining men of the front rank dived into them.

His line was gone. In its place were a half-dozen spurs with clear channels running between them. The company's firing weakened with their frontage so diminished, but their shots pushed the rampaging squig-beasts away to the side. The squig-beasts in turn confronted by these clusters of steel or the dark jungle beyond, shoved mercilessly on by their fellows behind, chose to make for the jungle, and crushed into the channels.

The men in each cluster pushed away from the beasts charging through on either side, pressing a dozen men into the space previously occupied by four, kneeling, crouching, packed tight together, contorting themselves to have every blade pointed out. A stumbling squig-beast ran itself into the bayonets on the side of one cluster. The force of the blow transferred through to the other side of the cluster where Private Geoffries popped out of the cluster like a cork from a wine bottle and was trampled underfoot, still grasping onto his comrades trying to haul him back in. One cluster dissolved entirely when an unlucky shot caused a squig-beast to cannonball into the front of it, knocking the defending Guardsmen to one side, whilst the Guardsmen behind were too closely packed together to shift their weapons round to defend themselves in time.

Roussell hauled his slack frame on top of his Chimera; from there he had a chance to see and be seen by his men. The guards he had posted inside the vehicle to watch Carson had had the presence of mind to man the turret multi-laser and some of the embedded lasguns that bulged from the hull, and had turned the dozen metres between the vehicle and the jungle into a charnel house.

The noxious smell of incinerated squig-flesh struck him as he clambered forwards. The men in the clusters saw it too. The closest ones tried to edge their groups closer to get behind the protection of the tank's hull; those further away stood no chance of running across as a single body and so lone troopers looked for gaps in the stampede and dived from cluster to cluster, ever closer to the Chimera, like children leaping across stepping stones.

Behind him, Roussell saw that Gomery's men were in a desperate plight. As for Gomery himself, it appeared his mind had finally snapped. He had not even drawn his gun. Instead he was shrilling away, blowing his officer's whistle as though calling foul on the whole attack.

It was nearly done, however. Roussell looked out to the south and saw that the shadows of the squig-beasts coming through the trees were thinning. He might live, he realised, and he grasped at the hope. He fired his pistol somewhere into the mass, the sound of the discharge lost beneath the hiss of burning air from the Chimera's las-fire beneath him.

In the corner of his eye, he noticed a shadow amongst the squig-beasts, a dark green shape running on all fours in their midst. He blinked and the shadow uncoiled into an ork warrior, which impaled its arm on the bayonets to sweep them aside and leapt into a cluster, punching, kicking and biting the trapped men.

They were everywhere, Roussell realised. The gaps amongst the squig-beasts were not empty spaces, they were filled by the ork savages who had started the stampede and driven the beasts straight at the Brimlock column. The squig-beasts were just to soften them up; now the true attack was beginning.

The orks were knuckling along at speed, keeping low on all fours. The men in their clusters had a mere split-second to fire before they were set upon. It wasn't enough. The orks shrugged off the snatched shots, grappled with the Guardsmen for their lasguns and brought bone-breaking blows down upon them with clubs, cudgels and rocks.

Well, damn them all, Roussell decided. An ork leapt onto the Chimera's roof. It turned and grimaced at him and he shot it through the head. Another with a stone hammer smacked the Chimera's lasguns from their sockets. A third mounted the front of the tank and tried to shove a rock into the barrel of the multi-laser only to lose its hand to the scorching red beam.

Roussell brought his pistol up to shoot it, but was punched from his feet by a blow beneath his abdomen. He tried to step back and regain his balance, but his legs refused to obey him. He fell onto his back, his pistol gone, and looked down his body to where a javelin had buried itself. Blessed Mother Marguerite, he thought, that's agony. He tried to say the same, but the words wouldn't form. He tried to reach out with his hands and pull the javelin free but his arms felt as though they were imprisoned in ice.

The grey sky was blotted out as the ork missing a hand leaned over him, peering into his face. Then it stood, gripping the javelin to hold him steady, and his last sight was a heavy green foot slamming down upon him.

'HOLD! HOLD, YOU milk-sops!' Forjaz berated his men as another band of ork warriors with the distinctive red vertical strip down across one eye threw themselves at the company. Carson's men, consigned to the rear, had escaped the brunt of the stampede. The orks coming after had not been so obliging.

'Hold formation! Hold formation!' They were huddled together, as were many of those still fighting up and down the trail, in three sides of a rough square. They had originally formed a line like the rest, but the orks had tried the end flank and so the men there had folded back.

Then Rosa had been overwhelmed ahead of them and the warriors there attacked down the column, forcing the other side to fold in. Only Frn'k's wild intervention had prevented the formation being shattered.

Stanhope was crouched in the front rank, gripping his lasgun as though it were his very existence. There was sweat pouring from every patch of his skin. His chest felt as though it was being squeezed in a vice. He had already retched up everything his stomach had held, so at least there was nothing more to come from there. His aim, at least, was still steady. He focused on the simple things; he saw an ork, he shot it, he saw another, he shot that. He just profusely hoped that the orks he was shooting were actually there.

Blanks, the bastard who had put him in this state, was crouched in the second rank right behind him. Stanhope got a knee in the back every time the barrel of his lasgun wavered off-target.

'Hold! Hold!' Forjaz called again.

'How bloody long for?' Blanks muttered too loudly.

Forjaz heard it and turned on the insubordination.

'What did you say, private?' he demanded. He only realised as the words were coming out of his mouth, that he had chosen exactly the wrong person.

'I said, how bloody long for, sergeant!' Blanks shouted and fired his lasgun again.

All conversation was then rendered impossible as Gardner, at the square's corner, opened up with the auto-cannon again. He kept the burst short.

'Running low! Only one can after this one's finished!' he reported.

Forjaz didn't deserve this. Booth dead, Red gone, prob-ably dead as well, Carson arrested. Why did fate decree that he had to be the one to preside over the compa-ny's last stand? A half-dozen men were dead, the same number wounded but fighting on. The unfortunate Zezé had been hit by a javelin and was shaking, laid out at Forjaz's feet. And Blanks wasn't even finished yet.

'We've got to move!' he said.

Forjaz couldn't ignore him. 'We hold!'

The orks made another rush, hooting and waving their clubs above their heads. The troopers grouped their fire by priority targets, hitting each ork not with a single shot that they could shrug off, but with three or four at once. One of the orks endured the pain and reached Stanhope. The major jabbed forwards with his bayonet, sticking it hard into the ork's torso, but the ork kept reaching forwards to smash Stanhope's head in. From behind Stanhope, Blanks struck, his bayonet punching through the ork's throat. Then he pulled back and fired a shot into its face that sent it reeling away.

Forjaz had hoped to get orders, but there was no vox chatter any more. There were no orders any more. It was every company for itself, but surely, if they could just hold out long enough, someone would come for them.

'We've got to move!' Blanks shouted again.

We're not going anywhere; that's what Forjaz meant to say. Instead, it came out as, 'There's nowhere to go!'

'The fort!' Blanks responded. 'Fort Eliza! We can reach it!'

'No, wait!' Gardner interrupted. 'Let's get back. Get out of the jungle into the fungus. A Valkyrie can come in there.'

This was bad, Forjaz knew, he was losing his grip. Troopers were not supposed to discuss, they were supposed to obey.

'Shut your traps!' he bellowed, but Blanks ignored him.

'A Valkyrie can drop into the fort as well,' Blanks countered. 'And it's where everyone else will fall back to!'

'Everyone else who thinks of it!' Gardner shot back.

Forjaz felt his authority slip away. 'No one's going anywhere!' He tried to reassert himself, but the men knew that no one was coming to rescue them, and Blanks had a plan.

Blanks stood up all the way and faced Forjaz. Forjaz had a sudden flashback to the orks Blanks had so easily killed the night of the ork raid. 'I don't want to fight you, Forjaz,' he said. 'And you don't want to fight with me.'

'So what?'

'So, we have an officer,' he said, and he reached down and hauled Stanhope to his feet.

Now it all fit into place in Forjaz's head, how close Blanks had made himself to Stanhope, how he'd looked out for him, got him eating out of the palm of his hand. He could never have done that with Carson, but as soon as Carson was out of the way...

Blanks smacked Stanhope around the head to try and shake him from his torpor. 'What do we do, major? What are your orders? Stay or go?'

'What's it to be?' He went to smack him again, but as the lazy blow swept round, Stanhope's hand came up and blocked it. He grabbed the hilt of his fell-cutter in his other hand and jabbed it in Blanks's stomach. Blanks, for once off-guard, flailed for a moment to catch it.

'Don't ever strike me again,' Stanhope told Blanks, and let the sword slide back into its sheath. Blanks nodded and Stanhope continued. 'We go.'

Blanks nodded again, satisfied this time. 'Right, to Eliza.'

'Yes, to the fort,' Stanhope agreed, 'but first, up there,' and he pointed up the trail to where the rest of the column was being massacred.

'You're mad,' Blanks said, and finally he and Forjaz

were in agreement. 'You can't save the whole regiment, major! You've got to save *your men!*'

'Yes,' Stanhope replied. 'All of my men.'

LIEUTENANT CARSON SAT in the dark waiting for the end. His three guards had been firing the hull lasguns, but after they'd been smashed in, and the driver and turret-gunner bailed out into the carnage outside, his guards appeared disinclined to open the rear hatch and fight on. None of the orks had tried to open the rear hatch. It was perhaps because they couldn't see anyone inside. Perhaps they didn't even understand that people could be inside. Perhaps they thought a Chimera was just as much a single living being as they were. It didn't really matter. They would figure it out soon enough.

That time appeared to be at hand. There was a groan of metal as something monstrous tried to rip its way through the rear hatch. The guards scrambled for their weapons and held them ready. A peak of light appeared, a silhouette beyond, and one of them fired. There was a deep, inhuman shout of alarm and the silhouette jerked back.

'Brimlock Eleventh, you idiots! Open up!'

One of the guards peered out of the hole and then quickly obeyed. Suddenly a half-dozen men poured into the back of the transport, grabbed the guards, took their weapons and threw them out onto the ground. They looked up to see the path to their Chimera lined with five Griffons, each one crammed to the brim with troopers.

One of the troopers grabbed the guard who had fired and lifted him up to his feet.

'You're damn lucky you missed!' Gardner spat at him and then showed him Frn'k looming over them both. The guard quickly agreed.

Major Stanhope stepped into the rear compartment of the transport.

'Lieutenant Carson,' he said over the sound the las-fire from the troopers holding the orks at bay.

'Under arrest,' Carson said back.

'From what I've seen, lieutenant, I believe that no longer applies. Now get up and jump on a Griffon, that's an order.'

'An order? From you?' Carson replied. 'How unusual. Such a shame I have to disobey it.'

Stanhope looked down at Carson in the gloom. He noted the uncomfortable pose, the odd positioning of his legs, the arms that hung like a dead weight.

'It happened again?' he asked

'They didn't need to restrain me to stop me escaping. My body took care of that all by itself.'

'Very well,' Stanhope said and turned away. He then handed his jacket to Blanks, returned, took a hold on the protesting Carson, heaved him up over his shoulders and carried him out into the light.

THE SMALL CONVOY rolled out back down the trail, the troopers on board shooting any ork that tried to pursue them. The Griffons were designed to carry a small mortar crew and so Stanhope had ordered everything inessential to be thrown off so as to cram all his men on board. Even so troopers had to cling on to the sides. Even the wounded, even the dying Zezé. Stanhope would leave none of them behind, not even Carson's three guards. As soon as Stanhope saw them, they became his responsibility as well and so somehow space was found to carry them too.

They turned off the main trail, heading towards Fort Eliza. The cohesion of the ork forces had crumbled. The warriors who had been fighting found themselves fixated by the weak creatures they had defeated and the strange items they wore and carried. The primitive tribes had earned a crushing victory over those aliens who had defeated the almighty Stone Smashas and their only thought was to get the choicest loot and to celebrate. Up and down the trail, the victorious orks had only a single chant:

'CHOP-PA! CHOP-PA! CHOP-PA!'

CHAPTER TWENTY-THREE

Blood Stripe camp, Tswaing, Voor
pacification Stage 1 Day 20

'CHOP-PA! CHOP-PA! CHOP-PA!' Mouse's ears were
filled with the chant. His eyes were filled with death. He
walked over yard after yard of bodies: orks, squig-beasts,
Guardsmen, all laid out together. The scavengers were
hard at work; the ork warriors had already taken their
trophies and now it was the gretchins' turn. Every pile
of dead, every platoon's last stand, was alive with them.
They snatched at everything they thought of worth,
digging their chipped fingernails into fabric to tear free
buttons, medals, crystals, anything that shone, to satisfy
their greed. Once done with that on a body they then
dug into its flesh to satisfy their hunger. Mouse could
only be grateful that the lengthening shadows hid the
results of their feasting.

The orks had tied his hands and put him on a leash to
drag him along like a pet. It was humiliating, but better
that than what had happened to his comrades. Red was
still in the cage. He was awake now. He held the torn

cloth to the wound upon his head as a makeshift bandage. The cloth was crusty and the side of his face was streaked in dried blood, but still he pressed it down. He wasn't moving.

During the battle he had gone mad. As he and Mouse had heard the sounds of carnage, Red had started shouting to try and warn the regiment. He had slammed himself into the cage to try to break free, the colour of his face going from flesh, to its customary scarlet, to a deep purple that Mouse had never seen before. He only stopped after the sounds of las-fire had ceased and were replaced by the orks' bellows of victory. It had been for nothing. It had all been for nothing.

'CHOP-PA! CHOP-PA! CHOP-PA!'

Mouse had tried to talk to him, had tried to explain, but Red had refused to listen. He had seen the comparative liberty that Choppa had granted Mouse and had fixed him with such a look of betrayal that it was as though Mouse were Horus reincarnated. Nothing Mouse had said made any difference.

Choppa called the procession to a halt. They had reached the remains of the armoured company. The grey hulls of the tanks were mottled black and ash-white from the fires that had burst from their engines. Their doors and hatches hung open; their shadowy interiors were gutted, plastic melted, metal scorched, steering columns and controls blackened skeletons.

Not every skeleton was merely mechanical, though. While the wounded had scrabbled to get out before they were cooked inside, the smell of charred flesh in the air was testament to those who had not made it. These were not tanks or transports any longer; they were carcasses.

Mouse did not know how the armour had been overcome so quickly, but that in itself did not surprise him. Guard doctrine taught the Imperium's soldiers ignorance and contempt for their enemies, not understanding and respect. True knowledge of the foe came only through battle, and there every lesson learned came at the cost of the lives of one's comrades.

Mouse remembered Azzabar. Back when they thought the fight was almost done, before the company even knew they were under attack, they had lost their commander. It had been Captain Sandys back then. He had been well under Carson's thumb and the company was getting on well. Then one night Mouse had seen him touring the defences when he had suddenly sat down. They had gone to his aid only to find blood bursting from his nose and eyes. He was dead in an instant and, moments later, the eldar, who were not even supposed to be on Azzabar, attacked.

Mouse did not have knowledge, but he had kept himself alive all these years by making very accurate guesses. Choppa's personal glyph totem was the key to it. It might be a weapon itself, or perhaps it was merely an object of focus for some psychic power, those same type of psychic powers that had reduced the brain of Captain Sandys to pudding without leaving a mark on him.

There was a commotion up ahead; the gretchin were squabbling over a body. The nearest ork waded in amongst them. It grabbed at their prize and held it up. The face was beyond identification, but Mouse recognised the insignia of a major. It had been Brooce. It was not the body that had caused the fracas. Brooce's uniform had been ripped open and beneath it were the regimental colours. He had tied them around his body to ensure they could not be captured while he still lived. And they had not. The gretchin had already bitten through the knot and so when the ork tugged at them they came away in its hand. It looked at the brightly coloured fabric for a few moments, not understanding what the banner represented, and then draped it around its shoulders like a cape.

'Chaffey,' a hoarse voice whispered his name. It was Red; he was standing up, looking at Mouse. His eyes were the same steely blue, but for the first time in all the years Mouse had known him, there was a frailty behind them. He was wounded, his face was pale. He was an old man and he knew his time was coming soon. Mouse drew up some of the slack on his leash and then crept over towards the cage, stopping a metre from the bars.

'Colour?' Mouse asked quietly. Red looked woozy, the blow he'd taken to his head was taking its toll. Red's lips were moving, but Mouse couldn't hear any words over the hooting and hollering of the rowdy orks. Red's body wavered and he started to slump against the cage. Mouse instinctively stepped forwards to try and keep Red upright. It proved to be a mistake. As soon as he reached the bars, Red's body snapped up and Mouse felt a hand close around his throat. Before he could react he found himself trapped in the iron grip of a very clear, very conscious and very angry regimental colour-sergeant.

'You rat-blasted,' Red raged at him beneath his breath. 'You dreg. You gopper. You don't say a word, you hear me? Don't you doubt for a single moment that even in here I can't pull out your throat. I can and I will unless you give me what I want. You hear that? What have you got?'

Mouse's eyes bulged as he struggled to respond. Red did not stop, however. 'You're a sneak and a thief and a coward, and the lieutenant only stopped me skinning you alive because you always had a trump up your sleeve. I need out of this cage, so whatever you have you give it to me.'

The grip tightened and the blood pounded in Mouse's head. He started to raise his tied hands. 'Slowly,' Red warned, and Mouse showed him the small blade he had tucked inside the cuff. Red took it and relaxed his hold. Mouse scuttled as far away as he could. He didn't want to be anywhere near whatever the colour-sergeant was about to do.

It took Red less than a minute to slice through one of the cage's ropes and escape. The orks were distracted by their celebrating. One of the gretchin did see and screeched, but the weak noise was lost amongst the general commotion. Red had his chance to run, to escape the orks, but he didn't. He ran right into the midst of them.

The orks noticed him then, but Red had a moment's grace before they could stop him. In that moment Red shoved his way through, booting the scurrying gretchin aside. Mouse gaped at his idiocy, Red had gone mad. He was trying to defeat the whole horde single-handed!

But Red's target was quite specific. The mob rounded on him, but he had reached it. The ork wearing the colours turned around and Red managed a single swipe, catching it across the face, before he himself was struck down from behind. Red stumbled, but as he fell he dragged the colours from the ork's shoulders. He clutched the precious cloth tight to him as he disappeared under the blows of the mob.

CHAPTER TWENTY-FOUR

Fort Eliza, Tswaing, Voor pacification Stage 1
Day 20

THE EVENING HAD fallen quickly over the deserted Fort Eliza. The clouds turned black and bulged with rain. Stanhope welcomed it. He welcomed anything that would hide them still further from any errant ork that happened to wander past. He kept his men away from the breach caused in the raid, kept them away from the bodies. The orks had been burned, whilst the men were quickly buried, but there was nothing to be gained by dwelling there. Instead he had occupied one of the towers, and used tarps attached between the Griffons and the tower to create a larger, communal tent.

The men had survived many rainy nights without cover before, but tonight he wanted everyone in the same place. Aside from Zezé, who passed into the light shortly after they arrived. Stanhope left Heal and a few of the other men to arrange for the body to be buried. Not many, for the company could not be allowed to forget that they were still in the midst of battle. Fighting and his orders came first; grief, mourning and loss all had to wait.

He was giving orders easily now. His self-imposed taboo had been broken and they were coming to him naturally again. One just needed to have the vision of how things should be and then impart it to the rest. But his orders carried the weight of borrowed authority, as Carson had said to him as soon as the opportunity to speak privately arose.

'I've been asking myself,' he had said, 'why was it that you came after me. I realised, you didn't come after me. You came after my authority.'

'I'm a major, lieutenant,' Stanhope had replied. 'I've commanded platoons, companies and regiments. I don't need your authority.'

'Yes, you do. Here, you do. With my men, you do.' Carson almost left it at that, but then he felt his body's weakness, the embarrassment of not being in control of basic functions. He knew that, right then, he could not lead.

'You can have it,' he added. 'Just take care of them. You damn well keep them safe.'

Stanhope agreed. He had taken weeks to accept the responsibility of these men's lives, and now he had, he was going to pull them through, no matter what it took.

One immediate disappointment, though, was that they were alone. When they arrived, it became clear that no other survivors had made for the fort. For a long while, Stanhope had to consider that his men might be all that was left of the column from that morning. Until finally, just before dusk, another unit had appeared.

'It's the cavalry,' Blanks had reported, coming down from the tower.

'The cavalry?' Stanhope had said. 'Blessed Marguerite, that's the last goddamn thing we need.'

Stanhope was not the only man of the company to think so either.

GARDNER SAT HUNCHED in the corner beside his autocannon and his ogryn. Trouble was dozing, the panic of the evening and the hardship of the night having had no effect on him. He had looked mournful only when Gardner had told him what little there was to eat. Such a straightforward life, so full of content and bliss at trivial matters such as food and companionship. What a fool, Gardner thought savagely and then instantly felt guilty about it. He could not help it.

The waiting was driving Gardner mad. He had stayed awake, pistol, knife and grenade ready, waiting for Reeve to send men for him. He must have already told that tin belly captain who had shot him. He had probably told him the day before, as soon as they had ridden him to safety. Damn cavalry. Damn Carson who had stopped him when they had been here last, when he had been ready, and when he'd had surprise on his side.

Now that was gone, now Reeve knew he was out to kill him. He knew it, and he would know he was here as well. The commissar was just toying with him, toying with him as he'd done on the Execution Boards with his brother. He was putting him through one last night of torment and then he'd have him seized before dawn, when all the rest of the company were asleep. He'd be put up against a wall and that would be it. The other brother dead. Another skull for his coat.

Damn him, Gardner decided. Hope: that was what they got you with. They let you think you had hope. Made it all the sweeter for them when they snatched it away. Well, this Gardner would not give him the satisfaction. He cast his hope aside. He knew he was a dead man in a few hours anyway. He would not be led like a lamb into the Emperor's light. He rose to his feet, a few joints cracking as he did so. He felt for the grenade in his pocket; that would do for Reeve. He felt the knife hidden at his back; that would do for any tin belly that got in his way. He looked down at his gun, too cumbersome. He looked down at Trouble, much the same.

Trouble would be okay, Gardner told himself. Blast it, give him a few extra portions at his next meal and he'd probably forget all about him. And if they came for him first, the ogryn'd probably get caught up and they'd take him down too. Best this way. Best this way for both of them.

He walked out and excused himself to Private Heal who was on sentry duty. Said it was a call of nature. Benefit of being a corporal, privates didn't question him too much. It was raining. Perfect. It would cover his footsteps and keep anyone else from wandering around. He walked blithely off until he was out of sight and then doubled back towards where Ledbetter had sited his men. Most of them would be in the main tent, little more than an awning really, set up against the remains of the fort's wall. Gardner bet Reeve would be there, briefing the men on the raid he wanted.

Gardner headed towards it, but skirted around where they had tied up the horses. He didn't want some panicky beast giving him away. He hunkered down against the sodden earth further along the wall and peered into the barracks. There were a few lights on, kept pointed down at the ground. Most of the tin bellies were lying down. A few were up, but Gardner could tell that none of them was Reeve, and he doubted that Reeve would be bedding down with them. He obviously wasn't there.

That made sense, Gardner realised. Reeve wouldn't call everyone together until the last moment. He'd be in one of the tents, telling Ledbetter his orders. He circled around, keeping out of sight of those locations where Private Heal and the other sentries were standing. Their attention should be focused out into the jungle, but with Emperor-only-knew how many orks prowling around, they'd shoot at anything they didn't recognise.

He closed on the tents. There was a light on in one. Dampened, but noticeable up close. That was it. He checked on his grenade. He could just toss it in from outside, but they'd still catch him anyway and he wouldn't see the look on Reeve's face when he saw his end. Better to make it quick. He'd just walk in there and–

'Bruvva?'

Gardner whirled around, then gasped and swore when he saw Frn'k standing a way off, dripping wet.

'You lefda gun? Isda danger? You needa gun?'

In the gloom, Gardner could see that Frn'k held the autocannon in his hands.

'Blessed Marguerite, Trouble,' Gardner hissed. 'Get back to the barracks!'

Frn'k could hear the panic in his friend's voice. Something must be wrong!

'Danger?'

'Be quiet!' Gardner rasped.

'Danger!' Frn'k decided and shambled over, looking all about for whatever was threatening his friend. 'Tell Trouble whereda danger!'

'You idiot! Get back! They're going to hear you! You're going to ruin it!' Gardner flew at the ogryn in fury, smacking him with the hilt of his knife, anything to try to get him away. Frn'k backed off, dropping the cannon, confused and stricken at his friend's assault. Why was his friend doing this? If there was danger then Trouble should be with him. They were always together. They were brothers, that's what he'd said!

Frn'k hid his face between his thick arms. 'Don't hurt

Trouble! Trouble sorry!' he whined.

'Get back!' Gardner ordered. 'Go back to the barracks! Leave me alone!' But it was too late; the men in the tent had heard the noise. Gardner saw the shadows shift and one of them emerge. It was Ledbetter.

Gardner swore again. They would have him for sure now. Just knowing he was there would force them to take him. This was his only chance. He sheathed his knife and pulled his pistol. He'd have to take that man out now, his bad luck, but he was only a tin belly after all.

A hand the size of an artillery shell gripped his pistol arm.

'What Bruvva doin'?' Frn'k demanded. 'Thatsa friend. You don't shoot friends. Bruvva told me thatsa bad thing!'

'Get off me, you stupid oaf!' Gardner stopped whispering as he erupted. He pulled to free his arm, but Frn'k held it with ease. If he'd had time he could have reasoned with him, but the tin belly had seen him and was about to raise the alarm. He reached up his left hand, tossing the unprimed grenade it held to the side, and grabbed the pistol from his right. Frn'k saw the grenade fall.

'Krumper!' he bellowed. He pulled Gardner in tight and turned away, interposing his own body to protect his friend from the explosion Frn'k thought was coming.

There was a roar, but not of an explosion. It was the roar of a human as Ledbetter charged in, chainsword whirling.

'Get your hands off that man!' he cried and brought the chainsword down on Frn'k's shoulder. The chainsword's high-pitched whine became a throaty drone as it chewed into the ogryn's flesh. Frn'k spasmed in agony, instinctively clenching tight. Too tight for Gardner in his grip; beneath the bloody chewing of the chainsword could be heard the sickening sound of bones breaking. The ogryn rolled away from the pain, his rain-slickened friend slipping from his grasp. He did not know why the grenade had not exploded, but someone was hurting him and he needed to get them to stop. He grabbed at the nearest weapon he could find.

'God-Emperor,' Ledbetter breathed as the monstrous ogryn raised the hefty autocannon in his hands. It wasn't loaded, but Frn'k didn't need it to be. He swung it like a bat, gripping it on the barrel, striking the cavalry captain with the heavy feeder system. The impact physically lifted Ledbetter a full metre clear of the ground and sent him sprawling back, unconscious, his chainsword automatically cutting out as it left his grip.

'Look out, he's gone berserk!' Frn'k heard someone shout, and then he heard the first shot being fired. It was being fired at him! He turned to face whoever had done it, but then another shot struck him in the back, struck him where Ledbetter's sword had struck. He bellowed in pain again. Many men were running at him now. They saw Ledbetter and Gardner lying prone at his feet. They shouted things at him. Blamed him for it. Called him things. He tried to find his words, but all he could think of was that he'd hurt his friend. He'd wanted to save him, but now he was hurt. *He* had hurt him. And the men all around him were blaming him for it, and shooting at him. He couldn't find his words. He couldn't explain. He had hurt his friend. He had been bad.

Frn'k opened his mouth and wailed out his broken heart. And then he ran into the darkness, while the stinging lines of light cut around him.

'Stop firing! For Marguerite's sake, stop firing!' Stanhope shouted as he came out onto the scene. He ran over to where Gardner and Ledbetter lay. Ledbetter was already stirring slightly, but Gardner was dead still.

'Medicae!' he called, and then cursed because they had no medicae left. 'Anyone!'

'WHO'S SEEING TO him?' Carson demanded, as Stanhope and Forjaz carried him out of the barracks.

'One of Ledbetter's men has some medicae training,' Stanhope replied.

'One of the tin bellies?' Carson said. 'Don't you realise that Gardner was probably out to–'

'*I* realise that. He, thankfully, did not.'

GARDNER WAS ALIVE and awake, but he would not remain either for long. The resigned look on the face of the cavalryman tending him told Stanhope that much.

'A lot of his ribs are broken, and I think he's bleeding inside as well.'

'What are you going to do?' Carson asked.

The cavalryman considered the question. 'I'm going to make him as comfortable as possible.'

'That's it?' Carson exclaimed. 'If that's what it is then get inside him and stitch him up. You're not just going to leave him. What kind of a medicae do you call yourself?'

Carson was an imposing man, and the force of his character was in no way diminished by the fact that he'd had to be carried in and sat down on the floor. But while many men within the regiment would have been cowed before him, this cavalry trooper was not one of them.

'If I was back in Dova, if I had the proper equipment and staff, and the proper supplies on hand… I still wouldn't know what I was doing! *Sir*. I know about your reputation, lieutenant, but there's nothing more that I can do. And I don't call myself any kind of medicae. I used to help them look after the horses. That's all. I don't know how to save him!'

The cavalryman's voice was tight with emotion.

Stanhope looked at him again and realised how young he was. He wasn't one of the veterans who had started from Brimlock, he was just old enough to be a man. He'd obviously been born on the crusade as part of one of the regimental families.

Carson was lost for words for a moment and so Stanhope took the chance to interject. 'Thank you for your efforts, lance-corporal,' Stanhope interjected. 'How is Captain Ledbetter?'

The cavalryman wiped the sweat from his face. His eyes were red. 'He's fine, sir. He's taken worse. There's really nothing more I can do. I have to get back to the commissar.'

Stanhope saw Carson's flicker of reaction at that.

'How does he fare?' Stanhope inquired politely.

'The conditions… they've aggravated his wound… I don't know that either.' The crumpled look on the young man's face spoke volumes about the weight of the responsibility that had been placed upon him. Stanhope dismissed him and he left.

Carson was talking to Gardner and Stanhope took his leave to allow them the moment. After ten minutes or so, Forjaz came out holding up Carson.

'He was trying to kill Reeve,' Carson said in a measured tone. 'When they find that out, whether he's dying or not, Ledbetter's men are going to come for him. I am not going to allow them to take him. I'm going to get my men ready.'

'We can't let this happen,' Stanhope said. 'This is my command and I will not let us end it all fighting each other!'

'Command then, major,' Carson replied. 'I suspect that Ledbetter's men will have the same preference for your authority as mine do.'

Whether Carson was spurring him on or merely

mocking him, Stanhope could not discern.

'Is Gardner still awake? I'd like to talk to him first.'

'Talk to him if you will. But I don't think he'll be inclined to reply,' Carson finished, and Forjaz carried him away.

Stanhope returned inside and settled himself next to the dying man.

'I know a little about what happened to your brother. Lieutenant Carson told me the night after we took the crater.'

Gardner didn't reply.

'He told me to talk to you if I needed to know any more,' Stanhope continued. What Carson had actually said was that he'd had enough of Stanhope's damn questions and that if he wanted to know any more he'd have to damn well talk to Gardner himself. 'I need to know more now. I have to try and stop what we both think will happen.'

Gardner, though, was evidently not in the mood to talk. He sat there, sullenly, staring only at his feet.

'I understand how it is,' Stanhope offered.

'Yes, sir,' Gardner replied, his voice dripping with scorn. Stanhope felt his temper rise, but he controlled it.

'I want you to think for a moment, corporal. Can you do that? I want you to think of everything you heard about me. Think of everything you know that I've done to myself, done to others, have had done to me. Think of it all, corporal, and then look me in the eye and tell me you think that I do not understand loss.'

Gardner thought, then blinked and looked away.

'I was there. On Cawnpore. I saw what they put us through. I know why Hacher was born and why so many men listened to what he said. I know they weren't traitors, they were just human. I saw what the Execution Boards did to people. I saw how they could lever a man open and what they could make him admit. Not for the sake of justice or truth, but simply to reinstate order and fear.' Stanhope knelt down on one knee and moved closer to the man. 'I know your brother wasn't a traitor.'

Gardner nodded, tried to swallow, then took a deep breath and stared straight at Stanhope.

'Then you know scrag all,' he said. 'Scrag all. That's what you know, you bloody carcass, you bloody shell. Because he was a traitor! You hear that? Can you understand that, major?'

Stanhope, surprised, stood up to go, but Gardner's anger pulled him up.

'He was a traitor,' Gardner ranted. 'I knew it. He told me. He told me how he had heard of Hacher and what he was doing. He told me how he spread the word of what was happening in the Sixty-Seventh all through the regiment. He whispered it to me at night just to show me what he could do. He was always trouble. Always. I started calling him Trouble when we were kids. He loved it.'

Stanhope backed slowly away. He'd hit the nerve and now it was angry, raw and exposed. He didn't need to push any more, Gardner would carry himself the rest of the way.

'No names, though,' Gardner carried on, 'I drew the line at that. I didn't want to know any names. I was too scared to know 'em. I thought if I didn't know the names then they'd never get me. I wasn't part of anything if I didn't know the names.'

Gardner gestured wildly and then froze as his memories slid on.

'But the black-coats didn't see it that way. After it'd all happened, I got called up before the Boards. Up in front of that one, Reeve, before he started wearing those skull-trophies of his. Back when he was just another black-coat. There were five of them. I heard they were brought in specially by Ellinor, to cut out the rot, so they said. Most of the time you hear of a mutiny, the black-coats just shoot every man still standing at the end. Sets an example to the rest, they say. Ellinor, though, the glorious bastard, didn't want to lose a dozen regiments just to send a message. He had plans for those regiments; he had a schedule of conquests to keep and not enough men for his liking. So these black-coats, they had a different method. They told me they believed me. They believed I wasn't part of anything. But they wanted the names of the ones who were. They wanted the rot.

'If I hadn't been gagged and bolted down I'd have laughed then. Give them names? They took the gag out and I gave them the name of every man who'd crossed me, every sergeant who'd chewed me up and spat me out, every officer who'd looked down his nose at me. They might all have been as pure as priests, but I didn't care. Let them defend themselves, it'd get me off.

'Then Reeve thanked me for my helpfulness, and he told me that he was certain my allegations would all be corroborated by the others. Because if they weren't, he said, they would have to conclude that I was naming innocent men because I was one of the mutineers. And if I was one of those, then it would be the cannon mouth for me... after they had finished a more *detailed* questioning.

'That was how they worked it. That was how they rooted out the traitors. They didn't accuse us, we accused ourselves. Everyone had to say a name, and if we refused then we were dead. If we said a name and others said the same, then we were safe. If we were the only one, we were dead again. Who was I supposed to choose? Who would everyone else pick? Who did I think someone else would accuse?

'Reeve asked me if I wanted to reconsider the list I had given him. I nodded and he ripped it clean through the middle. Then he asked me for the name. I should never have let Trouble get into it on his own! If I'd have been with him, I'd know the others, I'd have been able to save him. I told Reeve nothing. I said I didn't know anyone.

'Reeve went quiet at that and then I was unstrapped and taken out of the room. They took me out into the courtyard and showed me the cannon. I didn't say anything. They showed me the straps, showed me what was left of the one who'd come before me. I kept silent. They tied me over the mouth and lifted the barrel up. I pissed myself, but my mouth stayed shut. They called the order to fire and I waited, I waited the long seconds before I would feel the ball strike and tear me to pieces.

'The moment came, the cannon roared. I opened my eyes and I was still looking at the sky. They lowered the barrel and let me hang there on the straps, my trousers soaked, my face wet. Now I knew how it would be, I knew I couldn't go through it again. I said my brother's name. I said it, then they made me repeat it. Then they cut me down and took me back in front of Reeve and they made me say it again. Then they cleaned me up and took me back to my cell. And that's where I stayed until it was over. Fed, watered, and with nothing to do but listen to the cannon fire.'

Stanhope sat quietly while Gardner gasped and coughed at the exertion of telling his story. He knew there was nothing he could say. At Cawnpore, after he'd lost his regiment, there was nothing anyone could have said to him. They had trusted him; they had attacked that fortress because they had believed him when he had said the next wave was coming. He had betrayed them, just as Gardner had betrayed his brother.

But while Gardner had found a target for his guilt and

turned it outwards, Stanhope had kept it in. The only vengeance he had sought was against himself. He had not had the courage to defy the order to attack, nor had he the courage to end himself afterwards. Instead, he stepped out. He stepped out of his rank, stepped out of the Guard, stepped out of his life as far he could and waited for anyone to notice. He had held the gun to his head and waited for someone else to pull the trigger, but no one ever had. In his lucid moments, he had realised that someone was protecting him. Protecting, or maybe punishing him, by refusing him what he thought he deserved. It had taken him a year or so to finally realise who it was.

Of all those regiments on Cawnpore, there were only two that weren't brought up before the Execution Boards. The first were the storm troopers who had dropped into the citadel and caught the men who had called themselves Hacher. The second was the 1201st, or at least the only man who remained of it. The report of the display of loyalty by his men at that parade, their sacrifice on the slopes of the citadel, kept him safe, meant he was high above any suspicion. His men had protected him still, even after they were dead.

He had met Reeve then only in passing; he was one of the five that had questioned him, but that was all. The Board had told him that, because of the stigma that Cawnpore would forever hold, the 1201st would have it expunged from their record and instead it would show that they had given their lives fighting the xenos on Ghilzai. Stanhope, in his grief, could not have cared less.

Then, a few weeks later, he was transferred to the 99th and met Reeve again for he was the senior commissar for the regiment. Stanhope had thought nothing of it, and his slide began in earnest. Then he was transferred again, to the 263rd and there Reeve was again. Each time

Stanhope was bumped from regiment to regiment, Reeve appeared as well. He thought that Reeve had him under watch in case the mutinous virus should suddenly spring from him to his new regiments, and that belief made him sink lower and lower. But now, he looked back at those same events with an unclouded mind. Was it perhaps that Reeve was not *following* him, rather that he was *taking* him? Was he was carrying him from regiment to regiment as *he* was reassigned, ensuring as only a commissar can that Stanhope was not persecuted?

It seemed ridiculous. Amongst all the death on Cawnpore, why would Reeve pluck him out to save? He did not know. The two of them had never even spoken in private. But now here they were close to the end. The commissar was only a few metres away, perhaps dying, perhaps already dead; any answers he had already gone. And Stanhope was sitting with the man who had thought to kill him.

'How's Reeve?' Gardner asked, his voice weak.

'I'll have someone check,' Stanhope said and stepped out and gave the order.

'Wherever I'm going...' Gardner said when he returned, 'I better not see him there.'

Gardner was even paler than before, his lips going blue. Stanhope could see that he did not have long.

'You won't. Everyone knows that commissars don't go into His light.'

'Where...' Gardner croaked, '...then?'

'They stand in His shadow,' Stanhope said gently. 'So as to make sure of His loyalty.'

The corner of Gardner's mouth turned up in amusement and the two of them waited in silence for what news would come.

'Tell Trouble I'm sorry,' Gardner said suddenly, and then was drowned out by the noise of the rain as the tent flap opened and Blanks stepped inside. Stanhope looked round at him.

'Commissar Reeve is dead,' he reported.

Stanhope turned back to Gardner, but Gardner's eyes had unfocused and dimmed. They would not see anything again.

Stanhope released his breath and whispered a prayer. A prayer for them both. A prayer for them all. Emperor knew he had watched enough men die in the past, even die slowly before him. Here was the truth, the truth he would have told the next generation of officers had he ever been chosen to go home. The first is not the hardest. It's the last.

But Gardner would not be the last if his men and Ledbetter's now tore each other apart.

'Tell Carson to keep the men alert,' he told Blanks. 'I'm going to talk to Captain Ledbetter, and I will pray that his feelings towards us are gentler than ours towards him.'

CHAPTER TWENTY-FIVE

Fort Eliza, Tswaing, Voor pacification
Stage 1 Day 21

LEDBETTER HAD ALREADY taken the initiative. One of his cavalrymen appeared in his path, saluted, and then politely requested that he follow. His guide led him to the far end of their makeshift barracks. Stanhope entered and saw the body of Commissar Reeve. They had lifted it on its stretcher and put supports underneath almost as though it were the body of an Imperial hero, lying in state. Which, Stanhope supposed, Reeve almost was to these men.

A squad of the cavalrymen stood around him, reading softly from their prayer-books. Ledbetter was amongst them. He saw Stanhope, closed the small volume in his hands, crossed over to him and slowly saluted.

'Captain,' Stanhope said as he returned the salute.

'I wanted you to see him like this,' Ledbetter began, gesturing behind him. 'It is the best we can do, but a commissar of the Emperor deserves much more.'

Stanhope did not comment as he scanned the interior,

trying to count the men, trying to discern the weapons they carried, trying to sense whether there were any in hiding waiting to cut him down at a given signal.

Ledbetter had paused, waiting for a response.

'These are straitened times,' Stanhope finally produced. 'I am certain that he would understand that.'

Ledbetter stared coldly at him for a time, and then slowly nodded. 'You are right, major. He would have approved. For all his unshakeable faith, he remained a practical man. But I, in *my* faith, cannot leave him like this.'

Forty-two of them, Stanhope concluded, at least of those he could see. With Gardner dead, Carson immobilised and Frn'k gone, it would be a nasty fight. He had no certainty that his men would win. Of course, the faithful needed no such certainty.

'If you wish to transport him back to Dova, I am certain that we can make arrangements,' Stanhope ventured, trying to steer the conversation away from the precipice.

'His body is a shell, major,' Ledbetter swept on. 'It is his spirit that is my concern. And his spirit will remain restless until it receives its proper retribution.'

That was it then. An instinctive chill shivered up Stanhope's spine, but he blazed it away. He was about to die, but he could still provide one last service and create such a commotion as to put his men on guard.

'I do not think,' he said, playing for time as he lowered his body a fraction, 'that talk of retribution is particularly useful in the present circumstances.'

They would be watching his hands; he could not put them near his weapons. If he touched the hilt of his fell-cutter or his pistol, they would shoot him where he stood. If he charged their captain, however, they might hold off for a few precious seconds for fear of hitting him as well. There would be a signal; Ledbetter would want to ensure they struck only at his command. He had to anticipate it if he was to survive even a step.

'I agree,' Ledbetter said. 'Further talk is useless at present.' Then he took a step closer. 'But I want you to know now that when we return to Voorheid I will drag that Voorjer whore into the street and give her that same "justice" she gave to our commissar.'

Stanhope froze. 'Van Am.'

Ledbetter noted the slight tone of disbelief in Stanhope's voice, and inferred from it what he had expected.

'You cannot protect her, major,' he asserted. 'I know she is close to your company, close to your lieutenant. But she has forfeited the Emperor's mercy.'

He held up the small, crumpled piece of metal, half the size of a little finger, that had taken his commissar's life.

'A Voorjer bullet,' Ledbetter said. 'We dug it from his body.'

Stanhope took it and held it up in what little light there was. 'This was hers?'

'Of course it was, major. She either took the shot herself or gave the order to one of her men. She probably thought she could blame the orks, claim one of them fired it from those hunting rifles that the Voorjers conveniently lost from their first expedition to the rok.'

But it wouldn't have been one of the Voorjers, though, would it, Stanhope considered. They were outside of Reeve's authority; they were the only ones in that battle who did not have to fear his discipline. There was one man in that battle who most definitely did have a reason and who he had seen with a Voorjer rifle. Stanhope felt his body clench again. He continued to stare at the dented bullet as though examining it whilst his thoughts whirled and caught up. 'Could it not have been an ork?'

'The wound was to his back, major,' Ledbetter stated

icily. 'I saw the commissar when he fell. He was facing forwards. He only ever faced forwards.'

'Of course.'

'Do I have your word then?'

Stanhope looked at the man squarely. He was asking for his word as an officer. Stanhope wondered at him. How does a man survive twenty years of dirt and come out so clean? And why now did Stanhope feel soiled amongst these men of honour and long instead for the company of his rogues and killers?

'I cannot give my word, captain, knowing I may be ordered to break it.'

'Understandable, major. So, excepting if you are ordered, do I have your word?'

Just lie, Stanhope told himself. After what you've become, after the depths you've brought yourself down to, what is your word of honour worth?

Something, Stanhope decided. It's worth something.

Then who are you protecting? Your men, or the Voorjer girl? Your old regiment is dead. The man who may have been protecting you is dead. He died waiting for you to step back up. Become an officer again. Make the choice an officer should make. Protect your men, do what you must to bring them home safe or cast their lives aside here in order to protect the guilty.

'You do,' Stanhope replied. 'Once we reach Voorheid, I will not stand in the way of what you feel you must do.'

'Thank you, major.' Ledbetter shook his hand firmly. Stanhope responded without enthusiasm. It felt almost as an alien gesture to him now.

Stanhope took that as his opportunity to leave and stepped out into the darkness and the rain. Another cavalryman entered and passed a quiet message over to his captain.

'Major!' Ledbetter called. Stanhope stopped and

turned but did not step back inside. 'Your corporal, Gardener, was it?'

'Gardner,' Stanhope corrected.

'Gardner,' Ledbetter affirmed. 'I am sorry to hear he passed. When I saw that beast attacking him I struck it as hard as I could. I regret it appears I was too late. Do pass on my condolences to the rest of your men.'

'Thank you, captain. I'm sure they'll appreciate it.'

FORJAZ SAW STANHOPE return from the tin bellies. He motioned to them that all was well and Forjaz breathed a sigh of relief and relaxed his grip on his gun. Stanhope spoke briefly to Carson and left. Carson told them formally to stand down and the men around him, who had endured the devastation of their army during the day and were now rousted during the night to be ready for a savage close-quarter fight against their own, dealt with it all as only veterans could. They went back to sleep.

Carson called him over. Apparently Stanhope wanted a word in private. Forjaz helped him out and over to the tent where Gardner's body now lay covered.

'Sorry to put you to such trouble, lieutenant,' Stanhope said as they entered.

'It's no trouble,' Carson replied quickly as Forjaz sat him down. Forjaz knew the major had every excuse to keep Carson out of command, but Carson was determined to show no further weakness in front of the man.

Blanks was there as well, standing beside Stanhope almost as though he thought himself the equal of the rest of them. He had gambled on attaching himself to Stanhope when the major had been an outcast and that gamble was paying off. He and Stanhope sat on the ground as well, bringing them down to Carson's level. Forjaz followed suit, while Stanhope relayed what had transpired.

'So,' Carson summarised, 'you've sold her out.'

'She sold herself out by shooting Reeve,' Stanhope retorted, 'Or are you going to claim that you fired a second, freakishly ricocheting bullet from that Voorjer rifle you borrowed.'

Carson shut up at that and Forjaz watched the two of them consider their positions in a long moment of silence. Eventually, Carson started again.

'Did Ledbetter say why he thought she did it?'

'No,' Stanhope said. 'He only said he knew how close she was to this company. To you.'

'She didn't do it for me!' Carson protested. Stanhope arched his eyebrow.

'If I might interrupt, major, lieutenant,' Blanks began. 'I only ever heard Van Am speak of one thing: to keep Voor free, from the orks and from the Imperium as well. And there's no greater symbol of the Imperium than His commissars. If she knew we were staying, then she would have seen Reeve as the greatest threat. Without him, our garrison may have just served to protect them and nothing else.'

'Certainly the colonel isn't interested in spreading the Imperial word,' Carson agreed.

Even the lieutenant was listening to Blanks, Forjaz noted. The Guard had a rigid hierarchy, but in such a crisis as this, officers looked to those who stepped forwards. He'd never done so. It was only natural when you were standing in the shadow of sergeants like Red and Booth. But they were gone, he was the only one left, and even now he was being outstripped by a transfer of all people! His wife would never let him hear the end of it if Blanks was promoted above him. He had to make his contribution.

'More accurately,' Carson continued. 'Major Rosa wouldn't have been interested. He would have been the garrison commander. The colonel and Major Brooce would have headed home with the colour-guard.'

'A few slots open in that now,' Forjaz remarked, and then realised the other three were staring at him. 'But then again,' he thought out loud. 'No colours, no colour-guard, I suppose.'

Forjaz saw Stanhope look at Carson. Carson then looked at Forjaz.

'Thank you, sergeant,' Carson told him. 'Help me up, I want to check on the men.'

Forjaz did not understand, but he obeyed. Stanhope and Blanks were left alone.

'I should check on the men as well,' Stanhope decided and got to his feet.

'Carson is already doing that,' Blanks told him.

'I should do it as well. I need to know them and they need to know me.'

'No, they don't. They have their commander. You're not going to change that.'

'Then what should I do?'

'Go to sleep, Stanhope.'

'That sounded rather insubordinate, private,' Stanhope replied.

'It's not my order, major. It's your body's. It's been two days now since you last took the stuff. Two days for your system to realise you're not giving it what it expects any more. It needs rest more than these men need another man to salute.'

'I can't... I can't let these ones go, Blanks. I need to ensure they're safe.'

'Then sleep. I'll wake you if the orks come, or worse, the lancers.'

INTERLUDE

Execution Boards, Cawnpore – 656.M41 – Year 17
of the Ellinor Crusade

SENIOR COMMISSARS REEVE and Toklis finished their lunch as they watched the remnants of the bodies being removed from the mouths of the cannons. The rate of fire had slowed in the last few days and the tech-priests were complaining about the use to which the weapons were being put. Not for the loss of life, but rather that such firing was increasing the wear and tear on the machines.

They were complaining, but, Reeve had noted, not too loudly. The sheer scale of the judicial executions had overawed even the dispassionate members of the Adeptus Mechanicus. No one wished to raise their head too far above the parapet at present for fear of the commissars of the Boards.

Reeve was bored with it now. There had been a certain intellectual challenge at the beginning in devising the process by which the men would implicate one another, but now that was in operation, the interrogations, the sentencing, the executions had all become routine. There were no surprises, no shock revelations, just the inescapable grind from which, Ellinor hoped, some useful men might be salvaged.

It was on the last point where Reeve had one last spark of interest; a major of an auxilia unit which had been destroyed during the attack on the mutineers. The Board had brought him in this morning, questioned him briefly, and were ready to release him. The only pending vote had been Reeve's.

'I don't think there's anything more to him,' Toklis opined, popping the last morsel of food in his mouth.

'He's been sleeping a lot since we brought him here,' Reeve said.

'Goes to support his case, then. A guilty conscience would be keeping him awake. He's sleeping the sleep of the just.'

'The just?' Reeve questioned. 'He was ordered to stand and watch while his men, men he led for years, were gunned down in front of him. I do not believe he considers that there was anything just about it.'

'Well, then perhaps he's sleeping so much because he's hoping never to wake up. Either way, it's not our concern.'

'That always was the difference between us,' Reeve said to his colleague. 'You can only ever spot those who are a danger now; you can't see those who might be a danger in the future.'

Toklis adjusted the bionicle which covered his left eye. 'I see perfectly well, thank you. I suppose if you had been on Cawnpore from the start the mutinies would never have happened.'

'Of course they wouldn't.'

'And how would you have stopped them?'

Reeve did not need to consider it, he already knew. 'I

would have shot Carmichael.'

Toklis laughed in disbelief. 'On what charge?'

'The man could not even get his men to shoot a mutinous officer. What charge? Gross incompetence.'

The other commissar harrumphed. 'Well, Carmichael is no longer our concern and, if I may remind you, neither is Major Stanhope. There are a few more thousand of these to do and Ellinor's deadline is ticking down, so put Stanhope up against a wall if you feel you must, but get back to work.'

'I will be there shortly,' Reeve said, unwavering.

'Good.' Toklis left. Reeve did not head directly back, but instead took a diversion through the medicae ward. He went up onto the gallery and looked down at Stanhope's bed. The major had been woken, questioned and released less than half an hour earlier, and yet here he was asleep again.

Reeve waited, deep in judgement. He noticed someone approaching him. Reeve would have normally withered anyone who dared interrupt him. However, this one he was more charitably inclined towards: it was the colonel of the storm trooper regiment who had finally crushed the mutineers.

'Commissar?' the colonel asked. 'May I ask you a question?'

Reeve turned to him. Here was a true soldier of the Emperor, intelligent, effortlessly capable, his fealty and faith unshakeable and unquestionable. The kind of fighting man that Reeve himself had not been for many years.

The colonel stood calmly at attention, even though his torso was heavily bandaged from the wounds he had received. He had been respectful in his request, but Reeve made it a point of principle never to accede to another straight away. He found it encouraged undue familiarity. Reeve held the Emperor's authority and he would discuss what he wished before any topic of theirs. This fighting man might just have the insight to help Reeve make his decision.

'Do you know Major Stanhope down there at all?' Reeve inclined his head towards the bed beneath their feet.

The colonel looked. 'I'm aware of his situation. We don't typically fraternise with the regular regiments, though.'

A sensible precaution, Reeve knew, as it was the storm troopers who were deployed to bring those very regiments back into line, typically with overwhelming force.

'He, just as you, has performed a great service for the Emperor, but he has suffered a great loss as a consequence. I fear that his grief over that loss may lead him down a path of resentment and ultimately treachery. I would be interested in your thoughts on the matter.'

The colonel did not reply at once. He was not often asked his opinion on any matters outside of tactical deployment.

'It would depend on the man, commissar,' he replied guardedly.

'You should speak freely with me, colonel,' Reeve assured him. 'I have no doubts as to your loyalty.'

They were interrupted by the roar of the cannons firing again. The colonel took the moment to consider the matter further.

'I doubt,' he began, 'that any man who has been in this place and seen the consequences of mutiny could ever fall to that crime again.'

The colonel stepped beside Reeve and looked down at Stanhope. 'His men gave their lives to bring such abomination to an end. If he held them in any regard, he would never desecrate their memory. And if he truly loved them, then he would not blame his orders; he would only ever blame himself.'

Reeve thought on it. 'Perhaps, then, a bullet would be a mercy, if he is to carry such guilt.'

Reeve saw the colonel frown, but stay silent.

'I said you should speak freely,' he reminded him. 'What do you think of that?'

The colonel nodded slowly. 'It is possible. Yet… I believe, that is, I hope that the Emperor in all his Imperial Glory might sometimes deliver His mercy by other means than down the barrel of a gun.

'Not for traitors,' the colonel quickly added, 'not for blasphemers, not for those who refuse His duty–'

'But perhaps for the faithful?' Reeve interrupted briskly. 'Perhaps for good soldiers such as Major Stanhope? Perhaps for you?'

The colonel felt as though he had overstepped his bounds and snapped back to attention, eyes fixed blankly over Reeve's shoulder.

'No, no, colonel,' Reeve reassured him. 'Do not fear. You have given me something to consider. Now, what did you wish to ask me?'

'I merely wished to ask, commissar. I haven't heard from anyone else and I know you reviewed the battlesite. Did we at least get him? Did we get Hacher?'

'Colonel,' Reeve told him, 'there is no Hacher. There never was. He was a fiction. A construct for the mutineers to hide behind. Even the name itself, it's the Kartha word for chopping up, cutting up into pieces. Pieces. That's all Hacher was. Made up from bits and pieces from each one of them.'

'Yes, commissar,' the colonel said. Reeve could tell he was unconvinced.

'Colonel, did you kill all the mutineers there? Did you kill every traitor? Every last man and woman?'

'Yes, commissar. Those were our orders.'

'Then I assure you that Hacher is dead, and he will not rise again.'

CHAPTER TWENTY-SIX

THE UNEXPECTED PEACE along the trail did nothing to lessen its horror to those who were travelling it. The only noise Carson could hear was the Griffons' engines, and all he could see was the dead. Nearly seven hundred men had died on that trail in such a short time the day before, but it was not so much the number, it was the order.

So many of them had died where they stood that their formations still held. Men had fought so close together that as they died their comrades either side had held them up until they were struck in turn. Carson could tell at what stage of the battle each man had died based on how many of his comrades' bodies lay upon him. Sections, platoons, whole companies had been wiped out along the length of a few dozen metres. And Carson could put a name to every single grimy, pallid face he saw.

Gomery was curled up with a deflated Mister Emmett

under his head, almost as though it was a pillow. Colquhoun was half-in, half-out of a monstrous squig-beast the size of a tank which had fallen across his company. His halberd was still in his hands, jammed up through the roof of the squig-beast's mouth. Ingoldsby was still upright, impaled through the chest on a spear with a broken shaft; beyond him, running into the jungle, was a trail of the bodies of his men whom he had tried to protect.

The orks had used rope to hang some of the bodies, squig-beast and Guardsman alike, from the tree branches, like carcasses in a meat locker. There was no time to stop and cut them down and so some of the men began to try and laser the ropes as they went past. The sickening thump the first one made as it fell into a lop-sided ball discouraged them from continuing, even before Carson could chide them for wasting ammunition. The worst moments came as the trail narrowed and there was simply not enough space to edge around. Carson shut his ears at the crunch and pops as his Griffon drove over Brimlock dead. He had had to witness many dreadful sights in his time, but even he spared himself from looking back at the trail of the track-crumpled bodies of his former comrades they left behind.

It was a nightmare. It was his nightmare, to lose one's men and then to defile them in such a manner. He glanced over at Stanhope. The major did not even look, did not appear even the least bit concerned. Of course, Carson thought bitterly, he had seen it all before, hadn't he? But then the rancour vanished and, for that short time, Carson forgave everything that Stanhope had done to himself.

THEY HAD BEEN going for hours now and the mood amongst the survivors had lifted a fraction. They were long past the ambush-site, the orks had not attacked, and Dova, and safety, was close.

'Where in the Emperor's name have they gone, Blanks?' Stanhope asked rhetorically. 'They've just vanished.'

'It was the same after the night attack on Fort Eliza,' Blanks said. 'That night there was an army of them. The next day, when we were going through the fungus, they were in pieces. They can't hold it together for long.'

'I wonder why that is,' Stanhope said.

'I put it down to the Emperor, personally.'

'The Emperor?' Stanhope was surprised.

'He made it so that they might win battles, but that we would win the wars.'

They were both thrown forwards as the Griffon braked hard.

'Dova ahead!' the driver shouted back, excited. 'Thank Go– Oh, God-Emperor...'

Ahead of them was Dova, the bastion rising majestically from the jungle, just as when they had left it. But now the gates gaped pathetically open, broken off their hinges, and the walls were adorned with hanging bodies.

DOVA, Tswaing, Voor pacification Stage 1 Day 21

CHOPPA WAS NOT happy. The fighting the night and day before had been tremendous. Ripping. They had hacked the aliens to pieces and knocked their metal monsters over. But here had been losses. Of those amongst the warriors, he cared for little; he understood that was how his kind prospered. The strong survived, the weak died and spread their spores to grow new warriors who might be better. It was the losses amongst the meat-beasts that made him think. Almost every single meat-beast the savage tribes had owned, plus all those they had captured from the Stone Smashas, was dead. His warriors' stomachs were full now, but when that trail of meat-beast flesh was gone, taken or rotted, then they would become hungry and the tribes would turn on each other again.

Despite his victories, he felt his army crumbling around him. Nabkeri had woken him that morning with the news that more than half his warriors were missing. At first, Choppa believed it to be treachery, that they were planning a move against him, and he had stormed out with his weapon ready to cut the first challenger he saw in two. Nabkeri had calmed him down, though, and told him that most had just wandered away. Some had gone after the few meat-beasts remaining, the rest were simply sated with battle and food for a while and so had instinctively headed back into the jungle to the fungus fields that were their home.

Choppa did not want to return home, however; he wanted to go on. To have more boyz under his command, not fewer. He had not told them that, he realised. His boyz had gone home because they believed the war was over. Only he understood that the war was just beginning.

That was why Choppa had raised his standard here and called the tribes back to assemble. He wanted to show them what more this world had to offer.

STANHOPE WATCHED AS another ork warband emerged from the jungle and made its way across the flattened plain towards the desecrated walls of Dova. This one was larger than the last, over a hundred strong at least, and they brought with them a gift for their warboss. It was Frn'k.

The ogryn trod carelessly, placidly, being led along on leashes of ropes held by the warriors. He was still gripping Gardner's autocannon tightly in his arms. Stanhope noticed that, in all of their prodding and pushing, none of the orks came close to touching it.

It was time. Stanhope passed the monocular over to Heal to keep watching and walked back amongst his men, until he reached the tree which Carson was propped up against.

'Is it Trouble?' Carson asked as he approached.

'Unmistakeably,' he replied. 'How's Forjaz?'

'He's…' Carson didn't know how else to describe it. 'He's exactly as you'd expect him to be.'

Stanhope nodded and didn't say anything more. Forjaz had seen his wife, his daughters, his son in his uniform, all hanging from the walls. He had plunged from the lead Griffon and charged down the path towards Dova, shouting oaths of vengeance. It had taken Stanhope, Blanks and nearly a section of men to subdue him and prevent him from alerting every ork inside.

The families, the young, the invalids, and all the rest of the regiment's followers were not the only ones strung up. Stanhope turned away from Carson as he remembered Ducky, Marble and all the other injured that Carson had sent back to Dova for their safety. Stanhope could sympathise with them all, of course he could, but the shock had not stopped his mind working. When he saw the field of slaughter, the first thought to enter his head was how he would save his men now. Even as he held Forjaz to the ground, his mind was working as an officer's should, planning out the next steps they would take. His men would feel their shock, anger and grief, that was to be expected, but he could not allow them to be paralysed by it.

Blanks appeared, leading Ledbetter towards them. Stanhope had given his officers six minutes to react, feel, and calm their men. That was all the time he would allow. After that, the course of their expedition had to change and that required a new plan.

'I've asked Captain Ledbetter to join us. Discuss what's next,' Stanhope explained.

This time it was Carson's turn to hold his tongue as Ledbetter joined them. Blanks stayed close as well. Before Stanhope had begun, Carson interjected.

'Where's the colonel?' he asked. 'Is he there as well?'

Stanhope shook his head. 'He may still be alive, a captive,' he ventured.

'A Valkyrie is missing,' Blanks added, which was true; only two Valkyries were lying, burnt-out, on the landing pad.

Carson encapsulated his opinion of Arbulaster abandoning Dova to the orks in a few, succinct, earthy phrases. When he had finished, Stanhope began.

'We can wait here until the orks leave, but we have no way of knowing how long that will take. It may be days. It may be weeks. It may be never. So here's what I propose. We spend the night here and if the orks aren't making a move by tomorrow, we'll march. We'll affix a vox, set to transmit, to the top of one of the trees so that if the Valkyrie returns, they'll detect it and know where we've gone,' he said. He pushed the loose dirt between them aside and drew an outline of the continent in the soil.

'The only other place on Tswaing which had comms powerful enough to reach to Voorheid is here.' He pointed at a dot on the coast to the north. 'The original Voorjer settlements. We believe that this is where Van Am is heading. It's where she grew up so she knows the land. She must have some means of contacting Voorheid there. I doubt she'll take the trouble to destroy it before she leaves. These savage orks couldn't tell the difference between a vox-console and a tanna-brewer in any case.

'If we're truly lucky, we'll find boats there as well that can take us safely off the shore while we wait; perhaps they'll even be able to take us all the way back to

Voorheid. Even if there are neither, it's still a place that any rescue party will check, and where we are most likely to find supplies and a defensible position. It's a week's fast march, barring accidents and obstacles. We'll have to abandon the Griffons, of course, but the cavalry will be able to keep their mounts. It will be hard, but I believe we can make it,' Stanhope concluded. 'Any questions?'

Stanhope looked at the other two officers. Ledbetter's expression was unreadable; Carson was just staring at him.

'Yes. I have a question,' Carson said quietly.

'Go on, lieutenant.'

Carson opened and then clenched his jaw. 'Is this a joke?'

Stanhope looked at him hard. 'If you can see a problem with this, then tell us and we'll find a solution.'

'My problem…' Carson said and then set his jaw. He was furious, but Stanhope could not imagine why. 'My problem is that nowhere in your proposal is the part where we burn these murdering filth from Dova and bury them beneath its walls!'

Stanhope was taken aback for a moment. 'Lieutenant!' he snapped. 'We cannot contemplate an unsupported assault upon Dova.'

'I'm contemplating it,' Carson retorted. 'In fact, I'm demanding it.' He reached down and brushed aside Stanhope's dirt outline.

Stanhope was unimpressed. 'I'm trying to keep your precious men alive, lieutenant. That is what you wanted from me and what I have sworn to do. An all-out assault on a larger enemy force in a fortified position? They would be massacred.' Carson was shaking his head, but Stanhope barrelled on. 'Your first duty is to your orders. But now you have no orders, your next is to your men.'

'And I am fulfilling that duty,' Carson replied. Stanhope

made to stand, resolute, but Carson leaned forwards and grabbed his arm. 'No, listen to me, major. *Truly* listen for once. What have these men just seen? These men, *my* men, have seen the results of one massacre already. They have seen the bodies of the regiment's women, and their children, and the crippled. They know the killers are sitting on the other side of those walls. Do you think any of them care about their own lives any more? Do you think any of them wouldn't willingly sacrifice themselves to see justice done?' Carson could see his words were striking home. 'Do you think any of them could live with themselves tomorrow or any day after if they had seen such a crime and simply run away?'

Stanhope had no response to that. Instead, he merely turned to Ledbetter.

'Captain?' he asked. 'Your thoughts?'

'I completely agree with the lieutenant, major,' Ledbetter replied without hesitation. 'These xenos… *abominations*,' he spat, 'have committed an atrocity. None of my men will rest until it is revenged. As for–'

Ledbetter paused a moment, struggling briefly with the decision of whether to share himself with these others. 'As for myself. My woman is in there. She is beautiful and kind, and she has been quite the greatest blessing He has ever given me. And now I am sure that she is as dead as the others, but I do not mourn for I know we will be reunited in His Light. So, as for myself, I have no desire to delay that reunion a moment longer than necessary.'

Stanhope stared at the cavalry captain, but Ledbetter showed no emotion as he said those words. That was what such faith did.

'Very well,' Stanhope began again, sketching a new outline on the ground. 'This is Dova…'

* * *

THEY HAD A plan, Stanhope said to himself as he strode away. He walked quickly through the trees until he was out of sight of where the rest of his company was hidden. Then he could contain himself no longer, collapsed to his knees and doubled over. He retched a half-dozen times until finally he had anointed a tiny portion of Voor to be forever Brimlock. He shuffled away then shucked his uniform jacket off, took his knife and started to slice at it. He had the lining ripped, both cuffs opened, every pocket ripped by the time Blanks found him.

'Major!' Blanks said as he went to him. Stanhope whirled around wildly at the interruption, knife in hand. Blanks reacted without thinking, locking Stanhope's hand, stripping the weapon, and Stanhope suddenly found the point of his own knife at his throat.

Blanks threw the knife to one side and released his hold. 'Apologies, major,' he said, but Stanhope had more pressing demands. He grabbed the front of the trooper's uniform, both threat and plea at once.

'Where are they?' he asked. 'You must have kept some! Where are they?'

'Major?' Blanks tried to get through to him, keeping his hands high and open so as not to aggravate him any further.

'You cannot have got rid of them all. I've checked everywhere, but *nothing*.' Blanks saw Stanhope's hand go to his sword, but all he did was to wrench off the pommel and show the empty compartment inside. 'You can't have left me without any. You've got to have them.'

'I don't, major,' Blanks said calmly.

'I just want one, private. That is an *order*. I just need one,' Stanhope released Blanks and returned to his savaged jacket. 'It's happening again. It's happening again. I swore I'd never… but I have and now it's happening *again*!'

'Major!' Blanks said abruptly to capture his attention. 'It's not the same.'

'Of course it's the same. They'll all die. They'll all die again.'

'No, Stanhope,' Blanks replied firmly. 'It's a good plan. We have every chance–'

'We have no chance, Blanks. How many were there in that warband? A hundred or so? Almost as many as us? Emperor only knows how many more of them there are.'

'That's not significant.'

Stanhope stopped rummaging inside his jacket. He replied slowly, rolling each word around in his mouth. 'The fact that we will be... horribly outnumbered... is not... significant?'

'No,' Blanks said. 'A single bullet. That's all it can take to stop an army.'

'But not the orks, private. A single bullet isn't even enough to stop one of them.' Stanhope clasped something inside the lining. 'And there won't be merely one of them. There will be hundreds of them. And all our men, *my* men, will die.

'I told myself,' Stanhope continued. 'I swore to myself after Cawnpore that I would never do it again. I would never utter the order that would lead good men to cast their lives away for nothing. And then Carson came along and he's just as I was, just like that major of the 67th. Dedicated, determined, he died rather than murder his men, Carson is the same. I thought I was as well, but I wasn't. I fooled myself. I wasn't strong enough then, and I'm not strong enough now.'

Stanhope pulled his hand out from the lining; in between his fingers was a small, innocuous, dry leaf.

'No,' Blanks agreed. 'You're right. I can see that. You don't have to utter the order. Carson and Ledbetter are telling their men. You don't have to do anything any more.'

As Blanks reached in, Stanhope jerked the leaf away from him, but that was not his target. With a swift, smooth action, Blanks pulled the fell-cutter from its sheath and held it up in his hands. Stanhope reached after it.

'Give that back.'

Blanks held it away, twisting it slowly in his hand, admiring its construction. 'Why?'

'Because it's mine.'

'No it isn't. It belongs to someone else. You told me that.' Blanks looked at it again, catching the light with the blade. 'It belongs to a man who gave it to you to assure you of his loyalty. To tell you of the faith he held in you unto death.'

Stanhope dropped his arm down and waited. 'What's your point?'

'They knew, Stanhope. I can see it in you now and they could see it in you then. They knew what you were asking of them. The same as these men here. They know what their orders mean, but they'll follow those orders because they trust the men who are giving them.'

Blanks reversed the sword and sank it, point first, into the dirt of Voor.

'The only person you have left to decide for is yourself, major. When these men go into the fight, these men you say you've sworn to keep alive, who will be going in with them? The officer who earned that sword, or the trooper in hiding who's already gone somewhere else?'

At that, Blanks walked away, leaving Stanhope with his decision. A few moments later, the fell-cutter was pulled from the ground and down in its place fluttered a small, innocuous, dry leaf.

INSIDE DOVA, CHOPPA was fascinated by the gift that the war-party boss had brought him. It wore clothes coloured the same as the grey aliens, but it was far bigger than any of the rest of them. Just as size was of primary importance amongst the orks, perhaps it was the same amongst the aliens as well. Was this their warboss then? It did not act much like one. It was neither outraged, nor proudly defiant. There was nothing of command about it; it simply stood there dumbly, clutching that weapon.

Choppa told the war-party boss to bring him the weapon. It was much larger than the one his new alien boy and his grot had carried. Perhaps this one would be more robust than theirs. The boss baulked at the instruction. He told Choppa that the big alien had not allowed his boyz to take it away, and had killed one of them. Choppa was excited by that. He would see the big alien fight. He told the boss again to go and fetch the weapon and bared his teeth to underline the consequences of refusal.

The boss reluctantly obeyed and organised his boyz. At a signal from him, a dozen of them started pulling at the leashes to try and drag the big alien off balance. At the same moment, another dozen jumped at the autocannon to try to drag the weapon from its hands. It was dragged to its knees, but it held on tight. A few boyz grabbed for its arm, but it swatted them away, then took hold of one of the leashes and hauled. The boy on the other end was too stupid or too scared to let go and so was dragged from his feet. The others pulled all the harder and the big alien allowed them to pull him from the other boyz grabbing at the cannon. The boy who had been laid out scrabbled to his feet only to see the big alien running in his direction. It gave a little jump as it went and knee-dropped onto the boy's chest. There was a sickening crunch as his bones broke as the alien's full weight burst through his body.

Choppa called the boyz off and the big alien retreated

cradling the autocannon to itself. Choppa was not only impressed by its strength but also its cunning. The fight had also told him what the creature was. It did not fight as a warboss, it fought as a pet. That was what it was. And if it had been the grey aliens' pet, then it might be his as well.

It was exactly that possibility that Choppa was ruminating over when the first mortar shells fell onto Dova.

CHAPTER TWENTY-SEVEN

THE MORTARS WERE not intended to do much damage.
Their proper operators lay dead far back along the trail
along with most of their ammunition. Many of the
remaining shells had been ditched to squash as many
men on board as could be carried. The few shots that
Carson's men fired were only designed to get the orks'
attention.

In this they succeeded.

Orks poured out of the gates of Dova and onto the
plain. There were indeed more than a hundred, in fact
nearly five hundred emerged from Dova to do battle. But
it was not the distant Griffons that drew their attention.
From the jungle to the south emerged an ancient aspect
of war that was nevertheless new to these savage tribes.
It was cavalry.

Ledbetter formed the remains of his company up in
a single line, helmets and breastplates shining, their
weapons still holstered. The orks changed direction and

headed towards them. Ledbetter responded and his men pushed their horses to the walk. They were in no hurry. The orks picked up their pace in excitement at the violence to come. None of them had killed foes like these before.

As soon as the bulk of the ork force was out onto the plain, piling towards the cavalry, the other attack swung into motion. The Griffons burst from their firing points and motored out onto the plain. Their target was the gates, and they were not stopping for anything.

PRIVATE HEAL FELT a sudden surge of excitement as he crouched on his Griffon's weapon platform. He wanted to whoop with the thrill of the attack, but he suppressed the urge after seeing the serious faces jammed in around him. He could not help it, though. The horror was gone. The loss was gone. The uncertainty was gone. If these were to be his last few moments before being blown into His light and rejoining Zezé and Repton, then he wanted to live them out as he had wished to live every moment of his life. The joy he had never found in the squalor of his childhood or the back-breaking work resolving breakdowns on the Brimlock machine lines. Damn it, he said to himself, and he whooped. It was a whoop so quiet that no one heard it over the protesting engine, not even himself, but he knew it was there.

He held on tighter as the Griffons neared the gates. He felt the thumps as they smashed aside the orks who thought to try and stop them. Then he saw the broken gates of Dova flash past. They were inside; they were inside the walls! The Griffon slewed to a stop and someone was yelling at him to disembark. He placed his hands on the Griffon's tracks, praying they would not suddenly churn again, and vaulted over onto the ground.

His comrades were jumping down all around him.

The orks that had remained inside Dova had a moment's confusion before following their natural instincts. Heal saw one, brought his lasgun to his shoulder and fired. The ork stumbled, but held itself up. Heal fired again with the same result. He ran a few steps, closed and fired again. He ran closer and closer, firing and firing until finally the ork collapsed, its body scored with las-burns. Heal was not done. He grabbed his gun by the barrel and swung it down like a mallet on the back of the ork's head. It struck, but the skull still held.

Someone was shouting at him now to get back to the line. He would obey in a moment, as he had always done, but he gave the dead ork one last hammer blow and was rewarded with the definite crack of its skull.

That one was for Zezé, he said to himself as he spat on the body. Now for one more.

OUT ON THE plain, Choppa realised he had been out-flanked and turned back to the gates.

Carson's men had driven the Griffons just through the gates of Dova before halting. Carson and half his men stayed with the vehicles to defend the gate, while Forjaz, Blanks, and the other half stormed forwards to annihilate any ork left inside. The longer they had before the main bulk of the ork force returned, the better. That was Ledbetter's job.

As Choppa turned his orks away, Ledbetter sounded the charge.

'For the Emperor!' he called. 'Our faith, our shield and spear!'

The line started to run, and some of the orks turned back again, anticipating the combat. The horses raced forwards and their riders drew their lances. The explosive tips of their weapons detonated as their charge hit home, blowing ork bodies to pieces. The horsemen then threw

the wasted weapons aside, drew their pistols and tried
to disengage. Ledbetter, his chainsword whirling, carved
a path clear for his survivors, and led them round once
again.

Stanhope, meanwhile, had his own objectives. Whilst
Carson and Ledbetter's only goal was to wipe these ork
warbands from the planet, Stanhope had insisted that
he be allowed to do everything he could so that some
of them might still be saved. First he tried the gates, but
the mechanism was fused and useless. The wall-defence
guns were the same. How had the orks managed it? Stanhope wondered. To have taken Dova so quickly?

He then headed over to the Valkyries on the landing pad. The few orks, new-spawns who had been left
behind by the warriors, were easily dealt with. As he had
feared, though, when he first saw the Valkyries from a
distance, their internals had been gutted. Neither was in
any condition to fly.

From the landing pad, he could see out onto the plain,
to where Ledbetter's cavalry were fighting in the midst of
the ork horde; their horses jumping and swerving, their
breastplates shining with the reflected flashes of their
laspistols. They could not win, but they fought on anyway. In that instant, Stanhope remembered his margoes,
the fell-cutters of the 1201st attacking up that slope to
take the rebels' fortress. He remembered his second, Sub
Pagedar, as he held out his precious sword at the height
of the trouble on Cawnpore, as assurance that none of
his men would desert to the mutineers. They were dead,
just as proud Ledbetter and his cavalry would soon be.
Was the Emperor even aware any more, Stanhope wondered, of the gross injustices that good soldiers suffered
in His name?

The only excuse the Imperium had was that the alter-
native was far worse.

'There's nothing left for it,' Stanhope returned to Carson, as his men fortified the defensive line they had formed with the Griffons. 'We've got to take the vox tower.'

If they could take the vox tower then they would at least be able to send a message to Voorheid to warn of what had happened, and thereafter to Crusade Command notifying them of the failure of the Brimlock 11th. The difficulty was that the vox tower lay at the top of the central bastion.

'Forjaz and his merry band are already in there. Your man as well,' Carson replied, keeping his eye on the growing defences. He was slumped on the back of a Griffon's firing platform and leaned against the side. He had his arms folded and his infamous duelling pistols still in their holsters. Had these been any other circumstances, he would have been a picture of nonchalance. 'And look what they've already returned to me.'

Carson cupped his hand around his mouth and called out. Two familiar figures came over.

'Blessed Marguerite,' Stanhope said when he recognised Red and Mouse. 'They're alive?'

'Trouble as well,' Carson pointed to where the ogryn sat with the same glassy expression as before. 'His body at least. I suspect I know where his mind has gone.'

Then, as Red and Mouse stepped before him, Stanhope noticed red stripes on them, running from hairline to chin and crossing one eye. 'What's happened to your faces?'

'Heathen markings, sah. We'll be removing them as soon as time permits, sah.'

'So, it's true what they say, colour. Nothing can kill you.'

'Nothing has yet, sah. And nothing ever will.'

Mouse chipped in. 'Nothing can stop a righteous man

in the execution of his duty to the Emperor.'

'And that was you, was it Mouse?' Carson asked.

'No, sir. But I had one looking out for me.'

Red cleared this throat pointedly and shouldered his gun. 'On that note, Major Stanhope, as I understand that you're now the most senior officer of this expedition, I hereby hand over to your custody Private Rit Chaffey, commonly referred to by the vulgar epithet of "Mouse", and request he be charged with dereliction of duty, desertion in the face of the enemy and multiple counts of attempted theft and unauthorised salvaging. The penalty for each and every individual offence being immediate execution by firing squad. The men are a little busy at present, but I am happy to perform the sentence myself.'

Mouse started to protest and Red gave him a pointed punch in the kidneys.

Stanhope paused for a moment, taken aback. 'Thank you, colour-sergeant. I hereby order that all charges be dropped. You're a free man, Private Chaffey.'

'I thought I was a Guardsman, sir,' Mouse scowled, unamused, knowing that Red had been fully prepared to pull the trigger.

Stanhope turned to Carson. 'How long can you hold the line?'

It was a damned silly question; Stanhope knew as soon as he said it that Carson would hold it as long as he could. 'As long as it takes.'

'Thirty minutes, you think?' Stanhope asked.

'Oh, I don't believe you'll take that long, major.'

'Understood,' Stanhope said and very nearly left it at that, but Red spoke up.

'You're taking the vox tower, sah?'

'That's right.'

Red removed the heavy sash from over his shoulder and handed it to Stanhope. Stanhope took it, confused.

'The colours, sir,' Red said. 'Run 'em up the tower. Get 'em flying again.'

But Stanhope had a better idea. 'You're the colour-sergeant, Red. Come with us and raise them yourself.'

Red shook his head. 'Begging your pardon, sah. 'Fraid not, sah.'

'Red?'

The old warhorse looked over at Carson. 'Another fox-hole to keep my officer out of, sah.'

Red stepped away and headed back to the Griffon-line. The men gave a small cheer, half-ironic, half-heartfelt when he took his place amongst them and he bawled them out.

'Chaffey?' Stanhope asked Mouse. 'What about you?'

Mouse watched Red, his persecutor and defender, trot smartly off to the Griffon-line to aid in the increasingly desperate defence. He thought of what they had been through together and found that his decision was far easier than he expected.

'No troubles, major. I'm with you!' Mouse said.

'Good. Grab your pack, we might need your spares.' Mouse scurried off and Stanhope turned back to Carson.

'Anything more I can do for you, second lieutenant? Battlefield promotion?'

'Not unless you can promote me to colonel. With all due respect, Stanhope, I've had my fill of majors.'

Stanhope nodded. 'Anything else?'

'Just leave me with my men.'

The shout went up: the orks were heading back through. Whatever defences were in place had to be enough for these thirty men against five hundred.

'Of course,' he said and stepped down to the ground. 'Good luck, lieutenant.'

'Good luck, sir,' Carson replied.

* * *

STANHOPE AND MOUSE ran to the entrance of the bastion. The orks had broken it open in their attack and, like the gates, never thought to fix it. They headed into the gloom, making for the main stairwell. A chorus of echoing screams greeted them. A group of three of Forjaz's men, bleeding and bruised, stumbled past; the two walking wounded carrying the third.

'Watch out, major,' one of them warned. 'He's an animal. He's tearing the orks apart!'

The injured offered nothing more and stumbled outside. Stanhope and Mouse found themselves stepping over the dead and dying on both sides: orks charred and pierced by las-fire and bayonet, and the Brimlock troopers they had bludgeoned and battered with their crude weapons and heavy fists. Their blood pooled and mixed upon the floor. Some of the illumination still functioned, giving them hope that the vox tower might still have power as well.

The screams had stopped now, and in their place sounded inhuman bellows and grunts. They reached the bottom of the stairwell and there they found Forjaz's body, black with blood, ork flesh beneath his fingers and between his teeth where he had torn and bitten at everything he could reach. The orks had won. Mouse readied his gun and Stanhope pulled out his fell-cutter, preparing for the worst. They crept up the first flight of stairs and then they sensed the blood-dripping figure above them.

Stanhope swung his weapon up.

'The bastion is yours, major,' Blanks said in reply.

Mouse gasped behind him. Blanks crouched at the top of the stairway, looking down upon them. His helmet was missing. His armour was ripped, torn away in some places. His face was scorched. He was not covered in blood, he was drenched in it. None of it was his own. He sat there on his haunches, the only weapon in his hands his silver bayonet. He smiled.

'And, major, there's something you have to see.'

Blanks led the way, dodging quickly, silently over the bodies of a dozen dead orks, blood draining from their throats, eyes and ears where the bayonet had struck.

'I'm glad he's on our side,' Mouse whispered, and Stanhope could not have agreed more.

The something Blanks had alluded to was at the top of the bastion, up on the shooting deck. Stanhope halted them at the command section for the vox tower beside it. Fortunately, the orks had exhausted their destructive tendencies on the lower levels and so only a little damage had been caused. Stanhope set Mouse to get the vox working and followed Blanks up to the last level and onto the deck.

'I'll keep an eye on the defences,' Blanks said. 'Leave you two alone.'

'What?' Stanhope said, but Blanks vanished. He looked about the shooting deck in the dimming light. The canvas chairs were still there, some knocked aside by the orks. The giant map of Voor on the wall was untouched. The grand table in the middle of the room showed damage and was stained with blood at its four corners, but there was no one else there.

'Who... is there?' a weak, indistinct voice emerged from one of the chairs in a dark corner.

'I am Major Stanhope. Who's that?'

The voice groaned slightly. 'Stanhope... why... of all my officers... did it have to be you...'

'Colonel?' Stanhope exclaimed and strode over. It was Colonel Arbulaster indeed. What was left of him. The orks had not been generous in this regard. His arms and legs hung limply from his torso. Stanhope realised that where once his limbs had been now there were merely bound stumps. The actual limbs were only attached by crude stitches which gaped horribly. His fingers, ears and toes had been separated and then resewn as well. They had blinded one eye and the other was nearly swollen shut with bruising.

'It was the one with the bad leg…' Arbulaster burbled in way of explanation, 'I think… he was curious… why we don't heal the way they do.'

Mouse shouted up, 'It's working, major. Transmitting now!'

'The big one… all he did was stand in here… stare at the map…' Arbulaster continued. 'You'll have to keep… an eye on him, Stanhope…'

Arbulaster's face suddenly clenched hard and his throat let out a whimper.

'What is it?' Stanhope asked.

'Lost… the regiment… lost… the colours.'

Stanhope took off the sash, unrolled it a way to show part of the image of Marguerite, and held it up to Arbulaster's eye.

Arbulaster stared, then craned his neck forwards and buried his face in it like a child might with its blanket. His voice was muffled, but Stanhope could make out that he was repeating the same phrase again and again.

'Praise Him… praise Him… praise Him…'

Arbulaster's mutterings collapsed into a splutter and he pulled his face free.

'One last thing… Stanhope.'

'Yes?'

'If we should meet each other… in His light… do something for me.'

'Yes?'

'Don't stop… keep on walking.'

Stanhope heard Mouse shout again, even more urgent than the last time.

'Major, sir! I've got a message coming back.'

'From Voorheid?'

'No, sir. It's a Valkyrie, and it's coming in!'

The missing Valkyrie, returning from a run to Voorheid, had accelerated as soon as it had received Mouse's transmission. Now it was braking, banking, so as to stop and hover over Dova.

'Mouse, connect it through up here,' Stanhope ordered, and the rushing noise of a Valkyrie cockpit burst through the shooting deck.

'This is Major Stanhope, acting commander of Dova. Who is that?'

The pilot's voice came back over the sound of the wind.

'This is Flight Lieutenant Plant, returning with the colonel's cargo.'

'What cargo is that?'

'It's… My orders were only to report to the colonel…'

'Listen, man!' Stanhope snapped. 'Is it anything we can use to blow the orks we've got crawling all over us back into the jungle?'

'God-Emperor…' Stanhope heard the pilot gasp as the Valkyrie finally hove into view over Dova and he saw the battle raging on.

'Answer me!'

'No, major!' the pilot reported quickly. 'It's… crates of liquor, sir. Boxes of food. Tins of candied fruit. It's what the colonel ordered…' He trailed off.

In the corner, Arbulaster gurgled.

'…thought I should give the men a surprise…'

'What are your orders, major?'

'Dump it! Dump it all! Preferably on the heads of the orks! Then–

Mouse cut him off. 'Come in close to the vox tower and pick us up!'

'Ignore that, pilot. Mouse, shut up! Plant, drop inside

the walls and extract every trooper you can find!'

  'Wait! Wait!' Mouse started to shout.

  'Mouse, I said shut up!'

  'No! Serious! Serious! Don't get too close or they'll do it again!'

  'Do what again?'

  'What they did! How they took Dova!'

CHAPTER TWENTY-EIGHT

DOVA, Tswaing, Voor pacification Stage 1 Day 21

ON THE GRIFFON-LINE, Carson's men produced a blizzard of las-fire to try to keep the ork horde back. They had pushed through the choke point at the gates and now were piling up to the sides of the Griffons themselves. Some troopers thought to stand so as to be able to fire down at the orks who had made it into the lee, and they in turn became targets for the ork hunting javelins. The end was close, but not close enough for Choppa as he stepped between the gate posts. He held his totem high once more and struck it with his cleaver.

STANHOPE HEARD THE warning alarms blare in the Valkyrie's cockpit before the entire signal cut out. Mouse appeared up on the shooting deck.

'What in damnation was that?' Stanhope demanded.

'Something their warboss has. It's shorted the vox again!'

Damn the vox, Stanhope thought as he rushed across

to the edge of the shooting deck, what about the men? He grabbed the side and pulled himself up to see the Griffon-line, or where once the Griffon-line had been. The troopers had had their lasguns short in their hands and the Griffons ignite beneath them. The orks had been all over them in seconds and were triumphantly tearing them apart and racing for the bastion.

'Blanks! Blanks, get up here!' Stanhope shouted behind them. Mouse was at the edge beside him.

'Look, the Valkyrie!'

The Valkyrie had been hit, but not as badly. Plant was barely keeping her in the air. She was swaying from side to side as Plant fought with the controls. Mouse leapt up beside Stanhope and balanced on the window sill.

'Major!' he cried. 'Come get on the roof. We can get him down here.'

Stanhope turned back to Arbulaster.

'What about the colonel?'

Mouse's eyes flashed with anger. 'Personally I'd use him as a doorstop, but he's a bit bloody big. Let's go!' he shrieked, and scrambled onto the roof.

Stanhope heard Mouse's shouts to the Valkyrie pilot and walked over to Arbulaster.

'Colonel. Colonel!' he said, attracting his attention. Arbulaster looked at him.

'Would you like me to…' Stanhope began and drew the fell-cutter.

Arbulaster looked at it, then slowly nodded.

'So…' he muttered quietly, 'there it is…'

Stanhope swung.

'A good cut, major,' Blanks said behind him.

Stanhope lowered the bloodied weapon.

'I've blockaded the doors as best as can be done,' Blanks continued. 'It should give you a few minutes at least.'

Stanhope wiped the blood from his sword and put it

back in its sheath. 'Have you ever considered that it may not be entirely beneficial to your health to be constantly surprising people, private?'

'I find it's certainly less beneficial for their health, major.'

Stanhope looked back to the window. 'Mouse has the right idea. Let's get up there.' He tied the colours around himself again. 'Plant might not risk it for us, but he'll risk it for this.'

Stanhope went across and lifted himself up onto the window before he realised that Blanks hadn't followed him.

'Respectfully, no, major.'

'What's that?' Stanhope said, exasperated.

'You asked me who I thought I was.'

'Yes?'

'I don't know for sure, but I think what was done to me is only done to those who've committed some great sin. To give us the chance to atone for whatever it was. I'm not a person any more, Stanhope. I'm a weapon. And there's a whole army out there that isn't going stop here at Dova. It isn't even going to stop on Voor. But I can stop it here.'

'You can't stop an army,' Stanhope stated. 'Not even you, Blanks.'

'Remember what I said, it can just take a single bullet. If you put it in the right place.'

'You don't have a bullet,' Stanhope reminded him.

'I don't need one.'

Stanhope watched him walk down the steps and out of sight. He closed his eyes and said a prayer and then hauled himself onto the roof.

'He won't come down!' Mouse shouted. Stanhope looked up. Plant's control was still shaky. He hadn't moved off, but he wasn't descending either.

'Let's show him what we can offer then,' Stanhope said and untied the colours. He let the banner stream out in the Valkyrie's downdraught. That got a reaction. The Valkyrie started to descend, but only as far as the top of the vox tower. The array of antennae from the tower blocked him coming down any further.

'Looks like we're going to have to–' Stanhope began, but Mouse was already climbing the tower up to where the Valkyrie hovered. Its rear hatch opened, and there was a crewman inside, beckoning them up.

Stanhope fastened the colours and started to climb as well. As he climbed though, he felt his limbs start to weigh him down. First his legs, then his arms, then his head. He was tired. So very tired. He stopped for a few seconds to rest. He looked around at the stunning view all around him. The trail they had cut. The fort they had held. The crater they had taken. The ambush, the blood they had shed. He looked down at Dova and the faces slid before his eyes. Blanks. Booth. Ducky. Marble. Gardner. Forjaz. Red. Carson. The leaves. He saw a rain of them sheet past him. They would be there ready to catch him. They would have him again.

He pulled himself up another metre and looked up, at the Valkyrie above him. He saw on its underside those same markings as had been on Zdzisław's. After his crash, his pilots had painted them on their birds' bellies so that no commissar would see them, but they would know they were there.

He saw something drop beside him. They were giving him a lifeline. They were throwing him a rope. He took the colours from around him and tied them on. The Valkyrie lost height for a moment and jerked a fraction to one side. Stanhope felt the vox tower fly from his feet. He was in the air, his grip on the colours all that was holding him.

'You're going to have to hold on!'

Stanhope looked up, his vision swimming. In that moment, it was not the Valkyrie crewman reaching out to him, it was Blanks. Blanks would always pull him out.

...how...? he wondered.

'You're going to have to hold on, sir!' Blanks the crewman shouted.

Never called me sir.

'Hold on!' he seemed to shout again.

Don't have the strength.

'Hold on!'

Not strong enough. Can't survive again.

'Hold on!'

Can't do it all again.

'Hold on!'

Can't bear it.

'Hold on!'

Not again.

'Hold on!'

Stanhope relaxed and let the colours run through his fingers. He lay back into the air.

CHAPTER TWENTY-NINE

'BRIMLOCK ELEVENTH!' THE regimental sergeant major bellowed. 'Form companies!'

The troopers of the Brimlock 11th scrambled to obey, their own company sergeant majors worrying them into position as though they were dogs herding cattle.

Stanhope watched the carefully controlled chaos as, slowly, the individual companies started to emerge. He started walking down the front line, looking for his place.

He passed the cavalry and Ledbetter there dipped his lance in salute, then the artillery and Rosa gave him a wave, brandishing some kind of meat bone. Drum treated him to a blast of battle-hymns on his vox-amps and pranced a bizarre saluting dance on top of his tank. Stanhope acknowledged them all, but his place was not with them.

He passed Deverril, Wymondham, Ingoldsby, Fergus, Tyrwhitt, Gomery, Colquhoun, still no sign of his men. He saw Arbulaster, chest out, gut in, standing as proud as he'd ever seen him, Brooce by his side. Stanhope did not look his way, though, he just carried on walking. He passed Roussell, who did not seem able to stop adjusting himself. Stanhope saluted and Roussell scowled. There, finally, there he found his company. Zezé, Repton and Heal were deep in discussion. Marble was fiddling with his rifle. Forjaz was trying to fend off his doting wife and children, while Ducky took a few steps and hurled his lasgun away as he always did.

He gave a nod to Carson and took his place at their head. He shielded his eyes to see what their destination was, but could not make it out in the light.

'Major Stanhope, sir! Step out of that position!' Booth shouted at him. Stanhope turned, confused. This was where he belonged. Carson sauntered over to him.

'That's not your place, Stanhope,' he said. 'Someone's already there.'

'Who? I don't see them?' Stanhope queried.

'Of course not.'

The orders came through to prepare to march and Stanhope found himself moving aside. 'But I should be marching with you,' he said. 'You're my men.'

'No, major,' Carson told him. 'We only borrowed each other. Besides, there's someone waiting for you.'

The order to march came and the Brimlock 11th started to move out and leave Stanhope behind. One of the troopers broke ranks, however, and came running over to him.

'Major! Major!' Gardner said. 'I wanted you to meet my brother.' Gardner held his arm out into space as though he was gripping someone around the shoulder.

'There's no one there,' Stanhope told him.

'Of course he's there!' Gardner laughed back. 'He waited for me, didn't you?'

Gardner wrestled playfully with the air for a moment

and then turned away. 'Got to be getting back, major. Come on, Trouble.'

Stanhope watched the trooper, chatting away to nothing, run back to the company.

'Starting to figure it out, Stanhope?' a voice said behind him.

Stanhope turned around. The man Stanhope had known as Blanks was standing there. His face was the same, less the wide-eyed look that Blanks had occasionally had. His uniform was not.

'Major,' Blanks said.

Stanhope caught sight of his insignia.

'Colonel,' Stanhope replied and saluted. Blanks saluted back.

'Do you know why now? Do you remember?' Stanhope asked.

Blanks nodded.

'Was it a punishment?'

'No. It was a mercy.' Blanks looked behind him. 'The things I'd seen... It was His blessing.'

Stanhope nodded. Blanks glanced behind him.

'I have to get going. My men have been waiting for me.'

Stanhope looked. 'I don't see them.'

'You won't,' Blanks replied. 'You don't know them, that's why you can't see them.' Blanks saluted farewell and turned crisply on his heel.

'Were you him?' Stanhope called. 'Were you the mutineer? Were you Hacher?'

Blanks turned back.

'No,' he replied. 'We were the ones who killed him,' and he disappeared.

Stanhope looked about him, aimlessly. He should go on, but surely not alone. Then one last figure approached him from the haze. Just one at first, but then Stanhope saw the dozens arrayed in precise ranks behind him.

'We've been waiting for you, sir.'

'You've been waiting? All this time?'

'Of course, sir. We are your men.'

Stanhope nodded and, unseemly as it was, could not hold back the smile. He reached down to his belt and untied his sword and then presented it.

'I believe your word has been kept. This should be yours again.'

Sub Pagedar took it in his graceful hands and returned his major's smile.

'At your command, sir,' he said.

'Thank you,' Stanhope agreed. 'At my command.'

And ahead of them in the distance, Stanhope heard Private Heal strike up the song from his homeland, and he sang without restraint for the company's colour-sergeant was not there to quiet him. And the others raised their voices with him as the Brimlock 11th marched into the Emperor's light.

ABOUT THE AUTHOR

Richard Williams was born in Nottingham, UK and was first published in 2000. He has written fiction for publications ranging from *Inferno!* to the Oxford & Cambridge May Anthologies, on topics as diverse as gang initiation, medieval highwaymen and arcane religions. In his spare time he is a theatre director and actor. *Relentless* was his first full-length novel and his latest book is *Imperial Glory*.

Visit his official website at *www.richard-williams.com*